Peter Yeldham's extensive writing career began at the age of seventeen, and has included short stories, scripts for radio, and a spell as a columnist for a weekly magazine. He went to England 'to see what it was like', and stayed almost twenty years, becoming a leading film and television writer, with films like *Age of Consent*, *The Comedy Man*, and plays and major series for the BBC and ITV. He also wrote six plays for the theatre, staged in London's West End, America and Europe. Since his return to Australia, he has won numerous awards for his work, which includes screen adaptations of *The Timeless Land*, *1915* and *The Battlers*, and many original miniseries including *Captain James Cook*, *The Alien Years*, *The Heroes* and *Run from the Morning*. This is his third novel. He and his wife divide their time between a harbour suburb in Sydney and a property on the central coast of New South Wales.

*Also by Peter Yeldham in Pan:*

Without Warning

# Two sides of a
# TRIANGLE

# PETER YELDHAM

**PAN**
Pan Macmillan Australia

First published 1996 in Pan by Pan Macmillan Australia Pty Limited
St Martins Tower, 31 Market Street, Sydney

National Library of Australia Cataloguing-in-Publication data:

Yeldham, Peter.
Two sides of a triangle.
ISBN 0 330 35788 3.
I. Title.
A823.3

Typeset in 12/13 pt Bembo by Midland Typesetters, Maryborough, Victoria
Printed in Australia by McPherson's Printing Group

*To Lyn and Perry*

My deep thanks to Ray Alchin who first saw the interview and the possibilities for this story.

Also to Marjorie Yeldham, who read all the drafts, and contributed as she always does.

# PROLOGUE

## HONG KONG

FROM WALTER CHEN'S terrace high on the Peak, the city was like a blaze of diamonds against the night sky. Lights glittered from hotel towers. Electricity burned in a thousand offices on Kowloon where the staff had long gone, while, in narrow back streets, neons advertised garish delights outside tourist bars. The endless flow of traffic looked like irradiated ribbons that danced their reflections on the shadowy water of the harbour. Crowded ferries crossed between the terminals. Above them, a 747 came in over the sea towards Kai Tak like a falling meteor amid a luminous galaxy.

'We're ready,' Edward Burridge said, and the small group who were enjoying Chen's lavish hospitality while admiring the expensive view went inside to watch the videotape. There were six of them. Four were delegates from ASEAN law enforcement agencies. One was from Canberra and another, there as an observer, was an American.

The servants were dismissed, the doors were

locked and the tape began. For the next twenty minutes they sat watching the screen. It was a well-known current affairs program, an interview by a skilled and attractive reporter with an elderly man, and when it was over the lights were switched on and the drinks refilled by Chen himself. The doors to the room remained locked. The small audience exchanged glances but kept silent until Burridge spoke. It was a sure sign of their indecision.

'You're going to say it won't work.' He anticipated several who were about to say exactly that, giving himself a slight tactical advantage. 'But we're here to examine it, discuss it and, if we can, make it work.'

'Hardly feasible. Waste of time,' one declared.

Another, from Kuala Lumpur, supported him. 'It's impossible.'

'No,' Burridge disagreed. 'Difficult, I'll grant you. But by no means impossible. And certainly not a waste of time.'

'We could never raise that amount of money.'

Burridge knew he was on easier and surer ground here. He indicated their Chinese host.

'That's where Walter becomes a vital part of the equation.'

'I can arrange the money,' Walter Chen said, and went on to explain that while some of it would be his own, he would enlist the aid of other sources in various tax havens, assuring

2

them he had an intimate knowledge of even the tiniest, most remote financial shelters. His English was impeccable, the accent almost identical to Burridge's, for they had first met over forty years before as new boys at a minor British public school, and the bonds of friendship forged in sadistic initiation rites and the brutality of their peers had endured ever since.

The small group was impressed with Walter's air of quiet confidence. There was only one question.

'Mr Chen, you may lose a great deal of money. You certainly put it at some risk. So, with respect, what's in it for you?'

'A seat in the House of Lords.'

It was Burridge who answered and, because he chuckled, they were not certain if he was serious.

'I mean it,' he assured them. 'A life peerage. Such things can be arranged. After all, the late Harold Wilson ennobled the man who supplied his raincoats. But all that comes later. If you agree. If we succeed.'

'There are still many problems.' The senior law officer from Kuala Lumpur was determined to be intransigent.

'Of course there are,' Burridge considered him a crashing old bore, perverse and inflexible, but he smiled with diplomatic accord. 'That's why I made certain we got the very best brains together. If we can bring this off, the result will be a benefit to all our nations, quite apart from being a tremendous individual coup for each of us.'

They thought about the personal accolades it might bring, and liked the idea. He had them virtually running with him now. Before the meeting was over he would have their approval. It was all he required; once it was officially sanctioned he would not need them again.

'It's essential to find a wedge, and this could be it—the thin edge that splits the thing wide open. The money is guaranteed; we have a means of access. Not a bad start. With your consent I'll outline a scheme for us to consider, then try to recruit the right people.'

'How many would we need?'

It was Bradley Foster, of the Australian Federal Police, who asked the question. He was an ally, and they had rehearsed this over breakfast at his hotel.

'A small, tight operation, Brad. Very secure. Two people—as long as I can find the right two.'

He had no intention of telling them, but he already had one chosen. All he had to do was convince her. The Australians would provide the other. In a few weeks they would be here, and it would begin. The two of them wouldn't know, of course, nor would anyone in this

4

room, but the chances of their survival would be slight. It was the only way. They had to be expendable. He had long ago decided this, and he was not a man to dwell unduly on such a consequence.

Edward Burridge knew his strengths and his weaknesses. He had a driving ambition, a contempt for a large section of humanity, and was, nobody disputed, exceptionally gifted in the twin practices of treachery and deceit.

*But if he had known what was to happen, if he could have foreseen the outcome, would he have been swayed by this and made a different choice? Tried to terminate the scheme before it got out of hand? Those who knew him best thought not. They felt certain such a conniving, heartless bastard would have continued without hesitation, no matter what the cost.*

# PART ONE

## THE DECOY

1 BEN'S MARRIAGE WAS falling apart. He knew it and Deborah knew it, and even both their kids knew it. While there were no rows, no public slanging matches, while they still attended other people's parties and barbecues, arriving and leaving together, yet it was known they weren't getting on, hadn't been for months, and the end was inevitable, bound to happen soon. Better if it did. A clean break and start again. This way they were just prolonging what had become a poisonous situation. Their close friends were not the only ones who knew. Their neighbours knew. Some of Ben's group were aware of it, the special squad with their own agenda inside the department.

It was the job, he thought. The bloody job and its unrelenting stress. For two years now there had been so much he could not confide in her. Like Christine. Deborah knew about Chrissie, of course; knew they worked together, that she was in her twenties, ten years younger than him, vivacious and attractive. Deborah believed he and Christine were having an affair.

Which they were. *But if only it were that simple.*

'I'll be away for a couple of days at the weekend.'

It was after dinner. They were trying to decide if there was anything to watch on television. The kids were in bed.

'Where?' Deborah asked.

Once he could have told her. Now he simply said:

'A training course. They like to play silly buggers and keep the location secret. I think it's Leura or somewhere in the Blue Mountains.'

He sipped his coffee and avoided her sceptical glance. She knew he was lying. There was no choice; he had to lie. They had been given the word the previous night. He and Christine were to be on the early afternoon plane to Melbourne on Saturday. It was all set up. They would be contacted at their hotel. The money would be available, and a weapon supplied to take on board the aircraft, once they had passed through the security checkpoint.


She was waiting in the domestic terminal. They kissed each other while they stood in the queue to validate their tickets and send their luggage. They were aware of being watched by a man who dialled a number and spoke, but people with mobile phones were everywhere: in restaurants, bars, on the streets, at the beach—they were becoming a plague—and so they pretended to take no notice of him, even though he was almost certainly reporting they were on their way.

They passed through security and headed for the departure gate. He went into the men's toilet as arranged, and the contact was a Vietnamese with a whisk broom pushing a cleaning cart, sweeping up cigarette butts, wiping basins and collecting the wet and discarded paper towels. Ben was carrying a Qantas flight bag. The Vietnamese cleaner glanced at it, and went on working until a toilet flushed, a man emerged, washed his hands and went out to his flight, the door swinging shut behind him. The moment they were alone, Ben dropped his bag into the rubbish cart and accepted the identical Qantas bag the cleaner handed him. It was accomplished in an instant; the man nodded and their eyes met for the briefest of moments. The Vietnamese might have been trying to wish him luck, but there was no opportunity to exchange a word: the door swung open and two youths in their club's football colours entered, bringing with them the smell of stale beer and the gloom of an unsuccessful away match. While they were complaining about their team's performance, Ben slid out. He felt secure; the exchange had gone smoothly, their cover was immaculate. The bag he would take on board the plane contained fifty thousand dollars in used bills and an automatic handgun.

Christine was waiting for him at the departure gate where the flight was boarding. She wore a suede skirt, colourful fleecy sweater, and a matching scarf and beret. Chrissie Duncan looked, as she intended to look, like a pretty girl on an interstate weekend jaunt with a lucky man. The lucky man in question put his arms around her, and they kissed again like impatient lovers, so eager to be alone that they were unconscious of other people's envious or disapproving eyes. The kiss meant the switch of cabin bags had been successfully completed; it was also to allay suspicion, because no-one behaving so openly, attracting attention the way they were, would be likely to have anything to hide.

They were aware of the same man on the far side of the security barrier, again using his mobile phone. It was likely others had them under observation. There might be someone on the plane.

Ben kissed her again, and she responded. This time it was no exchange of messages; this was personal. In the time they had worked as partners, their feeling for each other had become a solace in moments of stress. The trip today was ultimate stress. The weeks of infiltration had finally paid off. They were going to bust him. It was very dangerous, and they were both long enough in the business and realistic enough to be scared. They knew, without having to express it in words, that if there was time after they checked into their Melbourne hotel, they would try to alleviate the stress by going to bed together.

'How long did you tell Deborah you'd be away?'

'Two, maybe three days.'

'Did she believe the story about the Blue Mountains?'

'No. Did Ken?'

'I just said it was weekend duty. He's good about not asking too many questions.'

They were lying naked in their shared hotel room. They had stripped off the moment the bellhop accepted his tip and left them, and made love with such urgency they had reached an excited, synchronous orgasm within minutes.

'Does he ever get suspicious?'

'All the time,' she said. 'I feel bad about it. I'd like to try to explain to him the way it is, but I wouldn't know how to begin.'

He knew what she meant. How could they

justify this to Deborah or to Christine's boy-friend? How could they make either of them understand that it was not really an affair, as such things went. It was nothing to do with love. Not even primarily to do with sex; what they sought in each other was relief from the fear they lived with, an emotional safety valve that meant little outside of this room. They could return home and leave it behind them, because they were working partners and friends, rather than lovers. They used their bodies to comfort and support each other at times like this, when they were nervous and afraid.

While it was true Ben's marriage was at an end, that was not a part of this; that was two ill-matched people who had once believed they could live happily together. His marriage was already damaged before he had met Christine, let alone begun to work with her.

The bedside phone rang, startling them, just when they felt a growing need to comfort each other again. Ben tried to ignore the warmth of her body and his rising erection. He accepted that it was possible to be friends and partners and not be in love, but she was attractive and he was fond of her, and it was wonderful the heat they could generate beneath a feather duvet in a hotel room a long way from home. With extreme reluctance he reached out to the insistent telephone.

'Dave Lennox,' he said, giving the name the

14

voice on the other end of the line was expecting. He listened and frowned.

'When? Where?' She watched him, as he
jotted something down on the hotel phone pad,
and hung up.

'A club in St Kilda. We've got about ten
minutes.'

'Bugger,' Chrissie said. 'I was just getting
randy again.'


It was heavy rock. Intimidatingly loud. The
music blasted their ears like a jackhammer, but
they played their role and danced to it while
they waited to be approached. The place was a
cellar club, a pick-up joint. A small glass of
warm sweet wine cost ten dollars. They knew
they were being watched, but dared not try to
identify their observers. It was one of the things
that rankled about this entire charade. Having
to pretend they were stupid.

After half an hour, when they were beginning
to wonder if the whole thing was a hoax, a man
appeared from an office behind the bar. With
him were two others who looked like over-
weight wrestlers, ridiculous in neat suits that
bulged as if the seams might burst.

'I'm Lennie,' the man said. 'Outside, now.'

The suited wrestlers fell in on either side of
them.

'Wait a minute,' Ben said, playing his role. It

would be wrong to appear complaisant. 'We're supposed to meet Lonsdale.'

'He's waiting for you.'

'Where?'

'Back at your hotel.'

'Then why the hell did you bring us here?'

'Just fucking move,' Lennie said, and they went out to a car. Ben was told to sit in front. Christine was squeezed into the back between the muscle men. They both looked with open lust at her tight skirt and stockinged legs, as if imagining themselves between her thighs. Chrissie was acutely aware of this; Ben could sense it. That was when he began to get an uneasy feeling about the whole operation.

There was no-one waiting for them in the lobby.

'He's upstairs,' Lennie said.

'Upstairs where?'

'In your room.'

Lennie was grinning, and one of his thugs pressed the elevator button. They rode in uneasy silence to the sixteenth floor. The wrestlers stood either side of Chrissie, each claiming her for themselves. Their lechery was so palpable that Ben's disquiet grew. The door to their room was locked. Ben used his key card to open it, and Lonsdale was sitting there, sipping a drink from the minibar and making himself at home.

'About time,' he said.

'We don't like the way you do business, Mick.' Ben didn't need much pretence to show the anger he felt.

Michael Lonsdale shrugged. In his late forties, he was lean with saturnine features.

'Being careful, mate,' he said.

Christine pointed at their ransacked suitcases.

'Does that include putting your dirty hands in my undies?'

Lonsdale ignored her as he took out a cigar and lit it. He looked at Ben.

'Where's the money?'

'Would I leave it here? Some bastards could break in and swap it for a bag of sugar.'

'You'll get what you ordered. A packet of white. Fifty grand's worth.'

'Let's see the goods.'

'Don't give me the shits. First I see your money.'

Ben made a show of reluctance, then shrugged at Christine. She opened her handbag and gave him a screwdriver. While the four men watched, he removed the air-conditioning grille and took out the cabin bag. He unzipped it to show them the bundles of dollar bills.

'Do we count it now?' Lennie asked.

'You count it when we see the delivery,'

Christine said, and when Lonsdale's eyes swivelled to consider her with more care, Ben felt the other's first hint of suspicion and knew her intervention had been an error. These were Neanderthals; in their world, women were required to be decorative and available—not give orders.

'I was talking to your boyfriend,' Lonsdale said abrasively, and Ben intervened before she could respond to this brusque dismissal of her.

'She's an equal partner,' he said, 'so she's entitled to have a say. How the hell else do you think I raised the money?'

'She may be equal, but she stays here while you and I do the deal.'

'That's not how we arranged it.'

'That's how it's going to be,' Lonsdale said.

'You make it sound like she's some kind of hostage.'

'Whatever you want to call it.'

'Jesus Christ, you've checked us out, Mick. You know we're buying a consignment from you to set ourselves up as retailers. It's a bit late in the day to start acting as if you don't trust us.'

'Sure, I trust you.' Lonsdale's smile did not reach his eyes. 'Only I never take risks. You bring the cash—we go downstairs.'

'Where?'

'The carpark. That's where we make the changeover. She stays here with the boys.'

He indicated the grinning wrestlers.

'Yeah, she stays here,' the first gorilla said.

'Here with us,' echoed the other, which seemed to please them both enormously.

'If everything's in order, we have no problems. We give you the smack, you give us the money, and then the boys leave.'

Ben thought about it. The more he did, the less he liked it. He looked at Christine. They both knew they had no choice. He could feel her growing tension.

'Let's get the deal done,' she said. 'The sooner the better.'

'No fooling around with my girl,' Ben told the gorillas.

'Who, us?' said the first one.

'No way,' said the second.

They went out leaving Christine with them, down the corridor to the elevators, Ben with the money in the cabin bag, Lonsdale on one side of him, and Lennie a close shadow on the other.

*Thank God,* he thought, *she has the gun.*


The wrestlers kept looking at her, their overt excitement and their exchange of smirks making her feel uneasy. She must not allow her nervousness to show. It had been one of the first lessons taught when she joined. Tension is contagious; if they realised she was frightened it would boost their confidence, they would have the upper hand, relish the feeling of power, crowd her into a corner and decide they should do their job properly and body-search her. Then she would either have to use the gun, or they would strip her, beat her if she resisted, and then rape her.

She tried not to count the passing minutes, but by now Ben should be in the carpark below. There was no reason why it should take long. He would simply pay the money and collect the heroin; Lonsdale would leave with the marked notes, and the special squad of federal police would pick him up the moment he reached home. If the operation was going as planned, an unmarked car would have kept them under observation from the time they left the hotel, and followed them back from the club. The occupants of the car would have shot videotape of the man called Lennie, as well as the two goons. There would also be a tape recording of the conversation with Lonsdale because, after they had made love and before leaving the room, they had installed a bug. A tiny, ultra-sensitive digital microphone. Provided, of course, that Lonsdale had not found it. The thought sent an icicle shooting down her spine, and made her shiver.

'Cold?' The largest of the two had been

watching her so intently he had immediately noticed.

'Easy warm you up,' the other said, which they both found highly amusing.

Christine remained calm. She picked up her handbag, opened it, glimpsed the gun nestling there and, as one of them made a movement which suggested he might check the contents, she casually took out a lipstick and mirror. They watched her apply the vermilion to her lips.

'Good sort,' one said.

'Bloody oath,' said the other.

'Be a great fuck,' the first one said, as if she wasn't there.

Chrissie knew she was going to need the gun.

2 IT WAS GLOOMY in the basement carpark. Lonsdale stood alongside Ben. Lennie was close on the other side, and it was no coincidence that wherever they moved, Ben was the one in the middle. It was looking bad. About as bad as it could be.

He had expected caution. That was natural. These people were tough, ruthless professionals. But this was not caution. This was suspicion. Hard-edged, hostile. He had been aware of it since they found Lonsdale in their room, and realised he would have had time to search for the bug. It was barely a centimetre in size and lying in a dish with some glacé fruit and chocolate peanuts. It looked identical, but anyone rifling through the dish would feel the difference. If Lonsdale had discovered it, everything since then was a masquerade, and Christine was in mortal danger.

Somewhere back in the shadows a car started. Lights on high beam dazzled them as it drew near. It stopped alongside. A dark blue Ford Falcon.

'All clear?' Lonsdale asked.

The driver nodded. There was another man beside him in the front seat. Lonsdale opened the rear door.

'Get in,' he ordered.

'What's this, for Christ's sake,' Ben protested. 'You said we'd do the deal in the carpark.'

'We changed our minds. Five minutes from here. Climb in.' Ben slid into the back seat. Lonsdale followed and sat beside him. Lennie remained behind, pushing the door shut.

'Seat belt on. Don't want to break any laws.'

Ben saw the driver's eyes watching him in the mirror. As he fitted the belt, a car came racing down the ramp, its tyres squealing as it spun in an attempt to block the exit, the two plain-clothes federal police in it already yelling and brandishing their automatic rifles.

*Jesus Christ,* Ben thought, *the fucking cavalry are early.*


Christine applied eye makeup, while they kept watching. It was important to sustain this air of provocation, to keep their minds focused. If lust was the only way to distract them, it was a risk she had to take. But it was a delicate balance trying to manipulate the feelings of two witless thugs. She knew she must keep them intrigued, tantalised, even hopeful, but there was a line she dared not cross. Anything too blatant would alert them. She had to be cool, even disdainful, and above all, completely casual. She put away her mascara. They were getting used to her removing and replacing things from her handbag.

So far, so good.

She stood up, expecting an objection. There wasn't one.

Both sets of eyes were mentally undressing her and the men were engrossed with imagining whatever sexual gymnastics might then follow. She moved to the table, looked at the dish of glacé fruit and coated peanuts, as though wondering whether to tempt herself, and saw with relief the chocolate-brown digital bug which was just a fraction larger than the others. She palmed it perfectly as she took several coated peanuts and swallowed them. The bug she still kept in her hand, as she selected a glacé mandarin slice.

'Sweet tooth, eh,' the first gorilla commented.

'Sweet looker, too,' the other said. 'Be sweeter still sucking on my dick.'

'You wouldn't do that, would you, darling. Not his great floppy tool. A horrible thing like that, you'd never know where it's been.'

'You're wrong, Chicker. I reckon she quite likes me.'

Christine did not bother to spare either one a

glance. She reached again into her handbag and this time brought out a comb as she dropped in the digital bug. It would still be recording, which was a pity, she thought, because she would not enjoy a playback of such comments in the interrogation room, or later in court.

She checked herself in a wall mirror and made an unnecessary adjustment to her hair. The glass reflected them both standing behind her, each watching her even more intently. One of them caught her gaze and gave her a foolish grin and, not for the first time, Chrissie wondered if they were hyped up on speed or coke.

She began to wish Ben would hurry. He must have completed the transaction by now, unless there was a hitch. She felt a hint of panic; she didn't know how much longer she could prolong this charade. She sensed they were becoming more confident, and her fear was tangible. Perhaps, like all animals, they had an instinct for such things. Ben's last look had been a clear and direct order to her. His expression had said: *To hell with the operation, use the gun if you feel in jeopardy.*

She felt in extreme jeopardy.

She had virtually decided that she had enough time to snatch the automatic and shoot them both, preferably in the balls if they tried to rush her, when there was a knock on the door. *Thank God,* she thought, and before she could move, one of the wrestlers went to answer it. He was flung back by the unexpected force of the door, as Lennie almost exploded into the room.

'It's a fix,' he yelled. 'Cops. This fucking bitch is the fucking drug squad.'


Ben was fighting for his life. The driver had reacted in a split second, his foot slamming down hard on the pedal, aiming the Ford at full speed towards the unmarked police vehicle. It hit the other car side-on and slewed in a violent skidding ricochet while, in the back seat, Lonsdale slammed an elbow into Ben's face and forced the two detectives to dive for safety as he brought out a handgun and shot at them. The man beside the driver turned, swinging a tyre lever, trying to hit Ben while he struggled with Lonsdale for possession of the gun.

The Falcon went up the winding ramp, burning rubber and cannoning off the walls. There was an elderly attendant in a booth at the top, stationed beside the barrier. They smashed through it, past the man's shocked and frightened face, speeding out onto the road mindless of other traffic or pedestrians, and headed right into Bourke Street. The car behind had clamped a siren to the roof and was in distant pursuit. By now, there would be urgent calls

message that Hammond's now unsuitable?'

'Because I think we can use the situation,' Edward Burridge said carefully. 'Unsuitable is not necessarily a word I'd choose. Your fiasco may not be such a disaster, after all. At least, not for me.'

He proceeded to outline what he had in mind.


The autopsy report was brief, and grudging with its lack of information. It revealed an unidentified woman had taken a massive overdose of heroin, and died accidentally by falling from her hotel balcony, while under the influence of the drug.

DRUGGED DEATH DIVE, one of the tabloids bannered the story, but most newspapers reported it less sensationally. It made the following day's television news when it was revealed the dead girl had now been identified, through a medical prescription found in the room, as Jill Morton. Since she had no apparent address, it was thought she might have been an overseas visitor, perhaps from New Zealand. She was too badly disfigured for any photograph to be circulated.

There was no trace of a man with whom she had booked into the hotel. He had registered as David Lennox, but it appeared that this might have been an alias. A credit card in that name was found to be false. The address he gave did not exist.

The lack of detail should have stimulated any keen journalist, but the story was overtaken by events. Yet another retired politician published his kiss-and-tell memoirs, and a former prime minister got drunk at a diplomatic party and made a clown of himself.

A week later the body of Christine Duncan was flown to Sydney and buried in a private ceremony. She had massive injuries, and the cause of death was given as a road accident. Only her parents, close friends and live-in partner, Ken Randle, were present.

Ben was advised not to attend.

He was also told he was on indefinite leave.

That day was the first time there was any mention of the missing money. When he asked what missing money, he was told to be patient. In due course there would be an inquiry.

4 THE SQUAD CARS came in over the rise of the hill and down towards the interchange. They crossed the road over the freeway, and headed like missiles in the direction of the rash of brick and tiled houses that made up the residential neighbourhood. The leading car set off its siren, and a moment later the others followed suit. They resembled a strike force of predators; lacking only the Wagnerian music to evoke memories of a famous but bizarre movie.

There were six cars.

Four officers to each.

It had to be a big operation.

The other drivers pulling over to give way, commuters lined up for buses, joggers, locals walking their dogs, all knew it had to be a major crime. At least an armed break-in, maybe a murder, an escaped prisoner or perhaps a hostage situation. They would no doubt find out more about it on the evening news.

The cars swung towards a housing development. The group leader sent a signal, and two of the cars diverted and took an outside road to cover bushland behind the area. The remaining four, two of them with detectives, the others with uniformed men, turned into the estate. It was a high-density mix of villas and bungalows, spread over several hectares, and consisted of four intersecting streets laid out in a grid pattern. Small front lawns, neat homes.

It was just after 7.45 a.m. Some of the residents were leaving for work, others doing last-minute chores, taking out dustbins, hosing gardens, or warming engines while waiting for their neighbours to share a ride to the railway station. Most of them belonged to a car pool. Their children were chatting and laughing as they waited for the school bus. The squad cars with their oscillating lights and wailing sirens created a stir. Houses emptied as people ran out to see what was happening. In the street, at the far end of the cul-de-sac, everything stopped as the convoy pulled up outside a modest brick home. Men sprang from their vehicles and ran with drawn guns, surrounding the house. Two of them made a display of ringing the front doorbell, then, without waiting for an answer, kicked the door open. They swarmed into the hallway where two children, who had been quarrelling throughout breakfast, were now understandably terrified.

Ben had not been able to tell his wife about Chrissie. On his return from Melbourne, after being swiftly removed from the hotel and put onto a flight leaving immediately, he was met at the Sydney terminal by an inspector who advised him what steps were being taken.

The inspector was routinely sympathetic. He said it was obviously a monumental cock-up, but that was for others to examine. He then explained that Christine would not be identified under her own name in the newspaper reports; a great deal of slick organising had been embarked upon by the Victorian police to arrange this.

Ben, still in deep shock, said he was glad the coppers down there had been slick and well organised, as Chrissie was dead because of those trigger-happy goons, and it seemed they were better at covering their arses than monitoring a covert action. He said they should be held responsible for her death.

The inspector seemed not to hear any of this. He made it clear Ben was to tell nobody what had happened. It had been decided that Chrissie's interests, and those of the department, would be best served by the cause of her death being a car accident and, apart from a few at the highest level, only Ben himself could link the detective constable who had crashed to her death in Melbourne, with Chrissie Duncan, sadly run over and killed in the same city. It was imperative he didn't tell his friends—or his wife. Ben had replied that would not be a problem.

The inspector had asked if he wanted a lift home. He said he would prefer to take a cab.

Seven days ago.

Christine had been buried. Ben had been asked to write his account of what had gone wrong, and had then been placed on leave until further notice. Deborah had naturally been surprised by this. When she asked him why, he was deliberately noncommittal.

'It's just leave,' he said.

'But did you request it?'

'No.'

'Then why?'

'Maybe they thought I needed a break. Chris being killed like that in a car accident . . . well, for one thing, they have to find me a new partner.'

'Why not team you back with Nick?'

Nick Feraldos was one of his few close friends in the squad, and they had formerly worked together. He shook his head, irritably. It was difficult enough to talk dispassionately about Chrissie being dead, to act out the lie invented for him, without this kind of domestic interrogation.

'I don't know, Deb,' he said, trying to appear calm but cutting short her questions. The kids were already in the family room. He could hear their raised voices, fighting over the cereal. 'They said go on leave. I'm being paid, so I can hardly complain.'

'It seems strange. They might at least have waited for the school holidays. That would have been more useful.'

'I'll cut the lawn,' he said, 'weed the garden. Do the shopping, if you want. When the department asks me to take leave, what else do you suggest I do? Tell them to shove it?'

'I just think it's peculiar,' she said, and when he made no further attempt to answer, she went off to cope with the children.

He sighed. It was almost a normal morning. He and Deborah disagreeing, the kids creating their usual bedlam, while she cut their sand-wiches, told them to hurry or they'd miss the bus, spearing resentful glances at Ben who had successfully immersed himself in the newspaper.

Dimly he became aware of a sound.

Police sirens.

And a relentless and unceasing family squab-ble. World War Three in the family room. Nine-year-old Daniel had kicked his sister beneath the table.

'Ouch.' Susan, aged ten, was not likely to let such an opportunity pass unnoticed. 'He kicked me.'

'Liar.'

'You did so.'

'Where?'

'Under the table.'

'Rotten whistleblower,' Daniel said.

'Daniel, stop it.'

'She is, Mum. She's a supergrass. A dirty informer, a stoolie.'

'Ben, are you going to sit there and allow this?'

'Daniel,' Ben shouted.

'Yes, Dad,' his son shouted back.

'Just shut up.'

For a brief moment, this had an effect. There was a lull in proceedings, and a temporary silence reigned. During it, the sound of the police sirens could be heard coming closer.

'It's unfair. It's victim . . . what's it called . . .?'

'Victimisation,' Ben suggested.

'Yeah, that's it. Victimisation,' he muttered, loud enough for them all to hear. 'Girls always pick on me. So do women,' he added darkly, glancing at his mother. Deborah ignored this and wrapped the sandwiches.

'Both of you, hurry up. Finish your breakfast, clean your teeth and get your schoolbags. Don't forget your homework.'

That was when the sirens stopped, and there seemed to be a commotion outside their house. The next moment the doorbell rang stridently but, before anyone could make a move to answer it, the door was smashed off its hinges and police charged into the house. Susan screamed. Daniel's face was frozen with disbelief and fear. Deborah shouted in shock at the intruders, something indistinguishable, some kind of astonished protest, and then more police were entering through the back unlocked door. Ben grabbed the nearest officer whom he vaguely knew.

'What in the name of God is going on?'

'Detective Sergeant Hammond?'

'You know that. Who sent you? What the fuck is this?'

'Check him for weapons,' the officer said to one of his men, 'and search the house.' To Ben he said: 'You're under arrest.'


It was on the midday news, and Superintendent Howard Morgan of the federal drug squad watched it with the state attorney-general in his spacious government office. He would have watched it with his boss, Bradley Foster, but the deputy chief commissioner had left for Canberra, and told Superintendent Morgan to liaise with the attorney-general, who had been consulted to give validity to what was being done. It was, after all, state police who were now involved, and the attorney-general was the state's senior law officer. Morgan knew how good his boss Bradley was at covering his back.

The news departments of several television channels had been tipped off, their cameras arriving in time to see Ben escorted from his house, angrily remonstrating while being hand-cuffed and then forced into the back of a police car, during which a long lens captured the dazed and frightened faces of his wife and two chil-dren at their broken front door, and the crowd of startled neighbours watching and speculating.

'A large squad of armed police,' the news-caster read from his teleprompter while gazing with deep sincerity at his audience beyond the camera, 'this morning arrested Detective Ser-geant Ben Hammond of the federal drug squad, in a sudden raid on his Sydney home. Although no statement has yet been issued, a police spokesperson said Sergeant Hammond is being interrogated on drug-related matters. It is believed he may be formally charged later today.'

The attorney-general used the remote control to turn down the volume, as several of the neighbours were interviewed. Morgan shook his head with disbelief.

'Jesus Christ,' he said.

'You don't approve?'

'You want tact, or you want the truth? I think it stinks.'

'You always speak your mind, don't you, Morgan.'

'If you're worried about me going public, I won't. But in the privacy of these walls, it was hamfisted, thuggish and quite unfair. It could have been done without publicly crucifying him, or his family.'

'Yes, the raid does seem to have been a trifle . . . excessive,' the attorney-general said.

'It was a bloody circus,' Morgan said angrily.

'Most unfortunate,' the attorney-general wanted to show he was a fairminded man, 'but the end result . . . that's what matters.'

'I don't even know what the end result is meant to be.' Morgan felt unable to take any more of the other's smug political clichés. 'But for whatever reason, we've chucked a man on the scrap heap. This seems like a nasty, dirty game, and I'm not at all sure any end result can be worth it.'


Ben's main feeling, apart from anger, was one of disbelief. He found it difficult to credit what was happening to him. Throughout the day he had been interviewed by a series of alternating teams, given coffee and a sandwich, but no rest, no chance to wash or shave, or to have a moment to himself, to try to fathom what this was about. No chance to guess who was orchestrating these accusations, and why. In eight years with the state police, part of this time with the major crime squad and four years with federal drug enforcement, he had never encountered any experience like this. At moments he felt physically ill.

His head ached with the repetitive questions.

'What happened to the money?'

'Why do you keep asking me? The money was in the car.'

'Not according to our information.'

'Then someone nicked it. It could hardly have been me.'

'Why not?'

'Jesus Christ, I was with those idiots who tailed us when the car crashed. How could I have hidden that much cash without them seeing it?'

'Unless the money was never in the car.'

'Of course it was. Where else could it have been?'

'You tell us. Fifty grand, gone walkabout. Can you explain that?'

Some were almost friendly; some hard and abrasive. He knew the tactics. He had used them himself in interrogations. Teamwork. One played the nice guy, the other the bastard.

'You were sleeping with Detective Duncan.'
'If I was, it's none of your fucking business.'
'Everything's our business.'

'Especially any fucking business,' said his partner, acting the hit man. Goading Ben about his relationship with Chrissie until he became enraged, lost his temper, tried to attack the man, and had to be restrained.

They called time out, and gave him more coffee. By now they knew he preferred it hot and black, no sugar. It came lukewarm, white, so sickly sweet he could barely drink it. That was only one of the humiliations. There were others.

When his bladder could no longer bear it, they took him to a toilet which was locked, and they seemed unable to find the key. By the time they had discovered it, the long delay and the nervous stress he was under had made him piss himself.

Later there were photographs.

Snaps of Chrissie: smiling, sunbaking on the beach, jogging, laughing at the camera, Chrissie looking wonderful. God alone knew where they had come from; they must have invaded her private belongings to find them. Ben even recognised some that he had taken with her camera. The photos were a cold and calculating tactic. They had more effect on him than anything else. She looked so young, so heartbreakingly alive that he wanted to weep.

He began to blame himself for her death.

The photos made him feel a bleak, desolate sadness.

5

A TELEVISION CREW was still staked out in the street. All the others had given up. They had done the mandatory interviews with neighbours, and now there was a stir as a car approached.

'It's the wife. Bringing the kids home.'

They had the camera rolling as Deborah stopped the car, and a bland familiar face with a handheld microphone was alongside her and the children before they could reach the house.

'Any statement, Mrs Hammond?'

'No,' Deborah said vehemently. 'Can't you leave us alone?'

The interviewer was well trained and accomplished. He'd been doing this for years, and one thing he knew—you kept hammering them with questions. Eventually they had to answer or run. Either way made him look good to his audience.

'How do you feel?' he asked. 'Did you have any warning of the raid? Is it true he's to be charged?'

'Please stop it.' Deborah was close to panic. 'Stop it!'

He turned to Susan and Daniel, as if she hadn't spoken. He gave them a big friendly smile.

'Kids, how was it at school? Any problems for you there? What did your friends say?'

*Hang on,* the cameraman thought, *that's going it a bit.* He choked back a laugh and kept filming as Deborah swung a shopping bag and hit her interrogator in the face. The cameraman, who had been hoping someone would do this for years, thought it might even rate the lead story on the six o'clock news. *Beauty,* he said to himself, and zoomed in for a close shot of the cut beside the famous one's eye.


There were a great many statements. They had a huge folder full of them, but they read out only selected ones.

'We knew Ben Hammond was on the take. Lotsa times he tipped us off before a bust, but you had to be real careful with him. He was in on the drug deals, only he kept that real quiet. He wanted a few runs on the board to get promoted. He was always a tricky bastard.'

'Harry the Hermit said that?' Ben was incredulous. 'And you call that evidence? Bloody Harry couldn't lie straight in bed.'

'We've got heaps more. Dozens. They can't all be wrong.'

He named a few, and Ben shook his head, disbelievingly.

'Pushers and pimps. The bloody dregs. All the rock spiders are being dragged out from under their slimy stones to set me up.'

'Maybe so. I'm sorry, Ben, but I have to say it looks like you're in deep shit.'


They charged him late that afternoon. Specifically they arrested him on charges of perjury and conspiracy to defraud, with drug-related allegations pending. There was no police opposition to bail, so he was brought before a magistrate who set his bail at a modest $10 000 in his own cognisance, and ordered him to report to his local police station each day. He was also to surrender his passport.

Outside were the TV cameras, photographers and a forest of thrusting microphones. They shouted questions at him. Ben tried to keep calm, knowing this would be seen in most homes across the city, and in particular by the families of his children's friends. He did his best. But the questions were abrasive and relentlessly intrusive, and it had been a terrible day. When one fiercely persistent female with a long-stem broomstick microphone told him she did not

51

believe his protestations of innocence, Ben yelled at her to shove the broomstick up her arse and fly away like any other witch would.

It had the benefit of enforcing a cut in the videotape. The news pundits could not allow their luminaries to be spoken to like that. At least not on camera in front of all those people.


Superintendent Howard Morgan sat watching the slaughter of Ben Hammond on the early evening news. To add to his disquiet, he was sitting alongside Edward Burridge. He didn't like Burridge. He thought him a cold fish, ruthless despite the suave and ingratiating veneer. He also felt a deep sense of anger at the way the Englishman had arranged the demise of Ben Hammond.

'It's in all our best interests,' Burridge said, reading his mind.

'Try telling him that. Nobody should be treated like this.'

Morgan had been warned this was merely camouflage for a major security operation, and the more realistic the better the chance of eventual success. He felt he had been coerced into this, without being entrusted with the full picture. He should have insisted. Now he was aware the other man had him categorised as weak and vacillating, and it annoyed him.

'He'll be looked after,' Burridge told him. 'I'll see to it.'

'In that case, God help him,' Morgan said. 'With someone like you on his side, what bloody hope has he got?'


Ben climbed the high wooden fence, and headed towards the back door of his house. The street was quiet. Television screens flickered behind drawn blinds in most of the houses. Down the road a neighbour's dog barked. He turned the handle, but the door was locked. He used his key and gently eased it open. He went through the kitchen. The house was strangely silent. Deborah was watching television in the living room, but the sound was off; she was really sitting there waiting for him. She used the remote control to dispose of the image.

'Where are the kids?' he asked.

'At Mum's place.'

'Must have been bloody awful for them. And for you.' He saw a newspaper on the coffee table. The late edition tabloid headline read: DETECTIVE FOR TRIAL.

'Ben, I packed some of your things.' He turned to stare at her, but it was not really a surprise. 'I'm sorry. It's a lousy end to a terrible day. It's rotten timing, but I just can't cope with it.'

He nodded and said nothing.

'It was going to come to this, anyway. Wasn't it?'

'Yes,' he said.

'We've had nothing going for us, the past few years.'

'No, we haven't. Have you told the kids?'

'Not yet. I'll explain you've gone away until the fuss dies down. Later, if we decide it's permanent, they'll be used to the idea.'

'I'll tell them.'

'Don't you think it'd be better if you stayed away?'

'Probably would, Deborah, but I'll tell them just the same.' He went through to the bedroom, where two packed suitcases lay open on the bed. She followed him.

'I'm sorry you're in trouble. I suppose you think I'm a bitch to do this, today of all days?'

'No. We both know it's been coming.'

'Can you find somewhere to stay?'

'A motel tonight. I'll look for a pad tomorrow. Better let the cops know, so they don't think I'm skipping bail.'

'Oh, God,' she said in sudden distress, 'I wish it hadn't had to happen like this. We should have been able to sit down and agree in a sensible way that we'd live apart.'

'Well, we're doing that now, aren't we? I'll leave you the wagon, and take the Mazda.'

'The exhaust needs fixing on the Mazda.'

'I'll have it done. I'll put it on the bankcard.' He shut the cases and took them to the front door. 'Have you got money?'

'Enough. I can draw at the automatic teller.'

'I'll let you know where I am. We have to sort out about finances, all that stuff.'

'Oh, Christ,' she said. 'I am sorry.'

'You don't have to be, Deborah. I know it's been hell for you, with the raid, the neighbours, the bloody media. I don't want you to keep saying you're sorry.'

He went down the front steps and put the two suitcases in the elderly Mazda sedan. She watched him from the door.

'One thing I would've liked, though. One thing you forgot.'

'What?'

'You didn't bother to ask me if I'm guilty or not.'

He started the car, as he saw her realisation, the look of dismay, her lips moving in a reply he could not hear over the noise of the motor, as he backed out into the street and drove away.

6 TERESA SAW HIM for the first time at her mother's funeral. It was a bleak day, the north London cemetery more than usually dismal with weeping grey skies, the crowd huddled beneath a canopy of suitably black umbrellas. She became aware of him because he stood alone, on the edge of the mourners, hatless and seemingly unconcerned with the light misty rain. He was tall enough for her to notice across the rows of faces fixed in suitable melancholy, some of whom were friends, some total strangers. He looked tanned, as if he had just come from abroad, and appeared to be in his early fifties. She realised his eyes were studying her.

'*In my Father's house are many mansions . . .*' the minister was intoning against the distant hum of traffic on the North Circular, '*I go to prepare a place for you . . .*'

Tess thought how much she hated funerals: the ritualistic, routine performance by parsons hired like the hearse and the limousines, clergy with no personal nexus or knowledge of the dead, winging it, as some of her theatrical friends might say, from a scrap of paper on which were scribbled down the necessary basic details of the departed.

'And to her devoted husband, Charles, and her grieving daughter, Teresa Francine, our thoughts go out at this time . . .'

*Francine*, Tess thought. *My God. I dropped that part of my name long ago. It's not in my passport. Even when I got married, I wasn't Teresa Francine. That was for my French father, twenty-nine years ago, at the christening font in Vientiane.*

The clergyman had garnered some facts, presumably from Charles, and proceeded to enlarge on them.

'Clarissa Lambert spent many years in the Far East, enduring the siege of Dien Bien Phu, and later lived in Laos, where her daughter Teresa was born. After several years in Thailand, she returned to this country to live in West Hampstead, where she and her husband shared a deep interest in the theatre, and local politics . . .'

With one mighty leap, Tess realised, the cleric had bridged the gap from Vientiane to West Hampstead, deftly avoiding mention of her long-dead father, or the parents' divorce, dwelling on the happiness of the current marriage, with no hint it had been preceded by one far less joyous. It was not a surprise there should be this tactful edit in her mother's epitaph. No doubt Charles knew her wishes; it was not something she would have wanted spoken of at her interment, reticent as she had been about it during her life. Tess had tried often enough, particularly during her teens, to find out more about her father, and had been told it was a painful subject. She was promised that some day they would have a good long talk about it. They never had. In time she had come to realise that they never would, and that the subject genuinely disturbed her mother.

Charles, of whom she was very fond, the kindest, nicest man in the world, had once said her mother cried and had restless nights each time she tried to reopen the subject. So from that time she had stopped asking. In fact, apart from some old photographs and details like the date of his death, Teresa had little real information about her father.

*'In the hope of the Resurrection, and of life everlasting, may the Lord God have mercy upon us. Christ have mercy upon us . . .'*

After another hymn, the ultimate prayer, the lowering of the coffin into the open grave, the first clods of earth, the last tears, the funeral was finally and mercifully over. The hired chaplain moved off to greet another cortege, and Teresa tried to steer her stepfather through the crowd of friends and acquaintances sympathising with their loss. In the process she met the man she had noticed earlier. He nodded, shook hands, and murmured his condolences.

'Burridge,' he said, and gave her an embossed card with his name, *Edward Adrian Burridge, United Nations Agency*, and addresses in both New York and Paris. 'May we meet?'

It was hardly what she expected at her mother's funeral, and he seemed to realise it. Charles had moved on to some distant relatives and for a brief moment they were alone.

'I apologise for the timing, but it is important. I need to talk to you, Miss Martineau.'

'What about?' she asked, wondering how he knew she had reverted to her own name after her divorce.

'About your father,' he told her.

'My father?' She was so used to evasion, the direct answer startled her. 'What about him?'

'Nothing I can discuss now. But we should meet as soon as possible. Perhaps tomorrow?'


She was still surprised that a day after her mother's burial she should be at Gatwick, collecting an Air France ticket to Paris, because of what some man she had never met before had said to her. On landing at Charles de Gaulle Airport she took a taxi to a building adjacent to the Jardin des Tuileries. In the foyer she showed her passport at the security desk, and after a muted phone call was admitted to the top floor with a view over the left bank and the Quai d'Orsay. A smart secretary greeted her with a welcoming smile, and told her Sir Edward was waiting. It was the first time she had known he had a title. She was shown into a large luxurious office, and coffee was brought almost instantly.

Burridge started to comment on the view, and pointed out the loaded barges making their way beneath the Solférino and Concorde bridges. Teresa decided she had not made this strange trip to spend the day being cultivated, or patronised.

'If you don't mind, Sir Edward,' she said, 'I've been to Paris many times. The last thing I need is a guide—or a tour, even if it's only making polite chat. You spoke about my father as if you knew him. I most certainly need to know about that.'

'I don't know him,' Burridge said, 'but I can tell you about him. For instance where he is, and what he's doing.'

'Where he is? What he's doing?' Teresa was confused. 'You make it sound as if he's still alive?'

'Well, of course he's alive,' Burridge told her. He seemed not to notice her shocked expression.

'No,' she said. 'I'm sorry, but you've made a

mistake. Or confused me with someone else. He died twenty years ago. I know that because I was exactly nine years old.'

'That,' Burridge said, 'was when your mother told you he died. That was when she wanted him dead.'

'What the hell do you mean?'

'She'd found a new husband. And your father was on the far side of the world. They'd divorced. She'd come home to England, to start a new life. It was simpler that he died.'

'But why?'

'I'm only assuming, but it seems a reasonable assumption, that she didn't want you romanticising a distant father—whom you some day might want to meet. You might even have preferred him. His being dead avoided such possibilities. It made life easier. If you asked questions, which I'm sure you would have when you were younger, what effect did it create? Did it cause distress? Tears and sleepless nights, perhaps? Did she try not to talk about him?'

It was so uncannily accurate that Tess began to shiver.

'It's not possible,' she said. 'He is dead.'

Sir Edward Burridge opened his desk drawer and took out a photograph. He held it in his hand before showing her.

'Do you have any old photos of your father?'

61

'One or two.'

'Is this the same man?'

He handed it to her. It was enlarged, a glossy black-and-white shot. In the background was a timber house with wide verandahs and tropical vegetation. In the foreground, a Thai girl and a man in his late fifties. Tess stared at her father. There was absolutely no doubt who it was. The few snaps she possessed, the very few her mother had reluctantly given her, were of a much younger man, but undeniably the same person. Her father was smiling, and his arm was around the girl, who could not have been more than eighteen years old. She had the feeling the picture might have been taken with a long lens, because they seemed natural and unaware of any camera.

'Well?' Burridge was watching her, but she knew he had already sensed her recognition.

'When was it taken?'

'As far as I know, about a year ago.'

'Where?'

'In Thailand.'

'Who took it?'

'One of our people. I'm not sure who.'

'The girl? Who's she?'

'I'm sorry,' Burridge said. 'I don't know.'

'Well, I'm sorry, Sir Edward, but I don't buy any of this. You have a picture of my father, yet you said you didn't know him. You can't tell me if that's a daughter or a girlfriend, or who it was that took the photo, but you can tell me he's in Thailand.'

'At present that's all I can tell you.'

'Why?'

'Because of what he does.'

'Which is . . .?'

'He works for us,' Burridge said.

'For the United Nations?'

'Yes.'

'Doing what?'

'It's not my department, so I'm not at liberty to say.'

He put out his hand for the print, and she reluctantly handed it back to him. She watched him put it away in his desk.

'You have to understand, Teresa—you don't mind if I call you Teresa, I hope,' he took her silent shrug as assent, 'that this is a huge organisation. We do a lot more than mount peacekeeping forces and listen to endless debates at the rather boring Assembly in New York.'

She was barely able to control her impatience.

'I am aware of that. I attended an Asia–Pacific conference of police chiefs with Interpol, as an interpreter for the UN.'

'Last year,' he said. 'In Cambodia. Phnom Penh.'

'Yes.'

'And previously you translated tapes we made

63

of an ASEAN meeting in Singapore. Just how many languages do you speak?'

'If you have a file on me,' Tess said, 'I imagine you would know that.' She was beginning to dislike him. Burridge smiled as if he had not heard the touch of asperity in her reply.

'I'm told ten, and you can manage others. Fluent in French, and the various French colonial patois one encounters in Vietnam and Laos. You speak Mandarin, Cantonese, Thai, German, Italian, Spanish, etcetera. You went to school in Bangkok as a child, so you grew up multilingual. Your stepfather, Charles Lambert, spent two years in Hong Kong after he married your mother, and you went with them—and learned what hardly any English people do: how to converse with the locals in their major languages. Later on, you studied at the Sorbonne. You're one of those naturals who goes to places, learns the language, and remembers it. I'm told you can hold a busy conversation with six or seven different nationalities, switching from one to another without any difficulty. You're on the books of a firm in Baker Street who supply interpreters, which means you travel a great deal, and apart from the two jobs for us, you've also worked for the French Sûreté, and for the Italian police in a Mafioso inquiry.'

'You make it appear as if I'm some sort of spy, up to my neck in intrigue. They were extremely rare occasions. Most of my work is for foreign business people, and usually boring. Last week, for instance, I was in Birmingham, with an industrialist from Taiwan, discussing the plumbing for his new factory with the local council.'

'You were also,' Burridge said, as if not considering this piece of information warranted a reply, 'a drama student after the Sorbonne, and then an actress. What happened?'

Tess studied him carefully.

'You seem to have an extensive file on me,' she said.

'The reports on your work for us were most impressive.'

'So that sanctions an investigation into my life?'

'Basic facts. No malice or any sinister intent.'

'I'm relieved to hear it. But for what reason then? I'm just a plain interpreter.'

'Certainly not plain, if I may say so. I would have thought someone with your looks would have had casting directors queuing. But you gave it up. Why?'

'Because I wasn't good enough,' she retorted. 'Looks have little to do with it. In the theatre I got stage fright, and on the screen I didn't enthral. I'm an expert interpreter and a lousy actor. Now if there's no more you can tell me about my father, I don't think I need to stay.'

'I'm sorry if I've made you angry.'

Tess decided not to answer this. She picked up her suede handbag and her coat, and rose.

'You see, I have a job I want to offer you,' Burridge said. 'It's a rather special job, so it required an intensive search of whatever was known about you. In the process, the computer linked you to your father. He's in Thailand, and that's where you'd eventually go—if you were to accept. You'd almost certainly meet him.'

Tess stared at him. She sat down again.

'Now tell me the truth, Sir Edward.'

'If I can.'

'When was that photo taken?'

'Last week.'

'After your computer made the link?'

'Yes.'

'Who's the girl? His daughter?'

'No.'

'Girlfriend? Or wife?'

'Not his wife. Apparently a girlfriend.'

'Well, at least I don't have a teenage step-mother. Did he know this was being taken?'

'No.'

'You needed it to show me?'

'That's right.'

'Without my father's knowledge?'

'I thought he might have reservations.'

'About meeting me? Or me taking the job?'

Burridge hesitated for a moment.

'Both,' he eventually said.

'Is it a dangerous job?'

'Not unduly.'

'But not as safe as discussing plumbing in Birmingham.'

'Nothing's as safe as that. Nor as dull.'

'Quite.' She almost smiled.

'Why don't we have lunch, and let me explain it to you?'

'First, tell me what my father does for the United Nations. You obviously have that knowledge.'

'Yes, I do,' he said, unequivocally 'But I'm not able to tell you. It's classified—on a need-to-know basis.'

'Don't play games, Sir Edward. I need to know.'

'No, you don't. All you need to know is that he's well and truly alive, and if you accept the job you'll meet him. I can promise you will. That's all you need to know,' Edward Burridge said.


She flew home that night, took the fast train to Victoria, a taxi to Drayton Gardens where she bought milk and eggs at the Indian supermarket, and walked the rest of the way to her flat in Bolton Gardens. It was the ground floor of what had been a London merchant's substantial home, long since divided into apartments, and she had bought a lease soon after property prices began to slump following the boom. At that earlier time, when prices had exploded beyond belief, there was no way she could have afforded it. Nor would Stephen have ever contemplated living here. Home to him was a smart modern townhouse with a terrace on Chelsea Reach, where other yuppies had lived and partied as if there were no tomorrow, and had played the house game, constantly trading up, just as they liked to say they turned in their BMWs when the ashtrays were full.

Stephen would have hated Bolton Gardens. Its main attraction was a fine large room with Georgian windows, the original living room of the house. There was a small bedroom, with an adjoining bathroom, and off the hallway a galley-style kitchen that led to the back door and a porch overlooking a tiny garden. It had been home now for two years, since the end of her marriage, and she always felt comfortable coming back to it.

Never more so than today.

*Why had her mother not told her? Why the strange, unnecessary pretence?*

She checked her answering machine. There were two messages, one from the office in Baker Street asking her if she was free to interpret for a Vietnamese cabinet minister in town to see the Board of Trade, and another from Tim, with whom she had had dinner twice, but not yet slept with, and not made up her mind how she felt about that. Deciding that they could both wait until tomorrow, and nothing was as important as this, she rang Charles.

'Are you all right?' she asked him.

'The place feels empty,' he said. 'I'm a bit lost. I don't suppose you could bear to drive over, and I'll cook you an omelette?'

'Of course I'll drive over,' Tess said, and then as casually as she could, she added, 'I want to tell you about my day. I went to Paris. I've seen a photograph of my father—taken last week.'

'Oh, Christ,' he said, and she knew then that Edward Burridge, whom she did not particularly like or trust, had told her the truth.


'I don't know why she did it,' Charles Lambert said. They sat in the kitchen of the rambling house in West Hampstead, where Tess had grown up, and his kindly face was more lined than usual, as a network of creases unfolded with his frown.

'Did you ever meet him? My father?'

'Never. Your mother and I met in Bangkok—after she'd taken you and left him in Vientiane. But I have to say this, darling—and you won't like hearing it. She hated him.'

'Like I hated Stephen, when we split up?'

'You didn't hate Stephen. You just couldn't stand living with the silly prat—for which I applaud you. But this was different, Tess. Your mother,' he hesitated, searching for a tactful word, but unable to find one, 'loathed him.'

'God,' Teresa said. 'I'm sorry to subject you to this.'

'I'm sorry I can't tell you any more. She would never talk about him even to me. It was obviously a very unhappy subject. And so, when she said he was dead, at least as far as you were concerned, I promised never to speak of it.' He sighed. 'I'd have kept that promise, but Clarissa's dead, and you know the truth, so there's no way I want to lie to you or lose you, Tess.'

'Thank you, Charles,' she said, feeling a great wave of affection towards him. 'But I don't entirely know the truth.'

'You know your father's alive.'

'Yes, I know that. But why mother hated him—their past life together—his present existence—I feel as if I know nothing.'

'Does it really have to matter?' he asked her.

'Yes,' she said, wishing she could lie to him, 'Yes, Charlie, I'm afraid it does. I can't just walk away—much as I'd like to.'

'You're going to take this United Nations offer?'

'Yes.'

'To meet him?'

'I'm taking the job. Whether that means I meet him or not, well, we'll see.'

'It's not dangerous, is it?'

His old eyes were anxious for her, and she loved him so much, and wanted to reassure him.

'Not unduly,' she said, then realised she had unconsciously echoed Burridge.

'Not unduly? I don't like the sound of that,' Charles said. 'You take care, you hear. Anyway, what sort of work is it?'

'Nothing important.' This time she was able to lie with impunity. 'Just another interpreting job.'

Burridge had an apartment in Paris. It was on the top floor of an eighteenth-century building in the Rue de Maubeuge, and looked down into the cloistered church of St-Vincent de Paul and up the slope of Montmartre towards the domed symmetry of Sacré Coeur. He finished breakfast, knowing it would be midafternoon in Hong Kong. He dialled the international code and listened while the phone rang in Walter Chen's house. Just when he thought they were out, Walter picked up the phone. He sounded breathless.

'Walter?'

'My dear fellow.'

'I didn't wake you, did I?'

'On the contrary—'

Burridge knew exactly what that meant.

'I apologise—to you and the lady.'

'I shall tell her.'

'No, don't. Don't mention it was me who rang. This is for your ears only.'

'As you wish. Any progress?'

'I met with Teresa Martineau two days ago. She called yesterday and accepted. So everything is falling perfectly into place.'

7 AT FIRST DANIEL pretended not to see them, then one of his school friends pointed, and he slouched reluctantly across the road to where Ben stood waiting, hand in hand with Susan.

'Hi.' He nodded at his father and his sister.

'Hi, Dan. How's school?'

'Okay, I suppose.'

They went to a coffee shop, and sat at a table outside in the sunshine. Susan had a lemonade, and Daniel a milkshake. He made a loud slurping noise as he drained the last of it through his straw.

'Daniel,' Susan said in protest.

He ignored her, and gazed at his father.

'Are you and Mum splitting?'

Susan was embarrassed.

'Cut it out, you little horror.'

'It's all right, Susan.' He was touched by his daughter's protective concern for him. 'We're thinking about it. People do separate.'

'I know. Half the kids in my class are one-parent families. That's what we'll be, won't we?'

'No,' Ben said carefully. 'You'll have two parents. Both of us will love you. We just won't be living in the same house.'

'Is it because of . . . of what's happened?'

Ben shook his head.

'Don't you like each other any more?'

'It's not that.'

'Have you got someone else?'

Susan threw up her hands in despair. 'Oh, God, you can't take him anywhere.'

'Shut up,' he said to her with sudden animosity. 'It's my life. He's my father. I can ask him a question.'

'Of course you can.' Ben looked at her, trying to convey he appreciated her loyalty, but this had to be discussed. They couldn't sit here and pretend nothing had happened.

'So what's the answer?' Daniel's grey eyes studied him from across the table.

'The answer is no. There could have been . . . but she's not around any more.'

'I think you ought to stop cross-examining Dad. He's had enough of that.'

Dan seemed for once to be in agreement with her, but then asked, 'Do you think . . . will they put you in jail?'

'Daniel . . .!'

'Will they, Dad?'

'I don't know, Danny,' Ben said. 'They might

try. I wish I knew why, because I haven't done anything wrong.'

He nodded, as if digesting this.

'I had a fight at school,' he said. 'Some kids said you were dead-set guilty, so I took two of 'em on.'

'What happened? Did you get hurt?'

'No, I won. Got told off by the teacher and kept in, but I won.'

'Good on you.' Ben smiled. His son grinned back at him. It was a moment to treasure, but he needed one thing more.

'I don't know if the court will believe I'm innocent,' he told them, 'but it would help a lot to know you two believe me.'

Susan said instantly: 'Of course we do. *I* do,' she stressed, and gazed at Daniel, waiting for his answer. It seemed a long time in coming.

'I'll tell you the truth, Dad. I wasn't sure. But I am now.'

He felt a great sense of relief and love for them both. He knew Susan was pleased at Dan's reply. Daniel himself took refuge in his milk-shake, and noisily slurped the dregs from the container. This time his sister smiled and made no complaint.

*It'd be some irony,* Ben thought, *if this trouble I'm in, and busting up with Deborah, made these two friends at last.*

● ● ●

The magistrate was a small neat man, who was not fond of the media. It irritated him to know he had a courtroom full of its representatives, and that he was about to give them a headline. He frowned again over the papers the police prosecutor had handed him, and asked Ben to rise. The public seats were occupied mainly by radio and print journalists. The cameras were waiting outside.

It was not a listed hearing. It had been brought forward, so word had clearly been assiduously spread. Someone was manipulating this like a public relations exercise. Ben again wondered who, and why, then realised the magistrate was speaking. He sounded acerbic.

'I am advised the prosecution is unable to proceed with this charge. It appears certain evidence has proved "unreliable". Some witnesses are no longer available.' He turned to spear a glance at the police prosecutor. 'Is this correct?'

'Yes, Your Worship,' the prosecutor said, amid a surprised outbreak of murmurs. The magistrate testily called for order.

'It is not the first time this court has been obliged to discharge an accused, after having been assured a case exists.' He gazed frostily at Ben. 'It is my duty to inform you all charges are withdrawn, and you are free to go.' He made it sound like a duty performed with considerable reluctance.

The media picked up on the resonance. It was yet another instance of the justice system failing. If a case had existed, why was it now withdrawn? In the public mind, the burden of proof had become a cumbrous millstone. Too many convictions being overturned on appeal. Witnesses failing to appear. So often the apparent guilty going free. And here was another. A suspect policeman on the take, mixed up in drugs, lucky or smart enough to walk away. Ben could feel the mood of mistrust in the courtroom. He knew the speculation and suspicion would continue.


They sat watching the satellite news, the Asia–Pacific service which Walter had taped earlier while Burridge was still aboard a flight from Paris, and saw the swarm of reporters, the intrusive microphones and cameras jostling for better and closer angles. A besieged Ben barely able to answer the stream of shouted questions, as he was asked if he was relieved to have the cloud hanging over him lifted—was it a police vendetta—a typical blunder—or just good luck that witnesses were unable or unwilling to turn up?

Pugnacious questions, a babble of insensitivity. Walter felt sorry for the man. He thought the press resembled a pack of rabid hounds, and

Ben Hammond was their fox at bay. He felt a rare surge of distaste for his friend Edward, whom he always knew could be ruthless, who had fought and defended him as a young and persecuted Chinese boy at prep school long ago, and so their friendship was firmly based and had endured a lifetime, but this was Walter's first glimpse of the world he inhabited, and he didn't care for it. *But after all, a seat in the House of Lords,* he thought, and knew it was not a false promise. Edward could and would arrange it. He left the huge glass-enclosed living room and went out onto the terrace.

Walter Chen looked down on the glittering lights of his city. It would not be his for much longer, but he was one of the fortunate. He had already made careful arrangements for whatever upheaval the imminent end of Britain's lease might bring. Walter was vastly rich. He had turned what was a relatively small inheritance into a development empire that had built shopping malls in Singapore and Sydney, and had been one of the earliest to discover the lucrative returns of up-market retirement villages. He had money in Jersey, the Caymans and Switzerland. He owned homes in Berkshire and Cannes, where he intended to spend the English winter. He would also have to acquire a London flat, close to Westminster and the House of Lords. The peerage. That meant he must choose a title. *Baron Chen of Hong Kong?* Perhaps. Whatever I call myself, he thought, knowing the English, the buggers will christen me *Lord Honkers*.

He wondered what Helene would say, once this was over and he could tell her. It was sometimes irksome not to be able to confide in her, but they had all been adamant about security. No-one outside the select group was to know; no-one was to be trusted, not even Helene to whom he had entrusted his heart.

Merely thinking about her brought sensual pleasure. He had divorced two wives, and known many women, but there had been no-one in his life quite like Helene Lee. Brought up in California, an exotic mix of Filipina, Chinese and American, she was deeply in love with him, and he was besotted by her. While he sipped a drink, the brilliant view spread below him, Walter no longer saw it. He was thinking of Helene's pliant lips, her slim vibrant body, the passionate climaxes, the tousled bed in which they had made violent love over and over again throughout the previous night. His stamina, which had once begun to cause him concern, now seemed inexhaustible. He hungered for her, and could even feel the memory of what had happened upstairs last night beginning to arouse him.

'Did you hear me?'

He realised Edward was there and had just spoken.

'Sorry—I was dreaming.'

'I said I'm sorry.'

'About what?'

'The treatment of Ben Hammond—it disturbed you. But we have to make this realistic.'

'I know.'

'The mess in Melbourne turned to our advantage. He no longer has to pose. In the public perception he's a bent copper.'

'You take awful liberties with people's lives, Edward.'

'In a good cause—ultimately.'

'Suppose, after all this, he refuses?'

'I'll have to see he doesn't,' Burridge said, and something in his voice made Walter want to shiver.

'It's a nasty, savage place, your world. I'd be useless in it.'

'You would. You have a gentle nature, old boy, except when it comes to battles over income tax.' Burridge smiled in a rare moment of genuine affection. 'But don't underestimate yourself. None of this would have been possible without the finance.'

'It's all transferred and in place. I heard from the bank. We have an appointment at noon tomorrow.'

'I'm very grateful, Walter.'

'My pleasure, Edward.'

'As to that, I believe your pleasure has just returned home,' he murmured, as a tall slim girl in a white cheongsam came out to join them.

'Sir Edward . . .' she nodded and smiled at him, and crossed the terrace to kiss Walter.

She was, Burridge thought objectively, a remarkable piece of crumpet. Stunningly beautiful. By far the loveliest of all Walter Chen's ladies. Over the years of their long friendship there had been an astonishing procession, ranging from a noted English duchess to a Thai barmaid. His chum had prolific tastes and a voracious appetite for the opposite sex. He had been the first boy at school to actually *do* it—with one of the local village girls—and had regaled the dormitory afterwards with the intimate details while they all masturbated furiously.

As Walter grew older, the women became younger. Helene had lived with him for the past six months, and gave every indication of being more permanent than most of her predecessors. In fact, Burridge sensed a quiet ambition in her to be the third Mrs Chen, and he wondered if Walter had yet woken to that fact. If this girl set her mind to it, no friend of Walter's would take the odds against him being single for long. And his elevation to the peerage, which was already subtly in hand, would make him even more desirable.

Burridge left them embracing and went inside. He hoped, if it came to wedding bells, he would not be asked to be best man yet again. He'd already done the honours for two matrimonial disasters. He dialled London, giving crisp instructions, then made a phone call to Sydney. He said he would be on the late afternoon plane.


'The rent's $250 a week for a short lease,' said the real estate agent, a ginger-haired friendly man who wore tailored shorts and long white socks, 'which is a steal because it's the off-season. You can have the place until the end of November. After that the owner gets summer rentals, upwards of a grand a week and twice that in the Christmas holidays.'

They had driven there in his new Mercedes, and parked at the the road's end, two hundred metres away. They walked the remaining distance along the beach. The cottage itself was unprepossessing, built as a weekender in years past, and showing signs of neglect. There was rust on its galvanised-iron roof, paint flaking from the fibro cladding, while the inside was basic: two small bedrooms, primitive kitchen and old-fashioned bathroom with faded tiles. But it was perfectly positioned, a picket fence and gate leading directly onto white sand which

ran down to the tranquil water. It was also iso-
lated. There were no other houses within view,
no marinas or picnic grounds, no people. They
stood on the tiny front verandah, and looked at
the expansive view.

'Most you'll see is a fishing boat or a few
yachts tacking out to the headland. No neighbours except the seagulls. If you like to fish, the
pelicans have an instinct. They'll fly from way
down Pittwater, from Bayview or Mackerel
Beach, and while you gut the catch they sit
waiting for a handout. That's if you like that
kind of thing.'

'I'll take it,' Ben said.

8 HE ASKED THE driver to wait, crossed the small front lawn and rang the bell. At first he thought there was no-one at home, although there was a child's bike propped against the steps and a car parked in the driveway beneath a metal prefabricated carport. He heard a movement inside, and knocked this time.

'Mrs Hammond?'

When there was no answer, he tried again.

'I need to talk to your husband. I'm nothing to do with the press, if that's your concern. May I put my card under the door?'

He had already selected which business card he would use. The plain one, containing his initials only, with the United Nations logo and New York address would be best. He stooped and pushed it beneath the doorframe, where there was just enough of a gap for it to slide. Part of it lay there visible for a moment, until it was picked up. A moment passed and then the door was opened.

Burridge saw a young, if wary and distracted woman. She held only the edge of the card, between her thumb and forefinger; the action seeming to portray her tentative and uneasy frame of mind.

'What do you want?'

'You are Deborah Hammond?'

'Yes.'

Her eyes looked towards the waiting car and driver, then back to him again. 'Would you please tell me what you want?'

'To speak to your husband.'

'He's not here,' Deborah said.

'Then I'm sorry for interrupting.'

Burridge proffered one of his most charming apologetic smiles, that brought no response.

'Can you tell me when he'll be returning home?'

'He won't be,' she said, and handed him back his card.

He heard the telephone as he cleaned the last of the fish, and threw the remains into the water. It was true about the pelicans. They had arrived like a squadron, one scout circling as Ben waded into the water to cast his line, then the others appearing once the fish started to take the bait. Now six of them floated majestically, waiting patiently, ignoring the scavenging and shrieking seagulls, while he gutted and filleted the flathead. He tried to feed all the pelicans in turn and, as if understanding this, they calmly kept their places, long beaks scooping up the meal of skin and entrails as it was thrown beside each one. When the gulls swooped, they beat at them with their wings, but otherwise their serenity and composure was remarkable.

*A very strange bird is the Peli-can,*
*His beak holds more than his belly-can.*

He used to tell his children the old jingle when they were younger. Maybe they'd go fishing when the kids came on Sunday, and he'd remind Daniel of it. But then he recalled Dan was nine, computer-literate, learning the guitar, and way beyond juvenile ditties. He'd no doubt manage a polite laugh, then exchange a glance with Susan that speculated on whether the old man was losing his marbles and into his second dotage.

Ben smiled. He felt relaxed and happy for the first time since he and Chrissie had set out for Melbourne. The weather was perfect. Warm and sunny, a mild spring day, the temperature in the low twenties, and a slight north-easterly breeze from the other side of the peninsula where the surf rolled in. It was a magical spot, and he had done his sums and worked out his future. He had made the big decisions; now only the small ones remained, like whether to have a cold beer with the grilled fish or else a white wine, or perhaps have a beer now and a chilled chardonnay later on the verandah, and watch the sun go down over the sea and turn it crimson. He felt lazy and content, which was when the telephone rang.

For a moment he thought about not answering it. But only two people had this number, and neither would call him without good cause. He threw a sack over the cleaned fish to protect them from the gulls, sprinted across the sand, stepped over the picket fence and went into the house.

'I was about to hang up.'

It was Deborah, and his instinct was dismay; she was going to tell him Sunday was off, and the kids had made other arrangements. But it wasn't that. She explained about the man who had come to visit, who had passed his card under the door, and asked to see him.

'I didn't tell him anything. But I've been thinking about it since. He might have been important.'

'Why?'

'I read the card before I gave it back. He's with the United Nations. A Mr Burridge. There was an address in New York.'

'Means nothing to me, Debbie.'

'I just thought you should know.'

'Thanks. The kids okay for Sunday?'

'Yes,' she said, 'but I wanted to talk to you about that, as well. I was thinking . . .'

*Oh God,* he thought, *here comes the first post-marital access row.*

'Thinking what?'

'Well, they're looking forward to it so much, do you have room for them to come instead on Saturday and stay the night?'

'Why, yes,' he said, surprised by the gesture. 'There's one spare bed, and I'll go into Avalon and buy a sleeping bag for Dan.'

'No need,' she said. 'There's an old one here. I'll give it a clean. You can collect it and some bedclothes when you pick them up. Do you want to take them for lunch Saturday?'

'That'd be nice. I know a good seafood place at Newport, but I suppose they'll choose McDonald's.'

'Bound to.' He had an impression Deborah was smiling, and knowing how he dreaded the prospect of a Big Mac, she probably was.

'Saturday then,' Ben said. 'About twelve.'

'They'll be ready. Ohh, and Ben . . .'

'Yes?'

'He's at the Park Carlton.'

'Who is?'

'This man. Burridge. That's where he's staying.'

'He can be at the Salvation Army hostel for all I care.'

'He insisted on telling me. He also gave me another number. He said he could be reached there.'

'Tear it up.'

'It's a number I felt I knew. So I looked it up in your book. It's Howard's office.' She waited for his response. 'Ben—are you there?'

'I'm here,' he said.

'Did you get what I said? Superintendent Morgan's office . . .'

'I got it—loud and clear. Your Mr Burridge can be found at bloody Howard Morgan's office. In that case, tear it up even more carefully and flush it down the loo. See you Saturday when I collect the kids. Tell them I'll have some pelicans drop in to say hello.'

'Some what?'

'Pelicans. You know . . . beak holds more than bellycans.'

'Have you been drinking?'

'Not a drop. But the air here is just like wine.'

When Nick Feraldos came home to their unit which overlooked the ferry terminal at Manly, the light on his vocaphone was blinking. His wife Jane, currently rostered on the overnight shift as head sister at the local hospital, was asleep in the bedroom, so he turned down the volume to replay whatever messages were on the tape.

There was only one.

It was a man identifying himself as Edward Burridge, asking Nick to kindly call him at the Park Carlton immediately he returned home. It concerned his friend Ben Hammond, and was a matter of some considerable importance.


'So you've lost him?'

Superintendent Morgan made almost no attempt to conceal his satisfaction at the thought. Burridge in turn found him a dislikable oaf, in his opinion the worst kind of Australian, with his truculent Welsh ancestry. He wondered how this stolid, unimaginative clod had become a quite senior and apparently well-regarded policeman. It was frustrating that he had to deal with the idiot—especially now Teresa Martineau was being processed in London for departure, and all was in readiness.

'I'm simply unable to locate him at this particular time. I don't know why that amuses you, Mr Morgan.' Burridge failed to conceal his resentment.

As if this gave him licence, Morgan did not bother to hide his own antipathy. 'I'm not amused, Sir Edward. Not the least bloody bit amused. One of my best officers has been de-stabilised.' He angrily lit a cigarette, in defiance of a notice thanking visitors for not smoking. 'You may not be aware, but he's resigned.'

'Resigned?' Burridge was startled. 'I thought he was temporarily suspended.'

'Internal told him it was indefinite, on half-pay, pending further investigation. He said, and I quote, to shove it up their collective bums.'

'Internal Affairs had no need to go that far.'

'You fitted him. You and your stupid mate in Canberra—'

'If you mean your own deputy chief commissioner—?'

'Don't bother to pass on the description. He already knows I think he's a bloody drongo. I've told him often enough. But you and he set this ball rolling, so don't blame Internal Affairs. They're paid to be predators, and here was a real chance for a feeding frenzy.'

'What absolute bloody rubbish.' Burridge was on the verge of losing his temper.

Morgan sensed this and seemed encouraged. 'That's the way I see it. It's how Ben's been treated. Chucked in the deep end, among the sharks.'

'Oh, come on,' Burridge started to say, but the other man was not listening. He wanted to vent his anger.

'And what really pisses me off is he blames

me. Christ Almighty, I like Ben Hammond. I disapproved of the whole bloody thing from day one. You know that. I haven't even been told the full extent of what you're up to, but I had to sit here like a dummy and take a mouthful, while he informed me what a bastard I'd turned out to be, and slapped his resignation on my desk.'

Burridge said, 'Well, in that case you have to know his whereabouts.'

'It was written on a plain sheet of paper with no address.'

'Don't treat me as a complete fool, Morgan. What about his severance pay and super-annuation?'

'What about it?'

'Your department must know where to send it.'

'We do.' Morgan seemed to relish his answer. 'He said to pay it to his wife, which we've done.'

'The whole lot, just like that?'

'Call me a liar. Ask my staff. That's how he wanted it. If they made private arrangements you'd have to ask him—if you can find him.'

'You do realise I want to help this man?'

'You could've fooled me,' Morgan said.

• • •

'I'm being heavied, Ben.'

'What's happening?'

'The Canberra creep—the great Bradley Foster himself—and this English guy Burridge are both trying to crap on me from a great height.'

Ben grinned. Listening to Nick Feraldos on the telephone, it was hard to realise he had spent the first third of his life speaking only Greek. He had been ten years old when his family had fled the bloodshed of an exploding Cyprus and he had learned his English the hard way, as an immigrant new boy in a Sydney school playground. He and Ben had been partnered when they first enrolled in the federal police, and had remained the closest of friends ever since.

'I've told them I haven't a clue where you are, but Burridge is a crafty bastard. He's on to me. Bloody Brad, of course, wouldn't know if a firecracker was up him.'

Ben laughed. Nobody in the squad had any liking or respect for the deputy commissioner. He was a notorious networker, who had used social and political contacts to manoeuvre his way to the top. He was not there yet; the head of the federal police was tough and capable, but no-one doubted in time Bradley Foster would manage to white-ant him. If he was aligned with this man Burridge, then the Englishman clearly had influence.

'What do you want me to do, Ben?'

'Hang on, I'm thinking.'

'I can tell 'em to get stuffed.'

'No. The Canberra creep would mark your card for that.'

'Maybe I'll join you, and seek early retirement.'

'You can't. You have a wife. How is she?'

'She's beautiful.'

'I know she's beautiful. But is she happy? Is she well?'

'She's terrific. She sends her love to you.'

'And mine to her. Tell her she's a Princess.'

'You deliver your own sexual messages, mate. So what do I tell these nongs?'

'Tell them you know where I'll be—after the weekend. But you won't have the details until Monday. Can you do that?'

'Easy,' Nick Feraldos said.


Susan and Daniel loved the cottage. Dan declared it was ace, and they fished from the beach until late, stopping finally to clean and gut their catch. Dan had never caught such large fish before and he was excited, while Susie said she felt sorry for the poor things and please couldn't they throw them back. Dan told her not to be a dickhead, and war was about to break out on the beach, but then the pelicans arrived.

Susan fed the pelicans. She waded into the water; they allowed her to come quite close as she tossed them the skin and fish gut, and Dan for once didn't try to be competitive but simply watched her with the great floating birds. His hand reached for Ben's, in a rare gesture, and he was silent for what was for him a long time. Then, all of a sudden he said:

> '*A very strange bird is the Peli-can,*
> *His beak holds more than his belly-can.*

Do you remember telling me that, Dad, when I was a kid?'

'Yes,' Ben said, not trusting himself to say more. He felt his son's hand in his, and watched his daughter in the water, and knew he had rarely been so happy.

9 THE TALL FIGURE looked absurd, trudging along the beach towards him, carrying his shoes and socks, wearing a tie, the jacket of his suit slung over his shoulder, his trousers rolled up to avoid the fine grains of sand. He appeared completely out of place.

From the corner of his eye Ben could see his progress towards the remote cottage on the tranquil beach, but gave the impression of paying no attention. He sat on a patch of grass inside the picket fence, apparently engrossed in the job of fitting a heavier sinker to the nylon line of his beach rod. He looked up with surprise as Burridge stopped, and mopped his face with a large linen handkerchief.

'Lovely day. Bit warm.'

'Fuck off,' Ben told him.

'I say . . .'

'Say what you like, mate, but say it somewhere else. Get lost.'

'Not very friendly, Mr Hammond.'

'I don't have to be friendly. This is private property. I've rented the place.' He went back to fitting the sinker.

'Let me come in and talk.' Burridge used the handkerchief again to mop his neck. 'I'd kill for a cold beer.'

'You think I'd offer you a beer?' Ben showed sudden anger. 'Not if you're the bastard who's been hassling my wife and friends.'

'It was crucial to find you. I'm sorry for any inconvenience I caused,' Burridge said, doing his best to look contrite. 'I heard of your trouble. I think you've been badly treated.'

'That makes two of us,' Ben said.

'I'd like to help.'

'How?'

'I'm in a position to offer you a job.'

'I think I've retired,' Ben said. 'There's this army of people called the unemployed. Maybe you've even heard of them. Since I'm now a member, I can draw the dole. Do lawn mowing or security work on the side for cash. Or I could start a private-eye business. Getting sleazy pictures of errant husbands doing it on the desk with their secretaries—or executive wives doing it with their male underlings. I have all these various options when my money runs out, so I don't need people to drop in and offer me anything.'

'Let me discuss it. Talk to you.'

'I don't think I want to hear anything else you might say.'

'Don't be such a bloody fool,' Burridge said, and tried to enter the gate. Ben grabbed his shirt and tie with one hand and hit him with the other. His visitor went sprawling back and landed in a heap. He sat up spitting blood and wiping off the sand, collecting his jacket and shoes from where they had landed, his pride more severely injured than his mouth.

'That,' Ben said, 'is just in case you're the prick who's caused me all this grief.'

If there was one thing in which Edward Burridge excelled, it was an ability to judge other people's emotions. The act of physical force had released tension in Ben Hammond; there were signs to indicate an easing of his anger. He was not, Burridge surmised, apart from the demands of his job, a violent man. The simmering hostility had cooled a few degrees.

'If that makes you feel better, I'd still kill for a cold beer.'

Ben shrugged. He neither responded nor moved.

Burridge said, 'And if you want the truth, yes, I am taking advantage of the situation you find yourself in. But I didn't cause it. The "grief", as you put it, began with your backup squad in Melbourne pressing the panic button and arriving too early. The real grief was your partner being pumped full of heroin and thrown off the sixteenth-floor balcony.' He saw Ben's reaction, and continued, 'Oh yes, I've read the file. The rest of the grief was some cack-handed concept that you'd taken the money, the fifty thousand, for which you can blame your boss, Superintendent Howard Morgan, the Welsh wizard who called in Internal Affairs. After which it was open slather—like a bunch of sharks at a feeding frenzy.'

He got a measure of satisfaction sheeting the blame to Morgan, and even cribbing and paraphrasing his words. It seemed to work. Ben turned and went into the house. He emerged a moment later with two chilled bottles, threw one to Burridge, who deftly caught it.

They opened the screw tops, and began to drink.


The lights were relentless. Like a high-powered modelling session or a film studio, Teresa thought, as the arcs came on again. This time she was photographed with her hair blonde, the rinse they had used still damp and causing ringlets, so that once again she looked quite different.

This was the fourth photograph: all showed diverse hairstyles or colours, while contrasting makeup created a total change of appearance each time. The young man with the clipboard, who had been deputised by Sir Edward to arrange the session, seemed more like an advertising account executive than an obscure assistant, controlling as he did a team that included two hairdressers, a makeup girl, as well as the photographer and his gaffer who operated the lights.

Amid this small crew, throughout one frantically busy morning, she was the focus of attention. Teresa Martineau—the star. The thought made her smile.

'I like that,' the man with the clipboard said.

'Like what, Andy?' His name was Andrew Sykes-Blair, but he insisted she call him Andy.

'I like the smile. We'll have one with the smile.'

They took one with the smile.

*God knows,* she wondered, *what the crew thinks of all this? Her crew?* It brought another secret smile, and the photographer's reflexes were sharp as he caught it for good measure. *Are they part of the Burridge empire, or just out-of-work technicians?* She guessed the latter.

Andy consulted his clipboard. He called her aside. 'You also speak Greek, it says here.'

'Yes,' Tess nodded.

'My God, you're talented. Can we have dinner—like tonight?'

'I can't,' she said truthfully. 'My stepfather's expecting me.'

'Tomorrow night?'

'I have a date.'

'Isn't it always the way? Some other night this week?'

'One of the hairdressers said you have a wife.'

'She's in Fuengirola.'

'Oh well—hope she's back soon.'

He sighed, and gave her a look of mute boyish appeal, clearly designed to either melt her heart, or beg her not to be old-fashioned. She just smiled, and asked, 'Have we finished?'

'One more.'

'What is it this time?'

'Greek piano teacher. Dark hair. We can use the wig. A rather severe look, I think.' He went to his attaché case and returned with a pair of horn-rimmed glasses. 'Try these.'

She put them on.

'Smashing. This time you're Aliki Hadjidakis, from Salonika.'

'Why do I need so many different passports?'

'Orders, poppet. Instructions from on high. Sir said at least five identities, just in case, and sir never leaves anything to chance.'

The screen flickered in the darkened living room, where Ben had drawn the curtains, while he watched the same videotape that had been shown in Hong Kong. After they had finished a second beer, his uninvited guest had asked him to view a cassette. When Ben said he had rented a television for his kids, but had no video recorder, Burridge told him it was not a problem.

'I brought one with me—just in case. It's locked in the car. Like to walk back with me while I get it?'

'Not particularly,' Ben said. 'You walk back and get it. I'm going to have a swim.'

Burridge shrugged, and handed him a business card. 'In the meantime, you might as well have this.'

Ben took it and felt the embossed printing: *Sir Edward A. Burridge. United Nations Drug Enforcement Agency. 1st Avenue & East 42 Street, New York.* Apart from the zipcode it gave telephone and facsimile numbers as well as a Paris address.

'Sir Edward?' Ben had a typical Australian disdain for titles. So many domestic knighthoods had been purchased under corrupt state administrations in the past. In one state it was said there were more knights than days.

'This is not the same card you gave my wife.'

'Not quite.' Burridge complimented him on his acumen. Ben was unimpressed.

'I have real concerns about any guy who hands out a series of different business cards. It's con-trick territory.'

'Not in this case. I can prove my credentials,' Burridge said. 'All I ask is you look at the video. And perhaps we could have a glass of wine while we watch the movie.'

The screen was rich with the beauty of Chiang Mai. The lovely reporter walked slowly towards the camera, using a technique she had made famous. Her name was Maria Novotnacov, and she had been born in Bosnia and brought by her parents to Australia as a child. Now she was a media luminary.

'Humans have been using drugs since they first crawled out of the swamp and learned to stand upright.' The camera enhanced Maria's angelic looks, while she punched facts in a staccato style that had endeared her to a vast public, and made her a ratings winner worth mega-bucks.

'But in the last twenty years the use of hard drugs has escalated, and with it the growth of powerful criminal empires. This is Chiang Mai, the gracious city in northern Thailand, near to the heart of the Golden Triangle. Somewhere north of here is the front line in what has become a war.' On the small screen, the city was replaced by a big camera close-up of Maria.

'The United States and the major nations are losing this war. Statistics reveal it costs an average two million dollars to catch and jail a single drug smuggler, and thirty thousand dollars a year to keep him in custody. Little wonder people are beginning to say legalise— forget it—turn our backs and put the money to better use: spend it to educate, to combat poverty.'

Ben was intrigued, despite the reservations about his visitor. He watched Maria being shown into a luxurious Thai home, shaking hands with an elderly man surrounded by a cluster of beautiful young women. Only in the far background was there a glimpse of an armed guard.

'This is Kim Sokram, the head of reputedly the world's biggest drug syndicate. He operates out of Thailand, a mere two-hour walk from the Burmese border, and distributes across Asia, the Pacific and Europe. In the world of drugs, only the Colombian barons are Sokram's equal. He has his own troops. He is a ruthless author-itarian who recruits children from the hill tribes and forces them to join this illegal army. To his own people, the use of opium or any drug is forbidden. If they are found out, the penalty is five days of solitary, screaming their withdrawal symptoms in a cage or a guarded pit in the jungle.'

As a series of graphics and statistics appeared, showing the growing spread of drug abuse,

Burridge used the remote fast-forward control to speed through it.

'This was about three months ago,' he said. 'I'd say agreeing to the interview was a whim or an ego trip for Sokram, but she got a great scoop. A real stunner, isn't she?'

'A stunner,' Ben said, trying to parody his English accent, and failing, as Burridge pressed the normal speed button. On the screen Maria was part way through an interview with Sokram.

'It has been suggested, the cheapest way to end the drug rings is to buy out the owners. If you were offered ten billion dollars to close down your operation, what would you say?'

They heard Sokram's robust laughter. He was obviously impressed by the beautiful westerner, and just as intrigued at the idea of playing the gallant.

'No-one has made me such an offer,' he smiled.

'I realise that. But if they did——?' As he hesitated, she persisted, 'Ten billion dollars to walk away. Which would obviously include a guarantee of no prosecution. Would it tempt you?'

Kim Sokram thought about it for what seemed like a long time. 'Perhaps,' he said eventually. 'After all, I am an old man with several young wives. I have many children and grandchildren.'

'It would make them all wealthy as long as they and even your great–great–grandchildren lived,' Maria said. 'Does it tempt you?'

'If I am honest, yes.'

'You mean that, sir?'

'You ask me the truth. The truth is that in life almost anything is possible,' Sokram said.

The rest was a closing summation by Maria, with stock aerial footage of the mountainous remote Golden Triangle behind her. Burridge turned off the television, then rewound the videotape.

'Since that interview,' he said, 'we've made indirect contact with Sokram. Via a source in Bangkok. We've come to the conclusion that he could be persuaded to meet.'

'Meet who?'

'Our emissary. In this case—you.'

'Don't be bloody ridiculous,' Ben said. 'You're kidding.'

He studied Burridge's face, carefully.

'You're not kidding. In which case, you're crazy. You're off the planet. So stop wasting my time.'

'It'll take only two weeks of your time,' Burridge said.

'I've got a lot of appointments in the next two weeks,' Ben told him. 'Fish to catch. Kids to meet. Anyway, if you close down one cartel, another springs up.'

'Then we deal with the new one.'

'Or else those bastards in Colombia would take over.'

'That's cocaine. This is heroin. One thing at a time. And the Americans will handle them. We have an agreement.'

'Jesus Christ,' Ben said. 'You really mean this.'

'I didn't come here to get a suntan,' Burridge responded. 'We close down Sokram—with or without you.'

'Try it without me. Ask Miss Novotnacov to show you the way.'

'Don't be so damned stupid,' Burridge said, finally allowing his irritation to show. 'She was flown by his own plane from a private airfield, she and her camera crew, and they met at one of his summer homes near Chiang Mai. If she could take me, I'd hardly be here offering you a good fat fee.'

'What's your idea of a good fat fee?'

Burridge hesitated, 'The job could have its risks. That's why we pay you a hundred thousand dollars, tax-free. Just for completing the mission. You get the same again, if we succeed.'

Ben stared at him.

Burridge continued, 'It's the middle of September. You'll be back before the end of the month. I doubt if anyone will miss you.'

'Maybe not.'

'On the other hand, you'll have enough in the bank to buy the kids surfboards, or take them skiing next year; whatever they want. You won't have to spy on husbands or wives having it off on their office desks.'

'If I agreed,' Ben asked, 'what happens?'

'We take some passport photos tomorrow.'

'I already have a passport.'

'These are additional ones. In case of need. We spend the following day having them validated and arranging visas. Then you fly to Hong Kong.'

'Let me think about it,' Ben said.

'I need an answer now. Why don't I make a down payment? To prove I'm genuine.'


Teresa had a quiet farewell dinner with Charles.

'I'll miss you dreadfully,' he said.

'Two weeks, Charlie. That's all.'

'I'll still miss you.'

He tried to smile, but it was more like a nervous grimace. Tess realised he loved her as if she was his own child. She felt a sudden responsibility for this elderly Englishman, and was unsure what to do about it. It was too late to change her mind.

'A fortnight. It's no time at all.'

'At my age it's fourteen days, and each one is

a bonus. You take care, you hear me?'

'I hear, Charlie.'

'God bless,' he said. 'Dearest Tess, God bless you.'


Deborah stared at the cheque he had given her. It was made out for fifteen thousand dollars. The children were at school. She and Ben were alone in the house. A taxi waited outside.

'Ben ... so much. Where did you get it? Is it ... all right? You know what I mean. Is it ... genuine?'

'You mean is it honest?' He tried without success to contain his disappointment. 'It's an advance payment for a job I've been offered.'

'What sort of job?'

'A legitimate one—as far as I know.'

'It's just that people are still saying . . .'

'I know what they're saying, Debbie. The mud will stick round here forever. I've endorsed it, so you can bank it. Tell the kids goodbye. Tell them ... it was a wonderful weekend.'

He went outside to the waiting cab. They drove by Daniel's school, which was only two streets away, and Ben asked the driver to stop. Children were filling the playground at the morning recess. He thought he saw Dan, but decided not to try to call him. It could only be a brief farewell, and might cause his son embarrassment. Besides, he'd be back in two weeks. He told the driver to take him to the airport.

# PART TWO

## THE BETRAYAL

10 THE BANK WAS on Nathan Road. Amid the relentless traffic noise and the belch of fumes, it stood back from the street, as though rejecting the neighbourhood and the clamorous shops selling everything from cheap watches to genuine jewels, from dubious antiques to expensive silk. The bank was a large sedate British building, its wide steps and symmetrical columns forming a portico that seemed to belong more to Lombard Street than the heart of Kowloon. Like the Peninsula Hotel, it had escaped the demolition hammers and survived as a reminder of more gracious times.

It was cool inside, the air-conditioning a relief after the blast of heat that had greeted him as he left his hotel two streets away. He asked for the safe-deposit vault, and was directed down a marble staircase to the floor below street level.

The flight had been uneventful, the service cordial and almost continuous in business class. His glass had been constantly refilled with a fine

Cowra Chardonnay, the meal was a great deal better than the plastic packages he was used to, and he managed to sleep during the movie. He had been woken by the announcement of their impending descent, and moments later the lights of Hong Kong Island and Kowloon had appeared like some magical kaleidoscope out of the night. A hire-car driver holding a board with his name on it had been waiting as Ben emerged from customs, and he was driven to a modern hotel in the heart of Kowloon, surrounded by a lush tropical garden. A bellboy took his luggage, a pretty receptionist checked her list and welcomed him, giving him his key card together with a message that Sir Edward Burridge would telephone in an hour. He had been ushered up to a large and luxurious room on the twelfth floor with a spectacular view of the island from Victoria Peak to North Point. He felt like a pampered tourist on an expensive holiday.

Burridge had not telephoned. He had arrived instead, soon after Ben had showered and changed clothes, handing him an envelope containing a key and telling him to be at the Royal South China Bank on Nathan Road at exactly noon the following day. He would be met there, and the person meeting him would have full instructions. The key was one of a pair required to open a safe-deposit box; the same person would have the second key.

'How do I recognise him?' Ben asked.

'Don't worry about that,' he was told. 'In the envelope with the key is a reference number— as well as a password. I want you to memorise them both, and destroy the paper.'

'You mean eat it? Like the spies do?'

Ben was relaxed from the flight; Burridge frostily unamused.

'When you see the contents, you won't make stupid remarks like that,' was all he had said, and told Ben not to be late.

The marble stairs were deceptively deep, ending far below street level. It was like a deluxe subterranean bunker. He reached the bottom where there was a formidable steel door with grilled bars, through which he could see an armed guard on duty. Another guard stood outside the door, a .44 magnum prominently holstered on his belt. His eyes assessed Ben. Above him a remote-controlled surveillance camera did the same. There was a push button, with an instruction in Chinese characters. As he hesitated, the guard nodded. Ben pressed the bell and, in a section of the wall beside it, a tiny TV screen lit. His own face gazed disconcertingly back at him. As the screen changed to a set of numerals, a voice from a speaker grille asked him to impress his reference number. He tapped in the seven digits he had memorised.

The massive door unclicked as easily as any security system at the entrance to an apartment block. The guard gestured, and Ben went into the vault. He had an impression of a vast underground repository, full of metal containers, rather like the luggage lockers of a large rail terminus, but he knew these metal boxes would hold a great many of the city's secrets, along with fortunes in jewels and illicit cash. Armed guards patrolled the aisles. The feeling was one of intense vigilance. A watchful middle-aged Chinese, a managing custodian, sat at a central desk. Beside him there was a younger man at a computer. Ben realised they were carefully studying him, waiting for him to speak.

'Password?'

The elder man nodded.

'*Chiengmalan.*' It was the word Burridge had given him, along with the pin number and the key.

The younger clerk typed Chiengmalan on his screen. Ben watched as it formulated into a file number, which was then replaced by a message. In front of the custodian was a slim monitor He turned it for Ben to read what was highlighted there. TWO KEYS REQUIRED. Ben nodded, but before he could explain he was due to meet another party who held the extra key, there was the sound of the main door opening behind him.

'*Chiengmalan*,' a soft English voice said, and he turned to see a dark-haired and slender woman, who nodded and murmured a greeting while the clerk typed it in, and the monitor dutifully supplied information that the file was available. The custodian asked them for both their keys and, together with one held by the bank, guards were sent to unlock the deposit box and return with it. They carried it into a private cubicle for them, returned each key, and left the room. As the door clicked shut, an electronic sign appeared on it: KINDLY PRESS BUZZER WHEN YOU WISH TO LEAVE. THE MANAGEMENT GUARANTEES THERE IS FULL PRIVACY. NO CAMERA SURVEILLANCE OF ANY KIND.

Walter Chen waited outside the bank. He had seen them both enter. Now, as his Rolls-Royce drew up alongside him, he climbed into the back seat and directed the chauffeur to head for home. When they turned towards the harbour tunnel, Walter used the mobile telephone. He knew Burridge was waiting for the call. He would be alone in the house up on the Peak. Walter had given the servants the day off, and arranged for friends to invite Helene to the races. When the phone rang, it was picked up immediately. Walter reported all was well. They had both arrived, and the people assigned to their positions outside the bank were in place. Whatever might happen from now on would be closely monitored.

The metal container sat between them, like some sort of mystery casket. They each held their keys. It was only moments since the two guards had carried in the heavy box and left them alone.

'Did Sir Edward tell you about me?'

'Sir Ted,' Ben said, 'told me absolutely nothing. He allowed me to think you'd be a bloke.'

Teresa laughed. Ben was conscious of even white teeth and an animated and attractive face.

'I'm Teresa Martineau,' she said.

'Spanish?'

'English. French father. It was Therese, but I rebelled.'

'Ben Hammond.'

'I know,' she said.

'So what do we do? Open the box?'

'That's the idea. We need both keys.'

It had two slots. They each fitted their keys and turned in unison. Ben raised the lid and they stared at the contents.

'Bloody hell.'

It was Teresa who whispered it. Ben just blinked and shook his head in amazement. The deposit box was packed tight with bundles of American dollar bills. They both stared at the solid mass of what seemed an impossible amount of money. More money than they or most people would see in a lifetime.

'Christ,' Ben said. 'There has to be millions. I couldn't even begin to count how much is in here.'

'No need to count,' Teresa said. 'It's twenty million dollars.'

He turned to look at her.

'Is that an official figure?'

'So I was told.'

'By His Eminence? Sir Ted?'

'Yes.'

'Have you known him long?'

'Not very.'

'But longer than I have,' Ben said.

'Apparently. Does that upset you?'

'Not a bit.' Ben looked at her thoughtfully.

'Not a bit—only what?' she asked.

'Only for a lady who knew it was twenty million, you gave a fair impression of being surprised.'

'I thought it'd be gold bars, or even bearer bonds. Not a great wad of cash in used bills like this.'

'Ted forgot to tell you.'

'Something's getting up your nose, Mr Hammond. What's the problem?'

'No real problem.'

'I get the feeling there is.'

'I just like to be kept informed. Why didn't he tell me who you were, or how much money we'd find? Why play silly buggers? Is that his style? Because it's not mine.'

'He's definitely upset you,' Teresa said, irritating Ben.

'He hasn't upset me.'

'I suspect he has. Which is pretty bloody stupid. Us sitting here on either side of a fortune, having an argument.'

'Well, they say that's what money does to people,' he said, and made her smile. 'So what now? He told me I'd get my instructions from you.'

'We count out fifty thousand dollars each. Then lock up the rest of the money and return it to the custodian.'

'Pity.'

'Are you tempted, Mr Hammond?'

'I wish you'd stop calling me Mr Hammond. My name's Ben.'

'I'll try to remember. Does all this money tempt you?'

'Even if it did, I'm not a thief.'

'Sorry,' Teresa said abruptly. 'It was only a rhetorical question.'

'Rhetorical?'

'You know. Not one expecting a serious answer—'

'I know what rhetorical is. It didn't sound like that to me.'

After a pause, in which she gazed at him, he asked her: 'Are we going to be able to work together?'

'I hope so. Shall we start counting?'

'It's going to take a while.'

'In which case, the sooner we start, the better.'

He commenced to count. He knew they had begun badly, and had a feeling it was more his fault than hers. On the other hand, this Teresa Martineau—he estimated she was nudging thirty, good-looking, but not exactly his style— was either nervous or else, for some reason, uptight. He got the impression she didn't want to be here any more than he did. He wished, if he had to sit in a marble bank vault in Hong Kong counting out fifty grand from the obscene stack of money in front of him, that he was here with Chrissie Duncan. Chrissie had always been fun, able to laugh, cute and witty and enterprising—and perceptive when it came to reading his mind. He began to think that perhaps, without realising it, he had loved Chrissie. He knew he missed her far more than he had ever thought imaginable.

'Bugger it,' he said aloud, and then glanced at her. 'Sorry.'

'What happened?'

'I've lost count.'

Teresa shrugged. She went on adding up her pile of notes like a bank teller. Ben gritted his teeth and began all over again.


Outside the bank a trishaw driver sat watching the entrance. A tourist couple approached. Anticipating them, he produced a sign and placed it on his window. In Chinese and English it said: NOT FOR HIRE. He shrugged apologetic gestures, indicating that he was already engaged and waiting for someone inside the bank. When the couple had gone, the driver took out a mobile telephone and made a call by simply pressing a preprogrammed redial button.

The phone rang on the terrace of Walter Chen's house. Burridge answered, listened, and was hanging up as Walter arrived home.

'They're still in the bank.'

Walter poured them both a cold beer.

Burridge stood at the parapet of the terrace, and looked down.

By night or day it was a view that never failed to excite him. He could see the glass and concrete towers along the shore, the track at Happy

Valley racecourse, and a small sea of floating restaurants and bazaars. Out in mid-harbour a dragon boat at training ran the gauntlet of ferries and container ships. Once, amid the phalanx of skyscrapers, there had been an emerald green oval. A tiny oasis with immaculate turf and an English pavilion. He felt sudden nostalgia for figures in white on Saturday afternoons, and the gentle sound of bat on ball.

'I miss the English cricket club, Walter. They did splendid afternoon teas—scones and cucumber sandwiches. Remember them?'

'No. We Chinese weren't allowed to be members.'

'Weren't you? Good Lord. What happened to the place?'

'We bought it.' Chen smiled. 'It's a shopping plaza now.'

Burridge nodded, wishing he hadn't asked.

They finished counting. They each had a bulky heap of notes in front of them. Teresa stacked hers into neat piles, securing them with the rubber bands. When she put her money in her leather shoulder bag, Ben took his wallet from the pocket of his jeans. He looked at it and shrugged.

'Fifty grand into that wallet won't go, will it?'

'No chance,' Teresa said. 'Apart from which,

you'd be a mark for every pickpocket in town.'

'Would you do the honours?'

She nodded and put the rest of the money in her bag.

'Now what?' he asked.

'We lock it up and give the box back to them for storage.'

They used both keys to relock the metal container, and pressed the buzzer for the door to be opened. One of the guards entered.

'We're finished, thank you,' Teresa told him in Cantonese, and he called his companion to help carry it out. The clerk recorded its return on his computer, and they were asked to sign a document guaranteeing the contents of the security box had been as expected, that it had been locked to their satisfaction before its return, and they had witnessed it being replaced in the vault. Teresa thanked him—again in Cantonese—and the main door was electronically opened for them. It automatically swung shut when they crossed the threshold on their way out.

The trishaw driver saw them leaving. He once again pressed the redial button and heard a voice answer. In this way he had no idea of the number he was calling, or to whom he was speaking. He was simply hired for the day, had already been paid half of a generous fee, and would receive the balance from a messenger at the end of the afternoon.

'Coming out of the bank now,' he said.

'Keep watching and don't hang up,' Burridge's voice told him.

The driver watched as Teresa and Ben walked down the steps. In the street near them was a tourist in linen slacks and a gaudy shirt, festooned with souvenirs, using a video camera and carrying a Nikon. He seemed to be taking footage at random, but the trishaw driver was a trained observer, and he saw how the tourist panned and then steadied the camera, his finger pressing the lever to activate the zoom lens as he focused on Ben and Teresa. They moved towards a taxi rank, and the tourist sauntered in the same direction, by now holding the automatic Nikon and managing a few casual snapshots of the street, one of which included the pair as they reached the leading cab. When it drove off, the same tourist was already hiring the next taxi on the rank.

The driver reported all this, was thanked for his time and told to be in the same spot at five p.m. when he would be paid the rest of his fee. Burridge put down his telephone. He was silent for a moment. Watching him, Walter Chen knew something was wrong.

'They were photographed—and they're being followed.'

'Are you going to tell them?'

'Not until I find out who it is, and what the hell happened to our security.' He noticed Chen's concerned frown. 'Don't frown, Walter. You're supposed to be inscrutable.'

'They might be killed. Doesn't it concern you?'

'Of course it concerns me. I'd have to find two new people and start all over again.'

Walter Chen sighed and shook his head.

'You know, you used to do this years ago—at school.'

'Do what?'

'Pretend to be a bastard.'

'My dear old friend, I am a bastard. Ask anyone. I expect that's why we always got on so well. You're the only one who never realised it.'


'We change part of the money into Hong Kong dollars and Thai baht. But most of it into traveller's cheques,' Teresa said. 'We make three stops. Any bank or bureau de change.'

'Why didn't we simply change it all back there?'

'I'm just following instructions, Ben. We keep the taxi for as long as it takes, after which he drops us back at the hotel.'

'Where are you staying?' Ben asked.

'Same place as you. The Maison Citadel.'

'Now that's what I mean about Burridge,' Ben said. 'Why the hell didn't he tell me? We could at least have met last night to get acquainted, maybe had a drink or a meal. I ended up with room service and watched the midnight movie. Some action-adventure epic. It was bloody terrible. Did you see it?'

'No,' she admitted. 'I had dinner with Burridge, who told me you were feeling tired after the flight and having an early night. I'm beginning to agree he's rather devious.'

'I think he's a prick. But maybe he fancies you.'

'Thanks, but no thanks,' Teresa said. 'Anyway, you're wrong.'

'How do you know?'

'I'm not an idiot. I can tell.'

'How? Is he queer?'

'I doubt it. Not that it's any of our business. I know he has no sexual interest in me. Can we please terminate this conversation?'

'Of course,' Ben said.

'But I do have news for you,' Teresa told him. 'We're having dinner tonight.' She tried to repress a smile. 'You, me and Sir Ted.'

'Oh, bloody wonderful. Some enchanted evening. I suppose there's no possibility we could dice him?'

'None whatever.'

'At least you feel he's devious. You're having doubts about him. You do realise it's about the very first thing we've agreed on.'

Instead of answering, Teresa spoke to the taxidriver in rapid Cantonese. They pulled in alongside a bureau de change.


It was at the second stop that Ben became aware of the taxi. He noticed a Caucasian in the back seat, who remained seated in the cab while he and Teresa entered the premises. When they came out, almost thirty minutes later, hands weary with signing traveller's cheques, the man was loitering outside a cheap jewellery shop. He was sunburnt, and wearing the kind of casual clothes that made Ben feel he was an Australian.

They climbed into their cab. The driver was enjoying his day, as he watched the mounting meter, and reflected on the strange ways of the *guailo*. Ben said nothing to Teresa, but took a seat so he could see the car behind in the driver's mirror. He watched the man rejoin his taxi. As they drove off he saw the other cab move out into the traffic to follow them.

11 VICTOR MENDOZA WAS, in police parlance, well known to the authorities. He had done two terms for breaking and entering, and one far longer sentence for a vicious armed robbery with violence. He would not have been released until after the end of the century but, having done two years with another six to serve, Victor had talked seriously to a member of one of the triads about money and jewellery he had hidden in his native Macao, and how the possession of such wealth was of no worth to him without his freedom. A deal had been struck, and Victor assigned to work on the sewage truck. The prison was not on a mains sewer, and each Thursday the truck collected the effluent drums, and took them out to a waste-disposal plant in the New Territories. Victor did the run six times and even the most suspicious warders had begun to feel perhaps prison had changed his ways, and they could relax on Victor Mendoza.

On the seventh run, he escaped.

By the time the guards realised he was missing, Victor had swum a nearby canal, and was in the boot of a car being transported towards the coast. A speedboat was waiting, and he was taken to Macao where he handed over the promised money and jewels, and was given papers establishing a new identity. He asked for enough of his own money back to get himself re-established, and received a sharp lesson in the ways of the triads. He woke up the next morning lying on a beach, with broken ribs and concussion, his clothes shredded by knife slashes: a clear warning that another time it would be his face that was in tatters. It was fortunate for him the triad members did not know part of the haul from his robbery had been stashed in another place. He waited until he felt certain it was safe, then collected it from a stormwater channel that ran by his mother's shanty house. There was a ledge, a cache where he had once hidden money stolen from kids at school, for Victor Mendoza's felonies went back to childhood.

He made no attempt to visit his mother; he would not be welcome, and had no wish to see her. Since one of Macao's main revenue sources was the licensed gambling palaces along the sea front, he left the jewels in their hiding place, and played roulette with the money.

The first night he lost regularly, and stopped

just in time to avoid complete disaster. He returned a week later, having carefully sold off most of the jewels, and this time converted ten thousand Hong Kong dollars into almost six times that amount, leaving the casino after midnight with a drunken callgirl from Lantau Island. They booked into a hotel and made love most of that night and the next day, until the girl, by then sober, tried to rob him.

Victor Mendoza left the hotel shortly afterwards. He hung a notice on the door saying DO NOT DISTURB, and told the receptionist he would be back early that evening. He took the hydrofoil and was in Hong Kong two hours later, where he disembarked into obscurity. The girl's body was not found until later that night. Her throat had been cut, and she had been stabbed repeatedly—'as if by someone in a frenzy', the coroner reported. No killer was ever found. Victor Mendoza changed his appearance by minor cosmetic surgery. For additional security he bought himself an American passport and established a convincing background as a teacher from Honolulu. He lived by robbing tourists, usually when they were drunk and alone, looking for a girl with whom to spend the night. These were invariably small amounts and in cash, and mostly went unreported because his victims feared the possibility of publicity and embarrassment.

He took no risks.

Now he was about to take the major risk of his life, for the ultimate prize. He sat in front of a screen, studying the video of Ben and Teresa outside the bank on Nathan Road, and on the streets of Kowloon. It had been delivered by a courier. Carmichael had dispatched it while waiting at a bank as the pair converted currency. Soon they should be back at their hotel and, if this Carmichael was as good as he claimed, he'd shortly know its location.

A few minutes later the phone rang.

'The Maison Citadel,' Carmichael said.

Victor was well pleased. Now if the others did as directed, within twenty-four hours they would have the two keys and the means to acquire the vast sum of money in the vault. Victor Mendoza would be rich beyond his wildest dreams. But it was not only the money—it was the thought of the alluring and passionate girl with whom he would share it, that made him smile with such anticipation.

Helene Lee crossed the spacious lobby of the Maison Citadel Hotel. It was crowded with tourists, many of them middle-aged American males who gave her admiring and slyly hopeful glances. She ignored them and approached the desk, selecting a young male receptionist on whom to bestow her most devastating smile.

'Good afternoon,' she said.

'Afternoon, ma'am. Can I help you?'

Helene produced two sealed letters from her handbag. They were free invitations to a fashion show she had earlier picked up at a shopping mall, and had addressed the envelopes, printing their names: *Ms Teresa Martineau, Mr Ben Hammond.*

'Would you look after these? Or else I could deliver them to their rooms.'

It was a remote chance. The clerk shrugged an apology, as she expected he would.

'Sorry, but you can use the house phone. Call the guests—or I can put them here for collection.'

'Collection's fine. That's really kind of you,' Helene said, giving him a radiant smile, as if she had a desire to linger. He checked the register and placed the letters into the appropriate boxes where keys and messages were left. She was able to read the numbers 1295 and 1184, though not able to tell which was the woman's room, and which the man's.

It was good enough. She gave him another smile.

'You wouldn't like to attend the show yourself, would you?' she asked, feeling it gave credence. 'It's for a friend of mine, and I'm trying to help her get lots of people there. There's free champagne.'

'Will you be there?' he asked.

'No, I can't make it.' Helene saw his optimism evaporate.

'Me, neither. I'm working,' he said.

'Oh well. Thanks, anyway. Have a nice day.'

'You, too,' he sighed as he watched her long legs and the trim buttocks as she walked away. He realised an elderly American couple were waiting for their key.

'Sorry, sir, ma'am,' he said, flustered.

'Can't blame you, kid.' The man had a broad midwest accent. 'She's got a real neat ass—and it kind of smiles when she walks.'

'Henry,' his coiffured wife reproved him, 'that's disgusting.'

'It may be disgusting, honey, but it's sure as hell true.'

Helene went to a public telephone and made a call to Victor Mendoza. She gave him both room numbers, after which she took a taxi to the house on Victoria Peak. A half hour later she was being caressed and undressed by Walter, while he expressed his joy that a marvellous girl like her could be so in love with him.

'Fuck me, darling,' she said, bored with his devoted adoration and knowing how her prurient demands aroused him, 'fuck me as long and hard as you can.'

Walter needed no urging; she began to excite him, whispering obscenities, entreating him to do all manner of impossibly erotic things to her. He reached a frenzied climax, made the more fervent by Helene's uninhibited cries as she simulated a tumultuous orgasm.

She thought it was one of her finest performances.


'The name Hong Kong means fragrant harbour,' Burridge said, 'but nowadays that's hardly accurate. I prefer it from a distance.'

He had reserved a table by the curved observation windows that looked down on the twinkling lights. He was immaculate in a tailored tropical suit and MCC tie, Teresa attractive in a strapless figure-hugging white sheath, while Ben, who had been less-than-subtly advised the Starlight Room preferred guests to come well dressed, had chosen Kmart beach trousers, a knitted shirt and Reeboks. Apart from a raised eyebrow by Burridge when they met at the bar, and courteous impassivity from the maître d, his minor rebellion seemed to have gone unnoticed.

He watched their host showering charm on the girl with the soft dark hair, and wondered about her background. Though they had spent the afternoon together converting money, they had conversed little, as if the strange way they had met and the bizarre task upon which they were engaged made it difficult to enjoy any normal social exchange. He had no knowledge of how she had been recruited, nor, apart from her obvious ability with languages, what was to be her role. The whole enterprise was highly peculiar. Yet here they were in the newest, most expensive hotel in Hong Kong, and this afternoon he had seen a deposit box in which, he had been assured—and had no reason to disbelieve—there was twenty million dollars in banknotes.

Instinct told him there was something wrong, a hidden agenda, but he had no idea what it could be. He still suspected Burridge had more to do with his own very public arrest and treatment, despite his denials. Ben also knew there was no way he'd be here, involved in this, except for a promised payment of a tax-free hundred thousand dollars and, if they were successful, double that amount. It would take a long time for him to earn so much money.

Burridge consulted the wine waiter, and thought they might have another bottle of the Lindeman's Padthaway. He said how highly regarded Australian wines were these days. Teresa agreed that in England they were popular, and the shelves in Sainsburys were filled with them. Ben was suddenly fed up with their pretence of a social occasion.

'Oh, for Christ's sake,' he said, 'let's cut the crap.'

'Something on your mind, Ben?'

'Lots,' Ben said.

'If you have problems, now's the time to air them.'

'Let's begin with today's charade. Why did we go round town like bunnies, leaving a paper trail? What were we doing?'

'Changing money, of course.'

'Come on, Ted, stop the bullshit. It's the electronic age, smart cards and all that. Besides, we could have done it all at the South China Bank. Was this staged to see if we were being followed?'

'Do you think you were?'

'Why not just answer the question. Did someone follow us?'

'Difficult to say,' Burridge replied and Ben knew he was lying, but decided not to pursue it for the moment.

'When do we leave for Bangkok?'

'In a day or two.'

'What do we do until then?'

'See the sights. Go shopping.'

'Play at being tourists? Why?'

'I want you to get acquainted with each other,' he said. 'A few days together—spend a little of our money. Not too much,' he smiled. 'Any objection to a few days in Honkers with such attractive company?'

'Of course not.' He thought: *what else can I say?*

'Good.' Burridge was amiable. 'Then enjoy yourselves.'

'I would,' Ben said. 'If I trusted you. I don't think I do.'

Teresa's mouth opened a fraction. Burridge seemed unperturbed. It was one of his infuriating traits, Ben thought, this aloof composure. An impenetrable shell from which he surveyed the world.

'Why don't you trust me?'

'Because the friendly uncle role doesn't fit. You're about as benevolent and avuncular as a bloody piranha.'

'Picturesque turn of phrase you have, old boy.'

'What's more, you're lying. We were followed.'

'Yes,' Burridge admitted, 'you were.'

'Then why conceal it?'

'So as not to spoil dinner—or cause unnecessary alarm.'

'Who was it?'

'A man posing as a tourist. He photographed you. We want you to remain here for the next few days, until we find out how it happened. Whether someone at the bank has breached security.'

He sipped his wine while they watched him.

'You're right. It was staged—to ensure no-one was aware of your presence here. Unfortunately, we proved otherwise.'

'I'm glad you're finally telling us the truth, Ted. Though I can see why you wanted to sit on it. Hardly a great start. How the hell could it happen?'

'I'm working on it.' For once he sounded tense. 'Believe me, you won't leave until we find out who—and immobilise them.'

'While we're in a truth mode,' Teresa said, 'why did we need so much money?'

'I hope you put it in the hotel safe-deposit.'

'Naturally.'

'You'll need it all. Someone in Bangkok will make arrangements to get you to Sokram. That alone will cost eighty thousand dollars.'

'Christ,' Ben said, 'for what?'

'For his contacts. His knowledge. There may be other ways to achieve the objective, but this is the most secure. You'll be fully briefed later. As you saw today, there's a great deal of money in the bank here. There's more in other banks, and you'll be given a list of them, and how the funds can be accessed. This is what you'll present to Kim Sokram.'

'If we get there,' Ben said.

'Of course you'll get there. I'll be your control—monitoring progress all the way.'

'Is that supposed to fill us full of confidence?'

Burridge ignored the remark. 'As far as the man who followed you today is concerned, he was observed by one of my people, and identified.'

'You mean you know him? Why didn't you say so?'

'His name's Carmichael. An Australian who owned a bar here.'

Ben sighed and said, 'Getting information from you is like pulling hen's teeth.'

'After the bar went bankrupt, he acquired a boat and went into the refugee business. He's a drifter, a nasty piece of work. We can haul him in any time, but we need to find out who's running him. Once we do, and eliminate that danger, we leave Hong Kong. Just you two—and me.'

'I thought my father was to be involved,' Teresa said.

'Only if we need him.' Burridge seemed disconcerted she had raised the matter.

'Your father?' Ben asked. It was the first time he had heard of this.

Burridge answered, before she could respond. 'He works for us. It is possible he may be of help.'

Teresa stared at him in surprise. 'That's not exactly the way you put it in Paris,' she said. 'You gave me the impression he was the key to my being approached.'

'You misunderstood,' Burridge forced a smile. 'I promised you'd meet him, which you will. I wanted you for your language skills and knowledge of the area. The fact your father owns a business in Thailand, and has performed jobs for us, was a useful means to attract your interest.'

'You mean bait?'

She was clearly angry, and Ben watched her and again wondered what qualities, apart from her ability as an interpreter, had brought about her recruitment. There had to be something else. Some other reason. If she and he were to be partners, he felt he was entitled to know.


The maid pushed her cleaning trolley along the silent corridor to the door of 1295, where she knocked. When there was no answer she used a pass key, and entered. She went to the telephone, dialled once, then hung up. She began to search.

There was nothing in Ben's clothing. In a compartment of his suitcase was an air ticket and some credit cards, but she was under instructions not to steal anything. The warning had been blunt; it was vital neither had any idea their rooms had been searched. On the bedside table was a tiny leather travel frame, with snapshots of two children in it. She carefully checked, but there was no key hidden inside it.

She heard a tap on the door, and opened it to admit a man in overalls, carrying a tool kit. He went to the telephone, unscrewed the plastic casing and began work.

• • •

'Coffee?'

Burridge suggested they might have it in the Empire bar, with a liqueur or a brandy, but Teresa stifled a yawn and said she thought it was her bedtime, and would they kindly excuse her. The restaurant was crowded, all the tables occupied, and she made her way through the large room in the direction of the elevators. It was then she had the odd feeling that a couple at a far corner table were observing her.

It was not something Tess would normally have noticed, but she was still disturbed by Sir Edward's apparent volte-face about her father, and unsure what to make of his equivocation. She also had concerns over Ben Hammond, which she was trying to suppress, but her nerves were ragged and on edge. The impression she gained was a subliminal glimpse of two faces watching, as if in some strange way they knew her, and then the moment of eye contact was gone, and they looked swiftly away.

*That's ridiculous*, Teresa thought, but her glance lingered on them for another moment, long enough to register the girl's astonishing beauty. She was young and partly Oriental, with a Mediterranean-like olive skin. The man with her was Eurasian, in his early thirties. As she headed for the elevators Tess had the strange feeling the man was watching her again.

• • •

'She's going to her room.'

'I'd say so. The other two have gone into the bar.'

Victor Mendoza sat with a view across the restaurant towards the window table the trio had occupied, while Helene was carefully positioned so that Burridge could not possibly have glimpsed her. If, by some remote chance, he had managed to do so, he would have been told the same story she had given Walter: she was burdened with the visit of a distant cousin from Macao, and having the obligatory family dinner with him. Walter had certainly believed it. Whether Burridge would was another matter, but this was one chance they had to take.

Soon afterwards Helene discreetly left the restaurant. No-one knew Victor, who remained and ordered himself another coffee. He had at least a half hour to wait.


As Teresa found her room key, the door opened and the maid came out. There was a moment of mutual surprise, then she realised the cleaning trolley stood nearby. The maid smiled, gave a brief nervous bow, wished her goodnight, then pushed the trolley along the corridor. Tess shut the door, and the lock clicked. She saw the bed turned down and, on her pillow, a single fresh rose with a liqueur chocolate beside it and the usual hotel benediction: COMPLIMENTS OF THE MANAGEMENT. PLEASE ENJOY A GOOD REST.

She hoped it would be possible. There was a great deal to keep her awake. If this first day was a sample of what was to come, she would more than earn the fee Sir Edward had offered. She made a mental resolution to stop thinking of him as Sir Edward, and to call him Ted, as Ben Hammond did.

Ben. There was another reason to prevent her from a relaxed night and an easy sleep.

She unwrapped the chocolate and ate it, slipped off her shoes and removed her tights, as she sat on the bed and thought about Ben Hammond. For what they had been persuaded to do, they required some reasonable rapport—and there was none. She had been singularly unimpressed by his abrasive manner in the initial encounter at the bank. She not only felt they were ill-suited, he clearly felt he had been coerced into this and was regretting it—just as she was. It was also beginning to appear it might be more dangerous than she had been led to believe.

If Tess had a choice, it would be to pick up the phone, make a booking on the first plane home, and tell Sir Edward—Ted—she had changed her mind. The advance payment he had given her was in her savings account untouched. It could readily be returned. But she had an uneasy feeling it would not be as simple as that.

The uneasiness persisted, and she felt a wave of nausea as the room began to sway. Her vision blurred. She tried to rise, and staggered as if she was drunk. She knew this was impossible, because she had only had two glasses of wine throughout the evening. She tried to reach for the telephone. There seemed to be three of them; she made a frantic grab and felt something solid that slipped from her grasp and spilled on the floor.

She realised that if she bent down to try to retrieve it, she would not be able to get up again. The last thing she was aware of doing before losing consciousness, was to clutch at her handbag, as if remembering there was something of value in there.

# 12

'DO YOU THINK you'll get on together?'

'I hope so.'

'It's important, Ben. You need her.'

'As an interpreter? Or does she have some other qualifications?'

'She speaks every language and even some of the hill-tribe dialects between here and Vientiane. You'd get nowhere without someone who can communicate and knows the terrain. She's also trustworthy.'

Ben shrugged. It was hardly the answer he had hoped for. If Teresa Martineau had other attributes, he wasn't going to be told about them. They were in his room, where Burridge had invited himself for a nightcap, saying the bar was a bit crowded and public and they needed to talk in confidence.

'What's this about her father?'

'It's not important.'

'Everything's important.'

Burridge explained sketchily, giving the bare

details of his meeting with Teresa after her mother's death and his revelation to her that her father was very much alive.

'Will she meet him?'

'Of course.'

'As a part of this?'

'Most unlikely. He's just an ordinary businessman. Lived there much of his life, and has an eighteen-year-old Thai girlfriend. He's been useful to us once or twice, but in a very minor capacity.'

'So she was right. You did use him as bait.'

'Don't be bloody stupid.' He thought about it for a moment, while he sipped a cognac from the minibar. 'Bait's a rather emotive word,' he said finally. 'I expect I made use of the fact that he's there. I wanted someone of her quality— and I make use of anything I can.'

'Like you made use of my situation?'

'You could say that.'

'And why was it you needed me in particular?'

Burridge hesitated. Then he said, 'The contact in Bangkok, the one who'll put you in touch with Sokram— he's careful, but he'll deal with you.'

'Why me?'

'Because he's heard of you. We made sure he did. He thinks you're a bent cop, keen to go into commerce and become a drug trader.'

'While we're being friendly over a nightcap,' Ben said, 'I'm convinced you set me up. No matter what you say, that's what I believe.'

'You believe what you like, sport,' Edward Burridge said with sudden surprising venom. 'The truth is you're on the bones of your arse—and I'm all you've got.'


Helene sat in a room of the Maison Citadel which she had reserved, and listened to the conversation from room 1295. The man who earlier that evening had installed a listening device in the telephone receiver sat with her. The clarity of the sound on the amplified speaker was superlative. The maintenance man—who had discarded his overalls and tool kit for a business suit—had a tape recorder, the spools of which were turning. Much of the content of what Ben Hammond and Sir Edward were saying was of little relevance to Helene, but later the recording could be studied in case there was some element she had missed.

She wondered about Victor, and what progress he had made in the English bitch's room on the floor below.


The maid knocked and, receiving no answer, used a pass key to enter. She beckoned to

Victor, and they went in and locked the door. Teresa was unconscious on the floor. The phone lay disconnected on the carpet, and her handbag was close to where she lay. Victor picked up the bag, and began a search of the contents.

'We find the key, and leave, yes?' The maid was nervous.

He paid no attention. There was little money in the bag, but he expected that. They would have left most of it at the hotel deposit. The key was a different matter. They had each been instructed to keep their keys with them at all times.

He started to rip the bag apart. There were a number of different passports, which he cast aside with barely a glance. There was no sign of a key.


At long last, Helene Lee heard what she had been waiting for. There was a sound of rustling, as if a piece of paper had been produced, and then Burridge's voice.

'The money is contained in these eight banks. Each has the same type of high-security safe-deposit vault.'

She heard Ben Hammond reading the names of the various banks, and then the cities in which they were located.

'Hong Kong, Singapore, Bangkok, Paris, London . . .' It was all perfectly clear on the tape, but Helene in her excitement was writing it down, until she realised there was no need.

'Zurich,' she heard, 'Munich and Edinburgh.'

'You have to memorise all the details of all those banks as well as the account numbers.' This time it was Burridge speaking. 'For safety, nothing can be written down. Learn it all, then burn it.'

'Shit,' she heard Ben say, 'that's not easy. And what about the different keys and bloody passwords?'

'They're all the same.'

'What do you mean?'

'The passwords, the keys—they apply in each of those banks. It keeps it simple. Easy to remember.'

Wonderful, Helene thought. All we need is those two keys. Then darling Walter will tell me the password.


Ben finished his cognac and yawned. He hoped it would serve as a hint, but Burridge seemed not to notice. Having finally begun to confide details, he seemed eager to continue.

'In those bank vaults, the various deposit boxes contain a total of a billion dollars. The real balance, the majority of the money, is in a special account in Credit Suisse, Geneva.'

'How is that to be accessed?'

'There's no way it can be, until you reach an accord.'

'And then?'

'If and when Sokram accepts, you hand him all the details of the banks, after which I meet him and give him the number of the Credit Suisse account.'

'So you're the only one who knows it?'

'I'm the only one I can trust.' Edward Burridge gave his best impersonation of a laugh, and finished his drink.

'Time I was in the cot, old boy. See you tomorrow. Sleep well.'


Victor had almost ripped the room apart. Clothes were torn, luggage cut to pieces as he wielded a lethal knife. The maid gave up her futile attempt to remonstrate. Her instructions had been explicit: to leave the room tidy—but this was not someone with whom she wished to argue.

Teresa was still sprawled unconscious. Victor knelt and grabbed her by the hair, violently pulling her up into a sitting position. He thought he heard a murmur of protest, and held his knife at her throat.

'You fucking bitch,' he said it softly, his lips

close to her ear. 'Where's the key?'

There was no response. He shook her then, brandishing the knife blade in front of her eyes.

'Your key to the bank. To the deposit box. Give it to me or I'll cut your face to ribbons.'

'She can't hear you,' the maid said.

'She made a noise a moment ago.'

'It was nothing. Just a reflex. She's in a very deep sleep. If she hears or feels anything, it would be like a dream. She can't answer.'

The woman posing as the maid was a hospital nurse, tempted by the money, and beginning to regret she was there. The girl who had contacted her with the offer had seemed civilised, and made it sound an easy task. But this man was something unexpected. She had not known it would be like this. She sensed he was sadistic, and she felt afraid.

'How long does this stuff last?'

'Two, even three hours.'

'Jesus. Couldn't you have used something else? I need her conscious.'

'That's what the lady—your friend—said she wanted. Two hours to make a search.'

Victor's knife ripped Teresa's dress. He tore it from her body, and examined it, but it was just a slip of material with no place to conceal anything. He slashed through the strap of her brassiere, and removed it. His hands felt under her breasts in case the key was taped there. The

152

breasts were small but perfectly shaped and firm, the nipples a vivid pink against the light tan of her body. Touching them had begun to arouse him. Apart from a pair of briefs, the girl was now unclothed. He felt another stir of sexual excitement. First he needed to get rid of the maid.

'I'll stay until she wakes. You get out of here.'

The maid fled without a word. She guessed what he intended, but was too terrified to protest. As the door clicked shut, he found the telephone on the floor and removed it from its socket. He took it into the bathroom and left it in a cabinet. Victor had no intention of the device inside the receiver allowing Helene or anyone else in the room upstairs to monitor what would happen next.

He had lots of time. If Teresa Martineau did eventually become conscious, so much the better. The sight of her lying stretched out on the floor, almost naked and completely helpless, stimulated him torridly. His blood began to pound, and logic and reason fled.

He removed her pants, and started to search her.


Both directional speakers were silent. Helene wondered what was taking Victor so much time, and why the woman posing as the hotel maid was missing. But her concentration was focused on room 1295. The revealing conversation with the names and details of the banks was long over, and Sir Edward had gone, no doubt on his way to the spare suite he occupied in Walter's house on Victoria Peak. It was 11.30 and she should not stay much longer, or else Walter, who was acutely jealous, would begin to have doubts about dinner with the cousin from Macao. But first she must ensure they had the other key, the one held by Ben Hammond.

She looked at the man who sat listening. He shrugged.

'No sound now for ten minutes. We know the girl ate the chocolate. If the man has, he should be unconscious by now.'

'I'll give it another five minutes,' Helene said. 'In case he hasn't eaten it.'

'People do. It's free and on the pillow. The way this place charges, the customers grab something for nothing.'

'I hope you're right. Five more minutes and I'll find out.'


Ben felt close to sleep. He was trying to read and memorise the names of the banks Burridge had given him, but it had been a long day, and his eyes were heavy. He lay on the bed. He had put the rose and the hotel blessing:

COMPLIMENTS OF THE MANAGEMENT. PLEASE ENJOY A GOOD REST to one side, and unwrapped the liqueur chocolate. He was debating whether to eat it before cleaning his teeth or afterwards, or else to hell with cleaning his teeth and just do what he felt inclined— which was to close his eyes and drift into slumber—when the bedside telephone rang.

His first thought was that it might be Burridge, but he was on his way back to the house where he stayed on Hong Kong Island and, as far as Ben knew, did not have a mobile phone with him. Which left only Teresa, Tess, as she had said she was also known—and so he picked up the receiver, expecting to hear her voice, and pleased that she had called him.

'Hi,' he said. 'How are you?'

There was a distinct silence.

'I beg your pardon,' a voice said. 'Wrong room number.'

It was a soft female voice, and sounded as if it belonged to someone attractive. The kind of voice that invited a response.

'Sorry about that. What number did you want?'

He was fishing—even flirting a bit. After the wine and the nightcaps with Burridge, he was in a mood to respond to a sultry voice on the telephone, so that when there was a sudden click, and he heard the dial tone in his ear, it

155

was like rejection. Rather like a slap in the face. Or else . . . what?

Something about the call made him uneasy. He almost dismissed it, but then saw the hotel notepad beside his bed where he had written Teresa's room number. 1184. He wondered if she was asleep by now, decided that if he woke her he would apologise in the morning, and dialled it. He heard a high-pitched signal. He checked the hotel directory, which said room numbers could be dialled without a prefix, and he tried again with the same result. He called the operator, who also tried, and said room 1184's phone seemed to be out of order, and she would report it. Ben thanked her, and hung up. It was then he noticed the tiny marks on the telephone.

They were like scratches, nothing particularly unusual, yet at once he was alert. He tried to prise the instrument open but, lacking a screwdriver or knife to force it apart, he smashed the plastic case on the edge of the table. As it broke in pieces, he saw the small electronic device and instantly knew what it was.

*Christ Almighty*, he thought, but there was no time to consider the full implications. Their rooms had been bugged. Someone had planted these while they were at dinner. And Teresa's phone was out of order.

Ben was out of his room, and running.

He went via the fire exit, not the elevators which were in use— taking the stairs two at a time. He reached the floor below and ran along the dimly lit and empty corridor. Breakfast menus hung on door knobs; on others were DO NOT DISTURB signs. There was one on room 1184, but he disregarded it and leaned on the buzzer. He could hear it ringing continuously inside, and hammered on the door, mindless of other guests.

It clicked open. Without a thought, he pushed it and went inside.


Edward Burridge felt relaxed, as he was driven up the winding road to Victoria Peak. He thought that after a relatively bad start, the latter part of the evening had gone well. In a day or two, once he had identified and secured the group who had followed them, the pair would be on their way to Bangkok. Forty-eight hours later, with any sort of luck, it should be over.

He made a decision that tomorrow he would use his influence with the Hong Kong police to have Carmichael arrested and fitted up with enough evidence to put him away for a few years. Then the small-time Australian crook could have a choice; face the charges, or accept a generous financial offer and protection in exchange for the names of those who had hired him. It should expedite things. This security breach had no doubt come from someone inside the bank, but the sooner the people involved were found and immobilised, the quicker the real matter could proceed.

Lights were on in the house. Walter was on the terrace alone. He said he was waiting for Helene. A distant relative from Macao, a cousin, had arrived for a visit and had taken her out to dinner. She should be home any moment.

*A cousin?* Burridge hoped it was true. If the delectable Helene was playing games, Walter would be devastated. Because so much of his friend's life had been a series of sexual pursuits—emotional excitements quite often followed by dejection and disaster—Edward Burridge merely speculated on whether the girl was cheating, and never contemplated any other possible alternative.

It was something he would come to regret.

*13* THE ROOM WAS in near darkness. Only a faint glow from the neons and lights outside reflected through a gap where the curtains did not quite meet across the window.

He could see the outline of a figure lying on the floor.

Ben switched on the lights and let the door swing shut behind him. He only had time to glimpse that the figure was Teresa, and that she was both unconscious and naked, then he felt danger behind him and tried to turn. A knife flashed as Victor launched himself from where he had stood on the blind side of the door. Ben dodged, stumbled and tripped, and his assailant was on him, trying to thrust the blade into his throat. He had the advantage of surprise, but Ben managed to grip his wrist and slowly force the weapon back, while with his other hand he stabbed splayed fingers into the face so close above him. He saw it hurt, saw the other's eyes dilate with pain, and he seized his opportunity as he viciously twisted the hand holding the knife, and it dropped onto the carpet. Ben knocked it away, then he rolled free and got to his feet. Victor was slower to rise, and Ben kneed him as he came upright. He hit him with a blow deep into the solar plexus, and heard the gasp as he winded him.

Victor backed towards the door. He tried to open it but Ben caught him, whirled him around, crunched a knee into his groin, jolted an elbow to his face and, as his head dropped in agonised reflex, he administered a coup de grâce with a ferocious rabbit-killer across the back of the neck. Victor collapsed.

Ben, enraged, almost out of control, was ready to continue, but he heard a murmured groan from Teresa. He turned to see her trying to stir. He took a counterpane and carefully wrapped it around her to conceal her nakedness, then lifted her onto the bed. Her eyes opened and she looked blankly at him. There was some expression he could not fathom; she seemed to flinch from him, as if in fear.

'It's all right,' he said, 'you're safe.'

He heard a movement behind him. Victor was trying to crawl towards the knife lying on the floor. Ben moved swiftly, grabbing him by the feet and hauling him back. He pinioned him face down, looked around for something with which to secure him, and saw Teresa's discarded pantihose. He used them to tightly tie the man's hands behind his back. As he stood, Victor lashed out with his feet, catching Ben a glancing blow on the knee.

Ben retrieved the knife, knowing he needed help. It could not come from Teresa. She was conscious, but unmoving, her eyes open but still blank. She began to shiver. Whatever the trauma she was reliving, she was in a state of total shock. There was no sign of the telephone with which to summon a security guard. He dared not leave her to find help. Already Victor's hands were working, trying to unravel the pantihose.

Ben saw a weighty armchair in the room. He moved it across, then lifted it and placed it across Victor's legs, effectively immobilising him, if only for a brief time. He hurriedly drew back the curtains and used the knife to slash lengths of the braided curtain cord, then set about really trussing the intruder. He wrapped the cord as tightly as possible around Victor's feet, then ran it tautly to a loop around his neck, so that his slightest movement would strangle him. Then Ben stared into his helpless and ter-rified face.

'Now, you fucking bastard,' he said, 'who are you?'

• • •

Helene knew something had gone badly wrong. She sat in the back of the Rolls-Royce, as the chauffeur drove her home. She realised her call to Ben Hammond was a mistake the moment she had chosen the wrong option and hung up. She and the maintenance man had heard Ben try to telephone room 1184, then ask the switchboard operator to help, and the confirmation that it would be reported out of order. They had heard the scratching as he examined his phone. So sensitive was the device they even heard his intake of breath, then the sudden crash as he broke the receiver, then a silence as he smashed the phone.

'I think,' the maintenance man said, 'it's time I left.'

When he had gone, she telephoned Walter's chauffeur, who had asked her permission to visit his family while she dined with her cousin. He arrived within minutes. As he drove her up the Peak road, she wondered about Victor. Why the long delay? Had he managed to obtain the key? There was no way she intended to go near the English girl's room to look for him. It had become far too risky. Victor would just have to take his chance. Besides, even if he had one key, it was no use without the other. And if it came to a choice between life on the run with Victor—and riding in the back of a Rolls with an unlimited charge account and a chauffeur at her beck and call, it was really no contest.

Twenty minutes later she was sitting on Walter's knee, hugging him, as she recounted what a really awful evening she had endured, and how her cousin was a dreadful bore, ill-mannered and conceited, and thank goodness Walter had not come to dine with them, or she'd have felt such a loss of face because the man was family, no matter how remote and insignificant—she could be most inventive when the need arose—and she sighed and hoped she would never have to meet him again, and wished she had not wasted a night with this smug relation when she might have spent it like this with her darling Walter.

Around 2 a.m. after they had made love for a second time, and Helene fondled him and incredulously he was hard again, as her mouth slid around him until he was breathless in almost unbearable rapture, after that, when she said he had been such a stallion that she still felt aroused, but perhaps they would sleep for a while and do it again in the morning, it was then that Walter Chen asked her to marry him.


'His name's Victor Mendoza,' the Chinese police inspector said. He was young and had a distinct London accent. 'Looks like you gave him a fair old going over.'

'Self-defence,' Ben said, and they both smiled. Self-defence it had mostly been, but each knew there were a few solid extras in there for Teresa Martineau.

The squad car was discreetly parked at the back entrance to the hotel, and beside it a defiant but battered Victor was handcuffed to a uniformed policeman, with another keeping watch on him.

'He's a nasty piece of work,' the inspector said. 'He's got the rest of his sentence to serve, and assault with possession of a knife should get him another five years.'

He handed the weapon, now sealed in plastic, to one of the uniformed men and gave a sharp order. Victor Mendoza was bundled into the back of the squad car and driven away. Ben walked with the inspector to his own vehicle. In recounting the details, he had given the salient facts, but managed to avoid any mention of telephone bugging, the keys or the bank vault. It had been an armed attempt to rob a tourist, who had been found naked and in a state of shock. Her room was in chaos, and it had clearly been a vicious attack. The inspector had been anxious and sympathetic, wanting Teresa taken to hospital for treatment, but she had refused. He had efficiently arranged for the hotel to provide her with temporary clothing, for almost nothing she possessed was left intact.

He had been thoughtful and concerned, and Ben appreciated it. Now they shook hands.

'She's badly traumatised. When you feel she can cope, try to find out all the details. Or, if she prefers, I'll send one of our female detectives to talk to her.'

'You think it was rape, don't you?'

'I'd say so. Wouldn't you?'

Ben sighed and reluctantly nodded.

'Looks like it, but I sure as hell hope not.'

'On the other hand,' the inspector said, 'if it was, we could put that bastard away forever.'


The lobby, thronged with clusters of tourists by day, seemed larger in the early hours of the morning when it was virtually deserted. At the main reception desk, a night clerk studied the racing guide for the Queen's Cup meeting, while he surreptitiously watched the lone hunched figure sitting in a distant corner. She sat without moving. She gave an impression of being dishevelled, although she was wearing new slacks and a shirt the assistant manager had supplied.

The hotel management were shocked and trying to hush it up. They had persuaded the police to park at the rear of the hotel so there would be no damaging publicity. The receptionist's gaze swivelled to the figure in cotton trousers and T-shirt entering from the back door. He recognised the man who had found her—apparently just in the nick of time. There had been a fight in the woman's room, and several guests, one in the room adjacent and one directly below, had rung to complain of noise. All in all, it was quite an evening. The clerk began to wonder if the local English-language newspaper had got hold of the story. If not, he had a contact there, and the night might yet be worth a few dollars.

Ben crossed the foyer and sat alongside Teresa. She looked jaded and forlorn. She gave no indication of his presence. He took her hand in his, feeling her flinch, sensing as he had when he wrapped her in the counterpane and placed her on the bed, some deep image of disgust that her mind was trying to reject. He knew she was still in shock. Yet she had refused examination by a local doctor or nurse, or counselling with a woman police officer.

'They've moved you into a new room.'

She nodded, and spoke without looking at him, 'I know.'

'Next door to me. Do you want to go there and rest?'

'Not yet.'

'Something to drink? The coffee shop's open all night. I'll bring you one. Or something stronger?'

'No, nothing.'

Despite her flinch and hint of rejection, she had not removed her hand. It was progress of a sort, he supposed, but wished he was more skilled at handling a situation like this.

'How do you feel?' He knew it sounded inept, but there was hardly any way to ask the question sensitively.

'Rough,' Tess said. 'Violated.'

Although it seemed like the answer the police wanted, he was uncertain of her precise meaning. So he waited.

'I feel hurt and unclean,' she said eventually, and for almost the first time she looked at him.

'Tess . . . did he rape you?'

He thought she was not going to reply. She shuddered as if troubled by the memory of a repulsive dream.

'He searched me,' she said. 'I felt his hands— the rest I don't remember. But he didn't find the key.'

'Where is it?' Ben asked.

In other circumstances, the expression on her face might have been a trace of a smile. But she merely said, 'It should turn up tomorrow. I swallowed it.'


The cable car came to a stop at the Peak. There were only a few passengers. Burridge stood waiting on the funicular's panoramic lookout, as Ben joined him. Below them was an endless vista of modern high-rise towers, all the way down to the crowded harbour.

'You know this place was once a barren rock, with just a few tribes of fishermen.'

'Must have been a lot nicer in those days,' Ben said, in no mood for one of Burridge's historical discourses.

'We—that is, Britain—seized the place as a base for our opium traders. Made us rich. We were a bunch of bastards, really. We built a great empire by commerce, a large part of which was made out of trading in slaves and drugs. Then we led the world in trying to abolish the trafficking in both. Always been good at dabbling on both sides, we Brits. How's Teresa?'

'Lousy.'

'Did she sleep?'

'Finally. She woke up with one hell of a hangover. Which is hardly surprising. The chocolate was thiopental, which is a very fast-acting barbiturate, laced with mescaline. The police lab tested mine, and said it was like a knockout drop combined with LSD. She feels sick, and she's also feeling scared.'

'Give her a day or two . . .'

'I don't think you're hearing me, Ted. I doubt if she wants to go on. Both rooms were

168

bugged, and searched. So someone knew all about those keys, which means a leak from your end. If it's like this in dear old Honkers, what's it going to be like at the sharp end?'

'The police have Victor Mendoza. They're interrogating him.'

'That bastard will tell them nothing—take my word for it.'

'We're checking everyone at the bank. I've asked the local police to pull in Carmichael, but he seems to have dropped out of sight.'

'Your security is ratshit. I think she'll say she wants out.'

Burridge was uncharacteristically silent for a moment, as if he was uncertain how to respond. Then he asked, 'If she pulled out, how would you feel?'

'I'd be sorry, but—I think this is out of her league. I know she's a top interpreter and you say she has other qualifications, but I don't think she's equipped to cope. It's not her fault. You made the wrong choice.'

'I chose Teresa before I heard of you—because she's exactly the right choice.'

Ben stared at him, puzzled. 'What does that mean?'

'She was always the first choice.'

'Then there's something you're not telling me,' Ben said.

'Teresa Martineau is vital.'

'How vital?'

'She and this job are incontrovertibly linked. If she pulls out, the job ends. There is no job. It's over.'

'What?'

'You'd be on tonight's plane to Sydney.'

'Shit,' Ben said.

'We'd pay your fare home, and that's all. No balance of the hundred thousand. No chance of twice that as a bonus for success. I expect we'd give you a cab docket from the airport.'

'What the fucking hell is this? Some kind of doublecross?'

'Without her we don't continue.'

'What exactly is so special about Teresa?'

'Her father,' Burridge said.

14 WHEN THE TAXI drew up at his hotel, he collected his key and went up to his room. There was a message from Teresa saying that she had asked for calls to be diverted so that she could sleep until after lunch. Would he meet her in the lobby at two o'clock? Ben was glad of the chance to have time alone, for he had a lot to think about.

Burridge had been reluctant to confide in him further, as if his revelation about Teresa's father had been a mistake. Ben had felt like shaking him. He had kept his temper only with an effort, pointing out that since he had made the statement, he either had to explain it or else Ben would take the next cable car down, and see if Tess herself could give him an explanation.

'That would achieve nothing,' Burridge had said. 'You'd unduly alarm her, and there's not a thing she could tell you. She knows nothing about her father. Until recently she believed he'd been dead for years.'

'Stop messing me about, will you. You said

171

she's so important that without her, we don't even go on. You also said she's important because of her father. So who and what is her father?'

'He works for us.'

'You've got to do better than this.' He was becoming increasingly angry. 'You told us that at dinner last night. But you played down his importance in front of her—and later told me he was just an ordinary businessman, and unlikely to be a part of this.'

'I lied,' Burridge shrugged.

'Seems to me you're full of shit, Ted. And full of lies.'

'There's no point in being hostile, old boy.'

'Not much point in being civil, either. Ask a reasonable question, and the response is at best some trumped-up bullshit or evasions. So it looks like I just kiss your scheme goodbye. Go home and be a private detective or a security guard.'

'All right,' Burridge had said eventually, and it seemed to Ben, grudgingly. 'Let's stroll to where I'm staying. I'll tell you what I can.'

They had walked away from the cable car terminus, and past massive homes that sat high above the view. It was humid, and both felt the moisture and the heat.

'Her father is a powerful man, with a lot of influence. He's a public figure who owns and runs businesses. He employs a great many people. For that reason, he has plenty of clout with the government, but he also has influence with people close to Kim Sokram. He has a lot of authority and prestige. When I said he works for us, the truth is we haven't used him in years. He's far too valuable to waste on routine matters. When it's known his daughter is accompanying a man who wants to meet and talk with Sokram, it should ensure you a safe passage, because the word I intend to spread is that you're lovers.'

'I see.'

'As Martineau's daughter, she's your protection.'

'Why not tell her?'

'It's better this way. I need her with you, as a shield. You need her, or you'd end up in a *klong* with your throat cut.'

'Thanks.'

'No disrespect to you, but no-one would get anywhere near Sokram without her special status. Surely you can see that?'

'Yes,' he had nodded. He could see it. Teresa had a particular value. Burridge had not been exaggerating.

'Was she to be informed we were supposed to be lovers?'

'I didn't actually intend to tell either of you.'

'Just proposed to move us around like pawns on your personal chessboard.'

'If that's how you see it.'

'Or a puppeteer, and we're the jerks on the strings. The ones who never get to be told anything.'

'Information should only be disseminated when there's a real need to know.'

'And in your world, you're the only one who needs to know.'

'Secrets are best kept by the least number.'

Burridge had an endless collection of cloak-and-dagger clichés. Delivered with a condescending smile, they could irritate Ben mightily.

'Some secret,' he said heatedly. 'Along came Victor Mendoza, and the whole thing is a mess. Because I don't see how you or anyone else is going to persuade Teresa to continue.'

'I think you underestimate yourself,' Burridge had told him.

'Not me, sport. I sympathise with her.'

'Which is why you're the only one she might listen to.'

'What makes you think I'm even prepared to try?'

'Because I think you need the money. I know you've handed everything else over to your wife. Superannuation, severance pay, the house, the lot. Even endorsed to her the cheque I gave you.'

*Fuck you,* Ben thought with sudden anger, *how dare you snoop into my life?* But he didn't say it, because he knew Burridge spoke the truth. In despair at Chrissie's death, and anger at the way he had been treated, he had recklessly given everything to Deborah. No waiting for judicial division by the family court. He was rejecting that sort of order and prescribed direction. *To hell with the law and its established rites and statutes.* He had kept only enough to rent the beach house and live simply until his tiny savings account ran out. *After that? Well, there was always one of the private police forces the rich were forming to protect their exclusive estates and their kids. Some crappy job or other.*

Trust bloody Burridge to be aware of this. He had begun to feel the approaching insecurity, and to count on this prospect of the big tax-free bonanza. It would set him up for a long time. He knew that secretly he didn't want Tess to obey her instincts and give up, because it would mean the end of his one chance for a reasonable future.

'How does it look?'

It was a silk trouser suit. She held it up against her body for his opinion, and he nodded approvingly. They were in a street market, raucous with a whole range of different nationalities bargaining, as Teresa went back into the fray against the Indian merchant who owned the stall. She was enjoying herself, Ben could sense it. The owner was trying to haggle with her in English, and she was disconcerting him by switching between Cantonese and Hindi, which he professed not to understand, but clearly did.

In the end they reached an accord, and she paid the price into his hand with the Indian lamenting loudly he had been robbed. Ben carried her parcels, and they headed towards another store. Tess was savouring her success.

'It's fun. I got it for half what he asked. Mind you, I bet he doubled the price before we got there.'

They bought her some underwear, jeans and T-shirts, as well as a pair of casual shoes, then moved up-market. In Lane Crawford's exclusive designer salon, she tried on a number of dresses, amid a cluster of sales ladies enthusing over how the garments fitted, and how elegantly she wore them. They were surprised and pleased when she replied to them in perfect Cantonese. Ben sat holding the parcels, watching while the sales ladies kept watch on him for his opinion. Finally one of them spoke to Teresa, and she approached to show off a slim cream linen suit.

'She said to ask my husband what he thinks,' Tess said.

'Did you tell her that I'm really your bearer? The bag man?'

She smiled. 'So what do you think?'

'I think it's very smart, and you look terrific.'

'Do I?'

'Truly.'

'It's ridiculously extravagant. And I don't even know if I'd wear it much—'

'Wear it tonight, and we'll have dinner at Aberdeen.'

'Will we? That'd be nice. But this thing costs a fortune.'

'Don't even consider the cost. The way it makes you look, you can't afford not to buy it.'

She laughed, her face alive with pleasure at the compliment, and he suddenly realised that while she was conventionally attractive, not as beautiful as Christine, but few were, she had something elusive he had been trying to identify, and to which he could at last put a name.

She had style.

He watched her walk back to tell the coterie of sales assistants how much her husband liked the outfit—she said it in English for his benefit—and they bestowed on him approving smiles to acknowledge his acute perception and obvious good taste. Yes, she had style.

The pity of it was, dinner tonight would more than likely prove to be their last meeting.

*15* ABERDEEN IS A floating village sprawled on the far side of the Island, sheltered by Victoria Peak: a cluster of markets, tiny dwellings and smart restaurants. Its eating houses are a tourist mecca, and on the sea breeze is a mix of exotic cooking, char grills and the occasional whiff of open sewers.

Ben and Teresa chose a seafood restaurant. She looked poised and elegant in her cream suit. It was less than twenty-four hours since her ordeal at the hotel, but as the day progressed she had seemed more at ease and relaxed.

'It was a nice afternoon, Ben. Thanks.'

'For what?'

'You were very patient, while I tried on all those things. Most men would've been sighing or checking their watches.'

'You take the wrong sort of guys shopping. I enjoyed it,' he said truthfully. 'I loved the bargaining, when you let them hassle you in English, then suddenly ambushed them with a stream of Cantonese.'

Her peal of laughter attracted smiles from adjoining tables. It was an uninhibited sound, rich and genuine.

'Ambushed them, indeed. I like that.'

'I wish I spoke languages.'

'I grew up with it. Not so easy to do that in Sydney.'

'No,' Ben said. 'When we were kids, we thought the rest of the world was too far away—so why bother? But it's changing. Kids today are more aware. One of mine is in his second year of learning Indonesian.'

She asked him how many children he had, and he told her about Susan and Daniel and showed her snapshots he carried in his wallet. She wanted to know about the kind of house and locality he lived in, and he briefly explained that he and Deborah had just come to the end of thirteen years together, and added they were mostly good years, except for the past two, and they were going to work things out so that the kids did not suffer. He told her about the beach house he had rented, and how it was remote and peaceful, and would be his for another two months until the high summer rentals forced him to find somewhere else.

'Sounds idyllic,' she said.

'It is. Maybe I'll try to rent it again, after the rich trendies go back to work. You can actually step off the front lawn onto the beach.'

'Heaven.'

He asked her where she livéd, and she described her flat in Bolton Gardens. Ben said he had only ever spent two weeks in London, the year after he and Deb married, a sort of delayed honeymoon, and he had found the city a bit cold and wet, and not all that friendly. He corrected himself and said that was not entirely true; people were friendly if you asked how to get somewhere, and would go out of their way to show you, but no-one had ever asked them home.

Tess explained that invitations like that took about two years; until then you were mere transients; and yes, it was often cold and damp, and there was more dog shit on the pavements of Kensington, the borough in which she lived, than in many entire cities, and yet she treasured the place and could not imagine a life spent anywhere else.

During the meal they reached an easy rapport, where he was able to enquire if she had other family. She found herself talking about Stephen; how he had been extremely handsome but a terrible mistake, their divorce a trauma upsetting her mother, but thoroughly approved by her stepfather, Charles Lambert, whom she loved dearly, and who, even if she met her real father, would always have a special place in her affections.

Coffee gave Ben the opportunity he needed.

'But you won't now, will you,' he said casually.

'Won't what?'

'Meet your father.'

There was a brief silence. Tess looked into her coffee cup, as if the answer might lie there.

'I don't know,' she finally said.

'I wouldn't blame you.'

'If I drop out, Sir Ted will find someone else to go with you.'

'He says not.'

'You mean if I don't go to Bangkok, it's all off.'

'Yes.'

'Why?'

Ben wished he could tell her the truth and repeat all Burridge had told him, but he had made promises and felt constrained by them. He resolved to keep as close to the facts as possible. If obfuscation proved necessary, at least there would be no outright lies.

'Matter of trust, I think. He's investigated you, and you get his personal gold seal of approval. Finding someone else would be too difficult, and take too long.'

'So if I don't go, you don't?'

'Seems that way.'

'You don't get to earn—whatever it was you were to be paid? Is that what you're saying?'

When he did not reply, she asked, 'How much was it?'

'Doesn't matter, Tess.'

'I think it does,' she said. 'How much?'

'For Christ's sake—it's not important. If it was me, after last night, I wouldn't go.'

She studied him carefully. 'Did Burridge ask you to talk to me?'

'Yes.'

'Convince me to stay here? Go on with it?'

'That's right.'

'Only you've changed direction. He wouldn't care for that.'

'This afternoon,' Ben said, 'I came to the conclusion I liked you. I'll tell you the truth, and admit that wasn't what I felt yesterday. But today I decided you were gutsy and brave—as well as attractive and clever—therefore a bit special. And that whatever you wanted, the hell with the consequences. I was on your side.'

The waiter came by and asked if they would like more coffee. Teresa seemed not to hear him. She was studying Ben, as if they were alone. Eventually the waiter moved on with his tray.

'Is that the real you talking,' she asked, 'or some scene you worked out with Burridge?'

'Stuff Burridge. I'm saying leave. Go home to Bolton Gardens, and I'll go home to my beach house. We'll send each other a Christmas card.

Only before you do, the inspector asked me to show you this.'

He reached into his pocket, and placed a police photo of Victor in front of her. She picked it up and gazed expressionlessly at it. She knew who it was. She had been conscious when the police had arrested and formally charged him.

'He said it might help jog your memory. He wants to get a rape conviction.'

'Whatever happened, I was out cold. I can't help.'

'And you don't want to remember?'

'That's not it. I can't, Ben. Stop leaning on me like a cop.'

'I'm sorry,' he said.

She looked carefully at the photograph again.

'I can tell you one thing, though. I did see him last night. I mean earlier. When I left the restaurant.'

'Are you sure?' Ben was startled.

'Yes. He was with a girl. Not that it helps the inspector, but that's something I can remember.'


In the middle of the night the phone rang. It kept ringing. Ben thought at first he was dreaming, then tried to ignore it in the vain hope that it might stop. Eventually he fumbled for it and answered.

'Did I wake you up?' Tess asked.

'Yes,' he said.

'Sorry.'

She didn't sound it. She sounded alert and positive.

'I've been thinking. The man's locked up in jail. And I came all this way to meet my father. So why should I go home to Bolton Gardens?'

Ben suddenly felt wide awake.

'Are you still there?' she asked.

'I'm still here.'

'We'll go and tell Sir in the morning.'

'If you're sure.'

'Couldn't be more certain,' Teresa told him.


They took a taxi to the house on Victoria Peak. A servant showed them into a marble living room, then went to find Sir Edward. Ben stood at the plate-glass windows and looked down on the immense panorama of the city and harbour below, then realised Tess was displaying no interest in the view. She was staring at a framed photograph that stood on a side table. She picked it up, frowning.

'What is it?'

'I thought for a moment I knew her.'

She replaced the photo on the table as Burridge joined them. He seemed tentative, until

Teresa broke the news to him that she felt able to continue.

'Splendid.'

He included Ben in a smile that assumed he had successfully negotiated this change of mind.

'I'll make arrangements for you to leave tomorrow. The man you have to meet runs a jewellery stall in Bangkok.' He went to a desk in a corner of the room, where he found writing paper and printed a name and address. He showed them what he had written: *Pandit Singh. Dealer in Fine Arts. Chakrawat.*

'You know the district, Teresa?'

'Know it? I went to school near there.'

Burridge sealed the envelope and gave it to Ben.

'I'll send word. He'll be expecting you.'

Ben nodded. Burridge made the obligatory offer of coffee or a drink, and they refused. Teresa indicated the framed photograph. She was still thoughtful: 'Very attractive girl, Sir Edward.'

'She is rather a dish, isn't she,' Burridge said.

'Who is she?'

'Helene Lee. She's just announced her engagement to my friend Walter Chen.'

They heard voices, and a grey-haired Chinese, immaculate in a blazer and yachting trousers, came to the open door and looked in. He nodded politely to them, and said to

Burridge: 'Just off, old boy. Sure you won't join us?'

'Thanks all the same.'

'See you for dinner, Edward,' a girl's voice called from behind, somewhere out of sight, and Burridge went out to acknowledge her.

Ben was hardly aware of him leaving.

*The voice,* he thought. *The bloody voice.* It had been just a few words exchanged on a telephone, but he knew that voice. Or thought he did. He had to hear her speak again.

They were engaged in a conversation by the front door. Ben approached them and then stopped, as if apologetic and embarrassed at interrupting. 'Sorry,' he said. And to Burridge: 'We're just off.'

'Be with you in a second,' Burridge said.

'I believe congratulations are in order,' Ben looked directly at the girl.

She gave a brief smile. 'Thank you,' she said.

*And thank you,* he thought, *because I'd know the sound of you anywhere. You may be the next Mrs Chen, engaged to Ted's old chum, but I'm bloody certain you're the reason we're in this shit.*

They took the funicular. Burridge offered to call a taxi, but Ben said Tess needed a walk in the fresh air, and the cable car was worth it for the experience, and he apologised for interrupting Ted with his friend and the fiancée—and wasn't she a striking-looking girl. Very pretty. The photograph hardly did her justice. A big age difference, of course. Was it his first marriage?

Burridge fixed him with an intent look, as if it was none of their business, and then reluctantly admitted she would be the third Mrs Chen.

'The wedding's in a few weeks, by which time I hope this will be over and we'll all be safely home. I'm to be the best man,' he said, with what seemed like a singular lack of enthusiasm.

It was then Ben told him he and Teresa didn't feel they could leave quite so soon. Not as early as tomorrow. They'd discussed it while Sir Ted was saying farewell to his friends, and Tess had made the point that she needed more time, a few extra days, in which to recover.

Tess had been brilliant. She didn't even blink. She looked suitably apologetic and said she was sorry to cause inconvenience. Burridge tried to curb his irritation.

'It's most urgent. I thought you said you've recovered.'

'I said I'd continue,' she corrected him. 'But not tomorrow.'

'It would be most unwise,' Ben observed, 'in fact pretty damn stupid, to leave here before she's fit.'

187

In the swaying cable car, on their way down, he told her about the voice. That he might be mistaken, could easily be; a few words on the telephone weren't evidence, but it was a fairly seductive distinctive voice, and they both knew it had to be someone close to Burridge who had spilled the beans. It might be Chen, or one of the staff.

Or the girl. Helene Lee.

Whether it was or not, Sir Edward Burridge had done a pretty ordinary job so far on security. Everything had been leaked; every move they made anticipated. Did Tess agree?

Tess did. But what was he suggesting?

'That we trust each other, and no-one else.'

'Are you saying that includes Sir Ted?'

'I'm afraid so. If the information came from that house, then Burridge is compromised.'

'Shouldn't we warn him?'

'You really think a supercilious prick like him would listen? Tess, I don't want to be alarmist. Victor Mendoza's in prison. But there are bound to be others—' He stopped in mid-sentence, aware that she was staring at him.

'Oh my God,' Tess said. 'The girl in the photo. That's where I saw her. With Victor Mendoza, in the restaurant. Not long before it happened. That's what I've been trying to remember.'

16 EDDIE CARMICHAEL PRIDED himself on what a newspaper once described as a chameleon-like ability to change his appearance and blend into the background. It had been his one asset as a con man in a not notably distinguished career. He had operated minor scams in both Sydney and Melbourne and, when caught, had pleaded guilty and asked for some additional offences to be taken into consideration. In fact there were thirty, but Eddie pleaded guilty to ten, and with the aid of a smart barrister and the use of his most effective expression—confused and bewildered innocence—he managed to be granted bail while the judge pondered on a suitable term of imprisonment. He was not entirely trusted by the judge; his passport was sequestered, and he was ordered to report to the police daily.

However, Eddie Carmichael had a collection of passports. He reported to his local station the following morning, and two hours later was at the airport, boarding a Philippine Airlines flight.

By the next day when he was due to report to the police again, he was on the island of Mindoro, having cleared immigration in Manila, his entry visa and residence permit both passing scrutiny. For two years he worked the bars, preying on tourists, and then decided, since the local police were beginning to take an unhealthy interest in him, that there were richer pickings in Hong Kong. In a side street off the Wan Chai market, he invested his money in an upstairs bar with a bunch of Vietnamese girls as his G-stringed hostesses. They were hard-working whores and for a time made him rich, for all were illegal immigrants and knew that if they did not perform to Eddie's satisfaction, they would end up in the detainee cages of High Island camp, one of the grim and dehumanising centres where sixty thousand boat people waited for deportation or the slim hope of being granted refugee status.

Two events occurred that contributed to yet another fall from grace in the life of Eddie Carmichael. One of his girls contracted AIDS and, stricken with horror at the diagnosis and guilt at the realisation she had doubtless infected others, she wrote of her plight to the newspapers, then killed herself in the most public way. She boarded a crowded Star Ferry in the peak hour. She stripped off her clothes in full view of hundreds of commuters, most of them too astonished to guess the purpose of the heavy chain wrapped around her naked body. Before anyone could prevent her, she had pushed her way to the bow, jumped over the side into the murky harbour, and disappeared from sight. A tourist had snapped her last moment of life; his photo made it a front-page story the following day—and not even the sergeant of police whom Carmichael paid could prevent him from being raided and closed down. He was, however, forewarned, and the cash drawer and his flat where he lived over the bar were both empty.

There was a comparatively healthy savings account in the Hong Kong and Shanghai Bank, and Eddie Carmichael was able to superannuate into luxurious obscurity. He rented a penthouse apartment, bought some blazers and cravats, and set about improving his image. That brought him his second misfortune. In the course of social climbing, with an eye to the main chance and the possibility of a really big sting on some wealthy sucker, he met and fell in love with Helene Lee.

She was, she said, a journalist, brought up in California, in Hong Kong here to write articles on the colony's imminent date with destiny: when the lease reverted to China. She was the most beautiful and exotic creature Eddie had met in his forty-five mostly ill-spent years, and he, who had so often used women to his own advantage, became a captive to her whims and fancies. Determined to impress her, they dined only at the most expensive restaurants; he leased a private box at the races so he could show her off; rented a yacht on which they gave parties, but which never left its marina; and took her for weekends to Singapore and Tokyo. In a whirlwind two months his bank account was depleted; he had enjoyed the most voracious and electric sex of his life, and then been quietly discarded in favour of an older, richer man.

She had simply announced one day that she had met Walter Chen, and was going to live with him. His rage left her unmoved. She told him in clear terms that he was a small-time crook and a poseur, and that Walter was rich beyond Eddie's dreams of avarice. She also said that if he behaved himself, they might occasionally meet and fuck, but only on condition that it was discreet. And then, two weeks ago, she had met him by arrangement, but not to go to bed. She had told him of Walter's English friend, Sir Edward Burridge, and a wacky and eccentric scheme to buy out one of the Thai drug barons. When he scoffed, Helene produced an audio tape and played it for him. Having no idea their conversation was being recorded, the two men had talked of staggering amounts of money. In particular they had discussed the contents of a safe-deposit box in the bank on Nathan Road.

Eddie Carmichael had been unconvinced at first. She could have all the wealth she'd ever need by marrying her rich man. Why would she take such risks? When she told him she could not bear Walter, his constant touching or endless declarations of devotion, that even as his wife she would always be little more than a pet harlot, and that she had already found and recruited Victor Mendoza, it was then that he began to believe her and envisage a change of fortune surpassing any of his wilder dreams.

He was not foolish enough to imagine a future with Helene; he soon learned that role was assigned to Victor, whom he distrusted and disliked. But he had agreed to work with them. If they succeeded, it meant at least five million dollars each—meanwhile he had spent much of his time speculating how he might outwit them and take it all. It would be a fitting climax to his career, and perfect retribution for the humiliating way she had treated him. But now, since the fiasco two nights ago and Mendoza's arrest, that objective had begun to change.

Ben and Teresa were festooned with parcels. They bought all manner of cheap clothes and souvenirs, not bothering to bargain with the delighted shopkeepers, who had all previously marked up their prices in order to reluctantly reduce them. After all, as Ben told her, it was just money. Not even theirs. Burridge had heaps more, so they might as well be Samaritans and spread it around a little. By the time they reached the Maison Citadel Hotel they looked exactly what they wanted to be: typical tourists, heavily burdened with packages and carrier bags.

He saw them enter the lobby, and became engrossed in a copy of the *South China Times* while he cautiously watched them collect their keys from the desk. It was important to take care, even though this new Eddie Carmichael no longer looked like the man who had followed them two days earlier. He wore a panama hat and horn-rimmed glasses, a neat jacket and tie. If required, he had identification in his wallet, a driving licence and a credit card in the name of Warren Bertram.

They had been shopping, which was a good sign. It meant they were relaxed. He saw the desk clerk reach for their keys—and was in a position to notice they came from pigeonholes adjacent to each other. So she had apparently been moved into the room beside Hammond. No doubt they had both been allocated new rooms, almost certainly shifted to a different floor. It would soon be checked, then all he need do was pass the relevant information on. He had already engaged a new team. One of them, in a bellboy's uniform, was in place near the elevator. Carmichael had started recruiting the moment he received word from Helene that Victor Mendoza had blown it and ended up back in jail.

Mendoza's arrest not only put Victor out of the way and made Helene more reliant upon him, but radically altered the situation. The English girl and the ex-cop were now warned, and bound to take precautions. Therefore, if he was to succeed, it left only one option.

For this amount of money, this once-in-a-lifetime opportunity, Eddie Carmichael was prepared to step into territory he had never dared venture before. His most important recruit had already agreed to a price. For twenty thousand American dollars he would kill the girl and secure her key. Then for another thirty thousand, he and an accomplice would kill the ex-cop. It was the only way. In each case, the rooms would be entered while they were at dinner, and the killings would occur when they returned, unsuspecting and vulnerable.

He was pleased how swiftly he had assembled the right people for the job. Helene had bought extra time by the charade of her engagement to

Chen. If Burridge had suspicions—and he must be checking all possible sources—she felt this might create doubt, at least briefly. Therefore urgency was an essential.

He had not let her down—and in time she would be grateful.

Tonight.

It had to be tonight.


There were others in the elevator, so they remained silent until they reached their floor, and the doors slid shut behind them. A bellboy got out at the same floor and headed briskly down the corridor. They stopped outside the rooms. Teresa felt reassured at his being so close.

'Did you see anyone?'

'No, but you have to trust me, Tess.'

'I trust you,' she said.

She opened her door and they went inside.

17 EDDIE CARMICHAEL WAITED for some time. He began to worry. What if they were attracted to each other, and spent the rest of the day upstairs in the sack? If he stayed here too long, he might become visible. Places like this were thick with house detectives, and the last thing he needed was to be quizzed on whether he was a guest and, if not, why was he spending so much time here?

It was then, with relief, that he saw a crowd spill out of one of the elevators, and they were among them. They had left their shopping upstairs, and appeared to have spent the past half hour showering and changing clothes. Both now wore typical tourist gear: shorts, sneakers and floppy shirts. She carried only her handbag. He held their room keys and had a camera. Carmichael registered these details as they crossed the foyer to the reception desk, left the keys, and gave one of the girls behind the desk their air tickets. He put aside his magazine, and strolled towards reception to study the pamphlets displayed there.

If Carmichael thought he was inconspicuous, Ben Hammond had been trained to spot a tail, without appearing to do so. He had been on the alert since leaving the elevator. He glimpsed a well-dressed man with a panama and horn-rimmed glasses, as he conversed with the girl to whom he had given the plane tickets. The man was now within hearing distance.

'Could you confirm our onward flights to Bangkok? The day after tomorrow, Cathay Pacific. Business class.'

'A pleasure,' the girl said.

'And could you get us a taxi to go to the Tiger Balm Gardens?'

She buzzed for a porter. The man appeared uninterested in the brochures; he strolled off to sit and read a newspaper. He looked different, but moved like the one who had followed them two days ago.

'The taxi's waiting,' the receptionist said. 'Have a nice day.'

'Thank you,' Tess smiled.

They headed towards the entrance. Carmichael, convinced of his obscurity, strolled in the same direction, to watch their cab leaving. He felt reassured. Their plane tickets were at the desk, and they were off to see the sights. He called the contact number, where Helene would get the message that all was well. It would happen as planned—tonight.


Ben watched him in the driver's mirror, as the cab pulled away. He was reassured the man gave no signal for pursuit, and there was no vehicle pulling out to follow them.

'Tiger Balm, yes?' the Chinese driver said. 'Very nice, Tiger Balm Garden. Good place for making photo.'

'No,' Ben said, 'I think we've changed our minds. Take the next street on the left.'

When the driver looked confused, Tess told him in Cantonese that they were going shopping instead.


The 747 took off, engines reverberating at full throttle as it lifted above the harbour with its ferries and sampans, and the crowded land with its mass of concrete towers swiftly became toy-like miniatures below. The aircraft turned to the south as the captain's confident voice welcomed them aboard, and a friendly stewardess in first class offered a choice of French champagne or anything else they wished to drink. Ben asked for an Australian chardonnay. Tess said she'd slum it with the Möet.

It had been a busy few hours.

When they left the hotel they had already made a phone booking for the afternoon flight to Singapore, leaving Kai Tak at 3 p.m. They had carefully selected names from the emergency passports Burridge had supplied, and were told to be at the airport to collect and pay for their tickets two hours before departure. They left all their clothes and other personal possessions in their rooms, as if they were returning. All they took with them was the money, much of it now converted to cash, and their various passports. Some of this had been strapped inside Ben's shirt, some in Teresa's bra, and the rest in her handbag.

They then visited a travel agency, where they paid cash for plane tickets in their own names to Sydney, on a flight leaving at 6.30 p.m. In the adjoining street at another travel bureau, they booked and paid for tickets, again in their own names, to Tokyo. If anyone was to feed their names into a computer, they could make a choice. The flights left within minutes of each other.

Afterwards they had gone to Kowloon's largest department store, where, in just over an hour, they had purchased clothes, underwear, shoes, a suitcase for each of them as well as cabin bags, while a contented taxidriver waited outside with his meter steadily ticking, and reflecting that life was good and his wife would be pleased with him tonight. When he got them to the airport with five minutes to spare, they paid him double what was on the meter, and he shook their hands and wished them a long life and great good fortune.

After all, Ben said, while paying for their first-class tickets—again in cash despite the ticketing officer's surprise—it was Ted's money. Not to go in style would be letting the side down.

Tess agreed as the friendly attendant refilled her champagne glass and handed her a large embossed menu for dinner. If someone else was paying, especially Sir—this was the only way to travel.

The first hint of anxiety came around six o'clock. Carmichael had assigned one of his new recruits, an attractive local girl, to take his place in the lobby. When he returned to join her, she reported they had not yet arrived back. He contacted the bellboy, who had now disposed of his uniform, and confirmed the new room numbers. He tried calling from the house phone. There was no answer. An hour later their keys were still uncollected at the reception desk.

Eddie Carmichael began to feel distinctly uneasy. He thought it was time he telephoned the emergency number to advise Helene Lee.

He was not looking forward to explaining to her they had gone out in their shorts around midmorning to visit the Tiger Balm Gardens, and had apparently found it so absorbing they had not yet returned.

The uniformed clerk on the hire car desk at Changi Airport was polite but inflexible. It was not possible to hire one of their cars by paying cash. A credit card was the only acceptable method. It was standard procedure. They would find the same rule applied at Hertz and Avis and all the other firms. Ben and Teresa already knew this, because they had tried them. It seemed, in the age of plastic money, there was nothing else that could be trusted.

Fortunately, they found there was a late flight leaving for Kuala Lumpur. They got the last two seats, the airline clerk frowning but finally deciding to accept US dollars, and they were in the Malaysian capital before midnight.

Carmichael had bribed one of the housekeeping staff to give him a key card. Helene was with him. They went into Ben's room and shut the door. They were baffled. Everything seemed to be in place. There was some laundry in cellophane on the bed. Jeans and a used shirt lay on

202

the chair. His watch was alongside it.

'See what I mean?' Carmichael was anxious to convince her, as well as vindicate himself. 'They haven't checked out. Their plane tickets are downstairs. Nothing's missing.'

Helene had been given a full report of everything the fake maid had found in the former room, two nights ago. She looked in the drawers of the bedside chest.

'Except a photo wallet,' she said. 'In his other room it stood there on the bedside table. Small, like a frame. It had pictures of his children in it.'


At times they moved slowly through the jungle. It seemed impenetrable, the passing branches and vines creating an illusion that they brushed against the windows of the train, while the rhythmic clatter of the wheels slowed its tempo as the engine's thrust laboured on the steep slopes. Approaching Ipoh, the jungle gave way to the symmetry of rubber trees, and occasional glimpses of plantation workers or the prosperity of substantial bungalow homes. Afterwards, near the coast, the line became a long stretch of level track with the Straits of Malacca to the west and the distant outline of Penang a visible haze across the opalescent sea.

Towards evening the train crossed the border

into Thailand, passing phenomenal limestone mountains that appeared out of the twilight, rearing up like rare scroll paintings.

'Unreal.'

Tess pointed, and they both stared in awe at this unique rock tapestry. Ben, remembering he still had his camera, took a flashlight photo. She smiled and said, 'If we'd gone by air we never would have seen that.'

'If we'd gone by air, we might have been met on arrival.'

The reminder of it spoiled her mood. 'They'll be looking for us by now, won't they?'

'For certain,' he said.

'And after two days it won't be in the Tiger Balm Gardens.'

'Relax, Tess.'

'I'm trying to. You try to remember I'm just an interpreter, and this sort of thing happens to other people.'

'You're doing so well, I keep forgetting it.'

She eyed him, about to retort to this blatant flattery. A dining car attendant came past beating a gong, preventing her reply.

'I'm starving,' Ben said.

'Ever eaten Thai food?'

'Of course.'

'In Thailand?'

'No, in Crows Nest.'

'Where's that?'

'Sydney, Australia.'

'You like chillies?'

'Within reason.'

'In Thailand,' Tess said, hiding a smile, 'chillies are not within reason. Have you ever heard of *gaeng phet*?'

He looked blank.

'It means hot curry. Most cooks add a few extra chillies, in case it's not hot enough. The chilli is small and green, and called *prik khi nu*.'

Ben started to laugh.

'You're joking.'

'*Prik khi nu*,' she insisted, straight-faced, 'is lethal. One *prik* crushed between the teeth makes your average *farang* take off towards the ceiling. And you rise like a rocket, not a soufflé. So—how about you let me order?'

'Please,' Ben said. 'Only no *priks*—nothing like that . . .'

'I promise,' she said.

They went through the train to the dining car, embellished with linen tablecloths and formidable menus. A waiter seated them at a table.

'You order,' he enquired in careful English, 'or you want I make suggestions?'

'I think we'd prefer to order,' Tess said in flawless Thai.

It was always the same reaction in this country when she spoke. A first moment of astonishment, followed by a warm smile of such

205

genuine pleasure it was like being welcomed into a family. The Thai people, hospitable, tolerant and charming, have a fierce national pride, and a foreigner who speaks their language is a true friend.

There ensued a lively exchange, to which Ben listened without the least idea of what either was saying, but he could tell it was cordial. The waiter went away beaming. Tess told him they would get the pick of the kitchen. The waiter would instantly make it known there was a female *farang* who had been to school in Bangkok.

'What are we eating?' Ben asked.

'We start with *gôong tawt kriep*.'

'Sounds great.'

'As an appetiser. I thought you'd prefer it that way.'

'I expect I would. What is it?'

'Deep-fried shrimp.'

'Nice,' he said.

'Then *gwûay dǐao pad thai*. Noodles with egg and bean sprouts,' she translated, seeing his blank expression.

'Great.'

'And—*khâo plow*. Everyone knows what that is.'

'Nearly everyone,' Ben said.

'Rice.'

'Of course.'

'With *gài yaang*. Chicken. Plus *núa pat namman hoy*. Beef in oyster sauce.'

'Love it. Can we eat all this?'

'Easily. Then for sweets we're having *khâo nĭao má-mwûang*. Mango and sticky rice with coconut milk.'

'Great,' Ben said. 'You can't beat a good sticky rice.'

The food was both delicate and delicious. During the meal the chef emerged to speak to Teresa, and ask if all was to her satisfaction. She assured him it was. Each waiter who passed nodded and smiled at them, as if they were old and close friends. A bottle of wine was sent to their table from the bar, compliments of Thai railways.

Ben felt like a goldfish in a bowl, or someone dining with a movie star. Teresa just took it in her stride, enjoying herself.

*Style*, he thought. *It's getting to me, this style.*

They toasted each other, then drank to the chef, the staff, and finally to the hope that no-one would be waiting for them in the morning at Hualumphong—the Bangkok central rail station.

18 EDWARD BURRIDGE HAD no idea that they were missing until they had been gone more than twenty-four hours. Satisfied that Ben had persuaded her to continue, despite the irritating delay, he had deliberately kept out of touch until he could reasonably suggest it was time to leave. It was therefore without any premonition that he put through a call to the Maison Citadel early the next evening, intending to invite them to dine and discuss the prospect of their mutual departure. In anticipation, he had already booked all three of them on a Cathay Pacific flight at ten-thirty the following morning.

His first intimation of a debacle was when, after no reply from either of their rooms, he was asked to hold on—and found himself transferred to speak to the assistant manager. She expressed her concern. In view of the attack on their guest, they had arranged to keep watch on Miss Martineau's new room. But apparently she had not returned to the hotel the previous day.

Nor had her companion. It seemed they had not spent the night in the hotel, and while they had left their air tickets at the front desk, these had not been collected. No clothes appeared to have been taken. They were last seen leaving the premises in shorts and T-shirts before lunch the previous day.

Burridge hung up in a rage. He had been too long at this game not to recognise the kind of underhanded and serpentine tactics he himself had used on occasion. Bloody Ben Hammond stipulating she needed time to recover. She was not fit to travel, he'd said.

Insisted on it. Not well enough to fly the next day.

*Fuck them,* Burridge thought. *She could not fly the next day, because they'd flown the same day. Probably an hour or two after leaving him. And that was now a day and a half ago. So where in the name of Christ were they, and why had they done it?*

He sat and thought about it, on Walter Chen's Italian marble terrace, and when his anger had cooled he began to realise there could only be one answer. It took him a long time to admit it, for he also had to face the unpalatable fact that it was largely his fault.


The train crossed the Chao Phraya River, with its network of *klongs* and river traffic. Minutes later they were in the vast terminus, Bangkok's Hualumphong Station. It was more than forty-eight hours since they vanished from the hotel, spending large amounts of Burridge's money to prevent themselves being followed. Whether that tactic had succeeded they were not yet sure. When they came off the train in the cavernous station, there was no way to tell if anyone was there watching for them.

It was a nervous and ominous feeling.

Their whole premise, the long journey, had been based on the assumption they were expected in the Thai capital, and that the airport would be watched, but an approach by train from Malaysia was so unlikely that no-one would give any thought to the idea.

That was their hope. Time would soon tell if it had succeeded.

The heat and the noise assaulted them as they left the protection of the station. In the street, taxis were queued up. Blaring car horns were a continuous and discordant symphony, while trucks passed with ghetto-blasters. It was chaotic bedlam—set against the splendour of the gilded spires and ancient jade temples glimpsed through the exhaust fumes.

Two taxis almost collided, as they jostled for possession of the emerging passengers. The drivers shouted abusively at each other, exchanging insults. While they did, a third cab arrived, unnoticed by the combatants. The driver had an engaging face; he grinned and gave Ben and Teresa a cheerful signal. He pressed a button, and the lid of his boot opened. They put their suitcases inside, shut down the boot and climbed into the back seat. The other two drivers saw this too late, and spat abuse as their cabbie drove them away. He laughed, and in an accent strongly influenced by Hollywood films, he told them to call him Joseph.

'You guys come by train, huh? Stay long?'

'Not long.'

'Ever been to Bangkok before?'

'No,' said Teresa.


Eddie Carmichael could sometimes get an erection by merely thinking about Helene, but he was also, when she was in certain moods, afraid of her. He was deeply afraid of her now.

'You simpleton,' she said. 'You dumb jerk.' She could use her voice like a knife. 'You sat there in the lobby on your fat bum, while they walked past you. Laughed at you. You fucking cretin.'

'Fair go,' he protested. 'They left their air tickets. Left their luggage. Who the hell could have guessed?'

'I could've,' she said. 'Victor could've.'

'Victor's so goddam smart he's in the

slammer,' he said, angered by her openly contemptuous comparison.

'Wrong again,' Helene said, with a look that made him uneasy.

'He's inside.'

'Correction. He *was* inside.' She looked at her watch. 'As of ten minutes ago, all being well, he is now outside. It's cost a lot of money, which will come out of your share, Eddie. That's if Victor thinks you even rate a share.'

'He's been busted out of prison?'

The news shocked him. He felt chilled.

She knew it—knew that he was afraid of Victor Mendoza.

Relished it, the way she smiled.

'Be like old times, won't it,' Helene said, 'all of us together.'

'Where?'

'In Bangkok, of course.'


The traffic was like a battleground. There was no relief from the tumult of car horns, the obscenities yelled by car and truck drivers at the tiny three-wheel samlors, oxcarts, or seriously endangered pedestrians.

Joseph—he said his real name was up there with his photo licence: Yung Li Hok Dan—but he said most *farangs* couldn't manage such a

mouthful of shit, so Joseph was a good name
for business with the tourists. He'd come by it,
he said, because his ma had shacked up with a
US soldier on R & R from Vietnam, and he
was the result—hence as a kid at school he was
called GI Joe the Yankee bastard, but when he
grew a bit and could beat up the other kids,
they settled for calling him Joe. Only he
decided the name Joseph had more dignity, and
his ma liked it because her favourite actor had
been Joseph Cotten in the movies, and she said
he had class. His ma would stay up till three,
four in the morning to catch some old Joe
Cotten film on TV, which made her a Cotten
groupie, and at her age, fifty, that was weird,
man, really way out and weird.

Joseph had a rich vocabulary of abuse and
profanity which he used against other drivers
incessantly. In between the story of his life, he
shouted invective, as if everyone else on the
road was his enemy.

'Hey, fuck face, you pig's arsehole,' he bel-
lowed at a cyclist, and went into a stream of
vilification in Thai. In the back seat Ben glanced
at Teresa for a discreet translation. She rolled
her eyes.

'Rude as it sounds?' he murmured.

'Worse.'

Joseph almost ran over a pedestrian, and railed
at him. He turned to grin at them over his

shoulder, a habit of his which Ben was beginning to find singularly disturbing.

'That's good, eh? I said his mother's a *kra-toey.*'

'What's a *kra-toey*?' Ben muttered the question.

'Transvestite,' she said, and this time Joseph heard her.

'Hey, you speak Thai.'

'Some,' Tess said, in English.

'Very pretty, the *kra-toey*. Can't tell the difference till the pants come off. Sometimes even then—you wanna see some?'

'No thanks. We want a hotel.'

'Hilton, Inter-Continental, Imperial? Which one?'

'We told you. Somewhere small. Quiet. Where the tourists don't go. *Off the beaten track,*' she added in colloquial Thai, which surprised him and made him turn to look at her.

'Hey, lady. You speak real good!'

'Would you do me a favour?' Ben said.

'Sure. You wanna massage parlour?'

'No, I want you to keep your eyes on the road.'

'I can see the road,' Joseph said. 'I know road backwards.'

'What I'd really like,' Ben said, 'is for you to get to know it forwards.'

'Shit man, I know it blindfold. Hey—how about a topless bar?'

214

'Not today. Just a hotel.'

'Little joint, eh? No other tourists. No Hiltons or Hyatts.'

'That's right.'

'Small crappy place.'

'You're getting the idea,' Ben said.

'Afterwards, we find massage parlour. Cheap. Two hundred baht.'

'No thanks.'

'Even cheaper. Special price just for you, boss. One fifty.'

'I don't think my friend would be interested.'

'Male masseur? Big guy, muscles like Mr Universe. No?'

'No,' she said firmly.

'Anything you like, pretty lady who speak the lingo. I aim to please. Whatever you wish—just ask. What can I do for you?'

'*Keep your eyes on the fucking road*,' Tess said in impeccable Thai.


It was in the afternoon newspapers. A small story on page four. A jail break from the prison in Caine Road. A prisoner who had previously escaped while serving a long sentence for armed robbery and aggravated violence had been recaptured after a sexual assault on a tourist. The jail break had obviously been planned with care, and with considerable inside help. There had been a small riot staged, some smokebombs and, when the emergency was over, the prisoner was gone.

The radio and television gave his name, and warned that he was armed and dangerous.

The Sala Sawan was no Hyatt. It had the air of a second-rate suburban brothel that had seen better days, and they had been long ago. Joseph stopped his taxi outside it and looked at them for an opinion. He shrugged; there was no accounting for taste.

'Small, non tourist. A real dump.'

They debated.

'Looks safe,' she muttered, then realised Joseph was watching her in his mirror, trying to lip-read.

'You guys running away from someone?' he asked.

'Only my husband,' Tess told him, and went inside to enquire if there were vacant rooms.

Joseph watched her. He turned to Ben: 'If I ever find a babe like her, I sure as hell don't bring her to a lousy shit-hole like this.'

The lobby was tiny. Flaking paint curled from the walls. The curtains were filthy. An overhead light shade was fly-stained, and the proprietor, who emerged from a beaded curtain that led to his living room behind the reception desk, was speculative and shifty.

She spoke in Thai, and asked if he had vacancies. He made a pretence of looking in the register and said he had. She took a twin room. She said it was probably just for the one night. She and her husband, Mr and Mrs Joseph.

Walter came in. He had been at his club, where he had played several games of squash, and had showered and had tea afterwards with some business friends. He was relaxed and looking forward to the evening. Helene had promised she would be home soon, and they would spend the evening together. She said they would dine early, and left him in no doubt how the rest of the night would be spent. In a happy frame of mind, he switched on the living room lights, and saw with surprise a lone figure out on the terrace.

'Edward?'

Burridge nodded to him as he came out.

'What on earth are you doing, sitting here in the dark?'

'Thinking,' Burridge said. 'Trying to remember.'

'Remember what?'

'How much we've talked about this thing

together. How much you know—that she might have learned.'

'Who?'

'Helene.'

'Don't be ridiculous.'

'Where is she?' Burridge asked him.

'She called me from Kowloon. This cousin of hers—she's gone to the airport to see him off. Thank goodness.'

'Walter, she hasn't got a cousin.'

'What?' Walter's bewilderment was genuine.

'I can assure you of that. I know a great deal more about her now than I did yesterday—and she has not got a cousin from Macao or anywhere else.'

Walter Chen was rarely angry. By nature he was even-tempered, an affable man. But he was incensed now.

'What the hell are you talking about, Edward? If you've been checking up on her—'

'I'm afraid I have. I've had a whole team of people checking up on her.'

'How dare you! And how dare you suggest I would've told her anything we discussed in private—or worse still as far as I'm concerned, that she can't be trusted.'

'I'm sorry,' Burridge said quietly. 'Please listen to me. Just sit down—and listen. Please.'

Walter sat down.

'Helene is not a journalist from San Diego as

218

she once told you. I've spent all the damn day on it, Walter, and it gives me no pleasure. No pleasure at all. She worked for an escort service in Vegas. I have faxes, details of a conviction for prostitution. When she first came to Hong Kong she lived with an Australian, a con man named Eddie Carmichael. She ditched him when she met you. But for some time—while living here—she has been in a sexual relationship with Victor Mendoza, who escaped from prison today. He was the man caught a few nights ago at the Maison Citadel Hotel, after he stripped and searched Teresa Martineau. He had one main purpose. He was looking for the key, Walter. Only two people knew about those keys. You and me.'

'And employees of the bank. You said there might be a leak—'

'I wish that was the answer. But it isn't. You clearly didn't tell her anything—I'd never believe otherwise—so she could only have set up listening devices here. I had a squad in to sweep the house which, as a guest, is unforgivable—but it had to be done. They found the living room, your study, guest quarters, were all wired. There was an infinity transmitter, in that ornamental flower pot, that could pick up every word spoken on this terrace. A digital Scoopman recorder, the size of a postage stamp, was on a shelf in the boiler room. The houseboy changed the tapes each day. Helene gave him money and promised him . . . other favours.'

In the span of a few moments, listening to this clinical recital of facts, Walter Chen seemed to have aged ten years.

'But only two days ago, she agreed to marry me. She was happy, like a kid about it.'

Burridge said, 'You're going to hate me, but I think the failure and arrest of Mendoza changed things. She was afraid of suspicion. She needed time. Perhaps the engagement was a means of gaining a few days time.'

'But in God's name, why? Jesus Christ, Edward—why did she need to do it?'

'Money.'

'But if she'd married me, she'd have had all the money anyone could spend in two lifetimes.'


The room was called a double, but it was cramped and the furnishings were cheap and rudimentary. The bathroom was at the end of the hallway. There was a narrow window on to the street that faced west, so that it took the brunt of the afternoon sun. Even now, long after dark, the heat remained. They lay on their twin beds, after they came back from a small neighbourhood restaurant. A fan turned, its blades clicking with monotonous precision overhead, but the air it circulated was warm.

'Joseph was right about this hotel. What a dump.'

'You don't mind us sharing the room, do you?' Tess asked.

'Of course not.'

'It felt safer.'

'Did you ask for twin beds?'

She nodded.

'You felt that'd be safer, too?'

She smiled. Then, after a moment asked, 'You think there'll be someone looking for us, don't you?'

'Yes. It's so much damned money.'

'At least they'll start looking in the tourist belt.'

'That might give us time to contact Singh and get out of Bangkok.'

'When do we call Sir Ted?'

'When we feel confident no-one is chasing us. When we're in a position to safely tell him his security is ratshit.' He handed her the Indian's printed address.

'Chakrawat. It's down by the river. A twenty-minute walk.'

'Did you really go to school near there?'

'Briefly—after my mother and father divorced. I must've been about six. We came to live in Bangkok. Mother married Charles Lambert and we went to Hong Kong for a while, then back to England.'

221

'And until recently—till Burridge broke the news—you always thought your father was dead?'

'Yes.'

'Must've been a shock.'

'It seems she didn't want me to have divided loyalties.'

'How do you feel about that?'

'Confused. I thought I knew my mother. I always loved her. We were very close. Yet for twenty years she allowed me to believe Daddy was dead. I'm still trying to come to terms with that.'

'Yes—I imagine. What did he do, your father?'

'Timber exports. He had his own mills. I don't remember this, but she—my mother— talked about it one day. All of a sudden. She told me about the teak and hardwood forests in the mountains of north Thailand. Told me how the loggers had to have permits so no-one could destroy all the natural wealth. I remember being pleased they were environmentally conscious before it became fashionable in the west. I was at university then, heavily into ecology and saving the planet.'

She was silent for a moment, then continued, 'Mother said the trees were so huge they had trained elephants to drag the logs to the river where they were floated down to the mills. She

222

said it was a strange magical place, rows of mist-covered mountains along the Mekong. She told me of the wild orchids that grew on the hills, and the gentle people who lived there. She talked of it just that once; it was as if I should know something about my father.'

'It sounds like she talked more about the place, than about him.'

'That never occurred to me, but I think you're right. And even telling me all this, she spoke of him as long dead. All those years, since I was nine, living a lie. What if he'd turned up, alive and well?'

'I guess she gambled that he wouldn't. Get some sleep, Tess. We'll go to see the Indian early tomorrow.'

'Goodnight, Ben.'

'G'night,' he said.

After a time, when he was nearly asleep, she said, 'She must have been very insecure—to pretend he was dead, and die without revealing the truth. Strange world, isn't it.'

*Stranger than you know*, Ben thought, but could not tell her.


Walter Chen was not, and had never been, a heavy drinker—but sitting on his expensive terrace, and looking down on his multimillion dollar view, he tried without success to drink himself into a stupor. He felt an ineffable sadness. As though, for all his vast riches, his life had been a complete failure. Somewhere along the way he had lost it, and he felt such anguish he could hardly bear the grief that constricted his throat.

Being Chinese in an English public school as bleak and obdurate as Newlakes Boys' College had not been easy. It had been worse when he first went to the preparatory school, enduring taunts and bullying. It was Edward Burridge who had one day thrust his way through the group who were chanting and mocking him: *Chin Chan Chinaman, pees and shits in an old tin can*—it had been Edward who had grabbed the ringleader by his hair and kneed him viciously in the groin, and had shouted and called them a bunch of little cunts—and ever afterwards, at least at prep school, he had been left alone.

Even at Newlakes, after the initiation year and the fagging and implied homosexuality, more implied than real, it had been intuitively understood that he was Edward's friend, and anyone who wanted to be racist or offensive had to deal with Burridge, whom everyone agreed was a real turd, a nasty and ferocious bastard, better avoided.

On that their friendship had been built, and had endured. For with all of Walter's renowned and successful pursuit of women, his wealth and hedonistic existence, his friendship with Edward Burridge had been one of the main pillars of his life.

And now it was ended.

Forty years. Walter had no-one closer.

Now it was finished.

Edward had packed his bags, said that it would be unfair to remain, in view of the problem with Helene and the certainty there would have to be an investigation, said it would be fairer, simpler, if he moved to the Peninsula Hotel. Walter knew what that meant. It meant his life-long friend would never be a guest in his house again.

He wished he could drink himself into a stupor. He had lost face, lost a friend, and lost a lover. That was what caused him the most distress. She never had been a lover. It was all a subterfuge, a lie.

Helene Lee had used him—made a fool of him.

That was the saddest fact of all.

Drinking slowly and steadily, he was unable to find oblivion. Steeped in melancholy, he was unable to cry.


They stole a car in Victoria, down by the docks, and drove up the road to the Peak. Lights were on in the house, but Helene knew that none of the staff were there. She had rung earlier, spoken to the housekeeper, told her that she would personally see the staff were paid a bonus for the celebration of the engagement—but she had one wish. That she and Mr Chen could have an evening alone. It was her special request, that they all go out tonight. Everyone. It was a surprise she was planning for him, so they were all to quietly leave the house after their supper. Enjoy themselves, stay out until at least midnight. Above all they must not tell him, or it would spoil the surprise.

They left the car outside the garages, and made their way across the lawn towards the main terrace.

He was sitting gazing into a glass of whisky.

He looked up and saw her, and then registered the two men. One of them, Victor Mendoza who had escaped from jail, had a knife.

'Hello, Walter darling,' she said.

He said nothing. Just stared at her, knowing that expressions of outrage or condemnation were useless.

'This is Victor, and this is Eddie. You're going to tell them about the Indian in Bangkok, who he is and where to find him. Then you're going to tell us the passwords to those bank vaults.'

'I'll tell you nothing.' He could hear the tremor of fear in his own voice. The others could detect it, too. Victor Mendoza smiled.

Helene took his drink from his unresisting hand. She let the glass drop on the marble tiles, where it smashed into fragments.

'I think you will, darling,' she said. 'Or else they'll kill you so slowly that you'll wish you were already dead.'

19 THE WAT PO TEMPLE was a revelation to Ben. He had heard much about Bangkok: its bursting vitality, haphazard and unpredictable nature, the city bisected by the Chao Phraya River, and the maze of *klongs* where small wooden houses were built on stilts over the water.

For those who had never been there, it was better known for its garish night-life, the streets of bars, nightclubs and massage parlours with touts hawking their attractions, and offering a mind-boggling selection of vices catering to every deviant taste. Ben knew of the profitable trade in so-called 'sex tours', and the depraved and well-protected pedophiles who came here to indulge their sick obsessive lust for young children. He had even been part of a team that worked on an investigation, probing an Australian group with a select membership, but to his annoyance and disappointment they had been unable to produce sufficient evidence to prove the case.

The Bangkok he knew, if only by repute, was a city of the night, a trysting mecca for sybarites, a perilous place where teenage—and even younger—prostitutes battled with transvestites for strategic street corners, and where AIDS was rampant.

The temple was like another world. Buddhist monks walked past in saffron robes. The compound extended over eight peaceful hectares in the heart of the city. It was filled with ceramic pavilions, porcelain spires, extravagant gargoyle demons guarding the gates, and the famed gigantic Reclining Buddha. There were acres of tiled courtyards, and displays of vivid colour in immaculate gardens. It was unlike anything Ben had ever seen. He was enthralled. He told Tess he could spend the rest of the day in this sanctuary, and to hell with Ted Burridge, Pandit Singh, and the whole bloody lot of them.

They had woken before dawn, unable to get back to sleep, and rather than face the prospect of breakfast in their hotel, they showered and dressed and decided to walk to Chakrawat. Teresa told him it was known as 'the thieves market', was close by the river, but since it was so early and the bazaar would not yet be open, why not detour and see the real Bangkok? It was a place she knew well for, apart from her brief two years here as a child, she had been back several times on interpreting jobs. It was a wonderful city, she insisted; despite its lurid reputation for night-life it had a tranquil and beautiful ambience. It would be a personal favour to her, she said, if Ben would come and see Wat Po, the temple founded when Bangkok was a fishing village.

Also, she reminded him, they had to discuss what to do about Burridge. On the walk through the quiet streets, the city barely awake, they decided to see the Indian first, and after that to call Hong Kong.

'He was tortured,' the young detective inspector said.

They stood on either side of the shrouded body. There was blood all over the expensive terrace.

'The poor bastard had his feet burnt, and his fingers broken, and then they used the knife.'

'To kill him?' Burridge asked.

'Eventually. But first they sliced him up. Took strips off his arms. Made incisions on his face. They also cut off his balls.'

Edward Burridge felt a paroxysm of hate and rage, while his mind tried to reject the horror to which his friend had been subjected. He was unable to do this. Try as he might, he could not prevent himself visualising the terror that must have confronted Walter Chen in the final awful moments of his life.

Chakrawat was a place of bazaars and open barrows. It was alongside one of the *klongs*; noisy, dissected by tiny alleyways; the stall owners Indian, Chinese and, to a lesser degree, Thai nationals.

They had found him without difficulty. It was a shop rather than a stall, a window displaying junk jewellery, cheap trinkets and tourist trifles for sale. He stood in the doorway, a Sikh, impressive with his beard and turban. Above the doorway was a canopy with his name: PANDIT SINGH. DEALER IN FINE WARES.

The premises were tiny and cluttered.

A room behind was equally small, with matted flooring. They sat on the rattan mats with Pandit Singh, sipping cups of tea, the heat of the day already rising, the room cramped, becoming uncomfortable and hot.

'More tea?'

'No thank you, Mr Singh.'

Teresa spoke in English. She knew Singh was proud of his English, and would prefer not to speak in Hindi. It was a factor interpreters had to assess for themselves; in a delicate negotiation, it could make a difference. Her job was not just a matter of knowing other languages . . .

few people realised that—it was diplomacy and protocol and a world of nuances that could enhance or ruin the result.

'Call me Pandit, please. We are on this earth for so short a time, we must not waste it in formality. We should all be friends.'

'Mr Singh ... Pandit,' Ben amended, 'you know who I am?'

'Indeed. I have been kept well informed.'

He produced a file of press clippings from Sydney newspapers, the largest of them a photo of Ben being hustled into a squad car with the glaring tabloid headline: DETECTIVE ARRESTED.

Ben sensed rather than saw Teresa's look of bewilderment at the sight of it. He realised she had not been briefed about this. Somehow he had taken it for granted Burridge would have told her.

'That was all a mistake,' he said.

'Of course.' Singh smiled, projecting an air of disbelief.

'However, you know I want to make contact with a certain man in the north.'

'I have been advised of this.'

'How soon can it be arranged?'

'Very soon,' Singh said. 'As soon as you wish. As soon as I am given the fee to arrange your various contacts and travel. There is a delicate network involved. Many people to be paid for their services. But you have been advised of the cost. This has already been made known to you. Eighty thousand dollars, yes?'

Ben hesitated. He exchanged a glance with Teresa. It was an issue they knew they would have to treat with care. There was simply not enough money left to pay his expected price. The need to escape, the costly smokescreen they had created with the plane tickets purchased for Tokyo and Sydney, the flights to Singapore, then Kuala Lumpur and the train journey, all this had used up an alarming amount. Added to it were the expensive clothes bought for Tess after the attack, not realising that the next day they would have to purchase a complete new wardrobe each, after leaving their possessions behind in the Maison Citadel Hotel. In their headlong flight for safety, the last thing on their minds had been to ensure they kept sufficient money for the Indian jeweller. As a result there was a distinct shortfall.

'Seventy thousand,' she said.

It was virtually all the cash they had left

Pandit Singh stared at her, no longer cordial.

'In the shop, I bargain,' he said. 'It is a game, yes? But in my house, in matters of this kind, there are no bargains, no games.'

'We had some unexpected expenses. Very heavy ones.'

'It is no concern of mine. I was led to believe we had a contract. I have been misinformed, embarrassed. People have been told to make themselves available for you. I've given my word, and they are waiting to assist you. This is a serious humiliation for me.'

'I'm sorry, but we're not trying to bargain. It's the truth, Pandit. Seventy thousand is all we can pay.'

The Indian took the teapot, and deliberately poured the contents into a slop bucket. It seemed an effective way of announcing the party was over. He told them if they could ever afford the agreed price, to come back and speak to him again.


There had been a fatal delay in alerting ASEAN police forces after Walter Chen's murder. The household staff had not returned to the house until midnight, and although they had immediately called the police, it was several hours before the homicide squad could begin their investigations. No-one at that time knew where to find Sir Edward Burridge. The servants all assumed he was out for the night: nobody had reason to suspect he had earlier vacated the private suite he occupied in a wing of the house.

It was not until it was discovered the suite was empty that a search had been instigated. Checking hotels, understaffed in the early dawn hours, took time which the detectives could ill afford, while their colleagues searched vainly for fingerprints. They soon realised the killers had worn gloves. It was only when Burridge was eventually located at the Peninsula Hotel that the link had been made, connecting the murder with Helene Lee and the two men.

Photographs of her, Carmichael and Victor Mendoza were found and faxed to all neighbouring countries, with special emphasis on Thailand, but by then the trio had long since landed and passed through immigration at Don Muang Airport in Bangkok. No trace of their arrival showed on the computer, nor would it appear on tourist registers at any hotel, since they had all travelled under different passports and in other names.

The phone rang and rang. There was no answer.

'We must have the wrong number. It's not possible the house is empty. Even if Chen's out, what about the servants?'

Suddenly he heard an operator's voice speaking in English: 'What is your name and what number are you calling?'

Ben told her. Tess stood alongside him, puzzled. They were in a glass booth, opposite the mosaic gates to the ancient Temple of

Dawn. Shaven monks in their robes walked sedately past. There could hardly have been a greater contrast than the porcelain splendour and towering central spire on one side of the street, and rows of people using modern telephone booths on the other.

'One moment,' the Hong Kong operator said. 'I'm having you transferred.'

'Why? What's wrong with the number?'

'One moment, please, sir.'

'What the hell is going on?' Tess asked.

He shrugged, then heard a male voice on the line. He put his hand over the mouthpiece:

'God Almighty, it's Burridge.'

'Finally! What's the matter—say hello to him.'

'I can't. It's a bloody tape.'

She leaned close, as he held the phone between their heads so she could listen. It was clearly Burridge on an answering machine.

'. . . and so I've been hoping you'd try to reach me. This call has been switched to a secure line. We've had trouble. Walter Chen is dead. Your friends may be on their way to Bangkok. We're not quite sure. I'm afraid the truth is, we've lost them.'

'Oh, brilliant,' Ben said, as if the recorded voice could hear him.

It simply continued in the same flat, emotionless tone: 'Your call is being monitored by a police officer. If you leave a message, it will be relayed to me immediately. I must know where you are, and how to reach you. ASAP. This is urgent—repeat—urgent. I stress again—it is vital you communicate at once. Give me sufficient information to find you. Make it clear and concise—after the tone.'

They heard the signal.

'What a stuff-up,' Ben said into the telephone, for the benefit of the tape. 'You couldn't run a chook raffle at an RSL club, you bloody drongo. We'll be at the American Express office at noon, tomorrow.'

He hung up.


They had two adjoining rooms in the Royal Thai, overlooking the river near the Memorial Bridge. Eddie Carmichael tried to curb his resentment as Victor perched on the bed alongside Helene and openly fondled her long slim legs, while she found the packet of photographs.

'Settle down,' she said to him, but made no attempt to remove his hand as he established proprietorial rights, knowing how it would anger Carmichael. She shuffled through the photographs, selected the best shot he had taken of Ben Hammond and the girl, and told Eddie to go and get more copies made at the photo shop in the hotel arcade.

'Fifty at least,' she said.

'Fifty? In this hotel? They'd be curious.'

'Don't use the hotel. Get ten copies at five different shops,' Victor said. 'Take a cab and be back here in an hour. Now move it.'

Carmichael resented taking orders from Victor, even though he knew these were more sensible tactics. He also knew the pair of them would be naked and in bed the moment he was out of the room. The twin thoughts annoyed him enough to ask, 'Why the hell do we need so many photographs?'

'Because I say so.' Victor smiled as he stroked Helene's nylon-sheathed leg, his hand beneath her dress, not even bothering to wait. Eddie Carmichael hated him, but he feared him even more. The way he had slashed and butchered Chen, the violence on that terrace, was still a terrifying, vivid scar in his mind.

Yet it had achieved their objective. The multi-millionaire had talked. He'd told them everything. The password, the elaborate financial mechanism he and Burridge had set up. He'd spilled it out in panic and agony, all except the details of the Indian jeweller here in Bangkok. He pleaded he did not know the name of the man and, in those final excruciating moments of his life, Carmichael for one had believed him.

'Well, what are you waiting for?' Victor said.

'I asked why we needed so many copies?'

'Because we give one to every taxidriver who'll co-operate. We also recruit a bunch of locals to circulate them to all the back-street hotels. That's where we'll find those two. Not in the ritzy tourist traps. In some little joint. So move your arse, Eddie. Fifty copies. When you get back, I'll have people set up to start searching for them.'

Carmichael went out.

Victor had one hand between her legs and the other removing her clothes the moment he heard the lock click.

'Wait on,' she said. 'Don't take me for granted, Victor.'

'Who's taking anyone for granted? You want to be fucked as much as I want to fuck you.'

'Like you wanted to fuck Teresa Martineau?'

'Who said I did?'

'I'm asking.'

'That's for her to remember, and you to find out,' Victor said.

'You bastard. You did.'

'You want me to tell you about it? Will that turn you on?'

She slapped him with sudden violence across the face. 'You blew the whole thing,' Helene said, 'all on account of that uncontrollable dick of yours. We wouldn't be on the run, we wouldn't have had to kill Walter, only you had to have that English bitch.'

She swung her arm to hit him again, but this time, forewarned, he easily prevented her. He used his strength to pinion her, then he smiled and said softly, 'Now you listen to me, sweetie. Don't talk bullshit. We would always have had to kill Chen. We had to get that password from him, and after that, no matter what, he couldn't be left to live. Alive he could alter arrangements at the bank. Shift the money. Dead, there's no way anyone has the authority. Not till the lawyers get it sorted out, and that'll take weeks. Long before then, we'll have their keys.'

'What if there's a watch on the bank?'

'Burridge can't have the bank watched, or it blows his entire scheme. We know that from what Chen told us. And the bank would never agree to having cops in their safe-deposit vault. Can't you imagine the protests? All those tax evaders and crooked police chiefs and bribed politicians losing their privacy. That's the really beautiful part of the whole thing. Once we kill them and get those two keys, we pick the right time to walk in and collect.'

'Who does? You and me?'

'I think you and Eddie. He's good at that sort of thing. Looks the part. And the guy who did the cosmetic job on me in Kowloon will work on you, so your own mother wouldn't recognise you.'

'She very rarely did,' Helene said enigmatically.

'What's that mean?'

'Never mind. Afterwards—what about Eddie?'

'I'll talk to him. Tell him how most of the money goes to you, because you set it up. And most of the rest goes to me. Eddie will get his fare back to Australia—if he behaves.'

She had given up struggling. His body straddled hers. His tight grip on her arms had lessened. The pressure of his crotch was beginning to feel pleasurable. He could sense her expectation.

'So now do you want me to tell you about Miss Martineau . . .?'

'You mean while you do it to me?'

'That's what I had in mind.'

'Then tell me,' she said with rising excitement.

There was one matter still to sort out, but it could wait. The way she felt, and the palpation she was getting from Victor, indicated that this time sex would not take long.


The Siam and First National Bank was on Thon Kai Street. He and Tess waited opposite for the traffic lights to allow them to cross. 'Are you sure about this?'

241

'It's the right name and place. And I have the file number.'

He had thought of that list of banks almost immediately after they had made the phone call. Realised that this was their solution.

'*The money is contained in eight banks. Each has the same type of high security deposit vault.*' He could still hear Burridge's words, and recall reading aloud the names and places in which they were located: '*Hong Kong, Singapore, Bangkok* . . .'

He had to memorise each location, plus their different access codes. Even though he was trained for it, and had a good memory, it had been a hell of a job repeating the details until they slotted into his mind. What had helped was the common factor of the password and the keys.

'*The password, keys—they apply in each of those banks. It keeps it simple. Easy to remember.*'

That's what Burridge had said, he explained to Tess, and, after she enquired directions, they walked the several blocks to Thon Kai Street.

'I mean are you sure we should try—without advising him?'

'How do we advise him?'

'We could try to call that same number again.'

'Not after the message I left on his machine.'

She smiled. 'Some poor copper will have to quote that to him. Imagine it. "Burridge here.

Any messages? Yes, sir. You couldn't run a chook raffle at an RSL club, you bloody drongo. Sorry sir, that's what it says here, sir." '

He laughed. Her mimicry was clever.

The lights changed to green, and they crossed the street. Teresa hesitated at the entrance to the bank. 'You don't think we should wait till he turns up tomorrow?'

'Sure, we can wait. Would you rather?'

'I'm not certain. Is it so important to have this money now, instead of delaying twenty-four hours?'

'I think so.'

'Why?'

'Singh won't touch us without the eighty grand. If bloody Ted had given us real protection, we'd still have that money. We'll wait— if you prefer. But I'll tell you what'll happen. His Eminence will look down his aristocratic nose, tell us we screwed up, and graciously allow us to use the bank. Since we happen to have the means of access, I'd like to present him with a fait accompli. Singh all stitched up. Us in control. It'd be a lot better than having him arrive to find us in a Mexican stand-off, so he can play God.'

'You've convinced me,' Tess smiled. 'Let's not hang about. Let's get cashed up.'

They went down the stairs to the vault. It was

like a replay; a feeling of déjà vu. Once again the vault was situated in a basement, with heavy grilled bars and a steel door. The guards this time were Thai. The security was almost identical: a series of remote-controlled surveillance cameras, the same kind of video screen which became a set of numerals, and a voice, in Thai, asking him for his reference. Tess nodded and Ben tapped in the seven-figure coded entry number he had memorised. The door unclicked, just as it had in Hong Kong—the difference this time being that they entered together.

They were both very tense. If this did not work, they were likely to find themselves in a police cell.

'*Chiengmalan*,' Teresa said, and it was typed, formulated into a file number and the Thai custodian looked at her.

'How many keys?' he asked in his language.

'Two,' she answered him.

They presented their keys, and waited while a similar-looking metal box was brought. The sight of it eased their tension. Suddenly they knew it was going to work. They started to feel relaxed as they followed the guards into a private room. The deposit box was placed on a table. The senior guard indicated the sign beside the door, explaining they need only press the buzzer and someone would unlock the door. Tess thanked him, and said she could read

Thai. The guards were clearly impressed, and approved of this attractive *farang* who spoke their language so well. Both smiled and went out. The door clicked shut and they were alone.

'Well,' she said, 'how about us!'

'It worked.'

'Clever clogs,' she said.

They were both on a high.

Almost in symmetry they raised their keys and fitted them into the box. They smiled and turned the twin locks, and opened it.

They stared at the contents.

Their first reaction of disbelief became total bewilderment.

The safe-deposit box was empty.

# PART THREE

## THE PURSUIT

**20** THE PLANE, DELAYED an hour in takeoff and forced to stack over the gulf, was consequently two hours behind schedule when it landed at Don Muang Airport. It did little to improve Burridge's mood.

He did not like Bangkok.

To him it had always been a frenetic city. Too crowded with tourists. Too brazen, its sex industry too overt, the eager, tenacious taxi-drivers forever importuning with offers of massage parlours, as if no-one came to this city for anything else. He sat trying to control his irritation in the oppressive heat and raucous traffic on his way from the airport.

'The Hyatt Imperial,' he told the driver, and when it was clear there would be no further conversation from this passenger, the driver shrugged and turned up his radio. Discordant music assailed them both, with strident inter-ruptions by male and female voices. Burridge could only assume these were commercials. He tapped the driver's shoulder, and gestured for him to lower the volume. The driver, by now aware he had a difficult fare and still hoping to salvage a tip, turned it to a more discreet level, chuckling continuously at what the voices were saying, and aggravating Burridge beyond measure.

He tried to shut it out, to focus on other matters.

He was still stunned by the extent of his grief at Walter Chen's death. He could not have guessed it would devastate him quite like this. He was at an age when friends and acquaintances died, some suddenly, others after lingering illnesses. There were occasional colleagues killed, because most of his life had been spent out on that edge of society where the dangerous games are played. Each year there seemed more funerals to attend, where one put on a mourning mask, feeling sadness, while relieved to be alive and able to attend such rites. One paid respects to the family, had drinks, met other friends, and went home feeling the onset of mortality to cross out another name from the address book.

But this had left him more distressed than anything he might ever have imagined. For almost the first time in his life, certainly since childhood, he had wanted to cry and, being incapable of doing so, felt such sorrow and remorse that his throat became tightly compressed, and he felt physically ill.

He knew it was his fault Walter was dead.

It had started three months ago when he had by chance seen the interview: the attractive Australian reporter, and her scoop with the drug baron, Kim Sokram.

The whole idea had come to him then. Like an ingenious scenario, perfectly unfolding. What was required, how to do it, each detail graphic and precise in his mind. He had spent the next month alone in Paris, ignoring friends, declining invitations, engrossed entirely. Slowly, with increasing elation, it had all fallen into place. Everything—except for the money. His budget, while ample for routine operations, could not even come close to covering this. And so, over dinner, he had confided in his lifelong friend Walter.

'I need to raise a great deal of money.'

'How much?'

'Ten billion dollars.'

Walter Chen had laughed. 'My dear fellow, what's mine is yours. But while I may be rich, I'm not that filthy rich.'

'Let's say I need to give the impression that I have access to ten billion dollars.'

'Ahh. Different. That, I daresay we could manage.'

Walter spent the rest of the meal explaining

251

how to do this. How to create the illusion of such vast wealth. What was required was a large amount of money in one place. Enough to impress and convince whoever it was that had to be impressed. A really serious amount that would lend authenticity.

'How serious?' Burridge wanted to know.

Walter suggested twenty million dollars was a serious amount.

'I can't get hold of anywhere near that much.'

'I can,' Chen had replied.

So Burridge had told him details of the idea.

Fortunately, he had not told him everything. It was not a question of mistrust. It was how Burridge had been trained to operate, the methods he had used all his life. Only one person should ever know the complete details. That person was him. Others—in this case a select group of senior national police chiefs— were told only the elements they needed to know. Walter Chen had not been privy to any facts outside the financial data. Which was just as well.

For he had died in such horror and pain, he could not have kept silent. He would have told everything he knew. Since his knowledge was limited, it did not compromise the ultimate operation. It created some problems, but Burridge was confident they could be handled. And if he could locate Miss Lee and her coterie, then that would be handled, too. Perhaps not according to procedure. Perhaps in some elemental payback way, far outside the rules.

He tried to resist the thoughts that tormented him, the image of the viciousness and cruelty, the knife that had sliced and carved his friend while he was still alive. *His balls*, for God's sake. *Stripped of all dignity, dying in such terror and abject humiliation.* Dying alone, with only his three assailants there to mock, and wound and laugh. The last sound in this world Walter Chen would have heard was their laughter.

He could not close it out of his mind. He knew it would be a haunting memory for as long as he lived. He wished to God he had never seen that taped television interview or contrived this scheme, but it was too late for regrets. All he could do now was to resolve it would succeed, no matter at what cost. If he had been determined before, success now was an urgent and bitter necessity.

The lobby of the Hyatt Imperial was crowded, with one group of package tourists arriving and another intrepid bunch of travellers being rounded up for departure. Burridge badly wanted a shower, but the flight delay gave him no choice. He had ten minutes to be at the American Express office, where he intended to give Hammond a real bollocking for leaving that message on the answering machine. It had to be printed out verbatim, and faxed across town to him by an embarrassed subordinate.

He managed to negotiate the crowd and check-in by giving the receptionist his Visa card, saying he would be back later to collect his key and sign the form, but meanwhile he was late for a meeting, and to please have his luggage taken to his room. He went out into the heat, and walked down the street to the rendezvous.

It was a few minutes before noon.

He found a chair, and a copy of the English-language *Bangkok Post*, and settled down to read. Half an hour later he tossed the paper aside and crossed to speak to one of the clerks behind the counter to make certain this was the only American Express office in the city. He was assured it was.

Later still, beginning to feel conspicuous, he went out into the street to watch for their approach, but the early afternoon heat struck at him like a blast from an open furnace. He retreated back to the comfort and air-conditioning of the Amex building, where he read travel pamphlets and tourist brochures, constantly checking his watch, determined to allow them ample time in case something had gone amiss.

He waited until three o'clock, by which time he had no choice but to accept that they were not coming.

21 'WHAT THE HELL is he playing at?' Ben said, not for the first time. They were having dinner in an open-air restaurant, where fish swam in small sculpted lagoons and along contoured canals, and tiny lights floated on miniature kayaks against the dark water, like a sky full of stars. It was a popular place, but they had not yet glanced at their menus. Neither had an appetite. They were still trying to puzzle out the empty box their keys had opened in the bank on Thon Kai Street a few hours earlier.

'If the pin number had been wrong—or the password wasn't accepted—or our keys wouldn't work, that I could understand. But everything was fine. Just like Hong Kong. The only difference being, the box in Hong Kong held millions of bucks. So what does it mean?'

'I still think we should call Burridge,' Teresa said.

'We're meeting him tomorrow. Noon at the American Express office. All we'll get now is that same answering machine. Besides—I'd rather confront him with this. It's too easy to bullshit over the phone.'

'Eight other banks you said.'

'That's what he told me.'

'Who's to say there's a cent in any one of them?'

'Christ. You're not serious?'

'I don't know, Ben. Let's order. The food here is for tourists—not too full of small green chillies.'

'What—no *prik khi nu*?'

'Only mild ones. Disappointed?'

They ate a small meal, and left early. They walked home in silence, both thinking of the forthcoming meeting with Burridge.

'What you said—about the eight other banks. That maybe there's nothing in them—'

'I was just thinking aloud. Running it up the flagpole as they say in the movies, to see if you saluted.'

He nodded, and was quiet for a moment, then he said, 'There's a well-known scam. A con trick. It's called the golden pot. You put a great deal of money in one bank account, then have many others, supposedly as well endowed. But the big wad in the first account is your stake money, your only real asset; the others are sucker bait. I wonder if we've been taken for a pair of dummies?'

'But why? He might be arrogant, but he's establishment. True-blue. Big job, big office in Paris.'

'All we've got is his card to prove it.'

'No, I've been there. I can vouch for it.'

'I wasn't even aware until I met him that the United Nations had any drug enforcement unit.'

'It has so many agencies, people don't realise its size. I've done a lot of interpreting for the UN. It's huge. World Health, World Bank, the IMF, OEDC, UNESCO; thousands of employees in Geneva and New York, and other major cities. I can believe a section linked to drug enforcement. Probably with Interpol and FBI affiliations.'

'And our own mob,' Ben said, remembering the phone number Deborah had recognised as Howard Morgan's. 'Okay, he's legit. But he plays games, and I don't like his games. So tomorrow—'

'Tomorrow he tells us the whole damned thing,' Tess said, and then realised Ben was staring towards their hotel.

By night the Sala Sawan was no more prepossessing than in the light of day. A small neon blinked ineffectually above the entrance, and shed pallid illumination over the pavement. A taxi cab stood there. Yung Li Hok Dan— Joseph—got out of the cab. He must have been watching their approach in his mirror.

'No thanks,' Ben said firmly. 'Absolutely no guided tours, no sex shops, no massage parlours.'

'No massage parlours,' Joseph said. 'Not tonight.'

He sounded different. He took a snapshot from his pocket. They recognised themselves leaving the bank on Nathan Road in Hong Kong. They felt an acute and immediate sense of danger.

'Where the hell did you get that?'

'People looking for you. Offer money. We gotta talk, guys. You and me, we got a big problem.'


It was, he told them, pure chance. He and some other taxidrivers, queued outside a hotel waiting for fares. These three, two men and a girl, a beautiful doll, meeting with some local hoods. He knew the hoods. Tough guys. Strictly for hire. Beat you up if the price was right. Kill you for a little extra. The dregs. The doll was handing out photographs. One of the guys, Victor, was giving the instructions—

'Victor,' Teresa said. 'Did you say Victor?'

Chinese–Portuguese guy, Joseph told her. Tough and mean. The other was a *farang*, tall and maybe Australian.

'Jesus Christ,' Tess said, and began to shake.

Joseph could see she was shocked, but went on expressionlessly. 'Giving them instructions, this Victor. Telling them to go look in the small hotels, back-street joints. Show the pictures. Check dosshouses. Cover the whole city. Find the bastards.'

'What time was this?'

Ben tried to keep calm. He needed to know how long they had. He could feel Tess trembling, and unconsciously took her hand.

Late afternoon, Joseph told them. Only he thought they still had some time on their side. The search was in the centre of the city. He estimated they had at least until tomorrow.

'*And why are you telling us this*?' Tess rapped out the question in Thai.

Joseph chose to reply in English, as if he wanted Ben included. The doll and the two guys had come to talk to the taxidrivers. Asked about two *farangs*. The cabbies all laughed. *Farangs*? Picked them up all the time. Their bloody country was full of *farangs*. How could they remember two, when they carried maybe hundreds?

The doll said they might remember the girl because, although she was English, she spoke perfect Thai. When she said this, Joseph knew who they were searching for. His face must have shown some reaction. He saw the mean guy, Victor, watching him.

'Ring a bell?' this Victor asked.

Joseph said he pretended not to know what this meant. The other guy, they called him Eddie, gave him a photograph and passed them around to the rest of the drivers.

'Have you seen them?'

Victor kept watching him. Joseph knew he was bad news, he could sense it.

'Don't think so,' he said.

Victor was staring into his face. A mean son-of-a-bitch bastard. Scary.

'You don't think? Well, I don't *think* that sounds too certain.'

'It's worth money to find them,' the other one, Eddie, had said.

'How much?'

'A thousand baht.'

Joseph had decided to be brave. He gave back the photo. He even managed a scornful laugh.

'Cheap shit,' he said. 'One lousy thousand.'

'Ten thousand,' the doll said. They were all concentrating on him, and he felt nervous. Mostly because of this Victor.

'Ten thousand. Okay, lady. I talk with you—not him.'

'You mean you've seen them?'

'No . . . but I'll sure as hell start looking.'

He took back the photo and studied it.

'Maybe I saw someone like this around the Royal Palace. On a tour. How do I contact you?'

260

Joseph said the doll took the photograph and put her name on the back. Helene Lee, room 503. He showed them the back of it. Her name was clearly printed there.

'This Helene baby and her buddies, they sure want to find you.'

'Where are they staying?'

The Thai cabbie did not answer Ben's question. 'So there you have it. That's our problem. I like you guys. I really wanna be on your side.'

They waited. He seemed reluctant to continue.

'But . . . I have big family. Gotta make a living.'

'What you mean is, you could be on our side for ten thousand baht,' Tess said.

'Nearly,' Joseph nodded.

'How much?'

'I got this wife and kids—'

'How much?' she insisted.

'Fifteen thousand.'

'How do we know we can trust you?'

Joseph looked at her, offended.

'What a thing to say. I'm your friend. Maybe the only one you got.'


The last of the men Victor had hired called in to say someone remembered them at the Wat Po Temple earlier in the day. Victor told him to stop wasting his time in temples, and comb every small hotel in every back street of the city and suburbs. When he put down the phone it rang again, immediately.

A voice asked for Helene Lee.

'Speaking,' she said.

'You made a call to Australia, earlier today.'

'That's right. I'm trying to locate Michael Lonsdale.'

After a moment, the voice said, 'You're talking to him.'

'Have you ever heard of an ex-cop named Ben Hammond?'

'Who are you, lady?'

'An interested party.'

'Yes, I know Hammond.'

'He's here,' Helene said. 'In Bangkok.'

'Doing what?'

'Attempting to make some kind of deal with Kim Sokram. You know who I'm talking about?'

'Yes.'

'A deal to buy him out. Now before you say I'm some kind of nut, I think there's slightly more to it than that.'

'You certainly sound like some kind of nut.'

'Do you want to listen, or shall I hang up?'

'I'm listening.'

'He's supposed to contact someone here. An Indian, a jeweller who can apparently provide a link to Sokram—but we don't know the man's name.'

'Fucking hell,' Mick Lonsdale said.

'You know his name? You sound as if you do. Because we need it. So we can stop Hammond making contact or, if he has, then find out where he is.'

Victor watched her, as the harsh voice on the other end spoke, and Helene started to write something down. She had made her first call to Australia earlier, soon after their frenzied love-making. While he was in the shower, she was already on the phone, trying to find this Lonsdale, a dealer in Melbourne she had once heard Burridge talk about.

'I didn't waste my time in that house,' she told Victor, and he could only agree. She hadn't missed a trick.

And now she had the name. She handed it to him as soon as she hung up. She had printed it on the hotel notepad: Pandit Singh, Chakrawat.

A flea market, down near the river. This Singh had a stall and a room behind it where he lived. But the truth was, according to Lonsdale, he owned a whole section of the market. Rows of shanties and bazaars. A regular land-lord. The Lord of the Fleas.

It took them a step closer to the couple. To the keys they held, and all the money waiting for them in Hong Kong.

But for Victor, it also meant something else.

A step towards Teresa Martineau.

He couldn't wait to get his hands on her again.


They slept uneasily. It was a single bed in a small room.

'You guys don't mind single bed?' Joseph grinned. 'Makes for friendship. Double bed, you can fight and turn backsides on each other. Single bed, you gotta stay friends.'

Tess smiled, despite her tension, and said a single bed was fine. Where would Joseph be spending the night?

Next door, he told her, with his girlfriend. It was her place he'd brought them for safety. Eighteen years old, a red-hot lover. He hoped they'd be able to sleep, because the walls were like cardboard, and he and his babe were noisy when they played house.

'So much for the wife and kids,' Tess said, when the door had shut behind him.

'Remember the cardboard walls,' Ben whispered, and offered to sleep on the floor.

'Don't be silly.'

The floor was dirty, and there was a dead cockroach on it.

'Sleep in our clothes, then?'

'Impossible,' Tess said. 'Too hot.'

She removed her jeans and shirt. She had no bra, just a pair of tiny briefs. Her body was slender, her breasts firm. Ben stripped to his Y-fronts. They filled the narrow bed, lying back to back.

'Comfortable?'

'That's a silly question,' she said.

'Maybe we'd have been okay back at the hotel?'

'Or maybe not. I doubt if we'd have been able to sleep.'

'Who says I'm going to be able to sleep?'

'I'm sorry,' she began to say, but he interrupted her:

'It's okay. Truly. No problems.'

'Thanks,' she said.

He felt her body turn, and she kissed his bare shoulder. 'Goodnight, Ben.'

'G'night,' he said, and lay awake for a long time, thinking about tomorrow's meeting at the Amex office with Burridge. He knew his preferred option. He wanted to jack it in. Tell His Eminence to stick the job up his backside. He was about to ask Tess how she felt about that, when he realised her breathing had become regular. She was sound asleep. But sometime before the meeting at noon, they would have to talk it over.

• • •

'You want to buy present? Souvenir?'

Pandit Singh felt uneasy about the two men. One was a tall *farang*, the other part-Chinese. Both had been perusing items in the shop for some time while he attended other customers.

'Rubies,' the *farang* said.

'No rubies.'

'Okay, diamonds,' said the other.

Singh forced a nervous smile. He hoped they were joking.

'Dealer in Fine Arts, it says out front. So where's the fine art?'

'Just sales talk, gentlemen.'

'Fleecing the public, Mr Singh.'

'One has to make a living, sir.'

'All right, let's cut the bullshit,' the Eurasian said. He produced a photograph of the couple who had come to the shop yesterday, and flourished it in front of Singh's eyes. 'You know these people?'

Singh had a moment to decide which reply was the safest. His instinct warned him to tell the truth.

'Yes,' he said. 'They came here yesterday.'

'Why?'

Again, he felt the man knew the answer and was testing him. 'They wished to meet a businessman in the north. I was to arrange it. For this they were obliged to pay me a sum of money.'

266

'How much?'

'Eighty thousand American dollars.'

'For an introduction?'

'No, sir. It was an intricate business. Guides to pay, village headmen to bribe. A great deal to arrange.'

'Did you arrange it?'

'No. They did not have enough money. They tried to bargain. I sent them away, told them to come back when they could afford my fee.'

'Will they come back?'

'I believe so.'

'Thank you, Mr Singh. When they do, you'll be able to help us, won't you?'

His breath caught as he saw the knife. The man smiled, and Singh knew, with a feeling of panic, how much he would relish using it.

'Won't you?'

'Yes,' Singh said. 'Of course. It'll be a pleasure.'


The sampan had a noisy outboard. Joseph sang as he steered. They left the main river and passed through a labyrinth of *klongs*, past floating markets and homes where women stood in the canals and did the washing, and children, wet from bathing in the river, waved to them from flimsy bamboo verandahs. Teresa smiled and waved back to them.

'Not far now, guys,' Joseph broke off his song to say.

They turned into another canal, and steered towards a tiny house. Thick poles supported it over the water. Steps led down to the *klong* from a wooden porch. Joseph cut the motor and they drifted in. He moored the craft and they climbed the steps. The house was made of hardwood, roofed with bamboo, and comprised a single room with rattan mats on the slatted flooring, below which canal water lapped from the sampan's wash. The primitive furniture consisted only of two upright chairs and a small table, with a double horse-hair mattress on the floor.

'No-one find you here,' Joseph said. 'Like it, boss?'

'What kind of place is it?'

'Short-time house—for the adultery. The marrieds come here to make a fuck—with girl-friends—or boyfriends. The owner, he's a cousin so I fix you special price. One thousand baht a night. Real cheap ... okay?'

Ben pointed out they may not need a refuge; after their meeting at noon they might not be staying in Bangkok.

'In case you stay,' Joseph said, 'you need a safe house. Best to make the arrangements. Only cost a night's rent—maybe thirty bucks in your money.'

Teresa agreed. She opened her handbag and counted out notes. 'A thousand for tonight's rent, just in case.' They both watched as she went on counting. 'Plus another ten thousand for you . . .'

'Hey,' Joseph's surprise was genuine. 'You already pay me.'

'So I'm paying extra. Ten thousand today, ten tomorrow if we're still here. The same every day we're alive, until we get out of this city.'

Joseph took the money. He seemed unable to believe his luck. He thought about the deal. 'This way, you make sure I stay friend.'

'That's right, Joseph.'

Tess smiled. Joseph nodded and smiled back. They seemed to understand each other perfectly.

'Smart lady, boss.'

'Yes.' Ben said. 'She is.'


The sampan chugged back to the jetty on the Chao Phraya River. It was after eleven o'clock. They decided they could keep Burridge waiting a brief time; it was best to pack their clothes and check out of the hotel before meeting him. Whatever happened when they met, they would not be spending another night at the Sala Sawan.

The taxi was waiting beside the pylon of a

railway bridge. The area around it was a wasteland of rusted trucks and cars. On the far side
of the river were timber mills, the sky smudged
by the soot of industry. Joseph removed the
outboard motor, then padlocked the sampan.
He opened the bonnet of the taxi to replace
various fuses and the rotor arm.

'Thieving bastards in this city,' he said cheer-
fully. 'I never take no chances. Man who takes
chances ends up pulling a rickshaw.'

Tess spoke to him in Thai, and he replied.
They both laughed, and he carried the outboard
to the back of the cab, stowing it in the boot.

'What was that about?'

'I asked him if he owned the cab. He said he
had a big loan, at high interest—but if we stayed
alive long enough he could pay it off.'

Ben smiled. Joseph was still at the back of the
cab.

'You enjoy handing out Burridge's money,
don't you?'

'Yes,' she said, 'if it's in a good cause.'

'Joseph's a good cause?'

'Our safety is. And, yes, I like Joseph—it'd be
nice to think we helped him own his cab, free
of the loan sharks.'

'If you think we might need his help, you
don't have much faith in Sir Ted.'

Teresa was uncharacteristically abrupt. 'I have
no faith in him. I think he's a dangerous

270

amateur, who nearly got us killed. And did get his friend Mr Chen murdered.'

'Then do we tell him to find two other people?'

'Trouble is, I could be just a day away from meeting my father. And I know you could use the money. Don't tell me you could get a job back in the force after those newspaper headlines?'

They had not discussed the lurid press reports, since their visit to the Indian the previous day. Now, before he could make any attempt to answer, Joseph climbed into the cab and started the engine.

'Let's go, guys. American Express, then the hotel? Or you want to check out of that craphouse first?'

'I want to check out,' Tess said.

'I'll go along with that. I also want to make a phone call.'

They drove to the hotel. At Ben's suggestion, Joseph dropped them on the corner, and agreed to return in ten minutes.

'Just playing safe,' Ben explained. 'If anyone comes looking for us later, we don't want that creep in there remembering your number.'

Joseph drove off. They walked along the shabby street.

'About those headlines,' Ben said, 'it was a fit-up. My partner and I—I'll tell you about it sometime. She was killed. They said there was money missing. I was blamed. Arrested very publicly. Grilled like a criminal. And then when it came to court, the prosecution said they had insufficient evidence. In the meantime, I collected media coverage like a pop star. And all of it fed by someone to Mr Singh.'

'Any ideas who?'

'Burridge. He told me. Singh would deal with me because I've been painted as a bent cop, wanting to get into the drug scene.'

'Good Lord.'

'You live in a nice civilised world, Tess—where people don't do things like that. It goes deeper. I think he arranged the fix. Once things went wrong in Melbourne, I reckon he used the situation. Took advantage. How do I know this? I don't, for certain. But it has his fingerprints all over it.'

She was shocked.

'And this is the man we're going to trust?'

'I'm not ready to trust him. No way. That's why I want to make a phone call.'

They had paused at the insect-smeared screen door to the hotel. The cramped vestibule seemed tackier than ever. A shaft of sunlight showed new stains on the peeling walls. Skeletal flies hung like warnings on the greasy light shade.

The owner seemed shiftier, if that was possible. 'You weren't back last night.'

272

He spoke Thai. Tess, knowing he understood, replied in English. 'Did you think we'd done a moonlight? A runner?'

'You stay?' He was surly, and seemed uneasy.

'No,' she said, 'we go. My husband wants to make an overseas call, then you can give us our bill.' To Ben she said, 'I'll grab a shower, then pack.'

She held out her hand for the key. The proprietor gave it to her. She went up the narrow stairs to the first floor as Ben reached for the telephone on the reception desk and began to dial the international code.

The corridor upstairs, even in daylight, was gloomy. There was a timer switch for the light.

Tess pressed it, and headed towards the room. The number five was in tarnished brass, and a screw that secured it was missing. It hung haphazardly, symptomatic of this unpleasant place. In comparison, the whorehouse on the *klong* seemed like paradise. She unlocked the door and went in, thinking only of a shower and a change into fresh clothes.

She closed the door and turned.

The scream never emerged from her throat.

In a flash Victor Mendoza had the knife against her face. His hand was clamped across her mouth, and his eyes warned it was worth her life to attempt to bite, or to fight him.

'Alone,' he said. 'That's nice. That's how I hoped it would be.'

He clicked the latch, so that the door was deadlocked. He kept the knife hard alongside her cheek where she could see it. His hand took her dress and ripped it. She was naked except for her brief panties.

'Now,' he said, 'let's start where we left off.'

He pushed her onto the bed. He was astride her, his bunched fist ready if she made a sound. She tried to scream and he hit her. In a haze of pain she saw the raised knife—and the look in his face. The expectation. The desire and antic-ipation in his eyes.

She felt as if she was dying all over again.

22 THE TELEPHONE RANG. It was answered and the machine said: 'Hi. This is Nick Feraldos. Jane and I are unable to answer your call at this time. Please leave your name and number after the tone, and we'll get back to you as soon as possible.'

*Bugger it*, he thought, then heard the signal. 'This is Ben. I'm in Bangkok. No phone number, so I'll call you later.' He was conscious of the proprietor making a pretence of not listening while he wrote out their hotel bill by hand.

'I need some info, Nick. Urgent. Anything you can find out for me on these names. The first is Walter Chen, deceased a couple of days ago, apparently murdered. He was a prominent resident of Hong Kong. The second is Helene Lee, who may show up in his dossier. The third, and most important, is Sir Edward Burridge. See if you can check his position with a United Nations drug agency based in Paris. I'll

275

give you the address and telephone number. Hang on while I read it out. Sorry to take up most of your tape, mate, but this is important.'

Ben read from Burridge's card, giving the addresses in both Paris and New York. He could feel the proprietor watching him. The man's forehead was beaded with sweat. Nervousness emanated from him like body odour. Why, Ben wondered.

He finished his message and hung up.

'Thanks. Put it on the bill, and I'll pay when we've packed up.'

'I can do it for you now, sir. Only take just a moment. I do hope you did have a pleasant stay.'

*There was something wrong.*

The man was scared shitless. He took out a handkerchief and wiped his face. The cloth came away damp. Behind him, the beaded curtain to his own quarters imperceptibly moved, as if someone stood obscured there. Ben tried to remain calm. He gestured for the bill, and casually, as if it was normal practice, he moved around to the other side of the counter to study it.

'I'll pay it now. I'll fix the cost of the call before we leave.'

As the proprietor gave him the account, Ben gripped his wrist. Quick as a flash, and using his other hand, he clamped the man's jaw, so he could not utter a sound. The dark eyes grew huge with fear as Ben tightened his grip, then lifted him—like a shield—like a battering ram—and crashed through the beaded curtain.

There was a young Thai there with a gun. He had time only to pull the trigger and fire one shot. It hit the hotel proprietor in the chest, then the youth was sent sprawling as Ben hurled the wounded man at him and was on him in a flash, stamping on the hand that still held the pistol as he kicked the gunman as hard as he could in the groin. His foot sank in deep. The other's face contorted in agony. The pain, like an explosion in his mind, made him release the weapon. Ben scooped it up. He knelt on the youth, who was writhing and gasping. He held the barrel hard against his cheekbone.

'Are you alone? Quick—or I'll kill you.'

The youth shook his head. His eyes lifted towards the ceiling, as he tried to gesture upstairs.

*Oh, Jesus Christ*, Ben thought. *Teresa.*

He hit the gunman with all the force he could muster. He wanted him senseless, and out of action, but he didn't wait to find out. Or to spare a look for the wounded proprietor, moaning and badly hurt.

He was running.

Up the stairs, heart pounding.

*Tess*, he wanted to scream.

He was already blaming himself for being so idiotically careless. *How could he have let her go upstairs alone? Why hadn't he first made a check? How long had he been making the call? How long dealing with the two below? Why was there no sound from inside their room?*

He tried the door. It was locked. He crashed his full weight against it, and felt a stab of pain in his shoulder. The door remained secure and invulnerable. He took the gun and shot at the lock, until it gave, then he kicked the door open.

The room was full of blood.

It was everywhere.

On the bedclothes, pillows, on the walls and the floor.

Blood.

The place was like an abattoir.


Joseph arrived back in the taxi. He parked down the street and waited. As time passed he debated what to do. Something had gone wrong. Joseph was worried; he liked them, especially the lady, who was really classy, but he would have been the first to admit that he was not a hero. If he went into the hotel, it would not only be apparent to the people in there that he was helping them—which might mean all kinds of trouble later—but what else might be there awaiting him?

If you were not a hero, there was no point in pretending to be one. He decided he'd better drive around the block a few times while he thought about it, in case there was someone watching the place.


She was still killing him. Still stabbing at his body with the knife, although Victor's eyes were now sightless and his arteries had drowned the room with blood.

'Tess.'

He knelt beside her. She seemed catatonic. Her gaze was vacant, bewildered and unfocused. He carefully took the knife from her hands as he saw recognition and sanity begin to return. She looked at the dead Victor and recoiled. There was blood all over her face and naked body.

'He was waiting, with the knife.'

She said it in a detached, nebulous way, as though confused how it could have occurred.

'My fault. I should have expected the bastard.'

'He tried to rape me. He said last time—'

'Talk about it later, Tess.'

'No.' She was determined. 'He said last time was just—just his hands—this time it'd be him. All of him. He seemed mad—as if—as if nothing else mattered. That's when he let go of the knife, to rip off my pants. That's when I got hold of it.'

She started to cry, silently, and he put his arms around her in an attempt to comfort her.

'I killed him.' The enormity of it was manifesting itself with her returning lucidity.

'You had to,' he said.

'He laughed—when he saw I had the knife. He laughed and started to describe how he'd fuck me, all the ways, make me crazy for him. I couldn't stand his voice saying such things. I stabbed him in the stomach first, and I thought I must have missed, because he went on laughing. But then the blood spurted. Jesus, the blood.'

'Tess.'

He held her, felt her body trembling, felt the fall of tears on his shoulder.

'The blood made him go crazy. He started trying to hit me, trying to grab the knife back. I knew he'd kill me. The only way I could stop him was to keep stabbing him. Just keep on— over and over—keep stabbing. And then there was a time when I think I knew that he was dead, but I couldn't stop stabbing him.'

'Tessa, listen to me.'

'Ben, I couldn't stop—'

'Listen. This is important. I'm going to pack our clothes. You're going to wrap this robe around you, and shower.'

'But the others—he said there was a man downstairs—'

'I'll take care of it. It's important we get away from here. But first you have to shower, and then put on clean clothes. Okay?'

'Yes,' she said, 'I think so.' She finally nodded. 'Yes, okay.'

She gazed down at the mutilated body, and shuddered. 'What about him?'

Ben grabbed a quilt and threw it over the bloody remains of Victor Mendoza. He deliberately turned Teresa away from the sight, as he draped a robe around her, and gave her a towel. 'Never mind about him.'

'Ben, I have to face facts. I murdered him.'

'No, you just did everyone a favour,' he said, intentionally tough and callous. 'They might call it murder, but when they find out the kind of shit he was, nobody's going to try hard to nail his killer. And even if you walked in and confessed, you'd go free. Because it wasn't murder, Teresa, it was self-defence. Got it?'

'I wanted to kill him.'

'Don't talk bloody garbage. You had to kill him. Or else you'd be dead—after he'd raped you, and hurt you, and done whatever else he wanted. Now are you going to shower, or do I have to carry you there and wash you?'

She took a toilet bag, and he escorted her along the bleak corridor to the bathroom. He made sure the water was hot, told her to lock the door behind him, then he ran downstairs.

The youthful gunman had fled. The proprietor was groaning and seriously injured in the room behind the reception desk. He was trying to crawl towards a coffee table on which there was a telephone extension.

'Sorry, sport,' Ben said, and ripped out the telephone cable that led to the switchboard. 'But you were the snide bastard who tried to earn a quick quid.'

He hurried back upstairs to pack their clothes. There were spots of blood on one of the suitcases, which he wiped off, and carefully checked for other traces. He left out a pair of her panties, patterned shorts and a colourful shirt. He wanted her to look casual and as much like any other tourist as possible.

He packed everything from the wardrobe and chest of drawers. He needed to change his own clothes, which were bloodstained from Tess's body. He threw the dirty trousers and shirt in the corner. They were better left behind: to take them would be dangerous. He carefully put her handbag containing their money on the suitcases, and beside it he placed his only spare shoes, canvas sneakers, to change into before they left the room; the others left an imprint of blood that would be like the trail of a fox in snow, and could only be discarded. Lastly, he found another towel, and wiped clean as much of the floor as he could, to give her space in which to change.

When Teresa came back, she had washed her hair, and scrubbed her entire body in an attempt to cleanse it. He gave her the clothes he had selected, and she put them on without a word. When she was dressed, he lifted the dressing-table mirror and held it for her while she brushed her hair; it was not possible to sit at the dressing table, because the stool had been over-turned in their struggle and, even if he retrieved it, she would have to sit too close to the covered body. He didn't want her to even look at it again, and she seemed to realise this. She found a lipstick and touched it to her lips, and finally nodded that she was finished and he could lower the mirror.

He stared at her. He gazed at a transformation. Her hair fell like silk and crowned her face. Her skin glowed from its fierce scrubbing, as if warmed by the sun. The trace of colour on her lips made her look very young and vulnerable, like a schoolgirl first experimenting with makeup. In that moment, he thought he wanted to spend the rest of his life with her. He had what seemed like a wild and irrational feeling that he had fallen in love with her.

'What's wrong,' she asked, conscious of his gaze.

'Absolutely nothing,' Ben said, 'just as long as you're all right.'

'I think I might be. Soon. Thanks to you.'

She did not wait for a reply, but went out of the room. He picked up the suitcases, and followed her, leaving the covered body of Victor Mendoza beneath its quilted shroud. Unable to lock the door, he pulled it shut to delay discovery, then went down the concrete stairs and out of the hotel.

'Jesus Christ,' Joseph said, 'what kept you?'

They had waited on the designated corner, concerned that he was missing until at last his taxi came into sight, and he pulled up alongside them. He pushed the button to open the boot, and Ben put the two cases inside. He climbed in the back seat beside Teresa, and tyres shrieked as Joseph accelerated away.

'I kept going round and round the block. Not sure whether to go in and find out if anything was wrong, or just keep driving.'

'We had a problem. It's okay,' Ben said.

Joseph had a distinct feeling it was not okay, but he remained silent. Ben told him to stop at a public phone box. When they pulled up alongside one, he got out of the car and asked Tess to accompany him.

'Can you do this, or else we'll ask Joseph.'

'Do what?'

'Call the emergency service—tell them to send an ambulance to the hotel. I hardly care, but if we don't bother that doublecrossing creep is probably going to die.'

'Of course I can do it. But it means they'll find the body.'

'They will, anyway, in time. We'll be well away.'

'Where?'

'I don't know yet. Let's see what Burridge suggests.'

For a moment she did not respond. Then she said, 'You think Sir Edward Burridge is going to get me out of this?'

Before he could reflect on her tone and what she had meant, she turned away to make the call. The emergency number, triple zero, was listed beside the instrument. She dialled and spoke briefly in Thai, then hung up. 'I said someone was very ill, and gave the address.'

He nodded. They started to go back towards the waiting taxi.

'Tess?' He took her arm, and they stopped. 'Are you telling me you don't think Burridge will help?'

'I don't know. The more I hear of him, the less I'm sure.'

'But he must. We've got to get out of this city. Who else is there to organise that?'

'Only us.'

'Us?'

'You and me. People we can trust. I trust

myself and I trust you. I don't think—at the moment—I trust anyone else.'

'I see.'

'You probably think I'm crazy?'

'No. I don't think that. Let's make another phone call.'

They went back to the booth and looked up the number.

'American Express,' a female voice answered.

'I need to talk to someone,' Ben said. 'He's waiting there to meet me, and I need to speak with him.'

'This is the American Express office, sir. We don't handle that kind of thing.'

'I realise it's unusual,' Ben said, determinedly polite, 'but it is urgent. His name is Burridge— Sir Edward Burridge.'

'But, sir—'

'I wouldn't be bothering you if it weren't important. I'm unable to meet him as arranged. I need to know which hotel he's staying at. So that I can make contact, later.'

'I'm sorry, sir, but this office is extremely busy. It's for people to make plane and hotel reservations and exchange money. We have no means of paging anyone.'

'He's a tall man, mid-fifties, English. Probably been waiting there some time. Over an hour. If you could just look around—'

He heard the girl apologise to someone.

There was a pause, then she came back on the line.

'I'm afraid there's no-one here fitting that description. I'm sorry, but I really can't help you any further.'

'Thanks,' Ben said, and hung up.

On the other end of the line, the Thai girl replaced her phone, and smiled at the couple who had been patiently waiting: 'So you'd like Phuket for a week. That's a good choice. It's beautiful at this time of year.'

She gave them each brochures and, as she began to organise their trip, she glimpsed a tall man entering. She remembered now that he had been waiting earlier, when it was less crowded. In fact he had been waiting for a considerable time. He was in his fifties and wearing a linen suit. He looked English, and he seemed angry.

*Oh well*, she thought, rueful at the timing, *not much point in telling him now. It's really none of my business.*


The taxi was cool inside. Joseph had kept the motor running with the air-conditioner working and had thus seen them talking and making both telephone calls, but had been unable to hear a word. He was puzzled and consumed with curiosity.

'Guys, you're late as hell to meet your friend. Is that where we go now? The Amex office?'

Ben glanced at Teresa. Since the idea of the phone call had failed, this was certainly the logical thing to do; it was reckless and unthinkable not to at least front the man and find out how to make later contact. But he saw the look on her face. She could not cope with it. She had already been through too much. Just because she was fresh and unmarked, her hair shining and her clothes clean, did not alter the trauma of what she had suffered.

She had to recover in her own way. Take one step at a time. Not be plunged into a confrontation with Burridge.

Because that's what it would be. He would want facts, details, the whole thing spelled out. There would be recriminations and argument about the way they had skipped from Hong Kong. Tess knew as well as he did: you didn't turn up an hour late to meet someone like Burridge—tell him you weren't staying because you distrusted him, and ask him for his phone number.

He almost smiled at the thought of it, and realised that Joseph was watching him instead of the road.

'Where, boss? American Express?'

He did something then, against all training and common sense, that was to have an effect on both their lives.

288

'No,' he said. 'Take us to the house on the *klong*.'

Teresa said nothing. But he knew, because they were starting to understand each other, that she was relieved and grateful.


Edward Burridge was unused to people not turning up. All his life, his father a landowner, his family upper middle class, had occupied their accepted place in the British social fabric. The Burridges were country bred; some of their progeny went to London and into the world of business; others adopted the law or the diplomatic service. Medicine was out, ever since the national health system. Doctors, unless they were clever enough to practise in Harley Street, were virtual public servants. The army was also in disfavour, since the likelihood for many years of being sent to Northern Ireland, and being shot by a sniper or blown up by a car bomb, was more than a possibility, while the Church, once a favoured refuge for the third son, was considered a hopeless deadend and no longer relevant.

Edward, in the early 1960s, after he had come down from Cambridge and was looking for a job, had met a cousin who was well placed at Scotland Yard. It was not something of which the family was particularly proud. They preferred their scions to be captains of industry, judges or ambassadors, not coppers. But it happened that Edward was not a snob, and he and his cousin formed a close rapport that endured, and when the cousin was eventually appointed chief constable of a county, and later moved into other, less outwardly visible activities, Edward Burridge discovered there were many more advantages to this friendship than he had dreamed of.

He never actually went through the routine of officially joining anything. It simply came to be known he was at the Foreign Office. In fact his varied career included a stint with MI6, and many years with Interpol. He enjoyed the stratagems, the tactics and secret manoeuvrings of the covert world. 'The cloak,' he liked to say to his colleagues, 'is infinitely more exciting and important than the dagger.'

He had a zest for the dangerous games, and relished the power he wielded; the surprising, at times alarming information on so many of his fellow citizens that he possessed. The world of concealment and masquerade suited him well. The essential ingredients for success were malevolence, callousness and a capacity for deception.

He was well qualified in all three.

Now, after so many years in the twilight and the shadows, he had come to the crest of his career. It was to be the peak moment in his life; he had planned it with ruthless efficiency. And for some extraordinary reason it had gone totally astray.

He went back to his hotel, but there were no messages. Though he expected none, it made him even angrier than the tedious and fruitless wait at the American Express office had done. He had tried to leave a letter for them there, but a senior male clerk had told him they were not a *poste restante* and had been singularly unimpressed by his United Nations business card or credentials.

He could have chosen to seek official help here at the highest level, but it was not the way he operated. The imprimatur of the Pacific Rim law enforcement agencies at the initial meeting weeks ago had been all he required. After that he set his own agenda, and it did not include liaison with ASEAN police. For one thing, they often played by the rules—which Burridge believed to be a hindrance and made to be broken—for another, when this was over, he had no intention of sharing the credit with any regional uniformed bureaucrat.

He sat in the cool of his hotel room, poured himself a whisky, and tried to think of the best way to proceed. Despite the setback, he had no doubt he would proceed. Nothing was going to jeopardise this. He had invested too much time and energy. It was a frustrating hiccup, that was all. He had picked his pawns, and the pawns were proving troublesome. They had always been, at least in his mind, almost certainly expendable.

Now, when that time came, he need have no regrets about it.

23 HELENE LEE HAD an instinct for survival that had often stood her in good stead. When Victor failed to return, she told Carmichael to use his mobile phone and make contact with the group of locals they had hired. He was to find out which district Victor had been searching—for a promising lead had come in around ten that morning, and Victor had gone to check it. She had been waiting with impatience ever since, and it was now almost mid-afternoon, and more than time to start taking precautions if something had gone wrong.

Within a few minutes, Eddie Carmichael returned with the news that there had been two deaths reported at a small nondescript hotel called the Sala Sawan. One, a tourist, as yet unidentified, had been stabbed to death. The other, the owner of the premises, had been shot, and died in the ambulance while being taken to hospital. A European couple, a man and woman who had occupied a room there, were missing and being sought for questioning. Reporters and camera crews already had the story for the early evening bulletins.

Helene knew it was time to move. If it was Victor—which was something her emotions would have to deal with later—if it was, and his face was on half the city's television screens, she had to be somewhere else very swiftly, where no sharp-eyed receptionist or hotel porter might recall their arrival together, and link them. She told Carmichael to get on his skates and check out, and arranged to meet him at the cab rank. She called the desk and said to send up a bellboy in five minutes, as she was moving to Pattaya beach. When she hung up, the telephone startled her by ringing almost at once. She debated whether or not to answer it, but felt it was safe; there was no possibility it could be the police yet.

In fact, it was Michael Lonsdale, calling from Melbourne Airport, where a Qantas flight was leaving in thirty minutes. He would arrive in Bangkok sometime after midnight. He had a vested interest in the man she was hunting and suggested they should meet for a late breakfast and an exchange of views. He thought it could be worth her while.

Helene said she was considering changing hotels, dissatisfied with the service here. She was not yet certain where she would be staying. It might therefore be best if she could call Lonsdale instead, provided he was already booked in somewhere. He told her he would be in his usual suite at the Oriental Hotel. He would expect her call soon after nine.

Water lapped gently below the wooden slats, and the dark water of the canal reflected the light of a quarter moon. Ben stood on the porch, where the breath of a cool breeze softened the night. Teresa was inside, by now asleep.

They had bought food at a noodle shop on one of the main canals, and brought it back here and eaten it with Joseph. During the meal Ben had warned him not to go near the hotel.

'Something happen there, boss?'

'Yes,' Ben said.

'Something bad?'

'Pretty bad. There was someone waiting for us. He's dead.'

It was all he said, not wanting to distress Teresa further by recounting the details. She had been silent, picking at the food. At the end of the meal, with Joseph preparing to leave, she went to her handbag, and handed him a wrapped bundle of Thai banknotes.

'Ten thousand baht, Joseph.'

He was startled. It appeared he might almost be embarrassed.

'But, guys—'

'Take it. We made a deal.'

'Okay.' He looked at her closely, while he folded the wad of notes and put them in his pocket. He seemed troubled.

'You sure you're all right, doll?'

Tess tried to insist that she was all right, but her voice lacked conviction. Joseph was astute enough to guess whatever happened had impacted on her emotionally. Now he was gone. They had stood and watched as he took his boat along the tranquil and deserted *klong*, towards the river and the city. He would soon find out the full story when he saw a paper or the television news. Ben began to wish they had confided in him more fully. For they were completely in his hands.

If Joseph wanted to rip them off, claim a reward from the police, or whatever he could wangle from Helene Lee, they were in trouble.

Teresa went inside. He heard her call good-night, and said he might stay outside a while. The light in the tiny house was turned out. He intended to sleep on the porch and give Tess the room to herself, but soon afterwards he heard the angry whine as hungry mosquitoes began to attack. He slapped at them, but they were relentless. He had to finally retire, defeated. At least the house had screens on the

296

door and the windows, and a coil burning in there to keep them at bay.

It was quiet and dark. He stripped off his clothes. Teresa was turned away from him, inert on the mattress, a light absorbent sheet spread across her naked limbs. He lay down as silently and carefully as he could, and was unaware she was awake until he sensed a movement. She reached out and took his hand.

She turned to him so that her body contoured against his. He could feel her warmth. She kissed him.

It was an almost chaste kiss, a mute appeal. She was seeking no more than comfort and companionship.

They each knew it. Or they thought they did.

The passion that energised as their bodies met startled them both with its intensity.


'Can't you sleep?'

'I don't want to, yet awhile. Do you?'

'No.'

She touched his face in the almost dark.

'That was lovely.'

'Yes. It was.'

'Unexpected, too.'

'Yes,' he said, knowing what she meant.

'I thought you'd stay out there all night.'

'I was going to. The mozzies drove me in.'

'God bless the mozzies,' she said

'You do realise this is a short-time house. I expect Joseph's on a percentage.'

She laughed. He liked the sound of her laughter. He sat up, and found the oil lantern that was the only source of illumination. He lit it, and looked at her. There seemed to be no need to say anything. He was so happy, it would have been superfluous.

Later on they talked. He told her about Chrissie. About how he felt, and the fiasco in Melbourne. He was able to speak about it for the first time and, in doing so, felt Chrissie vanishing from his life—and began to feel free of the guilt that had been a weight he carried since her death.

He talked in more detail about his trial by media, and his bitter resentment at the public arrest, the deliberate, calculating way it was done in front of his children, his wife, and the neighbours. How he had blamed his boss, Howard Morgan, but now wondered if he was wrong about that.

He even talked of Deborah, and the way their marriage had simply expired for lack of interest; of how he had given her the house and most of the money, because he felt the major guilt was his, and couldn't bear to barter over what had been, until recently, an amicable if unexciting life together.

He also mentioned the message he had left for his closest and most trusted friend Nick Feraldos, whom he would try to call tomorrow. Teresa picked up on the name, and asked if he was Greek. Ben said he was as Australian as a meat pie, but born in Cyprus.

'Ever been to Cyprus?'

'No. But I've heard lots over a few beers, when Nick starts on about how beautiful it is. He says it's beautiful and sad.'

'It is,' Tess said. 'He's right. All that wonderful Greek and Phoenician grandeur, but it's always been a battlefield. I spent a summer at Kyrenia, before I married Stephen. It's a very romantic place, Cyprus.' She snuggled close to him. 'Not remote enough for us, though.'

'Us?'

'We need to find a hideaway island. After we steal all that money in Hong Kong, and run away together.'

'Sounds nice.' He grinned. 'You're kidding.'

She merely looked at him, watching, as if assessing his reaction, saying nothing.

'You are kidding.'

'Of course.'

'I knew you were.'

'Just fooling.'

'Thought you were.'

'Or dreaming, Ben.'

'Dreaming?'

'Because where could we go?'

'Exactly.'

'No country in the world would be safe for us.'

'That's right.'

He was about to blow out the lantern. Tess said, 'But if you do happen to think of any place, let me know.'

'Shit,' he said, 'you really mean it.'

They could both feel the sudden tension.

'Don't be silly,' she said.

'You sounded like you meant it.'

'Perhaps—if it was possible. But it isn't.'

'That's right.'

'So let's forget I ever said it.'

She put her arms around him. 'Make love to me again. Leave the lamp on—so I can see you.'


In Sydney, it was midnight, and Nick Feraldos, who had come in off a late shift, hung up the telephone. He went in search of his wife, Jane, who was getting dressed to go on duty at the hospital.

'This is a bad week for making babies,' she said. 'We have to get our act together, and sort out these work schedules.'

He frowned, instead of his usual easy smile. 'I think Ben's in strife.'

'What's wrong?'

'This guy, Burridge. I called his Paris office. Nobody has ever heard of him. I called the number in New York. It's a delicatessen.'

'But he works for the United Nations.'

'So he said. Drug Enforcement. But the UN say they have no drug enforcement agency. And no Sir Edward bloody Burridge.'


Joseph cut the motor, and let the sampan drift gently in towards the wooden steps. He brought bread rolls, eggs, coffee and papaya, as well as the *Bangkok Post* and other morning newspapers. He watched their faces while they looked at the front pages. There were photographs of the Sala Sawan hotel, its dead owner, and one of Victor Mendoza from police files. In the *Post* an English headline was splashed above it: HONG KONG FUGITIVE MURDERED. TOURIST COUPLE SOUGHT.

'They don't print your names or your pictures,' Joseph said, 'but that's the only good news.'


Burridge saw it when the maid brought his breakfast. He swore violently, and read it with increasing consternation. God, what a mess. No wonder they hadn't turned up. His breakfast lay neglected and congealing while he put through an urgent call to Sydney using his own digital mobile telephone so that it would not go through the hotel switchboard. He simply announced he was unable to make contact with Ben.

'You mean you've lost him again?' Superintendent Howard Morgan could not resist it. 'To lose him once might be an accident,' he said, paraphrasing Oscar Wilde with considerable relish, 'to lose him twice seems remarkably like bloody carelessness.'

'Shut up, you stupid fucking Welsh git,' Burridge said with all the venom he could muster, which was considerable, and waited for a response but there was only silence.

'Morgan—are you there?'

He thought incredulously: *the bastard's hung up on me.*

Nobody had ever done that. There'd be a call to Canberra, to the Deputy Chief Commissioner, to sort this one out.

'Of course I'm here,' Morgan finally said. 'Just waiting.'

'For what?'

'For you to regain your cool. You're a bit of a worry. When you feel you can speak without going off your brain, you might care to tell me what's happened.'

Burridge managed through clenched teeth to explain some of the situation, at least since the death of Walter Chen. The way he told it made Ben appear to have acted impulsively and erratically. It was when he got to the Bangkok killings that Howard Morgan became concerned.

'I hope to God you've got influence, Burridge. They're rather serious about murder in Thailand.'

'Why do you think I'm trying to find him—and her? Do you imagine I called you to pass the time of day?'

'I'm trying to work out why you did call me. Ben's no longer one of my people, so what makes you think I could help?'

'Feraldos is still one of yours, and Hammond'll contact someone.'

'I'll ask. No guarantee Nick will talk, even if Ben's been in touch.'

'At least try,' Burridge said, with a trace of asperity.

Morgan heard it, and said, 'Don't blow your stack again. You told me there was a man in Bangkok—a contact Ben'd be making. Can't you get word that way?'

'Under no circumstances. It'd jeopardise the whole arrangement. Besides, I'm not even officially in this country.'

'Jesus Christ,' Howard said: 'If you were

asked the time of day you'd try to keep it secret. How do I communicate?'

Burridge reluctantly gave him the coded number for his digital phone. A call would reach him wherever he was in the city, at any hour of the day or night.

'It's vital I find them,' he added. 'I'm their only hope.'

'Then I wouldn't be him for quids,' Morgan said, and hung up.


Michael Lonsdale shut the bedroom door, and invited her to sit in the living room of his suite, but not before she had glimpsed there was a local boy in his tousled bed.

She shrugged. It was purely business, anyway, and ever since the confirmation of who had killed Victor, her search for Hammond and the interpreter had become intensely personal. If this man could assist in finding them—she wanted them both dead and after that there would be more than enough money to share around—then who cared about his sexual pref- erences? Besides, a predilection for boys meant she would not have to fend him off. She already had Eddie Carmichael trying to console her, hoping to move back in with her. She felt it was smart to play him along for the present, but Eddie was forever small-time, a loser, and once she had enough money she would pick and choose her own men.

Lonsdale asked what progress they had made. She debated whether to mention Victor. Although the English-language newspaper was there in the room with its lurid pictures and head-line, there was no reason for him to make a con-nection. But instinct told her this man had a great deal of power, as well as his own good reasons for finding Hammond, and only the truth would make them allies. So she explained about the back-street search of hotels, and how Victor had located them, but been knifed to death.

Michael Lonsdale studied the newspaper report. 'Doesn't seem like Hammond's style.'

'I think the English bitch did it. Teresa.'

'Why?'

She revealed the details of Victor's arrest in Hong Kong, and how he had lusted after this girl. Indifferent to such sexual cravings, it was not until she mentioned Teresa Martineau's full name that he showed interest.

'Martineau?'

'Yes. Do you know her?'

'I've heard that name.' He frowned. 'Who is she?'

'An interpreter—she lives in England.'

'How did she get into this?'

'Burridge. The man I told you about—he recruited her.'

'Tell me more about Sir Edward Burridge,' Lonsdale said. 'I want to know what he's up to. Everything about him. But first,' as she was about to answer, 'what news on Pandit Singh?'

'He's being watched. If they go anywhere near him, we'll know.'

'Good.'

He smiled. Helene Lee disliked the smile, which was artificial and distant. But then, she thought, he wasn't out to impress her, which made a change from men drooling and mentally wanking over her, and so she didn't have to like him at all.


'He's a phoney,' Nick said. 'Can you hear me?'

'I can hear you,' Ben said from the public telephone where Joseph had taken him across the river. 'Loud and clear, mate.'

'A bloody delicatessen, for Christ's sake.'

'Sounds a bit like his idea of humour.'

'Maybe, but I don't trust the bastard. Don't you trust him, either.'

'I won't. I haven't so far. What about Walter Chen?'

'Not much detail on him. Just that he was rich, and now he's dead. There are about thirteen cousins who probably never gave him a smile when he was alive, fighting over his will.'

'Already? Poor Mr Chen.'

'The girlfriend,' Nick said, 'now there's an item. Helene Lee. She was a hooker in Vegas. Lots of wealthy boyfriends since she retired from working on her back. She's hot stuff. You watch yourself, boyo.'

'I've got some news for you, Nick. I think I'm immune.'

**24** IT WAS THEIR third night. The place was beginning to feel like home. Tess cooked a meal of rice and vegetables, and they sat on the straw mats, eating with chopsticks. Outside, monsoon rain, the first they'd encountered, drummed on the bamboo and thatched roof, and dripped from the fronds of the palm trees. Warm and dry inside the house, the sound of it was a comfort.

It had been a strange time. They should have been afraid; at moments they were, but mostly they were quietly and joyously happy. If they were being hunted, they managed much of the time not to think about it. Teresa put her hopes for the meeting with her father on hold at the back of her mind, and Ben tried to forget that if he returned home unsuccessful, he would be penniless; they swam and washed in the *klong*, found a neighbourhood floating market where they bought fruit and fish, and Joseph came each day with the papers and his own brand of street news, and even though they paid him his ten thousand baht—a little more than four hundred dollars daily—they began to trust him.

It was a time of love and exploration. If they had remained as strangers sharing a room, they might have acted sooner; being lovers they wanted to delay as long as possible the moment of decision. They would have chosen—if any choice was possible—to remain there for weeks. But they realised that people were scouring Bangkok, and soon the search would transfer from the inner suburbs and cross the river to the network of canals, and the markets and wooden stilt houses along the maze of *klongs*. Even lovers had to make choices about such things.

'Soon there'll be talk,' Ben said.

'What sort of talk?'

'Speculation about us. Why do two *farangs* stay in a short-time house for so long?'

'If that's a trick question,' Tess said, 'I'll give you the simple answer. We cook, we eat, we make love. Day and night. We'd like to stay here forever.'

He looked at her, and could easily wish it were true. She wore a sarong and an embroidered silk blouse they had bought at the market, and the vivid colours enhanced her soft dark hair and blue eyes. He wondered why he had not realised how beautiful she was when they first met, and recalled in fact that they had not been the least attracted. There had been little rapport, even a latent hostility between them, both in the Hong Kong bank and during the long afternoon they had changed money in Kowloon. Now, little more than a week later, he was in love with her.

She wanted to meet her father, an opportunity she'd been denied since childhood. He would try to make it happen. He promised it, despite all his misgivings about Burridge. They both felt there must be a simple explanation for Nick's information. Burridge played devious games: they could not allow themselves to think it was anything else.

No longer feeling constrained by any pledge of confidentiality, he also told her why she had been selected.

'He chose me—*because* of my father?'

'Because he's influential,' Ben said, recalling what Burridge had told him. 'A public figure who has a lot of authority and prestige.'

'Is this true?'

Ben shrugged. 'It's what I was told. Your father works for the UN, but they haven't used him in years. Too valuable to waste on routine matters. Burridge said once it's known you're with me, I'd have a safe passage. He intended to spread the word that we're lovers.'

'Fancy that,' she said, and smiled despite her perplexity.

'He said you're my protection. Which may be true once we get away to the north, but not here in this city—not with Helene Lee and whoever else she's recruited.'

'So—we have to get out of Bangkok.'

'Soon as we can.'

'How?'

'That's the problem. We need Singh's help.'

'But we haven't enough to pay Singh. And he won't bargain.'

'Which brings us to it. We need cash. The vault here is a sham, but there's heaps back in Hong Kong. We have to get hold of some of it.'

'They'd be watching the airport.'

'Watching for two people,' he said.

'For sure.'

'Which is why one of us should go.'

She studied him. 'You mean one person take both keys?'

'Yes.'

'You've been thinking about this.'

'A bit,' he admitted. 'No reason why it won't work. We have the password, and the access number. It's all that's required. Both times they wanted the two keys. There was never any mention of two people.'

'Who'd go?'

'I would,' he said.

'They'd spot you a mile off. You wouldn't have a hope.'

311

'I'm used to this kind of situation.'

'In Australia, maybe. Not here.'

'Well, you can't go,' Ben said.

'Why not?'

'It's not your scene. I won't let you take the risk.'

'Don't try to be macho and protective. That's just dumb. I'm the logical one to go.'

'Why?'

'Because I have a bunch of passports, and all the languages necessary to fit the roles. Because I was in the theatre once; not a star or even a success, but I did learn makeup and character acting.'

She opened her handbag, and selected from the various passports and the diverse photographs taken of her so few weeks ago in London.

'This one, I think,' she said, showing him. 'That's who I'll be.'


The boat was a cabin cruiser, with powerful twin outboards. Lonsdale had hired it, along with a crew, and weapons. Some armalite automatic rifles and an Uzi. He told Helene to keep her people checking the hotels. He was prepared to spend as much as necessary to recruit extra locals so that they had teams watching the airport, the rail station and the main bus terminus in Phahonyothin Road. They'd also maintain a round-the-clock surveillance of the premises at Chakrawat. But the cruiser was his main hope.

'I don't think they're in the city any longer. The *klongs*, that's where I'd try to hide. That's where I'll look for him.'

'I get a feeling this is more than just trying to stop Ben Hammond. It's a lot more personal.'

'You're not wrong. The bastard broke my nose in Melbourne, and cost me lots of money. I'm a very bad loser.'


Teresa gave Joseph a list and he went to purchase the items she required. He was back by noon, and told her he had made her a booking on a Cathay Pacific flight for late afternoon. While they left her in privacy, they sat on the porch outside and waited.

'She go, you stay?'

'She'll be back tomorrow.'

'They watch the airport, boss, for sure.'

'Tess says she can handle it.'

'But how?'

'I don't know. She insists she can.'

Joseph heard the bamboo door slide open, and looked up. He gaped. Ben turned to stare.

'Jesus Christ,' Joseph said, 'who're you?'

He was answered by a stream of Greek. A

313

woman with jet black hair, heavy frame glasses and a long skirt gesticulated and continued to talk volubly, while they gazed at her, bemused. Then she looked down at Ben and murmured: 'You ever screw a Greek girl from Thessaloniki? If not, now's your chance.'

It was Teresa's voice, looking totally unlike Teresa.

'My God, Tess.'

'Tess? Who is this Tess?' The voice changed, became heavy-accented as she thrust out a hand and shook Ben's, with almost masculine heartiness. 'My name is Aliki Hadjidakis. I teach piano. If you wish to learn,' she said with severity, 'please understand that musical study is a serious matter. No jokes are allowed in my classes.'

She turned to Joseph. 'I am to Hong Kong going, to find students. You will please arrange for me the taxi.'

'Doll, you're a star,' Joseph said admiringly.

Teresa laughed. 'What a pity you weren't around, Joe, when I was trying to be one. I think we'd better go, before I lose my nerve.'


Ben stood on the bamboo porch and watched the sampan move away along the *klong*. Tess turned for a last look back, and waved, and he returned the wave and felt very insecure once the craft rounded the bend and was gone. He began to wonder if he would ever see her again. He wanted to shout to her to come back, to forget it, but it was too late. He stayed there, worrying, remembering her last words, as he put her luggage in the boat. The engine was ticking over, waiting for her.

She had kissed him and said, 'I wish it was safe for you to come with me.'

'So do I.'

'You know what we'd do? Take enough of the money in that box to last the rest of our lives. Then we'd keep going. Find our far-off hideaway island.'

'You're beginning to sound as if you mean it.'

'We wouldn't take all the money. Just enough to keep us in modest comfort—for our later years. Our superannuation fund.'

'Tessa—cut it out.'

'Dreams, Ben. I told you that.'

She kissed him again, and got into the sampan. Joseph pushed the control, and it chugged away. She would be back—if all went well—late the next day. He had over twenty-four hours to wait, to sweat and to do something he had not attempted since childhood.

Pray.

315

**25** A KLM FLIGHT bound for Amsterdam and London took off, heading westward into the afternoon sun. Only when it was airborne could they hear themselves speak. They were on the observation terrace above the terminal building. It was the first time Helene had introduced Lonsdale to Eddie Carmichael, who was booked on the next Cathay Pacific flight to Hong Kong.

'Why are you going back there?' Lonsdale asked.

'She insists.' Eddie answered. 'I'd say it's a sheer waste of time.' He was clearly unhappy. With Victor out of the way, he had ambitions of renewed relations with Helene; instead, he was being sent on what he considered a wild goose chase.

'It's not,' said Helene. 'There's every chance they'll go there.'

'Why?'

'Because the Indian said they didn't have enough to pay him. They won't find money in the bank here, we know that. By now they'll have guessed—it's all in one place, the South China Bank on Nathan Road.'

'You're certain of this?' Lonsdale asked.

'Positive. It was the last thing Walter told us before he died.'


Teresa changed cabs near the Erawan Hotel, nodded a nervous goodbye to an equally nervous Joseph, and flagged down another cab to take her to the airport. As she paid the driver, and walked into the terminal with some tourist accoutrements she had bought en route to the airport, she glimpsed Helene Lee and the man who had been on watch in the lobby of their Hong Kong hotel. Her heart lurched with fear. She had a moment of blind panic, but fortunately neither was looking at her. They were talking with a lean, saturnine man who sounded Australian, and several Thai men and women, all of whom had police-style radios.

She began to notice a number of other Thais with similar radios. They could have been airport security but at least two were studying photographs and, as she went past, she glimpsed enough to realise it was the snapshot of Ben and herself, identical to the one circulated in town, which Victor had used to track them to the hotel. Despite her bravado in the canal house, her stomach felt hollow, and her hands were damp. A trickle of sweat began to run down between her breasts. Her fear was so acute that she felt it must be visible to everyone around her.

She had to pull herself together. She went to the check-in desk where she had her ticket validated and was given her boarding pass and assigned a window seat in the main cabin. As she turned, she saw the same man two places back in the queue behind her.

Eddie Carmichael saw a flamboyant woman with black hair and prominent glasses. She wore a long skirt, sandals, a silk blouse that had tourist motifs all over it and, around her neck, she wore a string of junky beads. She carried an overnight bag, as well as a banana straw basket in which were souvenirs. He spotted a hand-crafted ceramic doll in traditional dress and a length of Thai silk, as she set the basket on the ground and peered at her boarding card with its seat allocation. He thought it was a pity about the glasses—otherwise she might not be a bad sort.

Tess realised from his brief appraisal that he had not recognised her. It steadied her nerves, gave her the confidence to remain there, creating the impression she was concerned about the seat she had been given while he stepped up to the Cathay Pacific desk. She needed to know where he was going and, if possible, his identity. Within moments she knew both, as the girl tapped his name into her computer—asked Mr Carmichael if he preferred smoking or non-smoking, and wished him a pleasant flight to Hong Kong. By the time he had left the check-in, Tess was in the duty-free shop studying the gemstones and apologetically telling the attendant that their black star and green sapphires were really magnificent—but she was just a simple Greek piano teacher and could not possibly afford such luxuries.

She saw Carmichael line up with the other passengers to board the plane. Fortunately she had heard him request a non-smoking seat and, after her foray into the duty-free shop, she went back and requested a change of seat to the smoking section. On the flight she endured chain-smokers on either side of her and her clothes smelt foul with cheap tobacco by the time they landed at Kai Tak. During the three-hour trip, one of the chain-smokers attempted a conversation. She looked vacant, explained in stilted English that she did not understand, and buried her head in a very boring Greek travel book.


Ben spent an almost sleepless night. He was missing her more than he could have imagined.

He had been in love only twice, he thought; once with Deborah when they met and married, the other time with Chrissie Duncan—but that he had only come to realise after her death, and may well have been generated by the sudden shock of her murder, and his devastating sense of loss and guilt.

This was quite different.

He had been scared every moment since she went. His mind was beset with images of disaster, visualising unexpected catastrophes. In the middle of the night, awake and sweating in the humid *klong* house, it seemed to him there was havoc waiting for her at every turn. It was not a lack of confidence in her; but she was, like most people, unable to deal with violence and danger. She was a talented interpreter with a gift for languages and a father who, for some reason, had caused Burridge to seek her out and recruit her. She was an amateur in his world—which meant she had no knowledge of the savagery, the viciousness, the corruption and spurious deceit, the whole filthy canvas of subterfuge and fraud which had now enveloped her.

He wanted her safe.

There was no telephone, either in the house or anywhere in the neighbourhood. He would need a boat to reach one, and Joseph was not due until the morning. If there had been a chance, he would have called her in Hong

Kong at the hotel she had selected, and told her to get out of there, to run, get on a plane to London or, better still, to Sydney, and to meet him there. He had sometimes been afraid for himself or, when they had worked together, for Christine, but this was different.

He had never been so sick with anxiety.

If this was love, it was absolute hell.


Teresa also slept badly, but it was excitement that kept her awake and stimulated, not fear. The fact of having been a passenger in the same plane as Carmichael, remaining unrecognised, had installed a feeling of elation that was dangerously close to over-confidence. She could hardly wait to tell Ben about it. The man had walked past her twice in the plane, the first time eying her, but with routine macho calculation, not suspicion, and when she had ignored him, he had shrugged and continued on his way to the toilet. The second time he hardly gave her a glance. Tess, buried in her book, pretended not to notice, secretly thrilled she had so obviously passed scrutiny.

However, despite the sense of chutzpah, she did take precautions. If Carmichael was to stay in Hong Kong, it could mean any number of things. The thought occupied her mind for part of the night and, early the next morning, she went to a shopping plaza beside her hotel. It took less than an hour, after which she checked out but left her overnight bag and straw basket at the porter's desk. If the day went well, she hoped not to be returning for them. If it went badly, she might not be able to return.

It was almost 9 a.m. She began to feel tense. The next hour might decide the rest of her life. She went outside to a waiting taxi and asked to be taken to the South China Bank on Nathan Road.

Dawn was lifting over the Chao Phraya River, still swollen from the last of the monsoon rains. Lonsdale watched as Sandy McPhee pushed the throttle and the cruiser surged forward. It cut a neat bow wave as it lifted onto a plane and flung a fantail of wash across the brown river, rocking small craft and laden barges, as well as ferries and fishing boats. People frowned at this discourtesy, but mainly expressed their displeasure in silence, for that was their way.

Only one buffeted sampan gave voice. Joseph, until then chugging placidly from his mooring, now discomforted and tossed about by the cruiser's trail, shouted at them:

'Fucking *farangs*. Lunatic bastards.'

His voice was drowned by the twin motors, and all Lonsdale and the others could see was a distant figure, shaking his fist. They laughed at the sight, and Sandy gave him the finger. Moments later they were out of view, even if the trough of waves they had created remained.

Joseph steered his way through these. He wondered about the cruiser. He had seen it late the day before as well. Some rich foreign bastards, but then if you're a tourist wanting to see the sights, why go so fast? The thought stayed in his mind, disturbing him slightly.

Further down the river, Sandy McPhee eased the throttle, and they settled down to a more sedate speed.

'No point in beating up too many sampans. Next thing we'll have the water police on our hammer,' he said.

McPhee, an Australian, was a former football star, now in his late forties. He was Lonsdale's main agent in Thailand, buying the heroin in the north, and finding couriers or freighter crews willing to take the risk; a man who prided himself on forever looking for new ways to beat federal police surveillance. He ran a bar and several massage parlours in New Phetchaburi Road, better known as The Strip, and had arranged the hire of the launch, selected the crew, and bought the guns.

'Slow down if you must,' Lonsdale said, 'but we wasted enough time yesterday. How much longer will it take?'

'Not long. A few hours.'

Lonsdale looked at him with surprise. McPhee explained, 'We didn't waste time yesterday. We eliminated the most likely areas. There's a hell of a lot of canals—this city's not called the Venice of the East for nothing, but I know the places to look. If these two are on the *klongs*, there'll be talk. We'll soon learn about it. If they're here, we'll have 'em before lunchtime.'

Carmichael sat in the trishaw and watched the doors of the bank open. A cluster of waiting people went in. A taxi arrived and a woman in an elegant trouser suit, wearing colourful butterfly glasses and stylish hat, paid the fare and entered the bank. She carried an attaché case and walked with an air of assurance, as if she possessed a sizable account and would be welcomed inside the Victorian facade with its grandiose and rather pretentious portal.

Teresa had not noticed him, so determined was she to arrive in style and not allow a moment of nervousness, not even a hint of hesitation. She swept inside, steeling herself to the role, hanging on to the character she had lain awake and created in the night. It was a sort of Sloane Ranger, one of those haughty, naughty Chelsea females whom the British tabloids loved and everyone else hated: money in the family, probably a Royal in the bed now and then, a 1990s younger version of Lady Bracknell was how she saw it, even if Oscar Wilde would have been upset. She had to grab hold of something, because already she knew what an ordeal it was going to be, and how easily any sign of nerves or fear could cause disaster.

So she looked neither right nor left but went autocratically and briskly down the marble stairs, deliberately disregarding the surveillance cameras. She pressed the bell and the instant her own face appeared on the TV monitor she was asked to indent her reference number, which she did with an air of impatience—sticking grimly to the script, acting the role—giving the impression it was all a dreadful bore. When the massive door unlocked, she entered in a manner that suggested she knew the place and visited regularly and, while a part of her consciousness recognised that it was the same custodian and clerk, the Sloane Ranger character she had adopted allowed no such recognition. When she gave the password, *Chiengmalan*, it was with a subtle air of irritation, a hint of how dare they ask her such inane questions, and she watched superciliously while the clerk typed into his computer, the file reference was formulated, and the custodian frowned and approached. This was the moment she knew had to come, the one which had kept her awake a large part of the night, and for which she had searched her mind and created the character.

'Madam, there is a problem,' the custodian said, deferentially, in English.

'No problem,' Tess said, like a duchess. 'I know that two keys are required. I have them both here.'

She produced the keys from her handbag, and handed them to him, as if bestowing a favour. She felt that he studied her for a long time, before he accepted them. In fact, her inner-controlled mind told her it was only seconds; he did not expect this, hence there was a brief surprise and a hesitation. Then he took the keys and gave them to two guards, who brought the deposit box. During this procedure she deliberately looked around with a contrived arrogance, somehow aware the clerk and the custodian were watching her curiously, and she therefore showed not the slightest interest in the proceedings until the box was taken into the same private cubicle and she was invited to enter. When she did so, it was with an assumed indifference, and the guard bowed and handed her the two keys, then went out and shut the door.

It was only when she was finally alone that Tess was able to release the breath she had held throughout, and to prepare herself for the next

326

moment of stress. She fitted the two keys. The feeling of tension was unbearable. She turned the keys and lifted the heavy metal lid of the deposit box.

It was almost an anticlimax. She sighed with a relief that made her realise the extent of her fear. The safe-deposit box was exactly as they had left it, crammed with an uncountable, inordinate number of American dollar bills.


Ben was on edge, and although he liked Joseph, there were times when he wished he was alone. Like now.

'Hong Kong time is 9.30, boss.'

'Yes, Joseph, I know.'

'Teresa, she finish the business soon. Be on her way back.'

Joseph had no real idea of what 'the business' was, and Ben had not the slightest intention of enlightening him.

'She doesn't leave until the Cathay Pacific flight at 1330. That's in four hours time.'

'You miss her like crazy, I think.'

'I'll be glad to see her,' Ben said, in what he imagined was the understatement of the year.

Out on the *klong* a luxury cruiser went slowly past.

'Pretty soon you guys have to quit Bangkok,' Joseph said. 'I get a real bad feeling it won't be long before Lee baby and her friends find you.'

Ben was about to reply; instead his gaze held on the craft. 'What would something like that be doing in this backwater?'

'Maybe tourists.'

'You don't sound convinced, Joseph.'

'Most tourists don't come round these parts. I seen that boat before. Out on the river, couple of hours ago, going like hell.'

'Slow enough now. Someone's taking a look at this house.'

Ben could see the glint of sunlight on binoculars.

'Developers come along the *klongs*, to look for land. Could be anyone. Just the same, we stay inside, eh, where nobody see us.'

They both felt relieved as the luxury craft picked up speed and vanished around the bend in the canal.

'I think we'll get the hell out of here,' Ben said. He had a distinctly uneasy feeling about the motor cruiser.

'Good thinking, boss,' Joseph agreed. 'You pack, I'll clear up. Be on our way in a few minutes.'


Teresa summoned the guards, saw them return the box and she completed the formalities by signing that the contents had been as expected, that it had been locked by her, and she had witnessed it being replaced in position in the vault. She felt exhilarated. It had worked perfectly. She nodded brusque thanks; it would not be in the character role she had adopted to show any particular gratitude, and certainly no elation. The main door opened electronically for her, and she made her way up the marble staircase to street level. Her attaché case was heavy with bundles of notes.

The heat of the morning was steamy, after the air-conditioning below. She paused between the fluted columns, as if to accustom herself to the change of temperature; in fact her eyes were checking the street.

It was then that she registered Carmichael, sitting in the trishaw directly across the street. He was gazing intently at her.


Down the *klong*, near a busy floating fruit market, one of the men McPhee had hired went ashore and asked questions. He came back excited. He murmured to McPhee, who translated it for Lonsdale.

'There's talk about a couple—a bloke and a girl, both *farangs*—who've been staying in a love house round here. A short-time joint, hired by the hour, but they've been there for days.'

'How far away?'

'Take us a couple of minutes.'

They went carefully along the canal.

Lonsdale got a feeling of absolute conviction the moment he saw the small stilt house. It was relatively private, no immediate neighbours although there were other bamboo houses nearer the *klong* market. A motorised sampan was tied up to steps that led from a tiny wooden porch. He studied the place through powerful field glasses, but could see nothing. Certainly someone was in residence; it was important not to alarm them. The cruiser was far too slow, the engines in neutral, the vessel just drifting past. Lonsdale, in the shadow of the deck canopy so he could not be recognised, gestured to McPhee who moved the throttle forward, and they picked up speed until they were out of sight around a bend. A short way ahead they saw a derelict jetty. McPhee pulled in there, and two of the men he had hired jumped ashore with automatic rifles.

They started running along the bank, heading back towards the house. Moments later, those aboard the cruiser heard shooting. McPhee slammed the boat into reverse then once clear of the jetty they churned towards the sound of the shots.

• • •

It was Teresa's feeling of triumph that almost brought about her undoing. The achievement, the thrill of success, made the shock all the greater when she realised she was staring directly at Carmichael. Even more alarmingly, he was studying her. Something about the way she had paused, her frozen stance in reaction to his presence, had alerted him. She could sense him speculating—about to start wondering. She had a split second to make up her mind.

She headed directly across the street towards him. Without realising it, she had adopted a limp. Too late she wondered if he had seen her enter the bank, sweeping in as if she owned the place; the limp was established and could not be changed now.

'Sir,' she called to him. 'Sir!'

Eddie Carmichael got out of the trishaw as she reached him. About to be suspicious, he was suddenly confronted by her. She thrust out her hand and shook his vigorously. In fluent Greek she asked if he was the man from the travel agency.

'What?' he said, bemused and not understanding a word.

In another burst of Greek, she asked wasn't he the man from the agency? Surely he spoke Greek? If not, what was he doing here like this?

To Carmichael it was complete and utter gibberish, his initial curiosity thoroughly dismantled by this aggressive approach, the strong handshake, the foreign language. The bloody woman was mad. Who the hell did she think he was?

'Sorry,' he said, 'I don't know what you're on about. I don't understand a single flaming word.'

She summoned up her most atrocious and fractured accent. 'I am Aliki Hadjidakis. You knowing my name?'

'Aleeky who?'

'Hadjidakis,' she said, as gruffly as she could. 'You are here for me waiting, yes?'

'Me?'

'You are Mister Georgio Sismaniis of the American Express?'

'No.'

'No? You must be.'

'I've never bloody heard of him,' Carmichael said.

'You are not for the touristica?'

'No.'

'Are you sure?' Tess stared at him accusingly.

'I'm bloody positive. Sorry, lady, you made a mistake.'

When she appeared not to understand, he said loudly and slowly, as if to someone dim-witted: 'You—make—mistake.'

'Mr Andreas in Salonika, you know him?'

'No.'

He was becoming angry. Tess was delighted. She continued, 'But he arrange I meet here with you. Mister Sismaniis.'

'Look, stuff off.'

'Beg pardon?'

'Get lost.'

'But I am lost.'

Carmichael had forgotten his first moment of speculation. He just wanted to get rid of this oddity.

'Please, you show me—American Express, where?'

'Uptown.' Carmichael jerked a thumb in the general direction. 'That way. Now excuse me—'

'Ahh, that way,' she said. '*Efcharisto*! Thanking you, sir. That way. *Efcharisto*.'

She concluded with a profuse stream of Greek, which seemed as if she was gratefully thanking him, but in fact she was nodding and smiling while she called him a two-faced pig ignorant son of a bitch, gesticulating happily all the while. She finally limped away as a relieved Carmichael got back into the trishaw.

Tess wanted to laugh, or run, and knew that she could do neither. As she turned the corner, and safely out of his sight, a cruising cab came past. She hailed it, and ran to where it stopped. She got into the air-conditioned taxi with relief, and said to the driver in Cantonese, 'I'll book

333

you for the whole morning, okay? The first stop is the Chase Manhattan Bank.'

A few minutes later Carmichael used his mobile, and made a call to Helene Lee in Bangkok. 'Nothing here,' he reported, and asked complainingly if he was expected to sit outside the bank the whole bloody day.

'You stay there until I tell you otherwise,' Helene said. She promised to call him if there was any news from Lonsdale, who also had a mobile phone aboard the boat.

It was when he hung up that Eddie Carmichael remembered the Greek woman's limp, and tried to recall, when she had first entered the bank, whether she had limped then or not.

Joseph was the first to see them. While Ben was collecting both his and Teresa's clothes and packing, Joseph went to lock the back door. He heard voices, glanced out, and saw the two men with rifles approaching.

'Shit,' he said, and slammed the door, as a burst of rifle fire smashed the tiny window alongside his face. He pushed home the bolt, and backed through the house. Ben was already trying to grab money and passports.

'No time, boss. That big fucking cruiser—we need a start.'

Ben knew only too well what he meant. If it

was the launch they had seen pass a few minutes earlier: they had no hope of escaping it in the open canal. They raced out the bamboo door and down the steps to the sampan. Even as Joseph pulled the starter, and the outboard caught, they heard the men with the guns smash down the rear door of the house. They threw themselves flat in the flimsy craft, as the gunmen started to shoot from the steps and bullets chipped and gouged the wood inches from their faces. Joseph managed to steer, while he turned the motor to its full revs. Already they could see the powerful launch behind them as it came in close to the stilt house and the two men leapt aboard, then it churned the waters of the *klong* as McPhee gave it full throttle.

It could only be a question of time. A few minutes more, and the cruiser could ram them, or the gunmen on deck could aim down into the sampan and kill them at close range.


Burridge had spent a frustrating and infuriating few days. There had been no word from Morgan, no trace of Ben Hammond or Teresa. He finally decided a risky move was preferable to inaction, and took a taxi to the Chakrawat market. He asked the taxidriver to wait for him, and made his way through the bustling and noisy bazaar. He saw the shop and paused, like any other tourist idling away time, to inspect the clutter of cheap trinkets in the overcrowded window. It all appeared normal. There seemed no reason for alarm. And, to give him his due, the prospect of danger had never discouraged Edward Burridge.

Above the doorway he saw the sign: PANDIT SINGH. DEALER IN FINE WARES. He tried the door. It was locked.

'Gone,' a voice said. It was a large lady with a sunny smile who emerged from an adjacent stall where sandals were for sale.

'Mr Singh? Gone where?'

'For holiday? For good? Who knows.'

'When did he go?'

'Yesterday. He locks the shop and says he's going to see his daughter.'

'Do you know where his daughter lives?'

'Near Kanchanaburi, I think. He once mention the bridge.'

'What bridge?'

'River Kwai. That bridge.'

'Oh,' Burridge said. 'But you don't know her address?'

'No.'

'Or when he'll be back?'

'Mr Singh don't say much. Keeps to himself. I know two men come to see him. One maybe Australian, one look like a Macao–Portuguese.'

'When?'

'Few days ago.'

*Blast them to hell*, Burridge thought, *it must have been before Mendoza was killed*, and he wondered how they had found out about Singh. It could not have been from Walter, because it was not information that Walter knew. He allowed no trace of concern to show on his face.

'You didn't hear what they said?'

'No. Whatever it is, he gets real worried. Each day I say good morning, and he don't hardly answer. Then, yesterday, he comes into my shop. Tells me people making trouble. He says men watch him. They won't go away. Asks me if he can leave by my side door after it's dark.'

'How could he do that, without them seeing?'

'We got a door between my shop and his. Mr Singh, he owns all this side of the street. I'm his tenant. So he can unlock the door between us, and talk to me, and the men watching don't know.'

'Did you see anyone watching his shop?'

'Sure. He's still there. Wearing baseball cap and blue shirt.'

Burridge glanced away, and saw the man loitering.

'Why don't you get rid of him? Call the police?'

'You think I'm crazy? Think I want to get

beaten up? Another one, he's waiting in the rear lane. I don't think Mr Singh is coming back.'

It was, Burridge thought, as he left his mobile phone number with her in the unlikely hope of Singh's return, yet another wretchedly disappointing day.

Without optimism, he rang Morgan in Sydney, who assured him he had talked with Nick Feraldos and asked him to co-operate— but there had been no word from Ben for days. If he chose not to call, there was absolutely nothing they could do to help.


A bullet hit the top of the outboard motor, and the ricochet went past Ben's face. If they opened up with full automatic fire, then he and Joseph were dead. But the cruiser simply increased speed and was only a hundred metres behind and closing the gap: fifty metres, then twenty, then coming alongside, when they reached a row of stilt houses, flimsy shanties that leaned against each other, where children played and swam, and women did the family wash in waist-deep water below their homes.

Ben looked up at the cruiser that had slowed to keep pace with them, dwarfing the sampan and, in that moment, he saw and recognised Lonsdale—there was absolutely no doubt it was

Lonsdale who had had Christine killed in Melbourne—glimpsed him raising a handgun to take aim. In the same instant Joseph swung the rudder sharply and the wooden craft veered towards the side of the *klong*, and ran beneath the houses. It dodged the bamboo poles that held the shanties aloft, swept past alarmed and shrieking children, Joseph steering and sweating as he tried not to hit anyone, but knowing this was the only hope—that the powerful launch could not reach them here, that the gunmen on board could not even shoot at them now, not with so many witnesses.

Ahead of them a naked mother scrubbed her infant baby. She screamed as the sampan speared towards her. Ben shut his eyes in horror. Miraculously, they missed her, but left behind them shouts of anger and outrage. Moments later they were in the middle of the neighbourhood floating market. Ignoring complaints and abuse from the fruit and fish vendors, they jostled their way through the boats, causing chaos on the barges where they were selling fried bananas and coconut milk, being yelled at by the women in their traditional straw hats on the rocking noodle sampans. There was no way the cruiser could follow them. They heard its klaxon horn, and saw it forced to reverse before it became blocked in the congestion of other craft.

'You beauty,' Ben said.

'They'll go round and wait for us at the river junction. We bought ourselves a few minutes, boss, that's all. It sure as hell ain't over yet.'

**26** 'MISS HADJIDAKIS,' THE bank manager said obsequiously. They were watching Chinese tellers counting bundles of notes as Teresa signed numerous traveller's cheques. They spoke in precise Mandarin.

'Yes, what is it, Mr Ling?'

'I compliment you. This is a very large amount of money.'

'So it should be,' Tess said.

'And why is that, ma'am?'

The bank manager was deeply impressed—with her beauty, her use of the language and, most of all, with the large transaction.

'Because,' Tess said in Aliki Hadjidakis's voice, 'I work at my job extremely hard.'

'And what sort of job is that, ma'am?'

'I am the highest paid callgirl in Athens.'

'Ahhh—,' said the manager, hopefully, but was interrupted.

'Mr Ling, please don't ask if I am free tonight. I am here on vacation.' She smiled sweetly at him, and continued to sign the various bank documents and the traveller's cheques.

'We'll cut the bastards off,' Sandy McPhee said, and although Lonsdale was furious at the way they had been outsmarted, he knew there was no way to continue the chase. And no reason to do so. At full bore they could easily catch them on the river if they tried to escape back to the city. But first there was a puzzle to solve: the girl, Teresa Martineau, had not been in the canal house, nor in the sampan. So where was she?

He told McPhee to go back and, soon afterwards, the cruiser waiting, they were inside the house. It was immediately apparent Ben Hammond had had no time to collect anything; all their belongings were still there, including a variety of passports. In the lining of one of the suitcases, he found a quantity of US dollars and an amount of baht, as well as traveller's cheques. But more than the money, it was the passports that interested him. Particularly Teresa Martineau's passports. There were several, with disparate photographs and various names and nationalities. It seemed she was a talented lady.

Now he knew why Hammond was here on the *klong*, and the woman was missing. He ran out to the cruiser and dialled his mobile telephone. After the first ring, Helene's voice answered.

'She's in Hong Kong,' Lonsdale said. 'You were right about the bank, but she's on her own. What time are today's flights back?'

Helene asked him to wait a moment while she checked a schedule, and told him there was a Cathay Pacific plane leaving Kai Tak in an hour, due to arrive in Bangkok at 3.15 pm. The next was a Thai Airways flight later in the afternoon.

'Right, here's what you do. Call Carmichael.'

'You want him on the plane?'

'No, I don't want him on the plane. I want to know if he saw her at the bank, and if not, why not? What the fuck has he been doing? I want him to go to the airport and try not to stand out like a spare prick at a wedding—to see if he can confirm she's on that Cathay flight. If not, then wait for the next departure. Or the one after, even if it's tomorrow.'

'Are you so sure of this?'

'I'm absolutely certain. She's there, and she's coming back, you can count on it. Tell Carmichael he's looking for a woman alone, and to forget the photograph; she'll be different to what he expects. She won't be travelling under her own name because her real passport is here, along with others. I think you've seriously underestimated her.'

Helene felt a surge of resentment, but kept silent. Lonsdale continued rapping out orders. 'Organise more people at the airport. Pull them off the railway station and forget about casing any more hotels. I want the biggest squad you can raise, all of them with radio communication, neatly dressed and able to pass for security personnel. No yobs or thugs. Get it? I want people all over that bloody air terminal. I want it wrapped up so tight, a fucking ant couldn't get in unnoticed.'

Carmichael knew, after a phone call from Helene Lee, that he was not the flavour of the month. He had been thinking deeply, trying ever since to remember his encounter with the Greek tourist, and had come to the dismaying conclusion that she had not limped when she arrived at the bank, and that he, who prided himself on his ability to pass for anyone from a businessman to a beggar, from a pilot to a priest, with the ability to change his appearance to fit every role, had been cleverly dudded.

The woman had been Teresa Martineau.

Instinctively he knew this, so when the phone in his pocket rang, and it was Helene calling from Bangkok with Lonsdale's news, it was also an unhappy confirmation of the fact. She had duped him. Even worse, Helene did not take long to realise this. The moment Eddie began to explain that perhaps she was posing as a Greek and to describe the way she looked, it was patently obvious he had seen her, and been outwitted.

Helene cursed him and called him a useless and gullible nerd. Since he was trying to help, doing his best to make up for his lapse, and the English girl had been convincingly brilliant, he thought this tirade of abuse not only unfair, but it did not augur well for a rosy future with Helene. It was perhaps time to cut his losses. He hung up on her, and switched off the mobile so she could not recall him. He thought if he was quick and lucky, he might be in time to catch Teresa Martineau at Hong Kong Airport, and put to her a private business proposition.


The barge was cumbersome and slow, with the heavy scent of a lavish funeral. It was laden with flowers being taken to the central street markets, a fragrant cargo of orchids and lotus, hibiscus, jasmine and bougainvillea. Sheltered below this canopy, almost suffocated with an abundance of incense, Ben and Joseph had done a deal, trading Joseph's sampan and outboard for a safe journey back to the city. The owner of the barge had the outboard motor stowed in the hold, and had left the sampan behind in the custody of a friend.

It would take them two hours, more than enough time to pick up the taxi and drive out to meet Teresa at the airport.

There was a warning rap on the bulkhead, and a voice called to them in Thai. Joseph replied, and told Ben there was a big cruiser in sight and fast overtaking them. They listened and soon heard its powerful motors. It was clearly travelling at full throttle. But, all of a sudden, as it seemed to be alongside the barge, the engines stopped.

'Shit,' Joseph whispered, and crossed himself. Until then, Ben had assumed he was a Buddhist.

They could hear the lap of the river, as both craft drifted side by side. A voice called. The owner of the barge replied. Ben was intently watching Joseph's face, saw the fear and tenseness replaced by relief, then heard the motors rev, and felt the barge start to rock in the churning wake as the cruiser sped away.

'They ask captain if he see sampan, with a *farang* and a Thai. Jeez, boss, gonna be quiet in this town when you guys leave.'

'Let's hope we can leave. I hope Tess is okay.'

'Anything else go wrong—maybe I have a nervous breakdown.'

Ben smiled. He moved to the tiny porthole in the bow, and risked a look. The cruiser was already far in the distance, speeding towards the silhouetted temples and the high-rise modern skyline of the city. Joseph joined him, peering out.

'Hell of a hurry, them guys.'

Ben nodded. He felt a strange disquiet.

'Maybe this Australian who knows you, he gives up.'

'Not him. He never gives up.'


Teresa was in the Sapphire Lounge, having booked a return ticket first class, when she heard the call. Among the frequent announcements of flight departures, came a soft, velvet feminine voice.

'Would Miss Teresa Martineau please go to the Cathay Pacific enquiry desk on the ground floor of the terminal immediately. Miss Martineau to the Cathay Pacific enquiry desk, please.'

She was sipping a lime juice; she almost dropped it. After a time, just when she began to think she might have been hallucinating, the call was repeated.

'Miss Teresa Martineau, will you please make contact with the Cathay Pacific desk at once. Thank you.'

The Sapphire Lounge was a deluxe and very restricted world, with spacious armchairs, courtesy phones, the day's newspapers and worldwide magazines, where passengers served themselves all manner of free drinks, and tea or coffee in china cups. There were savouries and plates of hors d'oeuvres and a discreet air of privilege; even the television sets were set at a volume that would not intrude on the tranquillity. It was on the second floor of the departure terminal; strict admission supervised by a hostess, chosen for her looks, diplomacy and charm, who took the guests' tickets, made them feel cosseted and welcome, and called them at the last moment when their flights were due to depart.

The hostess had Teresa's ticket, which now tallied with her passport in the name of Helga Gressmann. Helga had blonde hair and an accent from Bavaria to fit the role, and she wore a tiny skirt that was provocatively seductive and totally unlike the Aliki Hadjidakis who had flown in yesterday. Those who had met that original version of the Greek piano teacher were hardly likely to notice her legs, because they were bemused by the forbidding glasses, whereas those who met Helga—at least the males—could not testify to her features; they were so busy looking at the shapely legs.

Teresa had been pleased with her new role. Because of lack of time, she had been forced to buy a blonde wig, but it fitted perfectly; it had a flaxen sheen to it, and with the legs and the miniskirt, so micro it was nearly a pelmet, she felt confident and secure. But now, all of a sudden, there was a voice on the speaker calling her name.

There was no reason to panic. No-one here in this sanctuary would connect Teresa Martineau with a first-class passenger named Helga Gressmann, and yet she realised that someone was aware of her identity, and she had to find out who, and how much they knew, because it might mean a great deal when they landed at Dong Muang Airport in Bangkok. So she went to the reception desk, smiled at the attendant, said she was going to the duty-free, and walked in the direction of the escalator. Standing near it, she could look down and see the Cathay Pacific enquiry desk. That was how she saw Carmichael beside it. His eyes were everywhere, searching the terminal, but she moved back before he could look up towards her.

There were a number of things she could do. Firstly, she could ignore him, and get on the flight as Helga Gressmann. But blonde wigs and miniskirts could only create so much diversion; in the end there would be people waiting in Bangkok. She knew they would almost certainly be waiting anyway, but why give them a free kick by allowing Carmichael to telephone and alert them? Apart from which, she reminded herself, this man had been an accomplice in the savage torture and death of Walter Chen.

Teresa made her way back to the Sapphire Lounge. She asked how long before they were boarding. She had twenty minutes. She picked a courtesy telephone in the far corner of the lounge where there were no adjacent passengers to hear, dialled emergency, and asked for Detective Inspector Long. Moments later the young detective who had arrested Victor at the hotel came on the line.

'Inspector,' Tess said, accenting her voice so that he would not be able to identify her, 'at the airport departure terminal, there's one of the men who killed Walter Chen. I'll try to keep him here, but you have to get someone to him within a few minutes. Can you do that?'

'Who am I talking to?'

'That's not important. He's here, but you need to act fast. His name is Carmichael. Can you pick him up?'

She gave him Eddie Carmichael's whereabouts and description, waited only to hear the inspector had already relayed a message to radio control, then she hung up. She deliberately paused for a few moments, took a deep breath and dialled the Cathay Pacific enquiry desk.

'This is Teresa Martineau,' she said. 'You were paging me a short while ago. May I speak to whoever was asking for me?'

There was a pause, and Carmichael came on.

'Miss Martineau,' he said.

'Mr Carmichael.'

'You know my name.'

'What do you want, Mr Carmichael?'

'I'd like to meet and talk with you. I think we might be able to discuss a deal.'

'And if I was not interested, then what?'

'Then, lady,' Eddie said, 'you'd be in deep shit. There'd be some unfriendly people waiting there in Bangkok for Aliki Hadjidakis.'

'And who's she?' Tess asked. 'I've never heard of her.'

She started to become aware of the distant police sirens. She looked out the window and saw two squad cars coming into the airport. Behind them, more followed. It was already too late for him to escape.

'I'll tell you who's in deep shit, Mr Carmichael,' she said. 'You killed a decent man, and you have to answer for that. If Victor Mendoza used the knife, if he killed Walter Chen, you stood there and acquiesced. You're equally guilty. Nobody, inside or out of jail, is going to like you. And be warned, we're monitoring you, Mr Carmichael. The police have the terminal surrounded, and if you use the phone to warn Helene Lee in Bangkok, you'll be in a cell for the rest of your life.'

It was a complete bluff, but Carmichael was

intimidated. Tess realised it and hung up. She went to the window where she could watch the last of the police cars converging on the terminal. In the background, she became aware they were calling her flight.

There were over thirty of them. Helene had done well; most looked remarkably like airport security guards.

'Forget the photos,' Lonsdale said. 'Tear them up right now. She's not going to look like that, and it'll only confuse you. She could be a redhead, or a blonde, she might even be dressed as a nun. The point I want to make is that when this plane lands you detain *any* woman who is travelling alone. I don't care if she looks old, or is wearing Thai clothes, or in a wheelchair. We know she's on her own; we know she's smart; she walked past some of you yesterday and you never spotted her.

'Well, today it's going to be different. I repeat, she's on her own, so don't overlook anyone. Make what excuse you like; say you want to check her passport, or you suspect contraband or drugs. Work in pairs. If anyone protests or tries to run, you grab her.'

'But what if it's someone completely innocent?' one asked.

'I don't care if it's someone innocent. Every

woman on her own. If it turns out to be the wrong party, we can apologise later.'

The men and women, looking like an efficient security squad, moved off, and Lonsdale went to join Helene. They watched the arrival information board, as the letters and numbers shuffled to announce the Cathay Pacific flight from Hong Kong had landed on schedule.

'If she's on this plane,' he said, 'we've got her.'

27 TESS SIPPED HER champagne. A bulky man in the seat beside her seemed acutely aware of her, and she had the impression he hoped it was his lucky day. He had already monopolised the cabin staff, keeping them busy stowing his jacket, his suit in its zippered bag, and a number of parcels, making these peremptory requests in a loud English voice, with an accent she mentally classified as bombastic Birmingham. The thought made her smile; his assessing glance saw the smile and was encouraged.

'Going to Bangkok?'

Before she could reply, he said: 'I live there. My firm builds shopping plazas. Planning some sightseeing?'

She looked blankly at him.

'I am sorry,' she said in German, 'I do not speak English.'

She had bought a German magazine that morning, thinking it might be useful. Now she took it from her bag, and began to read.

The man shrugged. He asked the senior flight attendant for a *Financial Times*, and when she apologised that there was none aboard, he accepted the *International Herald-Tribune* with bad grace. Later, he was disagreeable over a delay in bringing him a large scotch, and complained about the meal which Teresa thought was excellent. He sighed constantly and seemed generally disgruntled.

He told a man in the seat across the aisle that he normally flew British Airways, and intended to do so in future. He didn't trust these wog airlines, he said, and announced he was chairman and managing director of Royalson's, who had built the largest shopping centre in South-East Asia.

He said Thailand was a bastard of a place to live in, but thankfully once the contract was up he could return to his manor house at Stoke-on-Trent, near Birmingham. Teresa, trying to sleep, at least had the satisfaction of knowing her reckoning on his accent was not far out. About thirty miles.

Poor old Stoke, she reflected, it deserved better. Throughout the three-hour flight she would gladly have requested a change of seats but, in the era of frequent flyer points and upgrading, the first-class cabin was full.

It was with relief she heard the announcement of their descent towards Bangkok airport, and the news they would be landing in fifteen minutes.


Ben was aware, from the moment he glimpsed Mick Lonsdale's face, that they were in deep trouble. He could only assume Chen had known more than Burridge had led him to believe, that Lonsdale's name had been extorted from him before his murder, and that after this Helene Lee had made contact with the Melbourne drug dealer. However it had happened, the hunt for them had now entered a new and potentially far more dangerous phase.

He sat in the taxi, parked anonymously among hundreds of vehicles in the airport's public carpark, while Joseph went to find out if the flight was on time. During the wait, he tried to predict how much they knew, and the way in which it might influence their actions. For instance, neither he nor Tess had doubted the airport would be under surveillance, but her pose as the Greek music teacher had clearly been adequate to pass muster. He knew this because she had called a number belonging to a friend of Joseph's late last night, and left a message that Helga would be visiting as planned. It meant she had arrived safely, all was well, and she would use the alternative passport she had taken with her on the return Cathay Pacific flight.

But all that was yesterday. Then they had been watching for two people. Today they knew Ben was alone; therefore Teresa was also alone. Lonsdale would have headed back to the house on the *klong* when they escaped his pursuit in the floating market. It was inconceivable he would not have found her assortment of passports, all of them with visas, and drawn the obvious conclusion that she had not left the country for long. Certainly not permanently. Not leaving behind most of her belongings, as well as so much money and those passports.

Ben had good cause to know Mick Lonsdale was no fool. He was as cunning as a rat—and he had been in a hell of a hurry out there on the river, to return to the city. The disquiet Ben felt then had grown into increasing concern. He had a feeling events were out of control, and there was no way Teresa could be warned.

He was certain she was in great danger.


The immigration officer scrutinised her passport. He studied her features, compared her with the photograph, thumbed through the pages and checked the computer to determine if she was listed there. He stamped her visa, and nodded a welcome to Thailand. She thanked him, and his gaze lingered a moment on the long tanned legs and the tiny skirt, as she walked towards the luggage carousel.

The odious passenger from Stoke-on-Trent was already there, waiting with a luggage trolley. Their priority bags would come off before the others. Tess had only a slim case to collect, one she could have taken with her in the cabin, but had sent it in order not to be the first to exit the customs barrier. She felt it more expedient to be part of a group, although there was no reason to expect trouble. No-one had seen her leave, nor could they know she would be on this flight. It should be a routine appraisal, with them using the same photograph, and she felt sure her new identity was different enough to pass scrutiny.

Beyond customs control she could see a small crowd waiting to greet arrivals. She looked for Ben, although aware he would be waiting outside the terminal as arranged, concealed in Joseph's taxi. It was the expectation of seeing him that made her hope he might be there, and the casual scrutiny caused her to notice a Thai man, talking busily into a two-way radio. He seemed to be looking in her direction. She felt a first hint of unease. Showing no trace of alarm, but with great care, she looked around. She encountered the gaze of another Thai, similarly equipped, and clearly intent on her. It was then she began to realise something was wrong.

The carousel commenced to move, and the

first of the suitcases tumbled onto the luggage conveyer.

They looked like a security squad being briefed outside the arrival terminal, but Joseph was street smart, and he saw the briefing was conducted by a *farang*. This he found strange, so he loitered and tried to watch. It was difficult to move close. They all had mobiles or two-way radios, and they seemed to be in touch with others inside the building. There was a lot of talking, and a sense of excitement. Several of the group went into the terminal. The *farang* was joined by a superb-looking woman. Joseph was instantly filled with lust and admiration, then a moment later he recognised Helene Lee.
'Oh fuck,' he whispered, and started running.

She knew there was no way out of this. Beyond customs, at least three others, all of them with the same mobile communications, were watching her progress and reporting. She picked up her case at the same time as the man who had sat beside her collected the last of his luggage. He had a trolley piled high with matching leather cases. She nodded sociably to him. He loftily ignored her. She tucked her arm in his, and smiled at his stunned expression.

'Sorry I was unsociable on board,' she said. 'May I join you?'

'No.' He was blunt and uncompromising. 'You may not. My wife's waiting.'

'Well, tough,' Tess kept smiling, as she placed her small case on the trolley, and tightly gripped on his arm, 'but I'm afraid I insist.'

'What the devil is this,' he wanted to know.

'Just relax,' Tess told him.

'Be buggered. What the hell is going on? You said you were a kraut, and couldn't speak English.'

He was indignant, offended, and about to start shouting at her. She knew this was the last hope she had. Her grip tightened on his arm.

'Shut up,' she said, softly and vehemently. 'Shut your stupid fat mouth and smile—or I'll yell cocaine. They'll strip search you.'

'What . . .?'

He was aghast, convinced he was being used for a crime. She made herself smile at him, much as she disliked the smug but puzzled face. She stopped the trolley and faced him. Her every instinct now alerted her that they were looking for someone alone, that they had pin-pointed her and a few other solitary women, therefore this was the only way.

'You are going to smile and be friendly, Mr Royalson from Stoke-on-Trent, or whatever your name is. You're going to pretend we're together. If you don't, believe me, I'll swear you're bringing in drugs. They'll detain you, take your clothes off, and put a torch up your arse. And when we meet your wife, I'll tell her how you had me in the first-class loo, and how you pulled my pants down and we joined the mile-high club.'

For a moment she thought he was going to hit her, and the bluff would fail.

Joseph drove the cab as close as he dared to the terminal entrance. He had his sign switched off, and to any observer he seemed to be alone. Ben was out of sight in the back seat. Joseph could see Helene and the *farang*, the one Ben called Lonsdale, with a Thai who was busily talking on his mobile and explaining something to them.

'What's happening, Joseph?'

'Nothing good, boss.'

Ben sat up. Joseph had an old baseball cap in the glove box. He tossed it to him. It was at that moment, as Ben put the cap on and fitted a pair of dark glasses, that they saw a large European man come out of the terminal, with a woman in a miniskirt clinging to his arm. In what seemed like slow motion, another woman crossed from the carpark and approached. Ben placed her as English, middle-aged and certainly showing signs of annoyance. Suddenly she began to shout. Then beyond the trio, Ben saw Helene Lee turn and recognise one of the three people. At this same moment came realisation.

'Christ Almighty, it's Tessa.'

'Where?'

'There, in the short skirt. The blonde. Go!'

The engine had been idling throughout. Now as Joseph hit the accelerator, Ben leaned over and touched the horn. It signalled Tess, who held tight to her handbag and ran towards the taxi. Ben had the back door open, and she dived inside. As Joseph picked up speed, the door swung wildly, hitting one of the Thai watchers who tried to grab her. Ben reached across her body and managed to pull the door shut, as he saw a tangle of legs and pantihose, and a blonde wig that had come askew like a hairpiece in a high wind.

Behind them, men and women with mobiles and two-way radios came running out of the terminal. Ben turned to see this, as Teresa disentangled herself and climbed from the floor, looking out the rear window, her face close to his as they watched Helene and Lonsdale run towards a limousine. They were accompanied by several of their squad. Lonsdale jumped into the driving seat, and the others climbed in the back. He reversed recklessly, and set out in pursuit. Joseph picked up speed, nearly hitting an empty tourist bus leaving the departure terminal. It blasted a loud outraged complaint.

Ben watched the receding limousine, now aware of Tess's warm cheek touching his. He pressed his lips against it, and she turned her face and kissed him on the mouth. Joseph glanced at them in the mirror.

'He's missed you, doll. Been real worried. Real unhappy.'

'Shut up and drive,' Ben said.

'Him a *farang* driver; got no hope. You guys hang on tight.' He laughed at his own wit. 'I mean hang on tight to each other.'

Joseph spun the wheel, and overtook a procession of two other taxis trailing an oxcart as they headed out on the feeder road towards the airport expressway. An approaching car had to take evasive action and almost went off the road. They glimpsed a frightened driver shouting abuse, but went past him too fast to hear the words. Ben took his eyes from Teresa's for a moment to glance back. The limousine was stuck way back, behind the taxis and the oxcart.

They reached the expressway ramp. Joseph went down it at speed, no thought of giving way to the stream of fast-moving traffic. Angry drivers forced to hit their brakes to avoid a collision sounded horns in furious protest. Joseph gave them a derisive wave, and began lane hopping, way over the speed limit, taking risks. He almost collided with a three-wheel *tuk-tuk*, which he said was not only illegal on the expressway, but endangering all their lives. Tess put her face against Ben's shoulder, and tried not to look. The notion of ending up a road statistic after all she had been through did not enthral her.

'Did it work?' Ben asked. 'The keys?'

'Like a charm.'

'No problems?'

'Only one.'

She explained about Carmichael, and their street encounter. By now they had lost the pursuit, and to her relief had left the highway exit at Ratchawithi Road, and were proceeding at a sedate pace in the north-west section of the city. She was able to open her bulky handbag and allow Ben to see the notes and traveller's cheques crammed inside.

He told her it was just as well; the *klong* house was gone, and with it all their belongings, passports, and a lot of money. It seemed, once again, they had only the clothes they were wearing. Tess's small suitcase had been left behind on the trolley. She thought about the man from Stoke-on-Trent and smiled. His astounded British wife had taken one look at her clinging to his arm, stared at her legs and short skirt, and had begun shouting at him, demanding to know what sort of floozy he'd picked up this time.

'What's funny?'

'I'll tell you later,' she said. 'In bed.'

Joseph heard this. He turned, oblivious to the traffic, and said, 'Only place that's safe tonight. You gotta squeeze into that single bed again. Gonna be real hard.'

Tess, unsure if he meant the blatant double entendre, stifled a laugh. She gave Ben a glance, in which her eyes sparkled and sent a message that she assuredly hoped it would be so.


The river police received a call from a fishing boat. Their nets had pulled in the body of a man near the mouth of the Chao Phraya River in the Gulf of Thailand. He was an Indian, whose throat had been cut, and could they please collect the corpse as it was seriously impeding them using the nets to meet their daily quota.

The police surgeon estimated the man had been killed early the previous day. Both the internal and external carotid arteries were severed and the body weighed down with chain. It had been a hasty untidy job, since most of the chain had untangled, and the corpse was rising to the surface when caught in the fishing nets. He said that in view of the decay and the nauseous gases given off by the bloated body, the catch should be impounded and destroyed, but was told it had already been delivered and was on sale at the fish market. The surgeon reminded himself not to eat fish under any circumstances, for the next few days.

The Indian's fingerprints were on file. He had a number of criminal convictions for petty crimes, receiving being the main offence, but was also linked to a drug network. He was swiftly identified as Pandit Singh, with an address in Chakrawat, and an hour later the police were there making enquiries. The two men watching the shop vanished during this, but two replacements came back later, after the squad car had gone. It was their reappearance, as much as the shock news of Singh's death, that decided the large lady who leased the sandal shop. She rang the phone number Burridge had left with her, and told him what had happened.

28 EDWARD BURRIDGE WAS not surprised by the news of Singh's death. It made it all the more urgent to find Ben Hammond and Teresa, and so far there had been a singular lack of response to his appeal for help from Howard Morgan. On an impulse he looked up and dialled the number he had listed for Nick Feraldos. He heard it ring for a time, and was about to give up when a woman's voice answered. She sounded so sleepy he checked his watch in case he had woken her. By his calculation it was only early evening in Sydney.

'Jane speaking,' she said.

'Mrs Feraldos?'

'Yes. Who is it?'

'I'm sorry if I disturbed you. I need to talk to your husband.'

'He's on duty. Till midnight. Then I'm on shift. Phone him in the morning.'

'Mrs Feraldos, I'm calling from Bangkok. This is important.'

She instantly sounded wide awake, as she asked, 'Who am I talking to?'

'My name is Burridge. Edward Burridge.'

'You're the one,' she said with sudden heat, 'the bastard who's made such a mess of things for Ben.'

'No, Mrs Feraldos. Listen to me. I'm trying to help him.' He was determined to keep his temper, no matter what she said.

'That's not what I hear. Nick's checked on you.'

'Has he, by God?'

'At Ben's request. That's how we know that you tell lies, Sir whatever-your-title-is Burridge. You give false phone numbers where you're not known, and places that don't exist.'

'Mrs Feraldos, will you listen? I personally gave those orders. I told Paris they didn't know me. I told my contact in New York to say it was a delicatessen. If your husband stopped to think—he'd know there are times when we have to work covertly. But something has gone wrong. Not exactly my fault; certainly not Ben's. I have to find him or he's going to walk into a bullet. Please, are you still there? Are you listening?'

'I'm listening,' she said.

'Your husband is my only chance. If Ben calls him—'

'If Ben calls him again, Nick will repeat what

he said last time—that you're a liar playing some double game, and not to trust you an inch.'

'Will you try to convince him otherwise?'

'I don't know,' Jane said.

'Will you try?'

'What are you asking me?'

'If he should telephone, tell him not to go near the Indian's shop in Chakrawat.'

'Where?'

'The market. He'll know where you mean. Tell him the man is dead. They cut his throat and dumped him in the river.'

He heard her intake of breath, and continued, 'There are men watching the place, for one purpose only. To do the same to him. Tell him that I suspect Lonsdale is here in Thailand . . .'

'Lonsdale,' she interrupted sharply, 'Mick Lonsdale?'

'Yes. So that ups the stakes considerably. I really must reach him, Mrs Feraldos, but I'm not necessarily asking you to trust me.'

'What are you asking, Sir Edward?'

'To write down this phone number. All you need do is give it to him—with the news about the Indian, and Lonsdale. After that, Ben makes his own choice whether he wants to talk to me.'

He thought he sounded reasonable. Unless he could find them, he might as well convene a meeting to admit his whole scheme had ended in disaster. No matter what might happen later, he needed Ben and Teresa Martineau alive, needed them urgently, and now.

'If we talk, he can decide if he trusts me,' he continued. 'Does that seem in any way unreasonable to you, Mrs Feraldos?'

When he put the phone down, he felt more confident than he had in days. It was lucky she had answered, not her husband. She was a nursing sister, and nurses were a damn sight softer touch and a lot more sympathetic than cops.


They had made love, trying to be as silent as possible because of the flimsy walls, but not actually succeeding because, when they reached a blissful orgasm and lay quietly together, they could hear Joseph and his nubile girl going at it, bedsprings squeaking rhythmically in the adjoining room. Tess got the giggles, and that was the end of romance for the night. When they found sleep impossible, she told him about the airport, the realisation they were searching for a woman on her own, and how she had coerced the man from Stoke into being the foil she needed for those precious seconds of indecision which helped her to escape.

Ben, in turn, told her about the narrow shave in the *klong*, and about recognising Lonsdale. It was Teresa who persuaded him to consider that this whole matter had moved up a gear; that if the man who ordered the killing of Christine Duncan was in the same city, even more than that, had hunted Ben and been with Helene Lee in charge of the squad at the airport, then it was time to seek help. And that meant making contact with Burridge.

'I don't know where the hell he is,' Ben said.

Teresa told him that perhaps there was a way to solve that. If she knew Burridge, he would have been leaving messages all over the place. At dawn, because of the time difference, he should call his friend Nick.

The telephone rang at eight the next morning, but it was a wrong number. Nick cooked himself some breakfast, expecting Jane back from the hospital at any moment. It rang again just as the eggs were poached to perfection. He turned off the stove and grabbed the receiver. It was a market researcher who asked if he was Nicholas Feraldos and said that she was Sandra. She did not volunteer a second name. She asked if Nicholas could please spare a few moments of his very valuable time to answer some really simple questions.

'I'm sorry. I'm rather busy.'

'We're all busy, Nicholas, but this is important research. A valuable survey. It's not something you can shrug off. We're putting the question to men—how do they feel about wearing condoms?'

'How we feel about it?' Nick asked incredulously.

'That's right,' the bright voice said. 'Would you say that wearing a condom enhances your sex life?'

'Enhances—?'

'Does it inspire and amplify your performance?'

'You mean this is important market research?'

'Absolutely.'

'You want my honest opinion?'

'Your honesty is vital to our study.'

'Well, in that case—I find wearing a condom about as much fun as washing my feet with a pair of socks on. However, if I was playing around, poking everything that moved, then I'd wear one out of fear. I hope that helps your really important survey. Have a nice day.'

He put the phone down. As he sat at the table to eat his toast and congealing eggs, it rang again.

'Christ Almighty,' he shouted, lifting the receiver as he said it.

'Is that who's running your new answering service,' said Ben's voice, loud and clear, as though speaking from nearby, instead of a street telephone in Bangkok.

'Thank God,' Nick said. 'Jane was sure you'd

372

call. She said I should shut up for once, and listen.'

'Did she? Tell her it was Teresa who said I should call.'

'Did she?'

'Insisted. Said it was the only way to find Burridge.'

'She's right. Sounds as if they might get along.'

'I think so,' Ben said.

'Are you two okay?'

'Well, apart from the last few days being the biggest fiasco since the fall of the Roman Empire, I suppose you could say we're both still in one piece. Which, around here, is something.'

'I've got a phone number where you can reach him,' Nick said. 'He persuaded Jane he's on the level.'

'Jane has a soft heart. She'd give money to Christopher Skase if he came collecting for the Majorcan refugee fund.'

Nick laughed and said, 'She would, too. Ben, listen. He told her two things she believes. Your Indian contact is dead, and Mick Lonsdale's in Bangkok. Her message is—Mr Burridge may be a thoroughgoing bastard, but you need him.'

'That's what Tess says. Let's have the number.'

• • •

A line of monks went past in sandals and saffron robes. Brown-skinned, heads completely shaven, they looked like young Buddha images, and moved with composed ascetic grace. Tess and Joseph stood watching them outside the walled splendour of the Grand Palace while, across the street, Ben talked on one of the public telephones. She could see by his stance and gestures he was incensed; if the body language suggested anger, his raised voice confirmed it.

'Big row, T'rees.' It was Joseph's newest version of her name.

'I would say so.'

'This the guy who's gonna help you?'

She shrugged to avoid an answer. She had persuaded Ben to make the contact, and it seemed Jane Feraldos felt the same way, which pleased her—but it did not appear too promising so far. As she looked again at the procession of robed devouts, Joseph said 'I used to think I might be one of them.'

'A monk?' She smiled. 'Doesn't sound like you, Joseph.'

'Nice, easy life. You walk round with a bowl—people give the offerings. Makes them feel good—earns brownie points with Buddha. And if you sit at anyone's table, they have to feed you.'

'What about the strict rules, Joseph?'

'What rules?'

'No sex, no money, no alcohol, no talking to a woman or you must do penance—plus your head and your eyebrows shaved daily.'

'No eyebrows,' Joseph said thoughtfully. 'You're right. My other idea's better. I open a massage parlour.'

'You're incorrigible,' she said, laughing.

'What's it mean?'

She switched into colloquial Thai, to explain he was perverse and unrepentant, a bit hopeless, in fact. Joseph seemed not displeased at the description. He said his aunt who was a fortune teller had once studied the leaves in his teacup and told him he was a bit hopeless.

Ben walked across the street to join them. He was shaking his head with disbelief.

'He's furious. The bastard is livid. He says it's all our fault.'

'Good God.'

'Claims we acted with irresponsible haste leaving Hong Kong, then made an appointment and never turned up, which left him at the American Express office looking like a dummy. I told him he looked like a dummy most of the time.'

'Probably not your most diplomatic remark.'

'Ohh, I dunno. It seemed appropriate to me.'

'Was that when you were shouting on the phone?'

'No, that came later—when we started to really insult each other.'

'You mean it got worse?'

'It got better. He called me an aggravating Australian arsehole, so I called him a poncing old pommy prick.'

'Oh, nice,' Tess said.

'I told him we've had a gutful. We're ready to pack it in.'

'What did he say?'

'That it seemed a pity, when we were so close to earning big bucks, and to tell you that you'd meet your father two days from now.'

Tess studied him carefully.

'You mean he's persuaded you to do something?'

'He's made a suggestion.'

'Like what?'

'It sort of depends a bit on Joseph.'

'How?

She looked puzzled. Ben was hesitant. Joseph was surprised, and already looking slightly nervous.

'On me?' he said.

'What's Joseph got to do with it?'

'Well, that's the awkward part.' He avoided her searching gaze and said to Joseph, 'I don't know how you're going to feel about this, Joe.'

'You tell me what it is—then I can tell you

how I feel,' the Thai cabbie replied with elementary logic.

'I hate to ask, but we need a really big favour.'

'Is it dangerous?' Joseph looked decidedly more nervous.

'Of course not,' Ben said.

Teresa was not sure why she knew, but she realised at once that he was lying.

29 THE ORIENTAL HAD colourful gardens along the Chao Phraya River, and historical links with Somerset Maugham and Joseph Conrad, both of whom had once stayed there. The legend of their visit was carefully nurtured, and some of their letters, newspaper reports of their arrival, and the visitors' books they signed were kept in display cases in the panelled hall. The Oriental preserved an air of nineteenth-century elegance, and while the Siam Inter-Continental could boast of its large grounds, pagoda architecture and miniature zoo, and other hotel chains built cathedral-sized vestibules and towering monolithic palaces for the twenty-first century, the Oriental remained smugly inviolate and genteel, with its river rooms offering the best view in town.

Joseph sat in his taxi outside the entrance, feeling terrified. He had his sign switched off, and was trying to read a newspaper, attempting to look like a cabbie waiting for his customer.

After a wait of several hours he saw her get out of a taxi that drew up in front of the main steps. He desperately wanted to drive off and forget Ben and T'rees; it would be the smart, safest thing to do. Yet, almost to his surprise, he found himself hurrying to intercept Helene Lee before she entered the hotel.

'Miss Lee?'

She turned at the sound of her name. What a great-looking babe, he thought; what a pity she was about as deadly as a cobra. She looked at him. This was the real scary moment. Would she recognise him from the airport? Ben had been sure she wouldn't; there had been only a glimpse, and their attention had been focused on T'rees, but the next few moments would tell. And T'rees, who had argued and been angry because she didn't want him to do this, had said she believed it was a danger.

'You Miss Lee?'

'Yes, what is it?' Helene showed no sign of recognition.

He felt an instant of relief, then summoned up his most eager smile, and knew he must make it realistic.

'Lady, what a bit of luck. I look all over town. I go to hotel where you stay. I call your room number—'

'What are you talking about?' She beckoned him away from the steps. Guests were going past, and the doorman was within earshot. 'Who are you? What do you want?'

'You remember me,' Joseph said.

'No. What's your name?'

'Yung Li Hok Dan. Taxidriver. Honest, you don't remember?'

'You tell me,' she said impatiently.

'Few days ago—maybe five days—you ask I look for two *farangs*.' He produced the photograph of Ben and Teresa. Helene's eyes brightened at the sight of it.

'You say girl speak Thai. On the back you put name and room number. Ten thousand baht you promise me.'

Helene took the photo from him, and looked at the back of it. She saw her own handwriting: Helene Lee, room 503.

'So when I find them, I go to hotel lobby and put through call to Miss Lee in 503. Only you ain't there. You move out.'

'Wait a minute. You found them?'

'Sure. Ten thousand baht, you promise. So I think shit, I lose reward. Then I'm waiting in the cab rank, and I look out and see you. So I collect, yes, after all? Ten grand?'

'You know where they are—right now?'

'Unless they move. I don't think they do.'

'You can actually lead me to them? Today? This afternoon?'

'Sure, babe—I mean miss. If I get paid.'

'You'll get paid—when I find out you're not lying.'

'Why would I lie, lady?'

'Come upstairs. Someone will want to question you,' she said, and Joseph felt afraid his bowels might empty and disgrace him.


It had been their first real argument, but surprisingly bitter for all that. Teresa had not wanted to use Joseph. She said she thought it was an underhand, scurrilous, typically Burridge scheme and, if Ben did approve, then she was surprised at him and disappointed. To which he replied that there was no compulsion on Joe, but it was about the only way they could get bloody Lonsdale and Helene Lee off their backs; and yes, it just so happened that Sir had come up with the idea when Ben told him about their taxidriver, who had in his possession one of the photographs of them which had been circulated all over the city, and that on it was Helene's hotel room number.

A phone call had swiftly established she'd moved out, a few hours after Victor's death, and there was no forwarding address.

'Good.' Tess had been openly pleased, and said that was the end of it. But apparently not. It seemed this had been expected, and there were two possible solutions. The first was to find out where she'd moved by questioning Carmichael in Hong Kong, and promising him a deal if he would co-operate. The second option was even easier.

Burridge used an Australian Federal Police source to check with the Thai immigration computer, and learned Michael Lonsdale had entered the country legally, and given his address as the Oriental Hotel, off New Road. If he and Helene had been at the airport together, then they were obvious associates, and a watch on the Oriental should produce a result.

Tess had developed a real affection for the Thai cabbie, with his grin, his frenzied driving and irreverent vocabulary. She knew, while he agreed to the idea, that he was very scared. She made no attempt to hide her distaste. As they were now in phone contact with Sir Edward, she called and told him that he was unfeeling, an unpleasant and callous drongo—to which Burridge laughed and said she was a nice girl, and must not pick up these crude colonial expressions, and that Joseph was just a pawn, and—while he would deny it if he was quoted—she and Ben were the king and queen, and he would always sacrifice a pawn to protect his main pieces. What's more, her concern for this local taxidriver seemed to him unnecessarily patronising.

• • •

The late sun reflected on the river. It touched a clinker boat at its mooring, a barnacle-encrusted landing stage. The surrounding riverside had once been a timber mill; now it was a wasteland, derelict with the rusted remains of abandoned trucks and cars. They were piled in untidy heaps, the discarded detritus of fatal smashes, insurance rejects, or metal fatigue; an unkempt testimony to the age of built-in obsolescence.

Across this arid moonscape two cars bumped their way over the dirt road, in the direction of the moored clinker. In the first, a hired limousine, Joseph sat frozen in the front seat beside the driver. Seated behind him were Helene Lee, Lonsdale, and a *farang* they called Sandy. Sandy had a gun: he had shown it to Joseph, and said if this was some sort of trap or a stunt to earn himself some easy money, then he, Sandy, would blow the Thai bastard's fucking head off. While Joseph was nervous of the gun, and of Sandy, it was Lonsdale who frightened him. If he had thought Victor dangerous and mean, this Australian, with his flint-hard eyes, was reptilian.

In his suite at the hotel, a big luxury penthouse with a view all the way along the river and a young and pretty boy prostitute sitting in a short kimono and watching as if it was an entertainment, Lonsdale had grilled Joseph until he sweated.

How did he know them? Where had they met? What kind of bullshit story was this, and did Yung Hi Lok, or whatever his stupid name was, expect them to pay him for this kind of crap? In the end, Joseph had convinced him by losing his temper. He had shouted that it was unfair—he had been promised ten thousand baht, and now they were going to renege. He said one *farang* had been in a house on the *klong*, only there had been a big boat chase. He had heard this from friends. And then late yesterday, he had seen them. The two of them, together. They had no luggage. They had hailed him, and said they wanted a place to spend a few days. So he had made a deal with them. *And if Mister Lonsdale with his young* kra-toey *didn't believe it, then he might as well take the boy into the bedroom and make him bite the pillow.*

He thought Lonsdale was going to hit him. Instead he stared at him for a long time. Finally he said, 'There was a taxidriver helped them escape us at the airport yesterday. I get the feeling he looked like you.'

'So what,' Joseph said, feeling the only way to get out of this was to be brash and daring. 'Maybe he did. Everyone look alike to you.'

That was when Lonsdale had nodded to Helene, who had used the phone and called up Sandy McPhee. And all three were now sitting behind him now, ready to blow his fucking head off. As well, in the car following them, were a bunch of armed Thai gangsters.

*Some really great idea this*, thought Joseph. He was too young, only thirty; he had a pretty wife, two nice children, and an eager eighteen-year-old mistress. He would soon be able to pay off the loan on his taxi. It was not a good time to die.


The cars converged on the moored boat, and stopped. They all got out. Sandy McPhee held Joseph by the arm, and laid the cold metal of the automatic across his neck.

For a moment nothing happened,

Then two people emerged from the cabin of the clinker. Ben leaned down and extended a hand to Teresa, and they both stepped ashore. As though they suddenly became aware of danger, they turned and stared at the cluster of figures.

Lonsdale smiled. He looked at McPhee and said, 'When she signals she's got the keys, kill them both. And this one.' He indicated Joseph, who was the only other person to hear it.

He wished he was a believer: in Buddhism so he could expect some life to come; or in Catholicism so he could repent. In anything.

He watched Ben and T'rees standing unprotected and helpless. Helene Lee walked to them, and he heard the sharp sound as she slapped Teresa's face.

'Now, you English bitch, I'll have the keys.'

'What keys?'

Joseph saw T'rees flinch as she was hit again.

'That's for Victor. Come on. We already know the password and the reference number. Walter told us.'

'Poor devil,' Ben said. 'It must have been a painful death. Did you feel any slight compassion, or did you just enjoy watching it?'

'Give me the keys—and you can go.'

'I don't think your friends would agree to that, Miss Lee.'

'Nor would the police,' Teresa said. 'They want to question you about Mr Chen's murder.'

'That's a bluff, you stupid lying bitch.' She attempted to hit Tess again, but found her arm in a vice as Ben held it. For the first time she seemed uncertain. 'What police?'

'The ones all around us.' Teresa said it loudly, as she had been told to do.

They waited for the bunch of armed police, a veritable army of them, to move from their arranged places of concealment behind the piles of wrecked and ruined vehicles.

Nothing happened.

There were supposed to be snipers who would fire warning shots from behind the mounds of debris. Detectives and uniformed police would swarm in and make the arrest. Neither of these things occurred.

Helene looked around and laughed, then she slapped Teresa's face again. Hard and violently this time.

Joseph felt the pain as T'rees was hit. He heard her cry out.

Afterwards, he could never quite remember how it happened, but he felt a rush of anger that blurred his mind. She was not only his friend, who spoke Thai better than any other *farang* he had ever met— she smiled at him, and shared jokes, and he knew she liked him. Also, he was half in love with her; the first time since puberty he had been a bit in love with a girl in an idolised, sisterly sort of way.

*And the bitch was hitting her.*

Joseph had to get McPhee's gun. But McPhee was holding his arm, and the gun was cold against the back of his neck. There was only one thing for it. He had seen this in a soccer game, in the last World Cup, when a goal was scored by a deft back chip, and he tried this now, but it wasn't a deft chip—it was a savage reverse kick with all the force he could muster. His heel caught Sandy McPhee in the groin. Joseph swung around and used his knee but by this time McPhee, in a paroxysm of pain, had crouched into almost a foetal position, and the knee caught him on the jaw and fractured it.

Before anyone could quite understand what was happening, Joseph had the gun and was firing wildly at Lonsdale. He missed by a considerable distance, but the melee of shots caused the armed Thais in the rear car to dive for shelter. And, as if this was a signal, police cars began to converge on the scene, bumping across the wasteland. Joseph became emboldened at the sight, and fired more shots towards Lonsdale. When McPhee tried to rise, Joseph kicked him in the head. Meanwhile Ben secured Helene, and the squad cars finally arrived, with uniformed men flourishing guns, and a braided and rather pompous inspector in charge, who spoke impeccable English and was determined to illustrate it.

'Helene Lee,' he said formally, 'you are under arrest pending extradition to Hong Kong to face murder charges. In addition, you have questions to answer regarding the death of Victor Mendoza.'

'Don't be stupid . . .' she began to say.

'As a known associate, you are believed implicated in his escape from prison. You entered Thailand with him on false passports. After his murder you left your hotel under an assumed name.'

Helene knew she should remain silent, but this was too much. Under suspicion for Victor's death? Her? They were insane. She angrily pointed at Teresa and Ben.

'You fool. They killed him. She did it.'

'We would have to seriously doubt that.'

She was incredulous; how could they believe she would kill her lover, the only one who could make her feel alive after old Chen's cloying affection. Yet how could she say he was her lover? It would leave her no escape from the other charges.

She stared at Teresa. It was a look of sheer hatred.

Lonsdale, who was stunned and furious at himself for allowing this to happen, did his best to regain his composure as Ben approached him with the same Thai inspector.

'This is absurd. I've never heard of Chen, and I barely know that woman. What's more, you can't arrest me without a charge.'

'The charge is conspiracy to murder. There may be others. We have statements from these witnesses you shot at them with intent to kill yesterday.' He indicated Ben and Joseph.

'Come off it,' Lonsdale snapped. 'He's a corrupt cop, who resigned before he was kicked out. No-one will believe what he says.'

'I believe it. And in addition, we have a witness in Hong Kong, a Mr Carmichael, who is most co-operative.'

A sergeant came and handcuffed Lonsdale,

while another took the injured McPhee into custody. In a few moments they were all gone, a line of police cars silhouetted across the wasteland. Before they went, Ben had a final word to the inspector.

'Watch Lonsdale. He's got influence and money, and he's an expert at hiring top lawyers who get him out of prison.'

'We'll do our best.'

'And where the hell were you? What kept you?'

'The instructions via your federal police were changed at the last moment. We were to wait until we heard shooting.'

*Bloody Burridge*, Ben thought, as he watched him drive away. He heard what sounded like a choking sob. Joseph was at the river, vomiting his heart out. Teresa ran to comfort him. She put her arms around him, held his head against her body, and wiped his streaming eyes and stained face. He shuddered and retched again, as food and bile spewed out. She murmured consolingly to him in Thai, then helped him to a car the police had left for them. She put him in the back seat, and returned to where Ben stood watching.

'How does it feel, Ben, to do that to someone?'

He wanted to explain the changed instructions, but had no opportunity. Teresa was not prepared to relent.

'Burridge is a shit. On that we agree. It was his lousy idea, but you went along with it. Like an obedient cop . . .'

'What?'

'Toeing the line.'

'Hang on, Tess . . .'

'You did go along with it,' she challenged him.

'I suppose I did, in a way.'

'In a way,' she said bitingly.

'Come off it, Teresa. We had to do it. We were always in trouble until we had those two in jail. For Christ's sake, aren't you relieved?'

'Of course I'm relieved. I hope they keep them in there forever. It's just the way it was done. Cold-bloodedly putting someone else at risk. That's Burridge's style. I never imagined it was yours.'

'Joseph was great . . . he was tremendous.'

'Joseph was terrified. You know that as well as I do.'

She went towards the car, where he was recovering, but still very shaken. She turned for a parting shot: 'We might have all been killed if it wasn't for Joseph.'

30 THEY SLEPT IN a quite different room from the previous night: a spacious bedroom in a penthouse apartment in central Bangkok. It was air-conditioned, secure, and a pleasing contrast to any place they had occupied for almost a week, but neither felt the least bit comfortable. They had twin beds, but were more estranged by the events of the day than by the space between them.

Teresa was unforgiving. Ben himself was disturbed and upset at the trauma he had caused Joseph, but that kind of stress and physical distress was not new to him. He had known shock himself; he had seen it in others. To him it had been necessary, and if Burridge's last-minute change of instructions via the federal police had been dangerous, at least the tactic had succeeded. They should be celebrating. He had attempted, without success, to point this out to Teresa. To her, it seemed Ben had bowed to pressure from Edward Burridge, and she still felt that subjecting Joseph to such stress was intolerable. The incident lay between them like a canker; it soured their feelings. At the very time when they should have felt relief and a sense of security, they were alienated and disaffected.

They had still not seen Burridge. After the arrests at the river, Ben called the direct number he had been given, and reported the outcome. He expected a meeting; instead he was told to buy what clothes they needed—casual clothes in which to travel—then they should make their way to an address which he was told to write down, to meet a Mrs Jessica Tate. Arrangements for their journey north would be made, and they would leave the following morning.

Two hours later they were in her spacious living room, sitting and having afternoon tea. Jessica Tate was a well-groomed Englishwoman in her sixties, who looked as though she belonged more in the pages of glossy magazines like *The Tatler* or *Country Life*. Her cultured voice came from another time and place.

'Weak tea or strong? Milk or lemon?'

They sipped their tea. Enjoyed a selection of thinly sliced tomato and cucumber sandwiches.

'Carrot cake,' she insisted, and told them she had made it herself that morning.

'Delicious,' Ben said.

'Thank you. It is one of the few things I cook that I'm rather pleased about.'

After the carrot cake, she opened the drawer of a bureau and gave them each an automatic handgun.

'You'll need these. And there's ammunition, and a backpack each. That's what you are— backpackers. You leave by bus tomorrow morning. You travel to here, to Lampang.' She had a detailed map of the country, and indicated their destination. 'You'll be met.'

'By whom?'

'More tea?'

They were perplexed; she was unreal, like someone in the cast of a stage play, a 1930s drawing-room comedy. When Teresa asked her who she was, she replied it depended upon who posed the question.

'I'm Jessica Tate, widow of Henry Tate. We were in teak. I also, when it's required, do odd jobs for Edward Burridge.'

She showed them to her spare bedroom where they would spend the night, hoping it was not inconvenient for them to share. The beds were twin, if that was unsuitable they could move them together. When they were alone, neither made a move to do so. For the first time in five dangerous but passionate days, they felt like uneasy strangers.

In the morning, they made their farewells to Mrs Tate, and Joseph picked them up in his taxi and drove them to the north bus terminus in

Phahonyothin Road. They had their backpacks, with the guns and ammunition among their clothes. Ben wondered, but didn't voice the thought, why guns were required, if Teresa's presence would be the protection Burridge had promised.

While they waited for the bus to depart, they stood outside with Joseph. He and Ben shook hands.

'I'm sorry about yesterday,' Ben said. 'It was unfair to ask you to do it—but you did it well.'

'I had the shakes. Nearly crapped myself. Sweated so much, I thought I was getting the Asian flu.'

He grinned his familiar grin, and Ben smiled.

'We have a lot to thank you for, Joseph. We wouldn't have made it to here without you.'

'You guys take care.'

'We'll try,' Teresa said. She kissed him. She gave him a small packet. It was wrapped, about the size of a paperback book.

'For me?'

'For you. Not to be opened until we leave.'

Beside them the bus was filling up. The driver signalled they were about to depart.

'I love you,' Tess said, and laughed at the surprised and eager look he gave her. 'Like a brother,' she said, 'like a friend.'

'That's good,' Joseph said. 'Sometimes I get

too much of the other kind. I don't have no sister, and not too many friends.'

He watched them, and stood waving as the bus pulled out. He felt a great sense of loss. He walked back to his taxi, illegally parked in a NO STANDING ZONE nearby. He opened the small present. His eyes dilated, and began to fill.

'Oh, holy shit,' he said. 'I'm rich.'

Inside the wrapping was a bundle of tightly packed American dollars. *Twenty thousand of them*, the note said. *Pay off your taxi, buy a house. No massage parlours, please.*

Twenty thousand US dollars. He did a rapid calculation and, by converting it to baht, discovered he was halfway to being a millionaire in local currency. A parking policeman shouted for him to move, and he started the taxi. He drove off, clashing the gears, because his eyes were wet with tears.

# PART FOUR

## THE TRIANGLE

*31* THE CHAO PHRAYA River is to Thailand like the Mississippi to the Southern United States, or the Nile to Egypt. On its rich alluvial plains is the granary where rice has been grown for centuries, planted before the monsoon and harvested in November. The river is the country's lifeblood; it irrigates and provides an artery down which the barges carry timber and farm produce; it bisects the country and flows into the Gulf of Thailand, fed by rivers from the north, among them the Ping which begins near the ancient city of Chiang Mai.

All the way north the road followed the river, and for hours they saw abundant and fertile plains, where water buffalo grazed or pulled ploughs. Emerald green rice fields flourished; thatched farmhouses, small but solidly built on stilts, amid them. Farm animals sheltered below the houses. Occasionally they passed through rural villages, and all along the roadside were tiny carved and colourful shrines, the spirit houses vivid with orchids and incense sticks, adorned with fruit and daily offerings to appease the spirits and to bring good luck to the family who dwelt there.

The bus stopped for lunch at a roadside cafe. Tess ordered them noodles with fried chicken, and a local beer. Over the meal she told him about the contents of the gift she had left with Joseph.

'Twenty thousand.'

Ben was determined to be agreeable, and heal the rift that remained between them. If he wondered why she had not discussed it with him beforehand, he merely said, 'Good. He deserved it.'

'I think so.' She picked at her meal, and added casually, 'I mean twenty thousand dollars, not local currency.'

'Ehh? But that's . . .'

'Six hundred thousand baht,' she said, before he could calculate it.

'He must have thought all his birthdays had come at once.'

'I hope so. You said we wouldn't have made it without him, and you were right.'

'And it's only money,' Ben said. 'Even better, it's only Burridge's money. Spreads a little joy and happiness.'

'That's right.'

He nodded, and ate some chicken. She

watched the beginnings of a slight frown on his face.

'You resent me giving him so much?'

'No.'

'Sure?'

'Positive. I'm glad you told me. Maybe we could have discussed it first, but I certainly don't begrudge Joseph anything.'

'I didn't tell you, because I felt you might say it was too much.'

'Why would I say a thing like that?'

'I don't know, Ben. I get the feeling you might have.'

'I get a feeling you're trying to pick a fight. And something tells me it's because of yesterday.'

'That's forgotten.'

'Is it? Why the hell should I object to Joseph getting a decent bonus. It was a nice thought, and I only wish I'd been able to share in the idea, instead of being told after the event.'

'It was from both of us.'

'No, it was from you—and now I'm being allowed to become a part of it. Well, you went to the bank, so you're the one who'd know if we can afford it.'

'Of course we can afford it.'

'Then there's no problem.'

'None. I drew extra money. It seemed stupid not to, after all the risks of going there.'

He wanted to ask how much extra, but decided against it. They finished the rest of their meal in silence.

Burridge sipped a whisky and looked out at the unique skyline where modern buildings jostled alongside the gilded spires and winged roofs of the temples. Though he had no liking for the city of Bangkok, he admitted the people had a rich tradition. Never subjected to colonial imperialism like their neighbours, the Thais had an independent spirit that enabled them to survive much of the turmoil endured by Cambodia, Laos and Burma.

Calm and courteous by nature, their women among the world's most beautiful, their dancers graceful, their art intricate with colour, their architecture elegant and distinctive, it was a pity their capital, where over seven million people lived, was one of the noisiest places on earth, dirty and fume-laden, a cesspit of vice and corruption, where children were sold as prostitutes and sex was the city's major industry.

'I don't know how you stand living here, Jessica,' he said, as she brought a gin and tonic onto the terrace to join him.

'Henry liked it. We spent so much of our lives in the East. I'm far too old to go back and start a new life in England now. I'd hardly know the place.' She took a chair. 'Edward, I'm worried about that girl.'

He raised his glass to her, and they sipped their drinks.

'Did you hear what I said?'

'Yes, you're worried about Teresa Martineau.'

'I liked her. I liked them both. I hope you're not going to get them killed.'

'One never intends people to get killed. You know that.'

'I know it's the result which is all-important to you,' Jessica Tate said, 'no matter what. It's always been that way.'

'What other way is there? I deal with vermin. I have to use their tactics.'

'You've changed, you know.'

'Have I?'

'You're far more obsessive. Not long before he died, Henry said you'd become so ruthless he scarcely knew you.'

'Henry was a gentle soul. Like Walter Chen. Both decent chaps. Both gentlemen. I never have been, but then I've always known and admitted my own lack of gentility.'

'What happens to Teresa?'

'When?'

'You know when.'

'I'm sure she can handle it.'

'I hope so. You take the most appalling risks, Edward.'

'Risks? What risks?'

'With people's emotions. With their lives.'


Lonsdale had been allowed one outside telephone call the previous night and, after an
exchange of money with the senior warder of
the remand block, he was on the phone to Melbourne. The recipient of the call was less than
enthusiastic, pleading a full calendar, with a case
before the High Court.

'You listen to me, you legal wimp,' he said,
'I don't care if you're defending Jesus Christ in
front of Pontius Pilate. I have one phone call,
and you're it. Start earning your big fat retainer
right now. Get the next plane. Get the best
local barrister in Bangkok. Get me out of this
bloody awful shitty place or I'll start talking—
all the details of our various enterprises and you
and your expensive law firm will be history.'

By noon the following day, Michael Lonsdale
was consulting with his legal advisers. Edmund
Pardy was a prominent partner with a Melbourne firm. He brought with him Mr Thon
Khra, barrister of the Thai Supreme Court
circuit, who told him it was likely bail could be
arranged.

'Bail be buggered,' Lonsdale said. 'I've committed no crime.'

'You're charged with conspiracy to murder,'

Thon Khra said. He did not like his client. But then he had no need to. The fee was adequate compensation.

'It's a load of bullshit. They can't prove a thing.'

'Nevertheless, there is a charge. Unless we could get a verdict of nullity, it remains on the statute. In due course, I can contest the facts and try to have it thrown out when it comes to court, but justice takes its time here. You wish to be out of prison as soon as possible. Bail is the best I can do.'

'What about McPhee?'

Pardy shook his head. He said, 'Sandy's too well known here. Mr Thon Khra's advice is not to prejudice your own chances.'

'Right,' Lonsdale said, 'then get on with it. How soon?'

'It won't be cheap,' the Thai barrister said, 'but I can organise a hearing today. You'll be free by late afternoon.'

There were flame trees that stretched across the streets like a canopy, shading the town from the afternoon heat. The bus drove off, heading north, leaving them beside the graceful, old-fashioned Hualumphong railway station. There were no taxis, but a line of horse-drawn carts stood in the shade, while their drivers sat beneath a tree watching villagers rehearsing for a music festival on local stringed instruments and flutes. Teresa gave the name of their hotel, and ten minutes later they were in a tiled foyer.

'Adjoining rooms?' she asked Ben, and he nodded.

The uneasiness between them remained. He hoped they could sort it out but, if not, if this reserve continued, it would be simpler if they were not committed to sleeping in the same room. They went upstairs, unpacked what few clothes they had, and Ben showered and changed. An hour later he had a call. It was Burridge, who said he had only just arrived and had a great deal to talk about, so they might like to meet him downstairs in the bar. Right now, if possible; the sooner the better.

'I'll see if Teresa's ready,' Ben said, hanging up, and reflecting that some people never changed. He knocked on the connecting door, and told her sir awaited her below.

'It's not locked,' she called, and he went in. The bathroom door was open, and he could glimpse her there, brushing her hair.

'His Eminence, or to give him his real title— God—requests our presence. In other words, get on our bikes and down there to meet him.'

She came out of the bathroom.

He stared, his eyes widening as his mouth stayed open.

She was naked. Smiling.

'Shall we call and tell him we're not quite ready yet? Or why not just make him wait.'

She kissed him and probed his mouth with her tongue.

'What a stupid idea,' she whispered, 'taking adjoining rooms.'


When they were at their most passionate, the telephone rang. It was like a distant sound, a bell tinkling, something happening elsewhere, as they became mindless and flooded together in ecstasy. They were rapturous, trembling with the intensity of their feelings for each other, and by the time they had subsided, it had long since stopped.

They lay with their limbs locked, her slender legs threaded through his, her breasts against his chest, reluctant to leave each other, not wanting to move from the bed, let alone the room. The idea of having to shower, dress, and go downstairs to the bar to meet Burridge, was low on their list of priorities.

'Did you hear the phone ring?' he said at last.

'What phone?'

'There it goes again,' he said.

She ignored the sound, as she held him tight and said, 'Don't ever let's have another row.'

'We're bound to. Everyone has rows. The

main thing is to promise they'll always end like this.'

'Yes, please.' She kissed him so ardently he felt his blood accelerate.

He scrambled out of bed. The telephone was still ringing. 'Look what you're doing to me.'

'Oh,' Tess said, eyes smiling. 'Nice one. And so soon.'

'Answer it, or he'll come charging up here.'

She picked up the phone and said demurely, 'Sir Edward? I'm so sorry. I'm waiting on Ben. He decided to slip into something comfortable.'


The helicopter hovered until the pilot could see the outline of the jungle landing strip. The men on the ground lit flares to guide him down in the failing light. In a few minutes it would be dark. When the pilot touched down, Michael Lonsdale ran, hunched and windblown by the revolving blades, towards the group of armed men waiting for him by the truck. They were accompanied by an interpreter, and introductions were swiftly made. They all watched as the pilot switched on his navigation lights, and the chopper slowly rose into the murky sky, and scudded back on the long haul towards Bangkok.

It had been a neat afternoon's work, Lonsdale thought, since the expensive and annoyingly uppity wog they'd briefed had appeared before a magistrate and secured bail. The chopper, the armed men, the interpreter, all these arrangements had been activated while he was still behind bars, triggered by a phone call made by Edmund Pardy, the Australian lawyer.

It was even better than that. A network across the north, from Chiang Mai to the Mekong, was now looking for Ben Hammond and the English girl. Sometime tomorrow they would find them. They were en route to a bizarre, apparently arranged meeting with Kim Sokram, to make him an improbable offer: several billion dollars to cease all production. Hammond must not be allowed to reach there. Because Lonsdale knew the reason given for the meeting with the drug baron was spurious. There had to be another agenda.

Unless he acted swiftly, they would achieve their objective. Lonsdale had remembered where he had heard the name Martineau. While he was with her, Ben Hammond was afforded protection. But not from him. Tomorrow they would be located, and he'd kill Hammond. That was certain. It would give him great pleasure.

About Teresa Martineau, he had not yet decided. In view of who she was, she might well become a vital bargaining chip.

**32** 'SETTLED IN, ALL right? Not too uncomfortable, the bus journey?'

He was smiling and polite, as if they had not kept him waiting more than a few minutes, as though they were old friends and he was delighted to see them. Immaculate as always, in a tan tropical suit, he was a distinct contrast to Teresa and Ben in their shorts, T-shirts and thongs. The bar was small and decorative with gilded scrollwork, and the lone waiter brought them cold beers.

'The bus was fine,' Ben said. 'How about you? Stretch limo?'

'Plane, actually. It was important we weren't observed travelling together. And vital we only meet here, for what will be the last time.'

'Is that a promise?' Ben asked, but was ignored.

'The hotel is what you might call a "safe house". If you see signs of any armed shadows around this evening, they work for me.'

'Secure and to be fully trusted, are they?'

'All right, Ben. Let's skip the needle. I'm sorry things didn't go exactly as planned.'

'That would have to be a bit of an understatement,' said Ben.

'If you'd trusted me, instead of vanishing . . .' he stopped with a shrug. 'Well . . . water under the bridge. I've been able to improvise new arrangements. We're back on track. I'm still your control, and you follow my instructions. If that bothers you, remember in another twenty-four hours it'll be all over, and you can both go home.'

'You mean after Teresa meets her dad, and we get paid.'

'Naturally.'

'What about Victor's death? Will there be an investigation?'

'Self-defence. No case to answer.'

'And Helene Lee?'

'She'll be extradited and charged with murder in Hong Kong. I apologise. She fooled me, and completely deceived Walter. He was a decent chap who didn't deserve to die like that.'

Tess felt the grief he would never reveal openly, and had a moment's sympathy for him. Ben was less compassionate.

'I know he was a friend. But that's where it screwed up. From day one, she and her lot were right on our hammer. So I want to be sure there'll be no more surprises.'

'Let's hope not,' Burridge said.

'For instance, where's Mick Lonsdale?' Ben asked. 'Still inside?'

'He was granted bail earlier today.'

'Terrific. Has he skipped the country yet?'

'We're monitoring the situation.'

'Were you going to tell me? Or didn't you think I had a need to know?'

'Forget Lonsdale. We'll look after him. You leave here at dawn tomorrow. I'll drive you to the airfield. A private plane will take you to Mae Chan. There'll be a jeep waiting. You'll drive north—the two of you—towards Mae Sai, right into the Triangle. It's mountainous, mostly unmapped, a wilderness of valleys and rivers hardly ever penetrated by outsiders. There's only one road as far as we know. It'll be rough and rocky in places, so it's going to be a bumpy ride. Somewhere along that road you'll be met.'

'By whom?' Teresa asked.

'By your father—or someone on his behalf.'

'My father? He knows I'm coming?'

'Yes. We got word through to him. He'd know by now.'

'How?'

'Via one of the distribution outlets that Sokram uses.'

'You reached my father—through Kim Sokram?'

'That's right,' Burridge said quietly.

Ben could feel the rising tension, see the growing bewilderment in her face.

'Who is he? Who the hell is he?'

'A chemist.'

'What sort of chemist?'

'A clever one.'

Ben said roughly, violently, 'Don't do this to her. Don't play games. Who the fuck is he?'

Burridge ignored him. He talked to Teresa, as if they were alone. 'Heroin is not a crop or natural substance as you may know. It's a derivative. The sap of the opium poppy contains alkaloids, one of which is morphine. Bonded with acetic acid, through a complex five-stage process, morphine becomes heroin. The Khmers and the hill farmers who grow the poppies, the thousands who harvest them, they're just the foot soldiers. The key figures are the chemists who manufacture the drug. You find them in laboratories all over the world: here, Marseilles, Mexico. Skilled pharmacists, with no morality, just a desire to get rich. They're the ones who refine the poppy into addictive drugs that destroy people. Some of these chemists make fortunes, then go home, buy a shop in Sydney or Munich or Detroit, and become your friendly neighbourhood dispenser.'

Tess shut her eyes. She wanted to run, to

block her ears, to shut out the sound of his voice. Burridge was relentless.

'Without the chemists, there'd still be opium and other drugs; we humans have always found the means and method to abuse ourselves with narcotics. But it was science that opened the floodgates to produce the so-called designer drugs, the hallucinogens, and all the names that have become fashionable through media use: *speed*, *ice*, *crack*, *ecstasy* and the rest. So there's a well-defined hierarchy to all this. The criminal mobs run the drugs, the couriers carry them, the peasants pick them. But the chemists create them.'

'My father . . . he does that . . .?'

'He does more, I'm afraid.'

Her pallor revealed the depth of her anguish. Ben took her hand. Burridge seemed not to notice; he simply continued, but his voice softened slightly, became less judgmental: 'Roland Martineau was a young man when he started to work for the Sokram family. Nearly thirty years ago. I don't know what he intended—perhaps he only meant to take up this line of work for a time, make some quick money and go home to France. He was newly married with a baby daughter. As a French colonial, he'd been dispossessed in Vietnam. Now the Americans were at war there. All over this area there was corruption. Governments were involved; the

Americans through the CIA; as well as the puppets in Saigon, the Thais, Laotians and the Burmese; everyone financed their wars and their coups by drug-trafficking. In those halcyon days, Sokram established his fiefdom. The biggest in the Golden Triangle. He ruled it like a feudal potentate. And your father didn't go home.'

He paused for a moment. It was very silent in the small bar. Far off, the slim barman polished glasses and waited for custom.

'I wish I could say he was prevented, but my information is it wouldn't be correct. He was promoted—became important to Sokram. The quiet man in the white coat, whom few people knew. He had drive and talent. Before long he was the senior chemist who not only controlled all the laboratories but also planned the new ones. His influence now is immense. It stretches far beyond the mountains along the Mekong. He's the one who establishes the new heroin factories in cities all over the world as the demand grows. He probably has more power than anyone except Sokram himself. Twenty years ago, he wasn't so important—but he also wasn't a timber exporter. I suspect your mother found out what his real work was, and that's why she left him. It's almost certainly why she wanted to make you believe that he was dead.'

Teresa was very still. They both wondered if

she was going to speak at all. She studied Burridge, as though he puzzled her.

'Then everything you told me in Paris was a
lie?'

'No, not at all. Certainly not everything.
Your father's alive. He lives here, in this region.
He has a young mistress. The house where the
photo of them was taken is one of his homes,
at Chiang Rai. He has another, but that's in the
village Sokram owns, somewhere deep in the
Triangle and beyond our reach.'

'Never mind what scraps of truth you told
me. Let's concentrate on the falsehoods. He
never worked for you?'

'No.'

'You're plausible, Sir Edward. You tell your
lies well.'

'If I'd told you the truth, would you be here?'

'Probably not.'

'I'm sorry,' Burridge said.

'No, I don't think you are. I think that's
another lie.'

'I'm afraid it's immaterial, what you may
think.'

There was a noticeably harder edge to Burridge's reply. Ben knew it was time to
intervene.

'Not to me it isn't,' he said. 'If Tess is upset,
if she doesn't want to see him, then we don't
go. It's that simple.'

416

'Really?'

'I mean it. We won't be on that plane. We'll be out of here.'

'I don't believe so,' Burridge replied.

He was faintly smiling. It should have been a warning, but Ben ignored it. He felt aggressive, wanting to hit out, to put a dent in that patronising demeanour.

'Stuff what you believe, Ted. Tell us about the bank. The one in Bangkok, with the empty deposit box. Are the rest all empty? That list you gave me—is it a scam? Because we think the only money is back in the South China Bank in Hong Kong.'

He realised he was still holding Teresa's hand, as she squeezed his fingers. It was a cautionary signal warning him not to mention her return visit to Nathan Road. Burridge seemed unfazed by the question.

'We moved the funds around. Decided the other banks were an unnecessary risk. The balance of the ten billion is safely in Switzerland.'

'That sounds like bullshit.'

'Nevertheless, it's what you'll explain to Sokram, when you meet.'

'No.'

It was Teresa, and they both turned to look at her, 'I'm not meeting anyone. Least of all my father.'

'My dear girl—'

'This is as far as I go. You never needed my skills, just my presence as some kind of shield. If I wondered whether I was being used, I could hardly have guessed the extent. *The daughter of the chemist who creates the drugs.* Well, for the past twenty years I've believed he was dead; so he can stay that way.'

'I'm afraid not, Teresa.'

It was the same smile, but this time Ben saw how counterfeit it was, and felt cold.

'You'll do as arranged tomorrow. Be flown to Mae Chan. Take the jeep. Meet your dear old daddy. Ben will put the proposal to Sokram. That's what will happen tomorrow.'

Ben felt it incumbent to protest, knowing it would be futile. 'Why the hell should we do what you tell us?'

'Because I wish it, old boy.' Burridge made no pretence of courtesy now. He spat his words like lethal darts: 'Because I insist. And if you fool around with me—after all the time and money that's gone into this venture, then I'll see you end up in a Thai jail with a kilo of heroin on your person—and if you behave and plead guilty, they might let you spend the next twenty years inside, but they'd rather shove you on a scaffold with a rope round your neck. Now in case you want to be heroic, in case you want to play the fucking sentimental knight errant because you fancy your ladyfriend here, because she's nice in bed, I assure you it would be a stupid gesture. She'll be picked up, too. For Victor's murder. And when it comes to being hanged in this part of the world, I'm told there's no sexual discrimination.'

He smiled. Ben felt shivers down his spine. He thought it was like being filleted with an ice pick. Burridge raised his glass.

'But we don't want this kind of talk. No need for silly threats. Let's all have a decent night's sleep. And it's not necessary for either of you to worry over unimportant minor details, like alarm clocks. I'll see to it you're called before dawn.'

He finished his drink and went out. They remained, not only stunned by his display of ruthlessness, but worse, knowing that no matter how irrational and deranged it sounded, he meant every word.

The voice on the two-way radio sounded excited, and the Khmer interpreter explained it to Lonsdale. The couple had been monitored since they first left the plane and headed north in the jeep. Now they were on the road that snaked its way along the floor of the valley below. They would be in sight within ten minutes. The tree had been expertly felled so that it completely blocked the road. The snipers were perched on the branches of the big teak trees, with a perfect view. They had their crossed-sights on the spot where the jeep would be forced to stop. Their orders were to kill the man, and make certain they did not shoot the woman.

Mick Lonsdale was going to do a deal over her.

He looked at his watch.

Nine minutes.

33 WHEN THEY LEFT the bar and went upstairs, Teresa undressed and got into bed. Ben switched out the lights and stood by the window, his eyes trying to adjust to the dark outside. There was a cloudy sky and no moon. By day the lawns of the hotel were undulating and manicured like a parkland, decorated with flame trees, oleanders, palms and durians. At night it was impenetrable.

'I won't be long.'

He touched his fingers to his lips, and went carefully out, via the connecting door and his adjacent room. She heard the lock click. She hoped he meant it, about returning soon; she wanted to stay awake but felt desperately tired. *Bemused*, she thought, and wondered if that was the correct word. Dazed. Yes, most certainly dazed.

Too much revelation.

West Hampstead, Charles, her flat in Bolton Gardens, the bleak day of her mother's funeral, it all seemed long ago and like part of another life. Good God, it was less than a month since that day in Paris when she found out her father was alive. Even more remarkably, it was only twelve days since she had left Heathrow for Hong Kong. *If she had known what she learned tonight, would she have come? No, she thought, but on the other hand . . .*

Without the truth, there'd have always been times she would ask herself what he was like, how they would have felt about each other. She had only a blurred memory of a voice reading bedtime stories to her; she recalled them mainly because sometimes the voice read to her in French, and at other times in English with a strong Gallic accent. A patois, she supposed, since he was brought up in Indochina. *What would she have done if Burridge had told her the truth that day . . .?*

While trying to make up her mind about this, she fell asleep.

In the garden someone coughed. A shadow moved. A voice murmured, a lighter flickered, and two faces were etched against the dark as both lit cigarettes and inhaled. A door opened and Burridge came out. Ben remained frozen. Burridge passed within a few feet of him.

'There's the flight plan,' he heard Burridge say, and one took it, the other shining a pencil flashlight while they both studied it.

'Any problems?'

'No. Seems straightforward.' The man had an American accent, but Ben thought he was a local.

'Where are they?' the other asked.

'Tucked up in bed together.'

'Lucky bastard.'

They both gave ribald chuckles.

*You pair of pricks*, Ben thought.

'Get on the phone,' Burridge said, but his voice was starting to fade as all three moved away, 'We've a lot to organise and . . .'

It was all Ben heard. He wondered if he could follow them, but it was as well he hesitated because the lights of a vehicle came on and he had to step hastily back into the shelter of a clump of palms. From there he could see—but not hear—one of the men dialling and talking into a radio telephone.

*A lot to organise.*

He wished he knew what that meant. He had a distinctly uneasy feeling, and wondered if he should share it with Teresa. On the way upstairs, he decided not to. She had had enough for one day, with the shock revelation about her father.

He stripped off his shorts and T-shirt, and slipped into bed beside her. He wanted to hold her, take comfort from her and perhaps in a brief while make love to each other, but she was sound asleep. He gently kissed her cheek, and she mumbled something that might have been his name, but did not wake.

*You were right,* he thought. *You and your remote hideaway island. We should have taken a bloody great big fistful of dollars, and run away to find it. Now it's too late.*

Burridge had some other agenda. His kind always did.

He wished Tess was awake, so they could make love. He wasn't sure if after tomorrow they would have another chance.


The plane set them down in a flat patch of farmland, within sight of a hill farmer threshing grain. Near him was an open-fronted shed, and they could see the jeep parked in there, waiting.

'The farmer has the keys,' the pilot told them, and said the jeep was gassed up. He was Burmese, the one from the previous night with the American accent. As they took their backpacks, he shook hands, wished them luck and pointed to the only road that led north towards the mist-covered mountains. While they stood and watched, he revved the motor, taxied, and the tiny plane lifted and climbed steeply away.

They went to collect the keys. Tess spoke with the farmer, who told her there was food and a flask of water in the jeep. He was from the *Karen* hill tribe, a Sino-Tibetan, one of the sects who cultivated their farms below the opium-growing districts. He had been told they intended to take photographs of spirit houses, then go trekking along the river road to the arch which told tourists they had reached their destination. Apparently, the farmer said to Tess, they would know it when they reached a concrete archway on the Mekong which said: WELCOME TO THE GOLDEN TRIANGLE.

'I don't believe it,' Ben said.

'He said it's true. People take minibuses or ride bicycles there.'

'Bicycles?'

'Groups even go on walking tours.'

'Good God. Has he been there?'

She shook her head. 'He's never been out of his village. And the arch and sign are just a tourist gimmick where people can have their photographs taken, like they once did on the Berlin wall. But just as they never messed on the other side of the wall, nobody finds the real Triangle. That's something else. A hundred and fifty thousand square miles of jungle mountains.'

'And somewhere in there is your dad.'

She involuntarily shivered, and moved closer to him. He took a hand off the wheel to put an arm around her.

'I wonder how long we keep driving?'

'No way of knowing,' he said. 'We stay on this road, until someone tells us to stop.'

'Ben, last night—I must have fallen asleep.'

'Yes.'

'You didn't wake me.'

He turned to glance at her, and the jeep hit a rock. They bounced and swerved, almost out of control.

'Sorry,' he said. 'I didn't see that rock.'

'I thought if I fell asleep you'd wake me. Nicely, with your hands all over me, and your tongue—well, almost anywhere.'

'Oh!'

'I was hoping. I wanted you to. I really wanted it badly.'

'Shit,' Ben said, 'now you tell me.'


'Four minutes.' The interpreter listened to the voice on his radio.

'Pass the word around,' Lonsdale told him.

He sat in the front seat of the truck, half hidden in foliage off the road, and watched the serpentine track up which the jeep would come. The snipers in the trees would wait for his signal, which would give him time enough to let Ben Hammond realise what was to happen. They were picked marksmen; his organisation in Bangkok had chosen and guaranteed them, and they would blast Hammond into oblivion. A hail of direct gunfire would slice his head from his shoulders.

Lonsdale particularly wanted him to know he was to die. He wanted his own moment of triumph, to see the bastard's realisation and terror, the bloody cop who had smashed his nose and caused a heap of trouble in Melbourne. He would revel in those last seconds, then give the signal. Just so long as they did not kill Teresa Martineau. Her father was going to show his gratitude, and Mick Lonsdale would soon be number one in the Australasian syndicate, and very, very rich.


The road had become a track. Dark and wet. The canopy of rainforest let in no trace of sunlight. For a brief time they drove with full headlights, then the jeep began to climb, and Ben put it into the low ratio and they ground their way up the rock-pitted slope. The sky began to show, and leaden grey mist hovered around the tops of the trees. The tangled jungle gave way to teak, a one-time plantation where battalions with chainsaws had moved in and wreaked havoc on the majestic trees. Teresa pointed at the scarred mountainside and the devastation. No-one had bothered here about new plantings. No reforestation. The road improved, as if those who plundered the area had used a grader to make better access for their machinery to violate the landscape. But the change to a smoother ride was brief, and again they were on rocks and rutted dirt corrugations, a bone-shaking surface with winding bends. There was a sharp curve ahead and, as they traversed it, they saw the fallen tree that blocked the road.

Ben hit the brakes, and the jeep stopped a few metres short. It had been expertly placed. There was no way past it, and little chance of reversing out of there. He knew immediately what it was, and glanced up to see the shapes of men perched on branches. There was nothing he could do. A figure moved from the undergrowth, and with a sinking feeling but no surprise, he recognised Lonsdale.

'You sit there, bastard. She gets out of the vehicle.'

He was using an amplified loudhailer, even though he was not far away. A normal shout would have reached them clearly.

'Take it easy, Mick,' Ben called. It was a futile gesture and a vain hope, but he had to try.

'Miss Martineau, move. Get out of the jeep.'

'No,' she said, but so softly that only Ben could hear her.

'For Christ's sake do what he says. You want him to kill you?'

'If I get out, what happens? They shoot you.'

'If you don't, they shoot us both. Now stop being such a stupid bitch and do what he says.'

She looked at him, and shook her head. 'No, Ben—'

'Tess, for Christ's sake—'

'Get out,' Lonsdale yelled, his voice almost out of control and so loud that the amplifier shrilled and created feedback and an echo. He signalled, and a shot rang out. One of the head-lights of the jeep burst in a hail of glass. He shouted again: '*Get fucking out!*'

*Out-out-out* the feedback echo resonated, as the trees exploded and the jungle around him ignited.

The gunship came out of nowhere.

They felt the detonation of the missile it fired before they saw the shape above the tree line and heard the thud of its twin rotors. The first missile hit Michael Lonsdale and instantly incin-erated him. One moment he was there staring at them, his arm about to rise, the next he was obliterated without a trace.

A second missile followed immediately. It demolished a tree leaving it a charred and defo-liated relic, petrified as if struck by lightning, killing all the snipers positioned in its branches.

Then the gunfire began. A lethal hail of tracer bullets sprayed the branches of the other sur-rounding trees. The crossfire was relentless, the gunners in the chopper determined to leave no-one alive. One of the armed men had time to scream as he fell. Two threw away their rifles and tried to run, but were cut down almost at once.

It took less than thirty seconds.

Ben and Teresa had not had time to move from the jeep. If they had been the target, there would have been little point to it. But although it happened so swiftly, they quickly realised the missiles and tracers had been directed away from them, towards those in the ambush.

Now the firing stopped. The blades started to whip debris around them, and they sheltered their faces as the ungainly craft with its long shape and twin motors descended. It had an oddly familiar look about it, and Ben realised it still had US Army Air Force markings, and he had seen choppers like it carrying troops and being used by medical teams in old newsreels and movies of the Vietnam War. So that was where the wartime salvage ended up. The litter and leftovers of lost causes, recycled from Saigon and transferred to another army. He wondered if Sokram had also bought tanks or artillery for his private militia, and who was the lucky American officer who had negotiated the arms deal? He would not have been the first, nor the last to do so.

The thud of the engines stopped. They stepped away from the jeep and watched as the rotor blades began to slow. A door slid open, a small metal ladder telescoped down and a man began to climb out. He was grey-haired, with tanned regular features, and trim-waisted. He moved with an easy assurance and wore light-weight tropical trousers, espadrilles and a batik shirt. Casual, yet smart. A good-looking man, Ben thought, and expected no less as Teresa went slowly forward to meet her father.

34 THEY WERE ABOVE the stronghold before they realised it. From the sky it looked like a mountain village, one of the very few they had seen during the brief flight over an endless terrain of thickly forested ridges and valleys, with occasional glimpses of the river. Once in a while there was open farmland, fields where the poppies were cultivated, and sometimes a cluster of thatched huts that comprised a hill-tribe settlement.

'Almost there,' Roland Martineau said, and that was what caused Ben to look down and glimpse gates and a rampart, and the roof of a house that would have been invisible had not Martineau's gesture indicated it. In fact, as Ben studied it, experience told him that a great deal of the roof of what must be a large mansion was obscured by the foliage of the trees, but the remainder was an enormous camouflage net expertly quilted with leaves. It blended per-fectly into the landscape. A squadron of spotter planes could have flown overhead and noticed nothing, unless they were grid-searching the area, or had the benefit of prior disclosure.

Teresa's father, now that they were closeted in the cabin of the chopper and face to face, was an impressive-looking man. He moved with an air of total confidence; there was a trace of French style in his walk, which could be read as arrogance, although he had been born and schooled in Indochina and had spent no more than a few months of his life in mainland France. He had a strong regional accent, but his English was fluent. In his late fifties, he was physically fit and had a vitality that a younger man might have envied. He appeared more like a former athlete or a man who earned his living outdoors, than any stereotype of a laboratory chemist. He seemed under the impression that Teresa had sought him out after her mother's death, and that she and Ben had first met in Bangkok and were lovers. By no sign or expression did she deny this.

It had been a strange period, little over half an hour since the missiles had saved their lives, when Tess and her father had exchanged a formal and rather stilted embrace, and she had introduced Ben, and all three had taken their seats while the crew dispatched a last projectile that blew up the jeep, after which they secured the doors and the ship rose and began to scud across the jungle. Thirty-six minutes since they had taken off. Ben had sneaked a glance at his watch as the motors started and, without appearing to do so, had kept a check of the time they were in the air. He could only hazard a rough guess, but estimated they had travelled about a hundred and fifty kilometres beyond the town of Chiang Saen, which put them almost exactly on the Burmese and Laotian borders.

It would compute with what the videotape had said.

*It operates out of north Thailand, a mere two-hour walk from the Burmese border.*

Two hours, in that remote and arduous terrain, was little more than a kilometre or two.

They were at the very tip of the triangle, perfectly sited for Sokram to operate with impunity in either Laos or Burma, able to take advantage of whichever political climate of the day was most to his advantage. The mountains were nearly impenetrable and easily guarded by his private troops, even assuming that the trinity of surrounding governments and their armies wished to invade. Which Ben knew was most unlikely.

The massive amount of money disbursed to guarantee the line of production was too well entrenched. It protected the entire system, from the crops still carried in by peasants on horseback, right down through the manufacturing process and the worldwide network of distribution. The recipients were in high places.

A phrase came to his mind. *Pyramids of corruption*, someone had once described the ever-changing regimes of Indochina; and the major drug barons had an elite payroll of diplomats and inspectors of police and army generals, all of whom knew that the tip of the triangle and the top of the pyramid had a related benefit for their future wellbeing.

He heard the engine change pitch, and felt the craft begin to descend.


'There's nothing left,' the young Gurkha sergeant said.

He stood on the jungle track where the tree still smouldered, and the metal remains of the jeep lay buckled and blistered in front of the roadblock. There were bodies all around him, but not the two he had been sent to find.

On the other end of the mobile telephone line, Burridge told him to see if there was any trace of Lonsdale.

'Not so far,' the sergeant reported. He suddenly asked Burridge to wait. He came back on the line a moment later.

'There's a half of a shoe. Made in Italy.'

'Well done,' Burridge said. 'Bravo. I think we can assume you've found the bastard, and he's been well and truly minced. Italian shoes, eh?

They like to ponce about in imported gear. No wonder the Australians have a balance-of-trade problem.'

The sergeant, who had done his training at Camberley in Surrey and knew his British masters and a cue for a laugh when he heard one, dutifully laughed.

'Droll, sir,' he said, and wondered if he'd gone too far.

*Droll?* Burridge thought. The sodding Gurkhas are supposed to be fighting machines. Not bloody comedians.

'All right, sergeant, stand by until you hear from me,' he said, and pressed the disconnect button.

Well, at least they weren't dead yet, he thought. It was fortunate they'd put a transmitter in the jeep. Even more fortunate that Martineau had taken their message seriously and monitored his daughter's progress.

He called the rest of the group—they were all Gurkhas—not only because he thought they were the best, but because they had no allegiances and they were honest, and he hoped they could not be bought. There was, thank God, only one comedian, and he would leave him guarding the Italian shoe.


The girl served them pâté and spicy savouries,

with a glass of white wine. Her father introduced her simply as Priya. It was the same girl as in the photograph, but in a different place. It was unlikely that anyone could get in here with a camera—certainly they would not get out again, for the short walk from the aircraft had shown them the place was a fortress and everywhere were patrolling guards with armalite rifles and American M60 submachine guns. Also, in the photograph, her father and Priya had been standing in front of a bungalow and, before Burridge confirmed it was a house they shared at Chiang Rai, she had already guessed it was in the lower hills because of the profusion of orchids and frangipani. This place they were in now was not a house. This was a luxury compound, his own quarters, a private secluded wing in Sokram's palatial mansion in the mountain village.

Tess felt disturbed and uneasy with him. They had formally kissed cheeks, clasped hands, spoken greetings in both French and English, although she could scarcely remember what had been said; doubtless it had to do with his timely arrival, and she recalled telling him of her mother's death, but there had been a constraint, a lack of affection in their meeting, for knowing what she did, she felt alienated, a stranger from this man who was her father.

She told him the story she had been coached to tell. Beginning with the truth. That her mother had always told her he was dead. That after her funeral, she had found among her private papers a sealed letter, a conscience-stricken apologia which contained the revelation that he was more than likely alive, and where he worked and what he did. That, as soon as she could, she flew to Bangkok to look for him and, in her initial enquiries, she had met Ben, who wanted to meet with Kim Sokram and needed an interpreter. As their destinations were the same, she agreed. Since then, she and Ben had become—close.

Roland Martineau listened to all of this carefully. It was difficult to determine if he believed it.

'How did you feel—about learning what I did?'

'I didn't want to make judgments, at least until I'd met you.' He made no response to this, so she added, 'I thought that only fair.'

'You were a beautiful little girl,' her father said, 'and you've become a fine-looking woman. But you're not a very good liar.'

It made her angry, and in a way it helped. This was no longer an examination of what Ben felt was their flimsy cover story. This was suddenly and intensely personal.

'I'm trying to be tactful—not to lie. If you really want the hard truth, the news revolted me.'

'What?'

He was startled by her hostility.

'The idea that you were a chemist who refines the sap of the poppy into a drug that destroys people made me feel sick. But even if my father had been Dr Mengele or Adolf Eichmann, I would still have wanted to meet him and ask why.'

Her bitterness was palpable. Martineau looked at her for a time, then he tried to shrug. 'You compare me with two very evil men.'

'Because what you do is evil.'

'What I do is a job.'

'If you think that, father, then I'm very sorry I came. What you do causes misery and death. It's one of the two scourges, the two plagues of our lives. The other is AIDS, but that's a disease. Your plague is contrived, it's marketed and packaged by criminals for profit, and sold to kids in the streets and schools, after *you've* processed and created it.'

The girl, Priya, had skilfully left the room without a sound. The wine sat in a cooler. Ben badly wanted to refill his glass, but he was mes-merised by what was happening.

Teresa gazed at her father, who seemed too stunned to reply. 'What you do is kill people. I can understand the hill farmers who grow it, because they make ten times more from poppies than from planting tea or grain. I can understand the foolish couriers who run crazy risks for a few

439

quick bucks. I can even understand the dealers, because they're criminals, they're scum, and don't know any better. But for an educated, intelligent man to apply your skills to a process which causes misery and death and ruins people's lives—yet go on doing *this job*, as you call it, that gives me a feeling of disgust with the whole human race, but especially with you. I have to tell you that I'm ashamed to be your daughter.'

*Jesus*, Ben thought, *we're in trouble. Where is she going with this?*

He felt a growing concern. He realised she had wanted to say these things ever since Burridge had told her the truth, and while he felt admiration for her outrage, he willed her not to go too far. Whatever he might try to do would not stop her now—but he desperately hoped she could stop herself.

'Don't you have anything to say?'

'You seem to be saying enough for us both.' Martineau's tone was formal and chilly. 'If you felt this, why did you come?'

'I had to meet you. To look at you.'

'Why?'

'If for no other reason, to perhaps rid myself of you.'

'Rid yourself?'

He stared at her.

Ben watched them both like an invisible witness.

'I'm afraid I don't understand, Teresa. What does it mean—to rid yourself of me?'

'Put it this way. Are you my father?'

'Of course I am.'

'Yes, of course you are. Somewhere I have a birth certificate and your name is on it. You're my father, because you married my mother, slept with her and made her pregnant. And, in a church in Vientiane, I was christened Teresa Francine, and no doubt you were there standing at the font to sign that I was legal. But so what?

'That doesn't make you a father—just a figurehead. I have another father. He lives in West Hampstead, in London. He married my mother—they had no children, but he looked after me as if I was his own—and he put up with my moods and tantrums, and sent me to school, ferried me there and back when I was too young to travel alone, helped me with my homework, consoled me over tiffs with boyfriends, did things a parent does. He really cared for me. He still does. That's my father. The real one, as far as I'm concerned. His name is Charles Lambert—and I love him. And if you promised me the earth, you could never take his place. You could never even get close.'

*I think you've just gone too far, my darling*, Ben said to himself, *but I also have to say I think you're pretty wonderful.*

35 THE MOUNTAIN CITADEL was ablaze with lights. Spotlights in the trees illuminated the main house. Inside the mansion, the palatial dining hall was lit by huge crystal chandeliers. Over fifty people were gathered, all hushed as they listened to a sound of a string quartet. The musicians, a harpist, a cellist and two violinists, were young Thai women. The music was haunting, the youthful players breathtakingly beautiful.

It was a glittering occasion. A scene of rare splendour. The guests were colourful in silks, the gowns embroidered with gemstones of red and electric blue. The tables were laden with delicacies. Heaped dishes of seafood, fragrant hors d'oeuvres and foie gras were a prelude to roast sucking-pig. There were trays of nectared fruit. For those whose religion allowed it, the finest French clarets and a choice of elegant Australian chardonnays were available.

At the main banquet table, Kim Sokram sat with his family. His wives, eight in all, ranged from the eldest in her sixties, to the newest who would soon turn eighteen. He had numerous children and a great many grandchildren, some of whom were older than the latest wife. It was the celebration of Sokram's birthday; he was eighty-two years old and, later on that night, the first and second wives would assist him to mount the new wife so he could leave his seed in young and vibrant ground. Sokram was a lusty and vigorous man who could easily perform this act without aid, but the thought of his first two wives being accessories to the act of deflowering, for the new wife had been examined and declared a virgin, caused him such images of sensual delight that beneath his robes he was already erect. Two women to assist and encourage, and a gorgeous new one to receive, would mean a night of hedonistic rapture and passion that would climax in the planting of new seed, and since he was fertile and lusty, the insemination was likely to add to his already significantly extended family.

Ben and Teresa stood among the main crowd of guests. She looked towards the long table, where the family sat. Among them—the only outsiders—were Roland Martineau and Priya. Her father was clearly one of Sokram's closest associates. It was the reason they had managed to reach here, and he had undoubtedly been pleased to receive the news of her visit and eager to welcome her; his monitoring of their journey which saved their lives demonstrated that. He had wanted her to accept him. To be his long-lost daughter, come to find him, after all the years of being deceived. He had wanted her to condone what he did, wished for some kind of absolution.

But she had rejected him. She hadn't even liked him—and he knew it. He had seen it in her face. He had become distant and angry, saying little more to her. He had abruptly excused himself, informing Ben that his servants would assign them a room, and they were invited—or was it ordered?—to attend the night's festivities, where Ben may perhaps be granted an opportunity to discuss his business, if Sokram so wished it.

The room they were taken to was in another building in the compound. It was a distinct contrast: bare floors, two narrow beds and barred windows. A tiny bathroom was attached. They tried not to form any conclusions about the bars while they showered and changed clothes. All they had were bush trousers and shirts. In the smart gathering they felt out of place among the elaborately embroidered *krapong phamai* and the silk suits of the men. They were conscious of frequent curious glances. She felt ill at ease, which was when Ben drew her aside and murmured to her that half these guests were drug dealers, enforcers or corrupt officials, so this elegant gathering was really just a bunch of thugs and racketeers, a crowd of cheap crooks—and not to feel inhibited or take any crap from them, because they were a nasty, worthless lot. However, since there were so many of them, and the place was lousy with guards and trigger-happy soldiers, he wouldn't make any official announcement of his opinion; he just thought she should know they were among a heap of shit.

Tess smiled and hugged his arm, and said she loved him. She wished they were somewhere else. Ben said he agreed, and was glad she loved him, because it was reciprocated. He suggested they should fill their wineglasses and get stuck into the seafood, because if the bars on the windows of their room were to keep them in, and this was to be a Last Supper, they might as well make the most of it. Which was when they looked across and saw Sokram studying them. Her father had joined him; they were talking together, then Sokram beckoned imperiously. They approached the table as Roland Martineau returned to his own seat.

Tess placed her hands together in a *wai*, a traditional greeting. Sokram nodded, but made no other attempt to respond, while his eyes surveyed her with approval. He spoke in English.

'So, you come to see your father?'

'Yes.'

'And your friend comes to see me?'

'That's right,' Ben said, and was ignored.

'How opportune that you should meet, when you both have the same destination.'

There was a trace of irony. Teresa ignored it, as she said, 'Fortunate for me, since we have become lovers.'

'Fortunate for him, since you have beauty, and unusual charm for a *farang*.'

*Dirty old bugger*, Ben thought, *he can't take his great orbs off her. I don't exist. But if he goes on perving like this, maybe he won't pull that flimsy cover story apart.* Though he doubted it. The story was bad. Too coincidental. It was typical Burridge, to lead them as close as Lampang, then saddle them with a cover that would not stand scrutiny.

Sokram gestured, and a servant brought a carved chair for Teresa to sit facing him. Ben was left standing. Sokram had barely looked at him, and was clearly interested in talking only to her.

'My looks are as nothing compared to your betrothed, *Khun*.' She deliberately used the venerated Thai mode of address.

'Your looks may be different, but nonetheless impressive,' he replied, and Ben began to think that at any moment this ritual word waltz would lead to Sokram propositioning her.

446

Tess smiled with polite appreciation, and decided it was time to change the subject. 'My friend Mr Hammond is here to make an offer. Is it permitted to talk of this at *sanuk*—while you celebrate at your family table?'

'What is permitted is decided by me. My table, my rules.'

Ben cleared his throat, to distract the old man, whose gaze was glued to Teresa. He started to say, 'The offer, sir, is—'

'Not you,' Sokram interrupted him. 'Her. I enjoy the sight and sound of good-looking women.'

'You are a connoisseur,' Tess observed, aware his compliment required an equally flattering response.

'I am an old man,' he said.

'With youthful eyes. And a young man's inclination.'

He smiled at that, and confided, 'The older I get, the younger my wives must be.'

'I commend you—on their beauty, and your virility.'

He chuckled. Clearly the brisk exchange and Tess's clever ego-massaging replies had put him in an excellent humour. He translated the comments for his wives on either side of him, who all smiled and made apparently admiring comments in Thai. They showed their surprise and pleasure when Tess answered in the same language. Ben, forced to be a spectator, wore a polite smile, knowing the dialogue was an obligatory preamble. He recognised her skill and fluency, and realised why she was in demand for high-level diplomatic occasions. He wished she was not quite so adroit; it would make it easier to ask her to share a beach shack with him, after they left here, assuming that the bars on their windows were only to keep other people out.

'What offer?' Sokram had decided the preliminary courtesies were over.

'Ten billion dollars,' Ben said.

'Let her explain.' He kept his gaze on Teresa. Ben felt as if he might as well have stayed back with the fish and the pelicans.

'An Australian television journalist came to visit you—with a camera crew. Three months ago. Do you remember?'

'Ahh.' He smiled. 'The lady with the blue eyes and dark hair. Beautiful. I flew her to my summer residence outside Chiang Mai.'

'She asked you if ten billion dollars would tempt you to shut down your drug empire. You said—perhaps.'

'I did. I recall that. I said perhaps.'

'Well, that's why my friend Mr Hammond is here. The money is available, most of it waiting for you in Switzerland, if you shut the jungle laboratories, and close down the manufacturing and distribution outlets.'

Ben watched the creased face, the momentary puzzlement as he stared at Tess. Then, as his mind translated the full extent of what had been said, he looked astonished and roared with laughter. 'Close down? Shut my business? Are you mad?' He called along the table: 'Roland, your daughter and her friend wish us to shut down.'

'*Merde*,' Martineau called back, and laughed.

'Just a minute, Mr Sokram,' Ben said. 'You were contacted by the United Nations—'

'Keep out of this,' Sokram snapped, and turned to Tess again. 'I made a mistake. I thought you are pretty and intelligent. You are pretty—and stupid. Shut down for ten billion? Our family can make that in a year. My father and his father before him sold opium. We have always been traders in the poppy—and always will be. I have ten sons and thirty grandchildren and, as demand grows, a billion dollars will be in each of their bank accounts every year for as long as they live. Do your sums, Miss Martineau. It is absurd.' He finally turned and faced Ben. 'I was not contacted by anyone. You have been misled.'

'I was told you were willing to meet us.'

'Then you are a fool to believe such a fantasy.'

'But I saw the interview. You did say perhaps.'

'I have agreed I did so.' He stood up, and they

realised he was an immense man. 'But what does perhaps mean to you? To me it means nothing. I was humouring her because she was pretty. It seemed like a joke—so I joked in reply. I would say that someone else has made a bigger joke out of you.'

He stared thoughtfully at Ben. 'Now why would they do that? Send you here with this lie, accompanying a girl who wishes to see her father after so many years? A daughter who then says she despises him. Who arranged this? I think you have more to tell me, and you should explain it—very quickly.'


They were taken back to the room, and this time there was no doubt the bars were to keep them from leaving. Two armed guards had been summoned, and politely escorted them. One had a bunch of keys but, before he could lock the door, Roland Martineau hurriedly appeared. He was agitated, lacking his usual self-assurance.

'You'll be questioned again,' he said to Ben, avoiding any glance at his daughter's face. '*Sanuk* is a tradition here. It is the Thai way, an ingrained joie de vivre, as Teresa can tell you. So the dinner of celebration will continue, long enough to save face, but not for long after that. Sokram will be present when you are interrogated, and you will tell him who sent you, who they represent, and the reasons why. It is obvious now that you accompanied my daughter because it would be a means of safe conduct, and the message I received of her expected arrival was a part of some conspiracy. In the meantime, we have alerted the guards and ordered extra troops in from their routine patrols.'

He went to the door, and hesitated.

'For God's sake, don't try to be brave,' he said. 'First of all they will inject Teresa with heroin, a little at a time until she is dead. Don't imagine because he admires her it will make a difference. They will destroy her mind, and force you to watch. And if you haven't told what they want to know by then, they will use a truth serum on you.'

'Your own prescription, father?' Tess asked, her voice harsh.

He did not answer her. He stared at Ben. 'I don't want her dead any more than you do,' he said, and went out. The guard locked the door and they were alone.

In the corner of the bare room, for the first time, Ben noticed the light of an electric surveillance eye.


An officer sat on duty, at a bank of security monitors. There were a dozen different pictures. Cameras watching the gates. Armed guards patrolling in the shadows. The duty officer ran his eyes along the screens. One showed the vast dining hall, where the celebration dinner was proceeding, and the main course was being served to the sound of the string quartet. Another screen was focused on a bare room, twin beds, with Ben and Teresa looking up at the camera. The duty officer blinked, as they seemed to vanish. A split second later he suddenly realised all the screens had gone blank. He snatched up the telephone.

In the dark a guard lay with his throat cut. A figure masked with a balaclava used a battery-operated laser to cut the powerlines. Near them were the telephone cables. He swiftly sliced through these with an oxyacetylene torch cutting off all external and internal communication.

The duty officer knew the telephone was dead. He urgently pressed the emergency alarm. Nothing happened. He ran to pick up the digital mobile connected to the inter-compound system. Even if someone had cut the lines, this was infallible. A matter of seconds and the alert would be raised. Unbelievably, something odd was happening outside. It must be reported at once.

The door to the surveillance suite opened, a figure took aim, a silenced gun coughed, and the duty officer never had time to know there was no-one alive to answer his call.

Dark figures slid over the walls and dropped onto the patrols below. Guards and young hill-tribe soldiers died, with a sigh, sometimes a grunt, never a shot fired or a voice crying out in warning. The small figures were relentless. They appeared from nowhere, killed, and were gone into the shadows. They had grenades, sub-machine guns, and pistols with silencers. But, above all, they had their knives, Toledo steel-bladed poniards, and these they used with lethal effect as they stabbed and moved on towards the darkened mansion.

In the massive dining hall, there was concern and annoyance at the power failure, but no time for panic. Sokram shouted for someone to use the telephone, and tell the duty officer there was a blackout. At that moment there was a reaction of general relief as the lights came on again. But these were not normal lights, they realised a moment later: these were huge arcs attached to their own power source. And behind the blinding glare were figures of men in balaclavas and jungle-dark clothing, with submachine guns. They began to fire. Their eyes intent, their hands steady, they raked the room with a hail of death.

The first to die was Kim Sokram, his bellow of outrage unuttered. His wives were shot to pieces, the oldest dying with the new wife in her arms. Roland Martineau tried to find Priya, but she was on the floor and bleeding to death. He tried to run to warn his daughter, but then realised, as they shot him, that she had been the means of bringing them.


In the dark room, Ben and Teresa saw the light on the surveillance eye go out at the same time as all the illumination in the compound failed. Soon afterwards they heard the first shots, then the steady indiscriminate firing of submachine guns and the thud of grenades exploding. When they heard the frenzied screams, they knew the people in the dining hall were being massacred.


Burridge stood near the main gates, receiving progress reports on his radio. Finally came the message that everyone in the compound, and at the banquet in the main house, was dead.

He gave the order to cease fire, and told his squads to search the village for the two people whose photographs he had issued to all the commandos.

If the pair of them happened to be alive, then he wanted to see them. If they were dead, cremate them with the others.

Buildings blazed. The surrounding jungle seemed to be on fire. A funeral pyre was already burning bodies. What they could see from their window was like a lurid Gothic nightmare. They heard running footsteps and a voice shouting at them to stand away from the door. A burst from a sten gun splintered the wood and smashed the lock to pieces, and they were ordered out.

The smell of smoke and burning bodies assailed them as they were escorted through the village. In the large mansion the power was restored as all the lights flared with a bright incandescence. Inside, no-one moved. The commando squad, unrecognisable in balaclavas and jungle fatigues, lobbed grenades through the shattered windows, and cheered at the sound of the explosions within. Ben and Teresa reached the end of the village, where a familiar figure, despite his commando-style garb, issued orders on a radio. He turned and saw them.

'Bravo. Well done, you two. A splendid job.'
Burridge put out his hand.

For an instant nothing happened.

Then Teresa swung her arm and slapped his face. A moment later Ben lashed out and hit him. It was a distinctly harder blow than he had given him a bare two weeks ago outside the beach cottage. It was as hard as he could manage, and Burridge went down in a surprised and injured heap. A hooded commando raced in, his hand on the trigger of his automatic rifle, ready to fire. Burridge stopped him with a gesture and climbed unsteadily to his feet.

'Don't shoot the stupid bastard.'

He looked at them both, and rubbed his jaw and his cheek. He said to them, 'No need to be upset. It's a bloody triumph.'

Ben knew it was a completely futile gesture but, for good measure, he knocked him down again.

**36** 'ARE YOU QUITE sure you won't have a drink?'

'No thank you,' Tess said.

'Not even a—' Jessica Tate was going to say not even a friendly one, but knew they would refuse. It would not be a good choice of words.

'We'll be going, if you don't mind.'

'We don't mind,' Burridge said. 'The sooner you're out of the country, the better.'

'That's just how we feel. We'll do our drinking on the plane. No offence meant to you, Mrs Tate.'

'None taken.' She went out, leaving them alone with Burridge. He was once again immaculate, in a lightweight tropical suit.

'I'm extremely sorry I couldn't confide in you both. Give you the big picture, so to speak.'

'You'd never have done that,' Ben told him. 'It's not the way you operate, is it, trusting people? *No need for us to know*, that's the motto. No need for anyone to know—but especially us, the bloody bellwethers leading you there.'

'Bellwethers?' Burridge seemed amused.

'Judas goats, if you prefer. Where did you put the transistors so you could track us?'

'One in the jeep. The others in your back-packs. Amazing what a good signal you can receive from something almost invisible.'

'Technology is a wonderful thing,' Ben agreed. 'In a few years time there'll be no such thing as personal privacy left.'

'It's called progress.'

Ben ignored this. He stared at him and said, 'You'll never admit it, but you set me up. Maybe some day, my kids will no longer be told by their friends that dad is really a bent cop who got off the hook by resigning from the force.'

'My dear chap . . .' Burridge seemed momentarily contrite, but Ben was not prepared to listen.

'And there was never all that money to pay Sokram. It was flimflam. Make-believe. Show us a great swag of cash, a list of banks around the world, and we buy the idea. You knew we hadn't a hope of persuading him to sell out—for ten times as much—that wasn't the scenario, was it? All you really wanted was for us to lead the way in. With those little microchips in our backpacks.'

'No other choice. He had too many people

in his pocket—too much influence. We couldn't even get close.'

'So you recruited us. The Judas goats. Two weeks work, and a big pay cheque—if we lived to collect it.'

'It was something of a risk, but our prime concern throughout was always your safety.'

'Bullshit,' Ben said.

'For God's sake, you came through. Flying colours, old boy. We won. Shut down one of the world's biggest drug syndicates. Destroyed his entire operation.'

'Congratulations,' Tess said.

'It's important, Teresa. I'm sorry about your father, but—'

'I daresay he deserved to die,' Tess said, 'but how about his girlfriend? All those wives and children?'

'It was a war. There are always casualties.'

She studied him, and shook her head, as if he perplexed her. 'The king is dead,' she said.

'That's it.'

'Long live the king.'

There was a brief silence.

'I always knew you were smart.'

'So who assumes the crown?' she asked him.

'It's irrelevant.'

'Someone you and your people control?'

Burridge gave a faint smile. 'Something of the sort.' He turned to Ben. 'You should look after this girl. Mind you, it's fortunate no-one will believe her story.'

'You mean you're taking over?'

'Not me. Not personally. No more than my chums in the CIA run any of the Colombians.'

Ben felt paralysed with the shock. *But of course. Why hadn't he seen it all along?* Burridge seemed amused at the realisation Teresa had worked it out and Ben was still struggling to come to terms with the idea.

'Think about it, Ben. Drugs will never go away. History tells us that. So all we can do is try to regulate the supply and demand. We've merely eliminated one man who was greedy and difficult to control, and replaced him with someone who will be more ... amenable.'

'You fucking cunt,' Ben said.

'If you insist.' He saw them to the door. Decided against offering a handshake. 'One thing. The keys to the deposit box—if you'd be so kind.'

They gave him their keys.

'Before you go, you do realise you can never talk about this. Not to anyone. Which is why I can allow you to leave. This whole matter never happened. You understand? It simply never existed.'

37 THE SUN WAS shining fiercely off the sand, and for a moment it seemed like a mirage. With a dismayed sense of déjà vu he saw the distant figure. It was definitely not a mirage. Coat over his shoulder, trousers rolled up, carrying his shoes and socks as he trudged through the soft sand. Looking as he had the first time, bloody ridiculous.

Tess was in the water with Susan and Daniel. Nick and Jane Feraldos were coming later for a barbecue. Tonight she was going to call her stepfather, Charles, and ask him to fly out to spend Christmas. She hoped he might like Sydney enough to want to live there.

'Even if he does want to go home,' Ben had said to her, 'you'll stay, won't you? I mean with me. For good.'

She thought about it.

'I'll stay a while,' she said, 'till the money runs out,' and now here was Sir Edward Burridge trudging along the beach, about to ruin the day. Tess saw him with equal dismay. She ran from the water, and Ben handed her a towel.

Burridge reached them and mopped his brow. 'Any chance of a beer, old boy?'

'Not a hope,' Ben said.

Burridge seemed unsurprised. He nodded to Tess and looked at the remote beach cottage. 'Charming spot.'

'We like it.'

'The agent tells me you're buying it.'

'I've made an offer,' Ben said.

'Well, we did pay you handsomely—you must admit that. And how are you both? You look remarkably well,' he said admiringly to Tess.

'It's the sun and the sea,' she said, 'and lots of sex. Awfully good for the skin.'

'What can we do for you, Ted? Apart from not offering you a beer—and asking you to fuck off.'

'We have a problem,' Burridge informed them.

'Nothing minor, I hope.'

'The money in the deposit box in Hong Kong—'

'What about it?'

'The accountants say it won't balance. There's some missing.'

They looked at him with astonishment.

'In fact, more than *some*. Rather a lot.'

'How much?'

462

'Well, after reconciling the first amount, then the additional sum you took for expenses . . . we are short of four million dollars.'

'Good God,' Ben said, amazed.

'Four million!' Tess whistled.

Burridge looked singularly unimpressed. 'I'm sorry, but you've clearly stolen it. When you went back there,' he said to Teresa.

'Is this a formal accusation?'

'In my opinion, you've been badly influenced. When I first met you, you were a nice girl.'

'When you met me, I was an innocent. I believed you.'

'I'm giving you the chance to return the money.'

'How?' Tess asked.

'You simply give it back, and it's added to Walter Chen's estate. Nothing more need be said. I could bring charges, but I won't—for old times' sake.'

'That's civil of you,' Ben said. 'Who inherits the estate?'

'It's in dispute.'

'All those cousins fighting over the remains. Poor Mr Chen.'

'That's as may be,' Burridge said. 'Let's get this sorted out.'

'But how?' Tess asked once again.

'Return the money.' Burridge was becoming terse.

'That's impossible.' Ben frowned, as though he was trying to explain something quite simple, and the other was being dense.

'Completely impossible,' she said. 'What four million dollars?'

'Don't let's sod about and play silly buggers. Part of the money that was in Hong Kong.'

'What money in Hong Kong?'

'How could there be money? The operation never happened. You told us that. Remember?'

'So who could have stolen anything?' Tess asked.

'Let alone a ridiculous amount like four million bucks?' Ben tried not to smile.

Burridge stared at them.

They looked innocent, so naively ingenuous. Ben took her hand. Burridge saw this. In that moment he saw a great many things.

'There'll be questions asked.'

'There can't be. None of us were there. It never existed.'

'You pair of dirty, doublecrossing bastards,' he said.

'Ted, old boy,' Ben told him with quiet satisfaction, 'I think that's the nicest thing you've ever said to us.'

Tess laughed then. Burridge turned on his heel and walked off, the soft sand making an angry retreat difficult. In that moment, despite his dislike, despite the treachery, Ben almost felt sorry for Edward Burridge. It would not have been appreciated, so he made no attempt to express it. Instead, he put his arm around Tess as they watched the tall figure walk away.

The children came, wet and refreshed from the water. Daniel submerged himself in his towel, then studied Teresa. 'Are you moving in with my dad? Permanent?'

'Daniel!' Susan said, despairingly.

Tess smiled, and ruffled the boy's mop of hair. Ben looked on with astonishment as his son accepted this gesture of feminine endearment without demur.

'Yes, Dan, I'm moving in. Okay with you?'

'Terrific,' Daniel said, and just to show he wasn't going soft, kicked a shower of sand all over his sister.

Peter Yeldham
**Without Warning**

*She woke suddenly. Someone was in the room...She knew she was in great danger. But if she called out, a blow across her throat could render her mute.*

*He said her name.*

*'If you try to telephone,' it was only a whisper, but she could hear him clearly, 'I'll kill you.'*

He was a man who wanted to possess her.

She thought she could handle it...but then the rules changed.

He lives a double life, trapped by a dark and guilty obsession. And he's about to jeopardise everything she holds dear – husband, children, closest friends.

As he pursues his relentless campaign, Megan is plunged into a terrifying urban nightmare, and she must enter the mind of a psychopath to survive...

David Sale
**Hidden Agenda**

FEAR
One day Dinah Lanyon is the wife of Australia's richest and most powerful man. The next she's living in terror.

MURDER
Dinah's fighting a deadly game with stakes higher than she could ever imagine.

BETRAYAL
In a world where power is the ultimate turn-on, everyone has a

HIDDEN AGENDA